EMPIRE OF DIRT

THE ECHOES SAGA: BOOK TWO

PHILIP C. QUAINTRELL

Copyright © 2017 by Philip C. Quaintrell
First edition published 2017.
Second edition published 2023.

Cover Illustration by Chris McGrath
Book design by BodiDog Design
Edited by David Bradley

ISBN: 978-1-916610-01-9 (paperback)
ASIN: B07656T32Q (ebook)

Published by Quaintrell Publishings

For Emma, Amy and David - my team.
I couldn't do it without you.

ALSO BY PHILIP C. QUAINTRELL

THE ECHOES SAGA: (9 Book Series)

1. Rise of the Ranger

2. Empire of Dirt

3. Relic of the Gods

4. The Fall of Neverdark

5. Kingdom of Bones

6. Age of the King

7. The Knights of Erador

8. Last of the Dragorn

9. A Clash of Fates

THE RANGER ARCHIVES: (3 Book Series)

1. Court of Assassins

2. Blood and Coin

3. A Dance of Fang and Claw

THE TERRAN CYCLE: (4 Book Series)

1. Intrinsic

2. Tempest

3. Heretic

4. Legacy

GRIMWHAL

BHAN DORAL

KHALDARIM

DHENAHEIM

SILVYR HALL

HYNDAERN

NIMDUHN

THE VENGORAN MOUNTAINS

THE KING'S LAKE

NAMDHOR

SKYSTEAD

THE WHITE VALE

KELP TOWN

THE KING'S INN

WOOD VALE

IKIRITH

GREY STONE

THE EVERMO

LIRIAN

SNOWFELL

BLEAK

THE NORD

VANGARTH

CARSTANE

THE WILD MOORES

ELETHIAH

WEST FELLION

THE NARROWS

THE MOONLIT P

QAININARAN

ILYTHYRA

LAKE NUBIA

TREGARAN

THE ARID L

AMEERASKA

THE HOX

THE OLD GARDEN

KARA

SYLA'S GATE

THE UNDYING MOUNTAINS

ITHILI

LAKE RAND

THE BLACK LAKE

DRAMATIS PERSONAE

Abigail Rose
A human mage and student of Korkanath.

Adellum Bövö
The late general and member of the Hand of Valanis.

Adilandra Sevari
The elven queen of Elandril and mother of Reyna.

Alidyr Yalathanil
An elf and master of Nightfall.

Asher
A human ranger and previous member of Nightfall.

Darius Devale
A human knight of the Graycoat order.

Elaith Nevandar
A human knight-in-training of the Graycoat order.

Faros Kalvanak
Boy Emperor of Karath and Lord of The Arid Lands.

Faylen Haldör
An elf and mentor to Reyna Sevari.

Gal Tion
The first human king of Illian, a thousand years ago.

Galanör Reveeri
An elven warrior.

Galkarus Vod
A human mage in the court of King Rengar.

Gideon Thorn
A human mage and student at Korkanath.

Gregorn Orvish
King of Grey Stone and Lord of The Ice Vales.

Hyvark
High priest and advisor to The Goddess.

Isabella Harg
Queen of Lirian and Lady of Felgarn.

Krenorak
A Darkakin warrior.

Lord Marshal Horvarth
Head of the Graycoats.

Merkaris Tion
King of Namdhor and Lord of Orith.

Mörygan Mörgö
An elf and advisor to Princess Reyna Sevari.

Nakir Galvörd
A General and member of the Hand of Valanis.

Nasta Nal-Aket
The Father of Nightfall.

Nathaniel Galfrey
A human knight and member of the Graycoats.

Ned Fennick
A human knight and member of the Graycoats.

Rengar Marek
King of Velia and Lord of Alborn.

Reyna Sevari
An elven princess.

Ro Dosarn
A human assassin and a member of Nightfall.

Samandriel Zathya
A General and member of the Hand of Valanis.

∼

Thallan Tassariön
A General and member of the Hand of Valanis.

The Goddess
The queen of the Darkakin.

Tobin Galfrey
Previous Graycoat and late father of Nathaniel Galfrey.

Tyberius Gray
The founder of the Graycoats.

Valanis
The dark elf and self-proclaimed herald of the gods.

THE
ECHOES OF FATE
THE PROPHECY

THESE FAVOURED ELVES FALL AND LOSE THEIR
WAY, AS MAN'S ANGER DEVOURS ALL DRAGONS'
FIRE. THE IMMORTAL MAN IS SET TO RISE,
BRINGING THE DARK ONE CLOSER TO HIS MOST
DANGEROUS DESIRE.

PALDORA'S CELESTIAL GEM GRACES THE DAYLIGHT,
AND IN ITS BEAUTY ORDAINS CALAMITY. ONLY
ALLIANCE AND TRUST BETWEEN TWO SHORES
OFFERS AN INTIMATION OF HOPE AND A GLIMPSE
OF ETERNITY.

CHILDREN OF FIRE AND FLAME OFFER GREAT
PROMISE, BUT ONLY ONE PERCEIVES THE TIME WE
WILL FALL. AS THE GODS RECAST THEIR FORTUNE
AND POWER, ONE WILL SUFFER THE BURDEN OF
DESTINY FOR ALL.

- NALANA SEVARI

PROLOGUE

I 000 Years Ago

The battle of Elethiah could be heard for miles around. The clash of elven steel resounded on both sides of the city walls, while catapults hurled giant flaming stones into the towering spires, creating chaos and raining debris on the citizens below.

The cries of death and rage filled the cool night air, as dragons swarmed the sky and set the battlefield alight with their deadly breath.

But Valanis couldn't hear any of it.

The king of elves, Gorvandil Sevari, lay dead at Valanis's feet, his queen not three feet away, having met a similar fate. The dark elf paid them no heed but, instead, looked long and hard into the startlingly blue eyes of Lady Syla, who gasped for breath in his merciless grip.

The elven hero had caused Valanis's campaign many set-backs

1

with her tenacity and legendary skill. It pleased the dark elf to feel her life ebb away, her eyes pleading to live. It only served to amuse Valanis all the more, to know that in their final moments, even the greatest of warriors feared death. Feared him.

"You cannot fight fate. The gods have already written the end of this story," Valanis whispered into her ear.

Before she could gasp her last breath, the dark elf broke her neck and dropped her to the cold floor.

Valanis stepped over the bodies and continued into the depths of Elethiah. The dark elf strode through the ancient halls with the whispers of the gods guiding his every step. He could hear them as clearly as he heard his generals in the Hand, advising him and offering their strength.

He had been chosen by the mightiest of beings to bring about a new world, fit for their return, and he would see it done.

A billowing black cloak trailed behind him, as he ascended the steps into the central tower. The bronze-tinted armour he wore was purely decorative, having no need of protection from anything as primitive as a sword.

Silky blond hair flowed down to the centre of his back, with a single braid running through the middle. He was attractive, even by elven standards, but he was beyond such trivialities now. Valanis only had one goal.

FIND IT!

A dozen voices cried out in his mind. Valanis could feel the power of Naius flowing through his veins, fuelled by the god's hunger to return. His body started to hum again and his skin adopted a golden aura.

Valanis had to stop at the top of the stairs and clench his fists with the enormous effort it took to control the magic within. The elf groaned and dropped to one knee, as the magic took its toll, threatening to burst forth and destroy him. He needed the gem, desperately. These fits had increased in frequency and intensity since his last submersion in the pools of Naius.

IT'S CLOSE!

Valanis had long discerned that particular voice as Paldora's, the goddess of the stars. Her gift would ensure his control over the magic of Naius. The elf looked up, through strained purple eyes, to see a teenage elf running across the landing, away from the Hall of Life. He couldn't conceal the pain he was in, but he recognised the elf as Elym, the prince of Elethiah. The boy stumbled at the sight of the dark elf, his eyes wide with shock and horror. Valanis couldn't maintain his gaze through the agony, however, his skin burning as if set alight.

FOCUS...

Despite the pain, Valanis could always hear the gods. Atilan, the king of the gods, offered him strength and courage.

The pain soon abated and he found control once more. The golden aura emanating from his body died away, returning his skin to its original, pale tone. The constant hum settled in his ears, allowing him to stand and regain his composure.

The prince had fled, leaving Valanis on his own. That was how he liked it. With every battle, the dark elf preferred to be unaccompanied. The only ones he truly needed were the gods, and they would never leave him.

The white ornate doors of the Hall of Life were soon before him, along with twenty elves, adorned in their usual white armour and blue cloaks. They stood defiantly with their scimitars raised and determined expressions.

There weren't many who would stand so defiantly before him, not anymore. These were among the bravest elves at the king's disposal. Valanis had always respected bravery, especially in the face of death, but in this particular case it was simply foolish.

"I have already slain your king..." Valanis's voice was not his own, at least not as he remembered it. He now spoke in deep intonations that reverberated with a dozen other voices, adding to his supernatural presence.

"I snapped Lady Syla's neck... what hope do *you* have? Join me and have your lives filled with purpose." The soldiers didn't move an inch.

KILL THEM!

Krayt, the god of war, hissed in his ear, as if he were standing next to the elf, urging him to let loose his rage and kill.

"So be it..."

Valanis lifted his hands, palms up, and unleashed his magic. Ten of the elves lost their blades when the swords leaped from their hands and took on a life of their own. The scimitars dashed and twirled around the hallway, cutting, slicing and hacking the soldiers to death. Blood was splattered across the walls, staining their white armour. Some of them were able to parry the floating blades, but even their elven speed was no match for Valanis's powers. In seconds they were all scattered throughout the hallway, dead.

The dark elf sighed; they would have made an excellent addition to his forces. But like him, they had made a choice, and standing against the gods was a *foolish* choice.

He strode over and between the bodies, until the double doors blocked his way. It took barely a flick of the hand to blow them open, using a wave of telekinetic energy.

The Hall of Life was a large circular chamber, supported by thick pillars creating an inner circle that surrounded a small podium. The far side of the hall was missing a wall where the balcony stretched out and hung over the back of the city. It had been designed with dragons in mind, so that they might sit in on the elders' meetings.

TAKE IT!

The voices cried out at the sight of the podium. Paldora's gem was finally his! Without a care, Valanis walked up to the podium and snatched the black crystal from its stand. He held it high, examining it closely; curious as to why he couldn't feel the artefact's power.

A TRICK!

This rock hadn't fallen from the heavens, but had simply been plucked from the ground. Valanis crushed the rock in his hand with his enhanced strength. He had been a fool, he realised.

Four elders, from the king's council, stepped into view from behind the pillars and surrounded the dark elf. They each wielded a staff that housed a crystal the size of a clenched fist. Rushing into their trap had been one thing, but not seeing the hulking creature that skulked above him was another thing entirely.

Garganafan, the oldest and most prestigious of dragons rested high up in the domed ceiling, his body wrapped around the pillars, with his claws dug deep into the marble.

Valanis killed elves freely, in the knowledge that the gods required the land to be cleansed before their return, but killing a dragon had always felt wrong to him. They were the most ancient of beings, and even though they had openly gone to war with the gods, long ago, before they ascended to the heavens, they were still the most magnificent of creatures.

He could always feel the gods' contempt for the beasts in the back of his mind, however, and often allowed that rage to spill out when he was forced to confront one. For that reason, he had killed many dragons since the war began, and would no doubt kill even more before his task was finished.

Garganafan ran around the pillars until his great bulk was on the floor. The ground shook when his claws dug into the marble floor and his long scaly neck curled around the last pillar, so that his head hung over Valanis.

"The gem is beyond your reach, Valanis!" one of the elders proclaimed.

The dark elf couldn't remember the name of the council member - they were all insignificant.

"Your crusade is at an end!" another stated.

"End?" Valanis laughed. "You think I brought war to your gates for the *gem*?" The dark elf laughed again, menacingly. "Paldora's gem is a means to an end. I *need* it so that I might serve the gods, but it's not what I *want*..." He looked up at Garganafan and smiled, mischievously. "Didn't you tell them?" A threatening, low rumble echoed inside the beast's throat. "Keeping secrets. Naughty dragon..."

Valanis readied himself with a plethora of spells and enchantments, but the elves were ahead of him, their staffs raised and their crystals glowing hot-white. The light blinded Valanis's senses, as if shutting him off from the world.

Their chanting quickly disappeared, lost in the rush of magical energy that raced about his body, ensnaring him. Valanis immediately fought back with every devastating spell he knew, but it did nothing when Garganafan added his own power to their spell. Waves of magic poured from the dragon's body and began to grind Valanis's will into the ground.

The dark elf could feel their spell building, the ensnaring energy continuing to expand from within Valanis, as if he was the centre of the spell. His vision was blurring and the world became as white as snow. He could no longer see the elven elders or the great dragon that bore down upon him. The last thing he heard was Garganafan's almighty roar, a sound so loud and powerful he thought it might bring down the entire Hall of Life.

The white light only encompassed his vision for a second, before the world returned in all its colour. Valanis looked from side to side in amazement. The Hall of Life was not as it had been only moments ago. The pyres were no longer lit and darkness had descended on the once great chamber. The domed ceiling had been poked through with jagged holes, surrounded by incredible cracks that looked to be threatening the hall's integrity.

Most surprising of all were the four elders surrounding him, encased in stone. Valanis looked up to see Garganafan, similarly entombed in dull grey stone. Life had left them all.

The Amber Spell...

Valanis had heard whispers of the council searching for the spell. Using the power of a dragon to see the magic through, however, had been an unexpected measure.

Valanis laughed to himself at the great sacrifice made to trap him. Not only had the elders died, but the most powerful of dragons had gone with them, and for what? He was free!

A dark thought crept into Valanis's mind... How long had they trapped him here? The state of the hall would suggest a long time. The elf moved for the wide balcony, but stumbled past the stone elves when his legs gave out, dropping Valanis to the floor.

"No..." That familiar hum returned in his ears and his skin illuminated the darkened hall.

Crawling across the marble floor, Valanis made his way onto the balcony, until he was under the light of the crescent moon. The stars shone in the heavens and Valanis pleaded to the gods to help him. He had failed to acquire the gem and without it he would never be strong enough to prepare Verda for their arrival.

A wave of nausea overcame Valanis and he rolled onto his back, his muscles succumbing to spasms. He screamed into the night and let just an inch of his power explode from his body. The energy washed over the balcony and cracked the stone, as well as destroying the railing.

He managed to get to his hands and knees when the episode dissipated. After taking a deep breath, Valanis stood and brushed his blond hair from his face.

At the edge of the balcony he looked down upon the ruin that was now Elethiah. His hope died when he saw the level of decay that had befallen the city. He hadn't been stuck in the Amber Spell for days or even years... he had been trapped in the Hall of Life for centuries.

The sky was devoid of dragons and the ground revealed no hint of his forces. Elethiah was now surrounded by swampland.

But where was Alidyr, his faithful general and head of the Hand? Where were any of his disciples?

It was possible they had all perished in the battle or in the days that followed, but he had gifted them all with a portion of Naius's power, as well as their magnificent weapons. They must be out there somewhere...

Valanis looked to the north, to the mountains of Vengora. His home and personal fortress, Kaliban, was hidden away, high in the snow and rock. More importantly, the pools of Naius were inside Kaliban. He needed to submerge himself in those enchanted waters: it was the only place he could rest and not have to fear the effects of containing the power of a god.

The dark elf pictured the cavern that housed the pools and opened a portal with the wave of a hand. He stepped into the inky abyss at the same moment another fit came on. Instead of walking into the cavern, Valanis stepped into a bog.

The herald of the gods and commander of the fiercest army in all of Verda was on his hands and knees in a swamp. The elf spat out the dirty water and crawled to the edge of the bog and rolled onto the hard ground, once again fighting the urge to unleash his power on the land, for it would surely take his life with it.

His cloak was sodden and heavy as he clawed his way across the dirt. Behind him, he could see Elethiah in its entirety. It was hard to judge which side had won the battle, let alone the war. The elves had certainly abandoned the citadel, but that wasn't to say they had lost to his forces.

Valanis roared into the night, using his rage to take control of the fit. In his short reprieve, the elf tapped into the magic gifted him by Naius, a magic he now shared in part with the Hand, and reached out across the ether.

He immediately felt the familiar aura of Alidyr, Thallan, Adellum, Samandriel and Nakir. They were all in different places, but they were alive!

He called to them. Their elation and surprise could be felt through the bond, but he quickly ordered them to find him for he didn't have a lot of time. He needed to reach the pools of Naius as soon as possible, before the next attack crippled him.

Through the magic of the pools, he could recover and learn what had become of his world.

PART ONE

CHAPTER 1
VALANIS

F*orty years later...*

Alidyr crouched by the edges of the shimmering pools of Naius and, with tentative fingers, the elf picked out a handful of crystals.

The glittering rocks formed the pools themselves, their liquid-like texture only solidifying once removed. The magic stored within each of the crystals was vast and capable of transporting Alidyr across the country in a single step.

Their glow vanished in his hand and he dropped them into a pouch on his belt.

"You're getting lazy..." Thallan Tassariön approached from behind.

The elven general appeared to be upside down to Alidyr, though unhindered by what should have been a twenty-foot fall.

"The pools of Naius are a gift, Thallan." Alidyr stood up to watch

Thallan walk between the stalactites and down the rocky column until they were side-by-side. "Any gift of the gods should not be overlooked."

Now that they were face-to-face, Alidyr could see the water dripping off Thallan's black cloak and armour. With his hood and mask pulled low, his pale face and bald head glowed in the light of the pools. Intricate tattoos lined his scalp in the script of the ancients.

"I can see from your appearance that you have met with the Mer-folk of The Adean." Alidyr turned away and slowly walked out of the gravity-defying caves, heading for the stone halls of Kaliban.

In truth, Alidyr was anxious to hear his brother's report, but he always took measures to appear composed in front of the Hand of Valanis - after all, he was the head.

"Indeed I have brother, but I have failed to bring good news." It was clear from Thallan's tone that he was happy to be the bearer of bad news. "The Mer-folk were insulted when I asked about Paldora's gem. They claimed that they would be aware if any such artefact was within their domain."

Alidyr looked away to hide his scowl. He had been a fool to believe that the ranger had truly thrown the rest of Paldora's gem into The Adean. At the time, Alidyr had been in possession of Asher's ring and a shard of the magical gem. He had been intoxicated with the power it granted him, not to mention the prospect of delivering it to Valanis.

Now, he would be made to look the fool in front of the Hand and his master. He wanted to order Thallan to return to the Mer-folk and tell them to scour the ocean again, but Alidyr knew the ocean dwellers were telling the truth. Valanis had established their fear of him millennia ago, if not their loyalty.

"I will inform Valanis immediately," Thallan continued.

Alidyr swivelled on him, blocking his path. "*I* will inform him. As head of the Hand it is my responsibility."

Alidyr could see the disappointment on his brother's face. For the last forty years, since Valanis had broken free of the Amber Spell,

Thallan had been placed in charge of the Hand, replacing Alidyr for his failure to find the gem. Returning the shard of Paldora's gem from the ranger had seen Alidyr elevated to his rightful position, above Thallan, once more.

"As you wish..." Thallan bowed his head and sank back into the darkness of the caves.

Alidyr took a breath to collect his thoughts and continued to navigate Kaliban's cold halls. The elf soon found himself at the grand doors of Valanis's personal chamber, a chamber his master had been unable to use until recently. Only with the shard of Paldora's gem was he able to leave the pools of Naius.

Alidyr paused in front of the door, considering his choice of words when delivering the news.

"Enter..." The beckoning voice was not that of his master, but melodic and female.

Alidyr rolled his eyes and entered the chamber, where Samandriel Zathya, another member of the Hand, stood defiantly before him. Samandriel smiled wickedly at Alidyr, always happy to challenge him when her famous double-ended spear was in hand.

Of all the Hand, Samandriel had always been the most protective of Valanis, guarding him like a father. Now, she stood in an empty room, a sentinel in front of the balcony door.

"Where is our master?" Alidyr inquired.

"He likes to watch the sunrise." Samandriel glanced at the entrance behind her.

Alidyr made for the balcony, but Samandriel stepped in front of him with blazing, golden eyes. Alidyr clenched his jaw, wondering if these games between his brothers and sister would ever end.

"He doesn't want to be disturbed..." Her tone wasn't to be argued with.

"I am the head of the Hand, Samandriel—"

"And you'll lose both of those parts if you take another step, brother."

Alidyr examined the tip of her spear and didn't doubt it. He had long wondered who would truly win in a contest between the two. For all his guile and strategic brilliance, his skill with a blade could be challenged by Samandriel at any time.

"Let him through, Samandriel..." Valanis's voice was but a whisper, yet it carried easily over the wind and into the chamber.

Samandriel cocked an eyebrow before bowing her head in respect. Alidyr caught sight of the familiar ancient script that lined her bald head. He had those same tattoos across his own head, but had chosen to hide them beneath his thick, black hair when he formed the secret society of assassins, known to Illian as the Arakesh of Nightfall.

Only after the doors closed behind him did Alidyr step onto the balcony. Even on a day free of storms, the view from Kaliban was only ever that of clouds and fog, though it gave the perfect view of the sunrise.

The ground would be forever hidden from the fortress's great height, however, along with the rest of The Ice Vales and Grey Stone below. That particular kingdom of man had been settled under the shadow of Kaliban for centuries, every king none the wiser.

Alidyr walked past the ancient armoured suits that stood either side of the archway. A wind, as cold as ice, whipped about his white robes, chilling him to the bone. The elf cared little for the temperature, however; he had been forged through pain and suffering until his master had granted him an inch of his godly power. Fire and ice were but elements to be controlled at his fingertips, and never to be feared.

The elf walked out across the balcony and felt the loss of one of his short-swords ever more keenly when in the presence of his master. The pair of magical swords had accompanied him everywhere for over a millennium, guiding him in battle and fuelling his bloodlust. Still, Alidyr couldn't allow for his discomfort to show. In the presence of Valanis, there could only be strength.

The herald of the gods stood on the lip of the damaged balcony, his dark form bridging the gap in the broken railing. Concealed in billowing, black robes that wrapped tightly around his waist, Valanis was hidden within a shadowy hood that struggled to contain the dark elf's long blond hair. Sleek, glistening armour protected his torso in layered plates, which rose into short pointed tips at his shoulders.

It wasn't the same design he had worn during The Dark War, Alidyr noted. Valanis's new appearance was subtler, yet more menacing somehow, as if the shadows themselves embraced the dark elf.

The hairs on Alidyr's body became rigid and his skin tingled as he joined his master. The magical aura that surrounded the herald was intoxicating, making Alidyr feel powerful in his presence.

It had only been a few weeks since Valanis had walked free of the pools of Naius. Somewhere beneath his armoured gloves was the ring that granted a portion of control over the magic that threatened to consume him. Alidyr could see that the shard wasn't enough though. Valanis's face glowed from within his shadowy hood and he had already seen the golden veins that ran across his master's face.

"Speak your fears, Alidyr," Valanis said, his gaze fixed on the sunrise.

His voice reverberated with what Alidyr had always liked to think of as the combined voices of the gods.

It humbled the elf to know that his master understood him so well. "I fear that the shard will not suffice, Master." He glanced at the golden aura emanating from within the hood.

"I too share that fear," Valanis surprisingly replied.

It wasn't in his nature to reveal fears or weaknesses, but then Alidyr realised how confident Valanis must truly be, even in a weakened state to voice such a thing. The herald of the gods was more powerful than any other.

"That is why I haven't left Kaliban," Valanis admitted. "I have stood here every day and looked out at the world, wondering if stepping into it will be the end of me. If I perish, the will of the gods perishes with me. Only I can bring them forth..." The dark elf turned to Alidyr and looked upon his acolyte with blazing purple eyes.

Alidyr bowed his head in respect and agreement. Valanis's vision for Verda was the most beautiful thing Alidyr had ever heard. He would do whatever his master bade to see it through.

"Now, tell me what *really* troubles you," Valanis commanded.

Nothing could be hidden from the master.

"Thallan has returned from The Shining Coast..." Alidyr reported.

The coast ran the entire length of the eastern shore of Illian: a place Mer-folk had been known to prey on unsuspecting fishermen for centuries.

"The gem is not in The Adean," Valanis concluded before Alidyr could elaborate. "You were deceived by the ranger."

"He was an Arakesh, a master of lies." Alidyr knew it was a mistake to create excuses; Valanis didn't tolerate them. "I was blinded by my arrogance and ask for no forgiveness but, instead, offer my life."

Valanis ignored his offer. "This ranger... The same boy who shared my slumber in Elethiah for a thousand years. The *immortal man*..." He continued to look out across the vista. "I have given this prophecy much thought since I awoke from the Amber Spell. The Echoes of Fate..." Valanis laughed quietly to himself, putting Alidyr on edge. "An apt title for godly words."

Alidyr was more than aware of the prophecy spoken by Nalana Sevari a millennium ago. It had been he who told Valanis of the princess's godly words, spoken not long after the Amber Spell was cast.

The immortal man is set to rise, bringing the dark one closer to his most dangerous desire.

Alidyr thought over those words for a moment, astounded by their accuracy.

"I've never thought of it before," Alidyr observed, "but why did the gods speak through Nalana Sevari of all elves? I know she was royalty, a Dragorn even..."

"The gods could not pierce the shroud of the Amber Spell to give me such foresight," Valanis explained. "But, in their wisdom, they found someone who could ensure their words rang out for all time, until they could reach my ears." The dark elf closed his eyes as the sun broke through the clouds and bathed his face in its warm rays. "We are all bound by fate and the destiny laid out by the gods, Alidyr. This ranger, *Asher...* he is still alive."

Valanis's bold claim gave Alidyr pause, for he had caused the collapse of Elethiah, the ancient citadel of the elves, and surely crushed Asher within, along with Princess Reyna Sevari.

"Only he knows the location of the whole gem, and the gods wish me to possess it. Find him and you will find Paldora's greatest gift. But, I cannot stay here any longer." Valanis turned and casually walked along the railing. "Forty years have I slumbered in this mountain. For decades I have sent you and your brothers and sister into the world to see out my commands. But, now I have returned to strength."

The dark elf held up his left hand and inspected the shard of Paldora's gem. "As I did during the war, I will lead our forces to victory; but no longer from the shadows. Let the world of man look upon me and shudder. Illian will see the true power of magic."

Hearing his master so enthused and full of life only enthused Alidyr all the more. The elf felt strong, invincible almost, next to Valanis. Finally, after a thousand years, The Dark War would return and consume all of Verda.

"Remain mindful, Alidyr. Even with the power of Naius we will be challenged for supremacy. We must ensure that events continue to flow as I have designed."

Alidyr walked alongside his master. "As we speak, three Darkakin armies march across Drowners Run. They will cross into Illian by the month's end, south of Syla's Gate.

"My spies have already reported that Malliath has been seen in Malaysai. That means King Elym is without a dragon and therefore unable to open the Dragon Wall. His army will arrive on these shores without the aid of the great wyrms. My Arakesh have already defeated the Graycoats, scattering them across the land."

"You are lucky that your schemes to retrieve the shard were successful," Valanis added threateningly. "Had you failed I would have commanded your brothers and sister to destroy you for the death of Adellum. Your words, however, appear to be as deadly as your *blade*."

Alidyr tried not to wince when Valanis emphasised the singular.

"That is why you sit at the head of the Hand. But never forget; your Arakesh are *mine...*"

Alidyr bowed again, apologetically. He had been expecting some repercussions for inadvertently causing the death of Adellum and losing one of his gifted blades. The elf was suddenly thankful that his only punishment was a few stern words, mixed in with thanks for retrieving a shard of the gem.

"Apologies, Master. The Graycoats are scattered and through King Merkaris Tion you already control the north. He will move his army on your command. When the Darkakin arrive from the south and the elves from the east, Illian will be plunged into chaos and blood. When the land is cleansed, the gods can return!"

Valanis didn't reply straight away, but stopped and mused over his thoughts. Alidyr knew better than to interrupt his master's thoughts.

"It has been a long time since Merkaris has visited the pools," Valanis finally said.

Indeed, it had been several years with Alidyr being the king's only connection to the dark elf. Alidyr could still remember Merkaris discovering Kaliban all those years ago, lost in his own little adventure through the caves of Vengora, the mountain range which dominated the northern lands.

The human was already twisted and depraved before Valanis brought him into the fold. The Hand had killed those travelling with the king and sent him away, the only survivor of a supposed Troll attack and now the new disciple of Valanis - a well placed one at that.

"Perhaps I should pay *him* a visit," Valanis continued. "Reward him personally for his defeat over Mörygan Mörgö."

Alidyr was aware of his master's dislike of the Mörgös. During The Dark War, they had served him covertly until his apparent defeat, after which they scurried back to King Elym, seeking forgiveness and telling lies of enchantments and spells put upon them by Valanis.

Mörygan had been travelling with Princess Reyna when Merkaris killed him, an impressive feat indeed... for a human.

"Is it wise to travel so far, Master?" Alidyr knew exactly how Valanis would journey to Namdhor, the capital of all the north.

Valanis placed a hand on Alidyr's shoulder, seemingly affectionately. "You worry about me so, Alidyr. Accompany me and see for yourself the power of Paldora's gem."

The dark elf waved his hand across the cool air and opened a portal darker than night. So powerful was he, crystals were not required to perform such a feat.

Before he made to step through it, Valanis held his arm out again, this time towards the main keep. The ancient armoured knights, standing either side of the doorway, began to shake. The helmet broke free of the nearest one and flew into Valanis's open hand.

In the master's hand, the air around the helmet became distorted. The steel lines that formed a pattern over the helmet glowed orange from the heat. Valanis was creating a new helmet as if his very hand was a forge. Soon, the helmet appeared new and stronger. Intricate patterns swirled across the surface, leading into a curvature of the cheeks and a mouth piece that sloped down past the chin.

Valanis pulled back his hood and illuminated Alidyr's face with a golden glow. The aura disappeared as soon as the dark elf placed the helmet over his head. Only the slightest hint of his purple eyes could be seen through the dark slits of the smooth, yet angular mask.

Alidyr felt it only added to his master's already menacing appearance.

"Come," Valanis's altered voice bade.

The two strode through the abyss-like portal and left Kaliban far behind. In a single bound they traversed four hundred miles north, into the region of Orith.

Alidyr looked about and recognised the gloomy interior as Merkaris's personal chambers. The morning sun shone through a divide in the heavy curtains, revealing the dust that floated across the room. The bed covers were strewn across the floor and a naked woman lay asleep atop the soft mattress, a plaything to the king of the north.

Both Alidyr and Valanis turned towards the bookcase behind them, their keen ears detecting the quietest of whimpers. They could see it for what it was: a secret door. Valanis didn't bother looking for the switch but, instead, swiped his hand through the air and opened the bookcase on its hinges with telekinesis.

The room on the other side was far gloomier than Merkaris's chamber. The stone floors were bare of any rugs or animal hides and the walls were hidden behind a plethora of torture devices and chains. The chamber was that of spikes and blades and the smell of old blood. Candles and torches cast shadows in every nook and corner.

"Please!" the man's agonised voice pleaded again and again. In the centre of the chamber, Merkaris stood with his back to Alidyr and Valanis.

The king was standing before a man who was chained to the ceiling by his wrists. Blood dripped down every inch of his naked body with several chunks missing from his ribs and thighs. Hooks dug into his mangled face, clawing at his nerve clusters. Alidyr recognised many of the torture techniques and was confident that Merkaris had learnt these particular skills from Samandriel.

"And who is this sorry soul?" Alidyr asked, taking joy in the fright he gave the king.

Merkaris swivelled on the spot, the shock still not gone from his face, and dropped to one knee in front of Alidyr. The king of the north was wearing nothing but trousers and a bloody apron, his golden hair splattered with blood.

"My lord..."

"I am not your lord." Alidyr stepped aside so that Merkaris might see the true herald of the gods.

Valanis's dark form shifted from the shadows, as if he had been made of them. Only his breathing could be heard through the heavy mask when he slowly approached the genuflecting king.

Merkaris's expression told of his understanding about who was standing over him. Anyone attuned to the magical world could feel Valanis's presence.

"Valanis!" Merkaris bowed his head to the ground and remained there out of respect, and no lack of fear, Alidyr suspected.

"Rise..." Valanis whispered.

The man hanging from the chains looked on, terrified, the sight of Valanis inciting darker thoughts of what horrors lay in store for him. It felt good to see others cower in fear of his master. For a thousand years his name had fallen into myth and legend, but now the world would remember what real fear felt like.

Merkaris rose to his full height, where he stood in a puddle of the man's blood, which was slowly seeping down a drain under his hanging feet. "You are free of the pools, free of Kaliban."

"Indeed. Are you ready to take your place by my side and reshape the world?" Valanis asked seductively.

"I live to serve you!" Merkaris bowed again.

"And so you shall." Valanis walked around the hanging man, taking in the various devices around the room.

Alidyr stood back, allowing his master to take the lead.

"The Graycoats are scattered and vulnerable, but they could still prove to be an untimely thorn in my plans. You are to use your influence as king to rally them, and then *destroy* them. Samandriel will assist you in overseeing their demise. Do this as you will, just ensure the task is completed."

"Of course, my Lord, I will see it done!" Merkaris replied enthusiastically.

Valanis paused for a moment, examining the various torture devices. "For forty years I have studied the history that followed my imprisonment. After The Dragon War, your ancestors plundered The Lifeless Isles, yes?"

Merkaris, clearly unsure where the dark elf was going, could only nod in reply.

"During a time when the race of men was fracturing, I would imagine that King Gal Tion, your ancestor, made scrupulous records of the treasures he discovered in the dragon lands?"

Again, Merkaris nodded, but now Alidyr was just as unsure as to what his master was hinting at.

"Do you still have those records?" Valanis asked casually.

"They are in the archives, my Lord." Merkaris was on edge. "Under this very keep."

"Excellent." Valanis stopped and turned towards the king, the hanging man between them. "You will show them to me, immediately."

With that, Valanis rested his gloved hand on the tortured man and unleashed a spell that slowly turned his body into a solid block of ice. The man groaned and screamed until his vocal cords froze and his entire body glistened. It was clear that Valanis didn't want the king to be distracted.

Merkaris quickly removed his apron and made for his chamber to change his clothes. That was when Alidyr noticed his master reach out for the nearest wall. Valanis staggered until Alidyr caught him and held him upright. He checked over his shoulder to make certain that Merkaris hadn't noticed.

"We need to return to Kaliban, Master," Alidyr said in a hushed but urgent tone.

Valanis inhaled a deep breath and stood up straight, lightly pushing Alidyr away. The hood and mask concealed his master's expression, but he could guess it to be a pained one, despite his outward posture.

"*You* will return to Kaliban," Valanis instructed. "Speak with Nakir."

"Master?" Alidyr was confused.

"You are aware of your brother's work in Karath?" Valanis asked.

Alidyr nodded, more than aware of Nakir's actions in The Arid Lands. Centuries ago, the elf had started a cult in the southern cities known now as The New Dawn. With his power and ancient knowledge, Nakir had convinced the upper echelons of Karath's ruling families that Valanis was their true god.

Through these families, and Karath's emperor, Nakir had steered The Arid Lands for years, fuelling their slave trade and bringing an end to their defence of Syla's Gate.

"When the Darkakin armies arrive at Syla's Gate, Nakir will need your help to open those ancient doors," Valanis explained. "The people of The Arid Lands will resupply and offer their lives to the Darkakin, swelling their ranks.

"Karath, however, has fallen into chaos and civil war of late. The slaves are finally fighting back. A failure on Nakir's behalf. Now, he is struggling to maintain control, and I fear that when the Darkakin arrive the emperor will have lost his forces entirely.

"I need those forces to join with the Darkakin. You are to send the Arakesh to Karath and coordinate with Nakir. See that the Darkakin's arrival is seamless and this civil war is quashed."

"Master," Alidyr started to protest. "I feel the skills of the Arakesh would be better used elsewhere."

"And yet you *will* send them to Karath. Nakir is in charge of the Darkakin and their arrival. Between them and the armies of the north, the free people of Illian will be trapped. This part of my plan is pivotal, and I won't see it compromised."

"But, Master, I have already had dealings with the Darkakin and their *Goddess*. Perhaps it would be better if I coordinated—"

The head of the Hand stopped short of finishing his protest when Valanis's dark aura threatened to overcome Alidyr and remove him from existence. No real show of power was ever required to get his point across.

"Forgive me, Master." Alidyr stood back and bowed his head.

Valanis turned and made for the door to Merkaris's chamber, their discussion at an end as far as he was concerned. The king of the north was already dressed and ready to go, the blood washed from his hair and face.

"Merkaris..." Alidyr turned to regard the naked woman in his bed. "No witnesses."

"Oh, she's been dead for a while..." Merkaris didn't even look at the woman, as he led Valanis from the chamber.

Alidyr examined the woman's body again, seeing now the indications that she was indeed dead. Merkaris Tion was more twisted than he gave him credit for.

The elf produced a portal, with the help of a small crystal, and returned to Kaliban, curious as to his master's interest in Gal Tion's records of The Lifeless Isles. Of all their conversations and his teachings over the years, Valanis had never mentioned the ancient home of the dragons with any significance before.

Curious...

Once back in Kaliban's cold embrace, Alidyr searched for Nakir to no avail. The elf was reaching for the diviner orb, hidden within his white robes, when Thallan came by.

"Where is Nakir?" Alidyr asked absently, his mind still wondering about Valanis's new interest.

"He had to leave for Karath," Thallan reported. "The city is falling into outright war."

Alidyr could feel his anger rising. Now he would have to portal to Nightfall to order Ro Dosarn, the stand-in leader of the Arakesh in his absence, to take the assassins to Karath, as well as portalling to the capital city to speak with Nakir himself. He wanted to personally oversee Nakir's efforts, something he could not do through a diviner.

The elf made for the pools of Naius again; he was going to need a lot more crystals. Now he had to coordinate their efforts in Karath as well as somehow find the ranger in all the chaos.

He still doubted that the man had survived the fall of Elethiah, but he wasn't foolish enough to doubt the word of his master.

CHAPTER 2
A ROYAL MEETING

K ing Rengar of house Marek strode through the lavish corridors of his palace, accompanied by Lord Marshal Horvarth and the Graycoat, Ned Fennick. A pair of Velian guards were stationed by every door to ensure their king didn't have to do anything as ordinary as use a doorknob.

The king of Velia glanced out of the passing window and caught sight of a stray row of celebratory bunting, blowing in the morning breeze. The king subconsciously clenched his fist with the irritation that rose to the surface.

He had been humiliated by the events of the past month. The moment in which history would have remembered his name had now passed. The elves had been driven from his city by assassins, Ro Dosarn had escaped his *inescapable* dungeons and, not only that, but the heads of every region in Illian had been personally invited to the catastrophe.

Humiliated...

Rengar entered the final room at the end of the corridor and tried to forget the embarrassment he had sustained upon announcing to

26

the city that the celebrations had been cancelled, and the kings and queens of Illian had left.

The room was a simple rectangle with no windows or decorations. The bulk of the room was taken up by a long table with six empty chairs, the only illumination from the torches mounted on the walls. A plain black orb sat in the middle of the table, the room's only ornament.

Galkarus Vod, Rengar's court mage, was already in the room, standing to one side in his usual robes and floppy, pointed hat. The mage's over-encumbered belt hung with herbs and exotic instruments, all of which made some noise when he bowed to his king.

"Are we ready?" Rengar asked the wizard.

"They are already seated, your Grace." Galkarus gestured for the king to take his seat at the head of the table.

Rengar took his seat and watched Galkarus stamp his staff three times onto the stone floor. The messy strands of wooden branches at the top of his staff glowed, as the crystal hidden beneath them offered its magical energy.

The black orb situated in the centre of the table gave an audible chime before the empty chairs became occupied. The wraith-like form of King Merkaris sat at the opposite end of the table, his strong hands clasped out in front of him, always the figure of composure. Rengar regarded the young king with caution. Something about the northerner always made his skin crawl and the hairs on the back of his neck stand up.

To Merkaris's right, King Gregorn Orvish's dishevelled form took shape. As always, the king of Grey Stone's scraggy greying hair fell to his shoulders with almost imperceptible braids woven throughout. The back of the chair could still be seen through the wispy fur that lined the cloak of his collar.

Rengar would never like the man, not after the wars their fathers had fought against one another. There was too much bad blood between their families to ever make lasting peace. For that reason, it was a good thing that the region of Felgarn, home to the kingdom of Lirian, separated their two lands.

Just as her kingdom sat between the opposing Mareks and Orvishs, Queen Isabella Harg's elegant features came to life between the two kings.

Rengar couldn't help but smile at the queen. He had always hoped to marry her and combine their kingdoms after her husband's untimely death. Of course there was the matter of his current wife to contend with but, if the opportunity ever arose to marry the queen of Felgarn, Rengar was sure he could deal with his conundrum.

To Rengar's right, the lanky form of Vizier Sivilis came together. A perfectly cylindrical beard protruded from his chin at an angle that was apparently fashionable in The Arid Lands. Rengar just thought he looked like a moron.

This particular moron, however, represented Faros, the boy-emperor of Karath, who never attended such meetings. He was always too busy playing with his toys, Rengar thought. In truth, the king was surprised that Sivilis had attended the meeting at all, given the state of unrest Karath was experiencing.

The last chair, in the corner, beside King Merkaris, remained empty as always. The elected leaders of Dragorn hadn't accepted an invitation to one of these meetings for years. It didn't bother Rengar anymore, who knew the elected leaders were simply criminals - like all the vagabonds that lived on that island, he mused. So far from Illian's shores were they, that the Dragornians considered them-selves a country unto themselves.

"Thank you for joining us, Rengar..." Gregorn said sarcastically.

Rengar had always liked to keep the others waiting. He wanted them to understand the importance of his presence.

Galkarus remained to one side, as did the other court mages that stood beside their lieges, hundreds of miles apart. Through the connection created by all five mages and the diviners, the rulers could see and hear each other. Rengar knew that through their eyes, he was sitting at *their* table with the two Graycoats behind him.

Vizier Sivilis sat forward. "If you have summoned us to apologise for our wasted trip to your kingdom, then please do not. Emperor Faros enjoyed his time away from Karath."

Because he lives under constant threat of assassination in his own land, Rengar thought.

"Get himself a new cuddly toy, did he?" the king of Velia muttered a little too loudly.

Though the others smirked and hid their amusement, Vizier Sivilis appeared shocked. "What did you say?"

"I said, I didn't summon this meeting to apologise," Rengar replied, allowing his impatience to be heard. "West Fellion has fallen." The king left his statement to hang in the air.

Gregorn's jaw dropped half an inch and he looked to the senior Graycoats, as if seeking clarification, while Isabella hung her head, no doubt already aware of their downfall. West Fellion sat in the southern region of Felgarn, Isabella's land, where they were most likely housing many of the survivors. Curiously, Merkaris's stony expression didn't move in the slightest.

"How has this come to be?" King Gregorn asked.

Rengar turned his head to peer up at the Lord Marshal. Horvarth sported a wound that curved up from his right cheekbone and over his eye. It had been seen to and stitched since the battle, but the Lord Marshal had been bedridden for several days in quite a daze.

Ned Fennick, on the other hand, looked to have escaped the battle and destruction of their fortress without so much as a scratch. Even more curious...

"My Lords and Lady," Horvarth began, "after West Fellion opened its gates to Princess Reyna, our home was set upon by an army of Arakesh." Instead of eliciting shock, Horvarth created confusion among the rulers.

"I'm sorry, Lord Marshal, did you say *army*?" Isabella asked.

"Yes, your Grace." Horvarth lifted his chin, fighting the shame of his great defeat. "Never before have they come together in such numbers. We were... outmatched. They appeared in the dead of night

29

without warning. Even now, there is no trail to suggest where they came from; they moved across the land like an army of ghosts. To have even reached West Fellion they must have passed several towns, and yet there are no witnesses. Five hundred warriors march over the land, and no witnesses!"

"Yes, they are light of foot," Rengar added impatiently, "as my own guards can attest to. Tell them the rest." The king didn't want Horvarth to go on and on, and he was all too aware that the Lord Marshal very well could.

"My knights are scattered," Horvarth continued. "Those who survived or fled have taken refuge in Vangarth, Whistle Town and here, in Velia."

Rengar cleared his throat deliberately, ushering the Lord Marshal along.

"Alas, I was injured: my life spared only by the grace of the gods."

And your cowardly friend, Ned Fennick. Rengar kept that thought to himself.

"The accounts from those who survived are all the same, however. The Arakesh were led into battle by an *elf.*"

Even Merkaris's ethereal body sat back in his chair at that news. Gregorn scoffed and Isabella lost control of her plummeting jaw. Sivilis only appeared intrigued, his immaculate eyebrows raised.

"With a single shot from a bow, this elf reduced the gates of West Fellion to rubble," the Lord Marshal went on. "Those gates have stood for a thousand years..."

Rengar cleared his throat again.

"All reports state that the fortress would have been overrun a lot quicker, if not for the efforts of the *ranger.*"

"The same ranger who accompanied Princess Reyna?" Queen Isabella asked, a little too intrigued.

"The same, your Grace. His name is Asher and was once a *member* of the Arakesh," Horvarth clarified.

"Oh, I am aware of the ranger's past, Lord Marshal. He saved my life and that of my son many years ago."

Rengar rolled his eyes. He didn't want to hear Isabella's recollection of Asher's heroics yet again.

"It is said that he stemmed the flow at the main gate single-handed," Horvarth explained.

Rengar glanced at Ned Fennick and saw the man's discomfort.

"There are few reports about what happened after the elf breached the main keep," Horvarth continued, "but those who have reported, tell of a battle between the elf and the ranger, with help from Princess Reyna and her companion, Faylen Haldör. Though they defeated the mysterious elf, it came with the price of West Fellion's walls."

"An *elf* led their army?" Gregorn was already over the destruction of West Fellion. "How many damned elves are there in Illian?"

Rengar straightened his back. "I am going to try and open communications again with King Elym Sevari. We will get to the bottom of this mystery."

"What is to become of the Graycoats?" Isabella asked, as if the two knights weren't standing behind Rengar.

"Lord Marshal..." It was the first time King Merkaris had spoken. "Get word to your wayward flock; instruct them to take The Selk Road north. I will have a place ready for them in Darkwell. It won't be as grand as West Fellion but my people there are welcoming. The Graycoats can settle there until you decide otherwise."

Horvarth puffed out his chest. "That is most generous, your Grace. I cannot thank you enough for your kindness. I will send word immediately."

Merkaris simply nodded in response.

Sivilis's ethereal form became animated. "No! Emperor Faros *demands* that every Graycoat left alive is to march to Karath at once. We contribute just as much to the peacekeepers of West Fellion, and their swords are required *now*!"

"As you say, Vizier Sivilis," Horvarth replied coolly, "we are peacekeepers. We are not soldiers bred solely to fight your wars."

"We are not here to discuss a few rebellious slaves," Rengar interrupted. He gave Sivilis a glare that told him to drop the conversation. "Now that we've cleared that up... there is still the matter of Princess Reyna. Since the battle she has been missing, along with her companion and the ranger."

"That's if they survived," Gregorn commented.

"If they escaped it wasn't witnessed," Horvarth added.

"I suggest we have our respective spymasters get the word out," Rengar said. "If we are to go ahead with our elven alliance, I don't want to have to inform King Elym that his only daughter is dead or missing in our lands."

"*Our* alliance?" Gregorn countered wickedly. "I thought it was all *yours...*"

Rengar ignored the obnoxious king of a land no one gave two shits about. He had more responsibility than the others since it was Velia which the elves had first contacted. The emphasis was on him to keep those lines of communication open.

"My people have no time to fear some ghost army!" Sivilis exclaimed, ignoring Gregorn's remark and Rengar's steely gaze. "The Arid Lands and the good people of Karath are under real threat. *The House of Owls* incites unrest and war against the great families! They are a cult!"

Rengar was already aware of the House of Owls, thanks to his network of spies in the south. He had taken an interest in them when rumours spread that they were responsible for the death of Emperor Faro's parents, the previous rulers of Karath.

Sivilis called them a cult, but the king of Velia knew full well that they were no more than a band of men, women and children - orphans all. As the unclaimed children of slaves, the group worked tirelessly to free those under the heel of the 'great families'. Ultimately, they were no threat to Rengar's kingdom and therefore of no consequence.

"Your country's civil war is a matter for *another time*, Vizier Sivilis." Rengar stopped himself from rolling his eyes.

"*Should* we fear this army of Arakesh, Lord Marshal?" Isabella asked.

Horvarth answered before Rengar could intervene. "I would suggest mobilising your armies at once and securing the cities. Complements from all will need to be sent to the towns, but I warn you not to underestimate the assassins. Though their number is smaller than any one of your armies, they are the most skilled of fighters."

"Yes, thank you for your strategical advice, Lord Marshal." Rengar held up a hand, signalling the man to remain silent. "We shall all remain ever watchful for their return, though it would appear that they attack with a specific goal, rather than aiming to conquer. Perhaps we will give it more thought when the princess is found. After her return to Velia we can discuss any extra guard that may be required from the other kingdoms."

"What makes you think she will return to Velia after nearly being assassinated within its very walls?" Gregorn spat.

Rengar couldn't even look at Gregorn for fear of losing his temper. "It was Princess Reyna's wish to return here and continue our discussions. You will of course be invited, as before."

A quiet tension overtook the small gathering. Had they actually been in the room, Rengar couldn't be sure he wouldn't have tried to throttle Gregorn.

"Do we even discuss Korkanath?" Isabella asked finally.

Rengar clasped his fingers over the table. "The timing is suspicious, but Magikar Pondaal has already returned to the island and is personally overseeing the investigation. The only thing we know for certain is that the dragon is gone." The lack of surprised responses was testament to the speed with which the news had travelled.

"Let the mages deal with mage problems," Gregorn offered ignorantly.

"Then this meeting is over..." Merkaris's ethereal body evaporated, followed unceremoniously by Sivilis and Gregorn.

"Until the next time, Rengar." Isabella faded away, leaving the king of Velia alone with the Graycoats and Galkarus.

Rengar hated it when the meeting ended on somebody else's terms. He always liked to have the last word, whatever it might be.

"I always thought the dragon was a myth," Fennick commented as they left the room.

Rengar ignored the knight's remark. "I would ask, Lord Marshal, that as your Graycoats travel north to Darkwell, they would look out for any signs of the princess or the ranger."

"Of course, your Grace," Horvarth replied, tracing the edges of his new scar. "If they're still alive, my knights will find them."

CHAPTER 3
BURYING THE DEAD

"They'll never find us," Faylen commented, upon observing the drunken Graycoats stumbling out of the tavern.

Asher pulled his hood lower to conceal his face, not wanting to take the chance. It had been his idea to keep to themselves and leave the Graycoats be.

Faylen hooked her arm under his and the pair drew closer together, as they walked the streets of Vangarth, posing as a couple. The ranger slung the sack of food over his shoulder and continued to head towards The Greenleaf Inn.

West Fellion was in ruins and the Graycoats dispersed, but Asher didn't fancy spending any more time in one of their cells, or the more likely outcome that he would end up killing them.

He still wasn't sure how he would react if he ever saw Ned Fennick again, his personal torturer. There was a time when Asher wouldn't have considered anything but killing the arrogant knight. His current company were changing him in many ways it seemed, some more subtle than others.

Faylen pressed against him within her dark cloak, having arranged her long black hair to cover her pointed ears. Asher felt uncomfortable with how much he enjoyed the elf's company. He had enjoyed the company of women before, but only for a night.

Taking comfort or joy in anything tasted like ash in his mouth these days.

Elaith was dead...

In keeping with Graycoat tradition, a pyre had been built by the companions and the young knight from Ameeraska had been cremated on the banks of The Unmar, ten days ago.

Asher missed the Graycoat's witty sense of humour and innocent naivety but, mostly, he just missed how she looked at him. Elaith had found the ranger to be fascinating and inspiring, never the killer the rest of the world saw.

How many Graycoats had died in the battle of West Fellion? Elaith would not have been the youngest to die at the hands of the Arakesh, though the young knight had been slain by a greater evil than the assassins.

Alidyr Yalathanil's smug face was burned into Asher's mind, not only by the many years he had spent being trained by the elf, but by the smirking expression as he told the ranger about the truth of his past, moments before the elf killed Elaith.

Asher was still trying to get his head around the idea that he had been standing still for a thousand years. For a millennium he had been frozen as a boy in the archway of Elethiah's oldest tunnels.

Any family he thought might still be out there, living inside The Wild Moores, would be long dead. It was even possible that his entire clan had been wiped out in any number of skirmishes between the wild folk of the woods.

More Graycoats rounded the corner in front of the couple. Asher glanced at them for a second, but was sure to keep from making eye contact. He had been trained vigorously in the art of blending in during his years at Nightfall, the home of the Arakesh. The ranger could move through any streets as if he was just another face in the crowd.

Faylen's beauty, on the other hand, was not something easily hidden. By any man's eye, the flawless complexion of an elf could not be ignored, and so the two Graycoats paused to take her in.

Asher held his breath and discreetly reached within his cloak for the small dagger that lay at the base of his back. It was the only weapon he had brought with him or, more to the point, it was the only weapon Faylen had allowed him to bring.

The elf had rightly pointed out that Asher had been seen by all the Graycoats, upon their entry to West Fellion, and that a man walking around Vangarth with a short-sword strapped to his back would gain attention. He had even left his quiver and compact bow behind, despite the fact that most of Vangarth's population wore both. It was a town of hunters, most skilled at navigating The Evermoore.

The ranger kept his head low and ushered Faylen along, turning the corner from which the Graycoats had emerged. He wanted to get her out of sight before one of them tried their luck. Though they were the famous knights of the realm, whose lives were one of honour and duty, he still didn't trust them. Especially now that their order was in disarray and their leaders scattered to the wind, or buried under West Fellion. Now, they were simply skilled fighters with no direction.

The sun hadn't long set and the cold night was quick to descend. Winter wasn't far off and they knew about it. Soon, the icy winds would travel south, off Vengora, and bring snow to The Evermoore.

The streets of Vangarth were still crowded, however, as the townsfolk prepared for the celebrations in honour of Ymira, the goddess of the harvest.

For the people of Illian it was as if nothing had changed. Asher looked around as everyone got on with their lives, putting up bunting and planting flags or building shrines to Ymira. They lived less than fifty miles from West Fellion where, only ten days ago, the largest battle in any of their lives had been fought.

The greatest knights of the realm, these people's self-proclaimed protectors, had fallen and seen their home destroyed. Not only that, but Elethiah, an ancient city that had stood for thousands of years, had been razed to the ground.

Nobody cared.

War hadn't been brought to their doors and Vangarth hadn't been destroyed. No one knew that Elaith had been killed by an elf, or that there even were elves in Illian. The royal families had kept that secret to themselves after the celebrations had been cancelled in Velia.

Considering everything they had gone through over the last month, being in civilised Vangarth seemed very surreal to the ranger.

Asher stole a glance over his shoulder to confirm that they weren't being followed. After cutting through the alleyway, the couple were back onto one of the main streets.

The town was predominantly made from wood, being surrounded by the largest forest in Illian. Vangarth was one of two towns that sat within the border of the forest and under the rule of Queen Isabella Harg. The queen ruled all of Felgarn from her throne in the city of Lirian, deep in the heart of The Evermoore and north of Vangarth.

"I need to pick up some more Evernight," Faylen said as they approached the herbalist.

"More?" Asher asked in his usual gruff voice. "You bought some a week ago."

The ranger didn't want to go near the herbalist. The little shop sat next to the hunters' lodge, which had been recently converted to house all the wounded Graycoats after the battle. The knights were always coming and going, visiting their injured comrades.

"I need it to make more elixir," Faylen explained. "You have no idea what it's like living among so many humans with an elven nose." The elf wrinkled her button nose in disgust.

"Reyna doesn't seem to mind." Asher couldn't hide his smile from Faylen, even under the cowl of his large hood.

Faylen offered a scowl in return. The princess's mentor still wasn't approving of the relationship that continued to form between

Nathaniel and Reyna. Asher was just thankful that the Graycoat had the elf to comfort him. After they left the swamps of Elethiah, Nathaniel had been a broken man, blaming himself for Elaith's death.

Asher waited outside the shop and sat on a nearby bench, next to an old man enjoying his pipe; sitting on his own was an easy way to stand out. A couple of Graycoats strolled by, but they took no notice of the hooded man.

The ranger sighed and sat back, tired of never being able to relax; no man should still be fighting into his fifties. Even though he hadn't told his companions, Asher had turned fifty three days past. He could never remember his actual birthday, but Nasta Nal-Aket had proclaimed the day he found Asher outside Elethiah to be it.

Asher didn't like to think about the fact that he was technically well over a thousand years old...

The ranger sat there, feeling the cold breeze settle into his bones, while his muscles continued to ache from his fight with the Arakesh and the dark elf, Adellum Bövö. Asher was used to feeling the after-effects of a battle, but Adellum had been a new challenge, not to mention the punishment he experienced at Alidyr's hands.

The ranger looked at his right hand and noted the absence of his ring. How many times had Paldora's gem healed him? Now he was without its magic. Now he was just as vulnerable as everyone else.

The neighing of a horse across the street broke his reverie. The large square door of the town's blacksmith blew open to reveal a rather frustrated horse resisting the smith's attempts to fit new shoes. Asher's eyes went wide when he saw the horse's chestnut coating and twin braids along its mane. *Hector*!

He eyed the smith with fury. "Son of a..."

The ranger shot up from the bench and stormed across the street and into the blacksmith's workshop. The horse tried to rear up in protest, but the smith's assistant held it down by the reins. Asher pushed the smith back and shot the assistant a threatening glare that saw him let go of the reins.

"What are ye about?" the smith bellowed, brandishing the horse shoe as if it were a weapon.

Though Asher appeared less threatening than usual without his assortment of blades and swords, he retained that look in his eye that gave even the most skilled of warriors pause.

"This is *my* horse!" Asher placed a hand on Hector's cheek and immediately calmed the animal.

"This here horse belongs to Mr Biggins, the stable master." The smith lowered the horse shoe and backed off a step. "He's had a load since that business down at West Fellion."

Asher sighed again, as the smith gave such little care or credence to the battle and all the lives lost.

"An' ye don' look much like one o' them Graycoats..." the smith added with confidence.

"Doesn't change the fact that he's mine," Asher countered.

"What's all this then?" an authoritative voice asked from behind the ranger.

Asher cursed under his breath; sure that he had just given himself away to the Graycoats.

"Do we have a problem here?" the voice asked.

The ranger turned around slowly and concealed his expression of relief at the sight of Vangarth's watch. Two soldiers, dressed in silver chainmail with green and yellow hauberks, were standing in the doorway. Each brandished a sword on their hip and wore silver helmets that revealed their faces. Dark green cloaks draped over their shoulders and collected mud at the bottom. The assassin in Asher had already assessed both men and decided where to strike to bring them down quickly and quietly.

But that was not his way anymore.

The ranger had his companions to think of now. If he started a fight here, it would compromise the others and put them at risk of being exposed. They had to remain hidden for now.

"He claims this 'ere horse belongs to 'im!" the smith exclaimed, his confidence now bolstered in the presence of the watch.

"Do you have any papers to back up this claim?" the soldier asked, sounding almost bored with the complaint.

Asher clenched his jaw in the sight of defeat. "No..."

"Then best be on your way." The soldier stepped aside and gestured for Asher to leave.

The ranger patted Hector one last time and left the blacksmith with a warning look. It would be the same look that gave the man nightmares that night.

Faylen met him in the street with a curious glance at the soldiers behind him. The elf quickly took his arm again and the couple disappeared into the lanes.

"What was that about?" the elf asked.

"I found Hector," Asher replied with no lack of frustration in his tone.

"You nearly got into a fight and exposed us all... over a horse?" The elf sounded bemused and annoyed all at once.

"*My* horse!" Asher replied a little too loudly, gaining the attention of a young man walking by.

Faylen gave him her usual condescending look and steered them into The Greenleaf Inn. The tavern that dominated the lower level was packed as usual, but there were no Graycoats in sight. They had picked this particular inn because of how far away it was from the converted hunters' lodge and surrounding inns.

Asher and Faylen moved through the crowd with ease, both experts in predicting body language. The ranger retrieved his key but Faylen interrupted him before he could press it into the lock.

"He's in *my* room..." she said with displeasure.

Asher smiled, putting away his key, and turned to follow Faylen into the room she shared with Reyna. Her elven ears proved true, as they entered and found the princess and the Graycoat sitting on a single bed together. Nathaniel made to stand up at seeing Faylen, but Asher noticed Reyna's delicate, yet incredibly strong, hands pull at the knight's arm and keep him in place.

The ranger paused, catching sight of the exquisite blade,

enchanted with powerful magic. Alidyr's short-sword was propped against the corner, along with Adellum's devastating bow. The sword's ornate, white handle curved slightly at the bottom, wherein lay a crystal the size of a thumb, fused into the hilt. The steel blade was hourglass shaped, just as his own was, and lined in ancient runes.

Asher could only see the blade spinning end-over-end until it found Elaith's heart...

"A productive trip?" Reyna asked, looking from Faylen to Asher, who was thankful for the distraction.

"We bought some food, I acquired some more Evernight root and Asher nearly got into a fight with the town watch over a horse." Faylen gave him another condescending look.

"You found Hector?" Nathaniel asked with forced enthusiasm. The knight was trying for the benefit of the group, but it was clear that he was still depressed. "He's in Vangarth?"

"Taken in by some stable master," Asher grumbled.

"I take it you already have plans to reacquire the horse?" Reyna asked coyly.

"Leave it to me." Asher's definitive tone ended the conversation and he dropped the sack of food onto the round table.

The group ate in relative silence, making small talk through mouthfuls of cold meat and bread. Asher couldn't quite believe how much meat the elves could eat. He was sure they put more away than a clan of Trolls.

"I overheard some disturbing news in the tavern today," Nathaniel said between mouthfuls. "Word has been sent from Lord Marshal Horvarth. Apparently he survived, and Ned Fennick with him."

Asher felt the echo of a hot poker burning his skin.

"They're in Velia," Nathaniel continued. "King *Merkaris* has offered a permanent refuge for all Graycoats in Darkwell."

They didn't trust the king of Namdhor. When Reyna and the others had arrived in Velia, it had been a complement of Merkaris's men that attacked them alongside Ro Dosarn. There was no evidence that Merkaris was aware of his men's deception, and certainly no link between him and Alidyr, but still, the king's generous offer to the Graycoats was not to be trusted.

"Will you go with them?" Asher asked, already sure of the answer.

Nathaniel looked from him to Reyna, before concentrating on his food again. "I've made my choice..."

The ranger was happy to hear it, if only for Nathaniel's sake. The Graycoats never accepted him simply because of who his father was. Tobin Galfrey had been one of the greatest Graycoats in history, but his public siring of Nathaniel tainted his reputation and humiliated the order. Nathaniel was nothing but a reminder of that to the other knights. Asher wanted his friend to be free of it.

The concept of friendship wasn't completely new to the old assassin, but he was coming to enjoy the bond that grew between them. Elaith's death, however, was a reminder of how much it could hurt to let someone else into his life.

For fourteen years Asher had roamed Illian as a free man, but he considered very few to be what others would call friends. He still couldn't deny thinking of Nathaniel as a friend, as well as Reyna and even Faylen, though the older elf was harder to read.

Asher just nodded his head in response to Nathaniel. The ranger had never been one for words, and hoped that his friend knew from the silent reply how glad he was.

Later that night, after leaving the elves' room, Asher didn't stop at the door to his room but gestured for Nathaniel to follow him outside. Curious, the knight followed him, asking all the while where they were going.

Asher walked through the near empty streets until they reached the edge of the town. The two paused in the shadows as a pair from the watch walked by on patrol. The ranger didn't want them to be seen leaving the town at night, a suspicious sight in itself. The two continued through the trees of The Evermoore until the lights of Vangarth were a dim glow in the background.

"What are we doing here, Asher?" Nathaniel asked again, frustrated.

"We're burying her..." the ranger replied solemnly.

Nathaniel looked confused. "Elaith? We built a—"

"The necklace," Asher interrupted, gesturing to Nathaniel's right pocket. "I saw you take it."

Nathaniel didn't even try to hide it. He reached into the pocket and retrieved a simple chain with a square piece of carved wood attached to it. The script was hard to see in the moonlight, but Asher knew it was written in Kilanti, the language of The Arid Lands and Elaith's birthplace.

"I didn't even know she had it," Nathaniel explained. "Graycoats don't have much in the way of possessions, especially from wherever they hailed from. We're told to leave it all behind and embrace the order." Nathaniel laughed with little mirth. "I don't even know what it says, but it was the only thing on her that was *hers*..."

"I don't remember any of the traditions of the Outlanders," Asher began, "but Nasta taught me some of the ways of *his* people."

Nasta Nal-Aket, the former Father of Nightfall and mentor to Asher had treated the ranger like a son during his time as an assassin. Before the destruction of Elethiah, Alidyr had gloated about killing him and dropping him into the pit, deep in the heart of Nightfall. In truth, Asher wasn't sure if he would have stopped the elf, had he been there.

"Nasta came from Tregaran, in the north of The Arid Lands," Asher continued. "It's not Ameeraska but their cultures are similar." Asher knelt down in front of Nathaniel and used his hand to dig a small hole in the soft muddy ground. "They bury their dead, but then they wait for the new moon until they bury their grief. They take something that belonged to the dead and they bury it, giving over their *grief* in the process. You need to leave it here."

Nathaniel looked down at the small hole and considered the necklace. "I failed her..."

"She was a Graycoat," Asher quickly replied. "Elaith died in battle, a warrior."

"I would rather she had died of old age."

"That's not how people like us meet our end." Asher stepped away from Nathaniel, giving him the space to consider the southern tradition. "Bury your grief..." The ranger left him under the dark canopy of The Evermoore.

It was some time before the knight returned to their room at The Greenleaf Inn. Asher kept his eyes closed and pretended to remain asleep, happy that his friend had perhaps found some peace.

Of course, Asher had no intention of burying his grief or searching for peace. Instead, he was going to find Alidyr Yalathanil and give the elf his blade back.

When the sun rose again, the four companions came back together to enjoy breakfast, and enjoy it they did. Nathaniel's renewed spirit infected them all, lifting the dark cloud that had followed them from Elethiah.

The knight wasn't completely back to his normal self, but his smile was genuine at least. Asher allowed himself to relax, for what felt like the first time in many years, and imparted on the group a few of his funnier tales from life on the road. They shared a laugh and the ranger even achieved a smile from Faylen, who never relaxed.

"So what do we do now?" Reyna finally asked in the inevitable lull.

"What can we do?" Faylen replied with a hopeless tone. "Valanis has been free for forty years. We have to assume he's been hiding in Kaliban. The legends say he built the fortress around the pools of Naius. Without the gem he must have been too weak after a thousand years in the Amber Spell, otherwise he would have been seen before now.

"But, with the gem, he could be anywhere now. Imagine what plans he already has in place with four decades of planning. You all heard Alidyr; he doesn't have an army, so he pits man against elf to do the work for him."

"He must have had the gem for ten days now," Nathaniel pointed out. "If he's as powerful as you say, why haven't we already heard from him? Why hasn't he destroyed Velia or Lirian or Namdhor? Alidyr brought down Elethiah with the gem; shouldn't Valanis be levelling all of Illian by now?"

"He doesn't need to," Reyna said. "He's already steered the course of the elven army. Valanis has but to stand back and watch."

"He doesn't *need* to, or he *can't*?" Asher emphasised the difference.

Faylen's eyes lit up, as if understanding his way of thinking. "Yes... He only has a *shard* of the gem." Faylen stood up from the table and began to pace. "It's possible he's still stuck in Kaliban or wherever he's been hiding all these years."

Nathaniel sat back and looked at his companions in quick succession. "Are we talking about going after Valanis?"

"No." Faylen stopped pacing. "Even if the shard of Paldora's gem doesn't restore him to strength, Valanis is still a powerful foe, with powerful allies. Wherever he is, you can be certain he's surrounded by those who would kill to keep him safe. We would need an army to march on Kaliban, if that's where he is, and no one knows for sure where it is!"

"There are five armies in Illian, not counting Dragorn," Asher said. "Should we ask to borrow one?" The ranger's attempt to add some levity was unsuccessful.

Reyna offered, "Perhaps we should simply give another army a singular purpose..." The princess looked to Faylen with a glimmer of hope.

"No," Faylen said without consideration. "There is nothing that

46

will stop your father from waging war with Illian. Knowing that Valanis is free will only increase his ferocity, and when he discovers that *you* have already been in danger he will invade all the sooner, I am sure. He won't wait for the dragons in Mount Garganafan to grow, and that's if Galanör even freed Malliath from Korkanath."

"Then we need more information." Reyna looked to the chest at the base of Faylen's bed. Its infinite depths contained most of their supplies, though Asher was unsure as to what Reyna was hinting at.

Faylen sighed and her shoulders sagged, as if she had come to some miserable conclusion. The elf sat on the end of her bed and looked at the chest with unease.

"What are you talking about?" Nathaniel asked for the two of them.

"We have a diviner," Reyna explained. "It allows us to communicate with other people who have diviners, but our one is part of a closed set. We can only talk to Galanör or my father." The princess didn't appear all that happy about the latter.

"I've seen these diviners before," Asher commented with a hint of distrust. "Anyone can listen in if they have one."

"Not these ones," Faylen finally spoke. "The three orbs were enchanted by our elders for many moons to ensure their security. It was to be our way of coordinating the invasion and supplying King Elym with information."

"Have you used it yet?" Nathaniel looked at the closed chest with interest.

"Not yet," Reyna said. "Mörygan was the last to speak with Galanör, though his diviner wouldn't work on Korkanath."

Asher thought about the elven ambassador, killed in his room in Velia. The ranger didn't know much about the elf except that he was supposed to be an expert in magic, and yet his room was testament to the battle of spells that had taken place. It continued to trouble Asher that they still didn't know who had killed the elf, but he could only imagine it to be one of the Hand, Valanis's generals.

"One way or another, you're going to have to speak with him,"

Asher said. "We need to know what kind of time we have before the invasion."

"And we need to know if we should expect dragons," Nathaniel added with wide eyes.

Faylen looked at them all before turning to the chest, her mind made up for her.

It was a strange thought to Asher that Faylen was about to speak with the same Elym he had met a thousand years ago, in the library of Elethiah. Their previous, if tenuous, link was a potential complication yet to be seen by the ranger.

CHAPTER 4
THE KING OF ELVES

D
espite the chilling breeze, the city of Elandril was encompassed in glorious sunshine. The entire valley sparkled amidst the dozen waterfalls that surrounded the elven city, pouring water from the river Nylla into the lakes that surrounded the land.

The tall trees of The Amara dotted the valley, until the great forest engulfed the horizon for as far as the eye could see, even an elven eye. King Elym Sevari looked out over the tops of those trees as if he could see Illian's shores, a thousand miles away.

The world of man was an ocean away, yet with every day the elves grew closer to reaching its borders.

Illian would be theirs again.

Elym rested his hands against the balcony railing and took the city in. What a beauty their home was. Over the course of a thousand years the elves had erected spires and towers of unimaginable height, as well as homes both humble and grand.

Their numbers had swelled over the centuries – no easy task when female elves could only bear children once every hundred years – and provided Elandril with an incredible population: every grown elf more than capable of wielding a sword or manipulating magic. No longer were they the peaceful folk of the wood, but a race to be reckoned with. It wouldn't matter how big the human armies were, because for every elf they would need twenty men to compete.

The king looked down from his balcony, set into the tallest tower in the palace, nestled against the high valley wall. His warriors were lined up in rows in the great courtyard below, training under the High Guardian, Varö Grövale.

Of all his advisers, Elym trusted Varö's word without question. The elf had achieved the highest rank within their army and his sons and daughters were all warriors born. Varö had no interest in matching his children with the highborn families or even the royals themselves. He would fight for Elym and the elven race until his life was claimed or Illian was theirs.

That thought led the king to dwell on Galanör of house Reveeri. The elf was the best sword fighter in all of Elandril, and easily the best choice to lead the mission to Korkanath, but he had failed to make contact via his diviner for several weeks. He should have returned with Malliath the voiceless by now...

Elym had personally taken the time to instruct Galanör on how to speak with the dragon and control his emotions. Though the king wasn't a Dragorn, Elym's sister, Nalana, had been one of the chosen for many centuries. Before her death, she had taught him about the ways of the dragons in the hope that one day, he too might become a Dragorn.

Of course, had he been born with that gift, as his sister had, he would never have chosen to live among them on their mysterious islands. Elym Sevari was born to rule.

"My Lord..." The melodic voice of Naywyn called to him from the doorway.

Elym turned to look upon his servant. The young elf presented the king with a wooden chest, carried in both hands. He had requested it, earlier that morning, to be brought from his private vaults; though now it was in front of him, Elym was hesitant to open it.

The rectangular box was engraved with ancient glyphs and elven symbols, an intricate spell that would keep the chest shut to all but him. His fingers ran over the polished wood, working through the hieroglyphs with great care. It had been centuries since he had looked inside.

As always, the chest had him thinking of Nalana, his sister. Her words had sunk into the very bones of his wife, Adilandra. How many days of late had he been frozen in place, fearful for the love of his very long life? Adilandra was in lands unknown, to the south of Ayda, seeking the last of the old dragons. A fool's errand, he thought. Their future lay dormant inside Mount Garganafan, with the unborn dragons.

Their last conversation had been an argument, and a great one at that, regarding her departure to the south. Before he could dwell on such depressing thoughts, Naywyn shifted her body and the breeze carried her perfume towards him. It reminded him of Reyna, his daughter. Another great love he had pushed away in pursuit of justice for his people. She too was in lands that carried great peril, though her mission was more important than most.

"My Lord?" Naywyn asked with concern.

How long had he been standing there, staring at the chest? He hated the box and its wretched contents; always taking over his emotions and dredging up memories. Before Elym could open the chest, his keen ears heard footsteps approaching the door to his chamber. Thankful for the disturbance, the king bade Naywyn to take the chest away as he adjusted his long robe and walked back into his room.

"Enter."

"My Lord." A member of his personal guard strode into the room, clad in white armour, helmet and blue cloak. Elym had always favoured the style since The Dark War and ensured the continuation of the tradition. "Forgive the intrusion, but the diviner has been activated."

Elym nodded curtly, containing any emotion in front of one of his warriors. "Gather the council and have High Guardian Varö attend." The guard turned on his heel and left immediately to see to his lord's command. Elym left soon after, looking back only to see Naywyn leave with the chest.

~

The circular chamber that housed the diviner had been enchanted with every spell imaginable to keep the room's secrets. No one could scry him from miles away or even listen in from the other side of the door.

The black orb sat atop an ornate pedestal, emitting a high pitched hum. Elym composed himself before placing his hand over the diviner, unsure as to whom he would be speaking with.

The circular chamber melted away, along with any semblance of reality. The king was surrounded by darkness and what felt like an encompassing tornado. Seated cross-legged in front of him was a ghostly image of Faylen Haldör, his daughter's mentor.

"Where is Mörygan?" Elym asked, all too aware that the diviner had been given to him and not to Faylen.

Faylen hesitated. "Mörygan is dead, my Lord."

At just over a thousand years old, Elym was an expert at guarding his reactions to any situation. As the king, his reactions alone could guide events in ways he didn't intend, and so he had learned long ago that keeping his composure was a fine way of keeping control.

"And Reyna?" Before they went any further, he had to know.

"She is alive, and here with me," Faylen explained. "We're safe, for now."

Elym clenched his jaw to conceal his sigh of relief. The thought of Reyna being harmed had opened a pit in his stomach that the king didn't think could be opened.

"How was he killed?" Elym couldn't believe that Mörygan Mörgö had died in any *accident*.

Even across the shadowy realm, Faylen struggled to maintain eye contact with him. "We don't know who killed him, my Lord. Whoever they were, they're in league with the Arakesh, the guild of assassins, here in Illian."

"I know of the assassins - humans all." Elym had been spying on the humans for years prior to enacting his plan, and knew a great many secrets. "How did one come to defeat Mörygan?"

"We now know that they are being controlled by none other than Alidyr Yalathanil, the head of the Hand."

Now, that he didn't know...

Elym looked away from her ethereal form in an effort to hide the shock and fear slowly building in his gut. Alidyr's body had never been identified among the dead after the battle of Elethiah. The elf deserved a truly horrible death for the terror and pain he had inflicted during those dark days. The fear that he or any of the Hand had survived had always lived inside Elym.

"You have proof of this?" he probed, still unwilling to believe.

"I fought him myself, in the Hall of Life..." Faylen continued to shock the king.

"You have been to *Elethiah*?" He couldn't help the anger creeping into his voice. "You were meant to stay in Velia and gather information. To assist Galanör in entering Korkanath. If the opportunity arose, you were to travel between the human kingdoms and inform us of their strengths and weaknesses. You were *not* meant to take my *daughter* to that graveyard!"

"There's more, my Lord." Faylen's mannerisms were so akin to Adilandra's that Elym couldn't help but think of his wife and the concern she would have for Reyna.

"You're going to tell me everything, Faylen, from the beginning..."

~

Later than he had intended, Elym joined the council meeting he had summoned. The heads of the seven highborn families were present, along with the four elders and High Guardian Varö.

The sleek chamber was filled with glowing orbs that floated around the room, though their light was barely needed with the midday sun flooding the room from the open balcony. Servants surrounded the circular table, each from one of the highborn families.

Elym walked up to his own place at the head of the table. His announcement was simple. "Valanis has been freed."

Along with the faces of every elf present, the king dropped into his chair, all composure forgotten.

"How can this be?" Varö asked. The High Guardian's long blond hair was tied up into a knot atop his head, so that not a single hair touched his pristine armour.

"It seems Paldora's gem never left Elethiah," Elym explained. Images of his sister, Nalana, flashed before his eyes, along with her blood on his hands. "My sister gave the gem to a boy, an Outlander..." The story was well known, but Elym was reliving accounts more for himself than anyone else.

"She thought he had a better chance of escaping the city unseen, and the gem with him. She was wrong. The power of the gem fractured the Amber Spell from within Elethiah's walls. It took a thousand years, but it finally freed him, along with the Outlander."

The king could hardly believe his own words. The pathetic little boy he had met in Elethiah's library so long ago, longer than some of these elves had been alive, was still walking around Illian, and now a warrior of capable skill, according to Faylen. That brought him to the next revelation.

"Not only is Valanis free, but the Hand has survived, or at least two of them have. Faylen Haldör claims to have seen Thallan Tassariön and has even fought Alidyr Yalathanil. Perhaps the wildest claim of all is that my daughter, Princess Reyna, has slain Adellum Bövö. Samandriel and Nakir have yet to make themselves known."

The elves sat in silence, struggling to take in such crushing news. It had been this council that had planned every detail of Illian's invasion. These thirteen elves had sat and planned the genocide of a race and the elevation of their own, along with finally defeating Valanis. Now, it seemed their greatest foe was still a step ahead of them.

"For the last millennium, Alidyr has been leading the notorious Arakesh," he continued, relaying Faylen's news. "He has been building this army in secret and teaching them our ways. They fight as we do, with some magical assistance. Their numbers are unknown, but Alidyr has pitted them against Faylen and my daughter, destroying the Graycoats in the process."

"The legacy of Tyberius Gray deserved such an end," Varö remarked. "Dragon-slayers all..."

"What of Mörygan, my Lord?" Petröna Mörgö, the head of her house and the aunt of Mörygan, asked with unease.

Elym was truly sorry that his family had to hear of his death this way; he would rather have conveyed the news in private. Though Mörygan's mother and father had been sympathisers of Valanis, and executed after the battle of Elethiah, the surviving Mörgös had done everything in their power to make things right.

"I'm afraid to say he was killed in Velia. His attacker is unknown but believed to be one of the Hand. My deepest sympathies, Petröna..." Elym bowed his head. Mörygan was the first casualty in a war that had yet to be declared, and wouldn't likely be the last.

"He died for the princess," Petröna said without pause, always ready to seize the moment.

"And the Mörgös will have the gratitude of house Sevari for all time," Elym replied with the only words Petröna wanted to hear.

"Forgive me." Tai'garn, the oldest and perhaps wisest of the four elders, looked to Petröna apologetically. "How long has Valanis been free of the Amber Spell?"

"Some *forty* years," Elym said. "But the worst news is yet to come." The king could barely bring himself to speak the words. "Valanis has Paldora's gem."

The table erupted into chaos, as every member of the council, the elders included, broke into arguments about past errors and future plans. Through it all, Elym could see the fear that drove them. It had always been Valanis's greatest weapon.

"He has but a shard of the gem," Elym went on. "Though it is unknown how this will affect his control of the magic that corrupts him."

"Where is the rest of it?" Tai'garn asked desperately, his youthful features contorted in dread.

"Lost, for now. Through some twist of fate, the Outlander has found his way, yet again, into the middle of our war."

"The boy?" Varö's sharp eyes focused on the king incredulously.

"A man now, freed at the same time as Valanis, apparently. He was raised by the same assassins that Alidyr controls." Elym could hardly believe Faylen's tale, especially the level of involvement from Asher. How could one man be so woven into their lives, the lives of immortals?

"Is this Outlander allied with Valanis?" Petröna asked.

"I doubt it," Elym replied. "He must have had the gem for some time and yet Valanis only recently gained possession. It matters not." Elym waved his hand to dismiss the topic. "The man is insignificant. What matters is what we do next."

"We cannot invade without the dragons!" Gadavar Reveeri sat forward in his chair. House Reveeri was the newest addition to the council, having only been given a seat thirty years ago.

"Your son is yet to deliver us one." Varö matched Gadavar's posture with a harder stare. "Galanör should have returned days ago, with or without Malliath. We should consider his mission a failure and assume he and his companions are dead. We need to invade *now*, before Valanis has any more time to gather his forces. Before he makes another attempt to kill Princess Reyna..."

Gadavar sat back in his chair with a sullen expression, except Elym knew it wasn't over the potential death of his son, but rather the way his failure would taint their family name.

"How do we know Valanis isn't controlling the armies of men?" Arion of house Kaidön asked. "If the Hand has survived all these years they could easily be manipulating the weak-willed kingdoms of man. We need more information before we launch our attack prematurely."

"We should attack now, I say," Elder Illithör Athatar offered.

The council looked to Elym for guidance. "We must immediately increase our efforts constructing the fleet." The king looked to Therö of house Velanii.

"We are yet to harness all the material, my Lord." Therö looked to others on the council for support. "We thought we would have *decades* before..."

Elym held up his hand to silence the elf. "We must assume Mount Garganafan will remain closed to us and the dragon eggs with it."

Elym could feel his plans unravelling. Without Malliath he could see no way of opening the Dragon Wall and retrieving the eggs hidden within. He had planned on raising the dragons over a period of years, while the fleet was constructed and his army fully prepared to go to war against a possible six armies. All the while, Valanis was supposed to be trapped inside Elethiah.

Now, his daughter was being actively hunted down, Galanör hadn't been heard from, Valanis was free of his tomb and Adilandra was still missing...

"Therö, you will have the assistance of all to construct the fleet - *all* will help." The elders looked to protest but Elym silenced them with a look. "From this moment we are on a war footing. There will be no more talks with King Rengar and the human kingdoms. We take Illian *now*." With that, the king rose from his chair and turned to leave, ending the council meeting.

Elym waited for an hour to pass before having word sent to Varö and Tai'garn to return to the council room. The king waited for them on the wide balcony, lost in thought.

"You summoned us, my Lord." Varö appeared behind him with Tai'garn by his side. Reading his king's expression, the High Guardian went on to add, "We were discreet. No one knows we are here."

"Faylen had more to say," Elym explained at once. "Alidyr's wicked tongue has worked against him. He has boasted that Valanis intends to use our war against the humans to weaken us before he strikes."

"With what army?" Varö asked. "The Arakesh are too small to pose any real threat against an army, especially an elven one."

"I have no doubt that Valanis has more going on than we can see. Forty years is a long time to make plans. My immediate concern is that he will find Reyna and use her against me." Elym put aside thoughts of his daughter's potential harm and focused. "A small band can pass through the land unseen and get into places no army could. Tai'garn, you are to leave at once for Illian and find the princess. Keep her safe until we arrive in force."

"My Lord..." Tai'garn bowed, his obedience unquestioning.

"Varö, you are to provide Tai'garn with a small group to accompany him." The king turned back to the elder. "Do not concern yourself with hiding your heritage; your reason for being in their lands is warranted and it may grant you access where it would otherwise have been rejected."

"Why the secrecy here, my Lord?" Tai'garn asked, always perceptive of his king's decisions.

"Trust, Tai'garn. Both you and Varö have my trust. But I learned today that Valanis broke free from Elethiah *forty* years ago, and exactly forty years ago, members of that council came to me and persuaded me to invade Illian..."

CHAPTER 5
THE REMNANTS OF HOPE

Nathaniel watched as his brothers and sisters said their farewells to the people of Vangarth. Carts and horses had been supplied to transport the wounded, along with healing elixirs and potions to see them through, until they reached Darkwell, in the east of Orith.

The town's lord embraced forearms with a Graycoat Nathaniel recognised as Elijah Bennett, a good knight by his recollection. It appeared that Elijah was now leading the ragtag group in the absence of Fennick or Horvarth.

"Last chance," Reyna said, eyeing Nathaniel with a coy smile.

Nathaniel returned the smile, aware that the princess already knew of his intentions to stay with her and the others. He couldn't deny that there was still a part of him that wanted to go with them, but he had chosen to forsake his duty in favour of a higher cause. His oath to the order had died with Elaith.

At least with Reyna and the others, he could make a real difference in Illian, possibly even help to avoid a war. There was also the matter of his feelings towards the princess to consider.

"Let them go their way, and I'll go mine." Nathaniel turned away from the departing crowd of knights and wandered back towards The Greenleaf Inn.

In the weeks since the battle of West Fellion, Nathaniel's usually shaved hair had grown somewhat, though not enough to conceal his identity. He was careful to keep his hood up and his face low, as Reyna did with her long blonde hair flowing out over her chest.

The knight was unaccustomed to his new attire and didn't care for loose-fitting clothes and a cloak. He longed for the comfort of his thick coat and missed the authority it granted him. Nathaniel especially missed carrying his sword and bow. Asher had warned him about keeping the sword in particular, due to the Graycoat sigil etched into the end of the hilt.

What did feel good, however, was the warm elven hand clasped in his own. They walked hand-in-hand back to the inn, a real couple who caught no one's attention. This was a life he could get used to.

That thought turned sour when he considered what a life that would really be. In ten, maybe fifteen years, there would be a notable difference in his human appearance. Reyna looked to be in her early twenties and would do forever, but he would grow old and die before she reached her first century of life. She would remain strong when he would grow weak, healthy when he would become sick. What life would that be, for either of them?

Eventually, he would hold Reyna back with his increasing age, and cause nothing but grief and sorrow for her. And he would have to live with knowing that she could be doing so much more instead of caring for him.

Nathaniel squeezed her hand a little tighter for a moment, appreciating the moment and savouring the feeling of youth. Leaving her now would be the easiest way to prevent so much grief in the future, but leaving her just didn't seem possible.

When they finally returned to The Greenleaf Inn, it became apparent that a heated discussion was taking place inside Reyna's room. It wasn't entirely unusual to hear Faylen disagreeing with Asher, but this time it sounded the reverse.

"...It might be the only way!" Faylen was saying, exasperated.

Nathaniel and Reyna walked into the room and observed the man and elf standing by the window, brows furrowed.

"Trust me, it would be suicide!" The ranger appeared more concerned than angry. "Did you get it out of your system?" He directed his question to Nathaniel with the same tone he had been using to argue with Faylen. It quickly became apparent, however, that he regretted his harsh tone and choice of words.

Nathaniel was learning to read Asher's expressions and body language very well. "The Graycoats have left for Darkwell," the knight replied, using his expression alone to convey his acceptance of Asher's unspoken apology.

"And what are you two discussing so... *passionately?*" Reyna asked.

Faylen looked to Asher and the two took a breath, as if for the first time. The ranger collapsed into one of the tattered, yet comfy, chairs in the corner, while Faylen bit her lip, carefully considering her words.

"We have to stop the invasion," the older elf stated flatly.

Nathaniel took his cloak off and walked into the middle of the room. It had only been a few hours since Faylen had spoken to Elym Sevari, the king of the elves, and told him of recent events. Even though they couldn't see or hear the conversation between them, it was clear how it had gone when Faylen's consciousness returned.

The king wasn't happy...

His attitude towards Faylen had been one of the reasons that Reyna chose to go out with Nathaniel to see the Graycoats leave. The elven princess couldn't stand anything to do with her father and had needed the fresh air.

Of course, Faylen's conversation with the king led the group to discussing what they should do next. Faylen was convinced that the invasion would come sooner, but no one knew what had happened to Galanör or the outcome of his mission to steal Malliath the voiceless.

"I *told* you not to tell him that Valanis was free!" Reyna said for the third time that day. "It will only give us less time."

"I agree," Faylen quickly replied. "But the truth is; if Valanis *is* manipulating events, our people might be the only ones who can stop him."

"At the expense of everyone living in Illian," Nathaniel added. "The elven army won't come all this way and stop at killing Valanis. They'll invade..."

"That's why..." Faylen gestured to Asher, her frustration rising again.

Nathaniel was getting used to the heightened levels of emotions that elves displayed. They reacted to everything with more zeal than humans, even sad emotions. Reyna's urges didn't take so much getting used to as they did energy.

"What is it?" the princess asked, looking at them both. "What were you discussing?"

"If we can kill Valanis we might still be able to avert war." Faylen had a hint of hope in her eyes.

"It's suicide." Asher remained seated, staring at Alidyr's short-sword in the corner of the room.

"What's he talking about?" Reyna asked.

"Valanis has a *shard* of Paldora's gem," Faylen explained. "If we can get the rest of it, we might have enough power to destroy him."

"But you said you threw it in The Adean." Nathaniel walked between Asher and the short-sword, focusing the ranger's attention.

"He was lying..." Faylen stated confidently.

The news appeared to excite Reyna, who flew across the room until the table stopped her from pouncing on Asher.

"Where is it?" the princess demanded with half a smile on her face.

Asher looked up slowly. "Beyond all of our reach."

"Asher," Nathaniel said softly. "This might be the only advantage we have over Valanis. Who knows what plans he's already made?

Whether the elves come or not, it might be too late to stop him if we don't act now."

"You're all insane if you think that the four of us can stop the most powerful elf who ever lived." Asher stood up from the chair and made for the window.

"The four of us beat Adellum," Faylen offered.

"Five..." Nathaniel added. For the rest of his days he would make certain that the world remembered Elaith Nevandar.

"You're not talking about challenging one of the Hand," Asher continued. "You're talking about fighting the other four *and* Valanis *and* every Arakesh *and* who knows what else."

Reyna circled around the ranger and looked at him with her brilliant emerald eyes. "I know you're not afraid, so what's holding you back?"

Asher hesitated. "Everything in me, everything I know tells me to blend in, be a face in the crowd, disappear. What you're talking about is going to put us out there for all of Illian to see. There will be no coming back from this. We're going to have to fight and fight and fight, until *they're* all dead, or *we* are."

"If it's fame you're worried about then it's a little too late," Nathaniel replied with a smirk. "As if fighting Ro Dosarn in the halls of the Velian palace wasn't talked about enough, your efforts at West Fellion will have you known across the land. And before all that, you were already infamous for saving Queen Isabella so many years ago." Nathaniel paused to ensure he had the ranger's full attention. "The assassin is *dead* and the ranger has *risen*..."

Asher didn't look convinced.

"What will the ranger do next?" Reyna added in her melodic tones.

Asher took a slow breath and met all of their eyes. "I threw it in the pit."

Nathaniel's expression of confusion was shared with Reyna and Faylen. During his time as a Graycoat he had been to a lot of places and seen a lot of things that most men would run away from, but he had never heard of the pit.

"When your training is complete," Asher revealed, "there's one final test that every student must pass to become an Arakesh. The pit is located deep in the heart of Nightfall. It was built centuries ago, probably under the orders of Alidyr. Every student has to go into the pit and find a way out on the other side. It's pitch black down there, a place where sunlight has never touched. A true test to ensure your bond with the Nightseye elixir is everlasting.

There are monsters under Nightfall that have never been seen before, nightmares that cannot be described. It's one of the reasons why the Arakesh are so few; only a handful of those who descend into the pit find a way back out."

"And you dropped Paldora's gem in *there*?" Faylen asked in despair.

"I knew it was magic, and powerful." Asher leaned against the window ledge. "I was younger back then, more competitive. I didn't want any of the others to find it and use it, and the gem had already gained the attention of a few of the others. I cut a shard off, crafted the ring and threw the rest away." The group stood in silence for a moment, digesting the ranger's words.

"So, we're going to Nightfall..." Nathaniel just had to say it out loud to believe it.

"I told you: suicide," Asher replied dryly.

"Where is it?" Nathaniel asked. For the first time in his life, he didn't really want to know. As a Graycoat he had been driven to locate the ancient school for assassins, but now, after hearing Asher's description of the pit, he wasn't so sure he wanted to find it.

"The only place farther south is Syla's Gate," Asher said.

"The Arid Lands?" Reyna exclaimed. "I've never seen a desert!"

"Nor do you want to," Asher continued. "The only creatures that thrive there are predators, the people included. The desert makes you hard. If we're actually going to travel there we'll need supplies, lots of supplies. We don't want to be stopping in Tregaran on the border. We need to head straight for Karath, the capital, and head east from there."

"That could be a problem." Faylen dropped a small sack of coins on the table. "That's all that's left."

"We could stay in Vangarth for a while," Nathaniel suggested. "I'm sure there's work for a group of our skill-set."

"That would take too long," Faylen quickly replied. "A journey that far south will take many days; we need to leave *soon*."

"We won't last long if we leave in haste and without supplies," Reyna countered, coming to stand beside Nathaniel, as she often did.

Asher cleared his throat. "I know a place where we can get coin *and* supplies." All eyes fell on the ranger, who, it seemed, would always have an edge of mystery to him. "Stowhold has one of their banks in Lirian, and I have friends there that can meet our need of supplies."

"A *bank*?" Reyna asked.

"Friends?" Nathaniel echoed in disbelief.

Asher responded with a knowing smile, as if he too was aware that the likelihood of him having other friends was slim and hard to believe.

"I have an account within Stowhold. It was part of my deal with King Rengar for escorting you to Velia. We can take enough coin to buy our supplies and find an escort through The Moonlit Plains."

"He gave you an account at Stowhold?" Nathaniel knew well of the prestigious bank and the privileged members that held accounts therein. Only the request from a king could have got Asher's name on the ledger. "How much did he give you?"

"No limits..." Asher replied with a wide smile.

Nathaniel whistled and turned to Reyna. "He really wanted you at his party."

"King Rengar considers himself a good judge of character," Asher continued. "He thinks of me as a simple man with simple needs. His children probably spend more in a week than I could spend in a lifetime, though something tells me he'll have people watching the account to ensure my tastes remain cheap."

"Why must we pay for an escort through The Moonlit Plains?" Faylen asked. "Surely we four can handle a few wild Centaurs."

"Only fools travel through those plains in numbers this small," Asher explained. "Best we pay for escorts or offer to *be* escorts. The larger the caravan the better."

Faylen looked to the setting sun. "We've already lost too much light. We use what coin we have left to buy four horses and leave at dawn."

"Three horses," Asher corrected with a wry smile. "I'll take care of the fourth."

"So, that's it then," Reyna announced eagerly, as if Asher's description of the pit had never been told. "We go to Lirian, pick up supplies and coin, travel south to Nightfall, enter the pit, find the gem and kill Valanis."

Asher groaned and pinched his nose. "We're all going to die..."

CHAPTER 6
THE SPECTACLE OF DRAGONS

S crambling over the lip of the last rock, Gideon tried to ignore the pain in his hands and forearms. It had taken him almost an hour to navigate the floating boulder, but the climb had been made easier by the thick roots that rose from the ground and wrapped around the slab of rock, as if it had been ensnared by a giant octopus.

A simple spell had turned the palms and fingers of his hands into rough calluses, increasing his grip. He could have used other magic to levitate himself to the top of the boulder, but he enjoyed testing his physical limits.

The surface of the boulder was covered in a thin layer of green moss and sporadic patches of grass, which made it soft underfoot. The mage adjusted the staff on his back and looked towards the horizon, his eyes fixed on the magnificent landscape around him.

"Incredible..." he uttered.

In the heart of the giant crater, known as Dragons' Reach, Gideon stood atop one of the dozen floating rocks that made up the home of the oldest creatures in Verda. The magical epicentre was surrounded by lush forestry and fields of green, an oasis in the middle of The Red Mountains.

Beyond the tips of those mountains were The Flat Wastes and The Great Maw, a dense jungle that swallowed up the Darkakin city, Malaysai. Thankfully, that nightmarish place couldn't be seen from this paradise. The only sound came from the roar of the waterfall that cut through the heart of Dragons' Reach.

The sun was only touching the tops of the distant mountains, turning the sky into shades of burnt orange and lilac. The beautiful sunset wasn't enough to capture Gideon's imagination, however, for all around him were dozens of dragons flying and gliding over the trees and piercing the clouds. The mage had been watching them for days now, and still he couldn't take his eyes off them, entranced as he was.

"Magnificent, aren't they?" Galanör sat on the edge of the boulder with his legs hanging over the side. The elf apparently had no fear of heights.

"No creature can match their grace," Gideon replied, taking a perch next to the elf. In truth, he had climbed the floating rock to speak with Galanör, before the landscape distracted him.

"I've been around creatures that exude a magical aura before," Galanör continued, "but I've never experienced..." The elf looked at his hands in disbelief. "I can feel their power rolling over my skin, as if my entire body is vibrating."

"I feel it too," Gideon replied, except for the mage it felt as if a warm aura had settled inside his chest and continued to pulse throughout his body. "Being here, I feel safe and content... happy even."

"I know what you mean." Galanör's smile didn't reach his eyes. "But you can't be sure can you? *Do* you feel safe and content, or is your happiness a simple reflection of their own."

Gideon looked from Galanör to the dragons flying above. He had already thought about the elf's comment and wondered if the dragons' unique method of communication was affecting his own emotions.

The beating of mighty wings preceded the melodic voice of Adriel. "I assure you, Galanör of house Reveeri, when a dragon wishes to communicate with you, you will know about it."

Both Gideon and Galanör rose to their feet as a dragon, coated in ebony scales, that glittered with silver, landed atop the floating boulder. Its thick neck drooped and lowered a head the size of a horse, allowing them a better view of Adriel, who was astride the dragon, between two spikes. The last of the Dragorn slid from his perch and landed gracefully between the dragon's chest and wing.

"This is Galandavax." Adriel stepped aside and swept his arm to encompass the spectacular creature. "He and I have been paired for seventeen hundred years now."

Galandavax shook his mighty head, before arching back on his hind legs and taking off into the sky.

"Alas, he would sleep now. I apologise for my absence. I realise that you both have a lot of questions and I left so suddenly after you arrived. Galandavax and I have always hunted together you see, and when he decides to hunt there is nothing that can stop him."

"You've been hunting for *ten days*?" Galanör asked.

Gideon could hear the frustration in the elf's voice. For ten days they had been left to their own devices in a land they didn't know, surrounded by the best predators in the world and no answers as to why Dragons' Reach even existed.

"Galandavax requires several tons of meat to sate his appetite." Adriel walked over the soft moss with bare feet.

Gideon took special note of the green moss that grew in abundance around his feet, as if drawn to Adriel. The elf's usual flowing robes were now fastened tightly around his waist with several belts. The elf had no weapons but a simple, yet ornate, dagger sheathed across his waist.

Adriel placed himself in the centre of the boulder and sat cross-legged, his wild blond hair blowing gently in the breeze. The elf had an air of calmness to him that put Gideon at ease, almost imitating the way of the dragons and casting his own empathy over them.

Galanör stepped closer to Adriel, but remained standing over the Dragorn. "We have a lot of questions but, more than that, we are running out of time. The queen, *our* queen, Adilandra Sevari, is a prisoner of the Darkakin! She is being kept in the palace in Malaysai. I don't know how long they will keep her alive. Before we found her she was forced to fight in their barbaric arena..."

Galanör couldn't go on and Gideon could hear the despair in his voice. They both knew there was a good chance Adilandra was dead by now.

"No." Adriel stated flatly to the unasked question.

Galanör glanced at the flying dragons in disbelief, before turning an angry gaze on to Adriel. "No? How can you say no? There are enough dragons here to raze Malaysai to the ground!"

With a look of caution, Adriel raised his hand to stop Galanör from shouting, but it was too late...

The boulder shook as a dragon came to land behind the ancient elf, its emerald head pointed low and golden eyes fixed on Galanör. The striking green scales and sheer size of the dragon gave away its identity as Rainael the emerald star, queen of the dragons.

On the other side of Adriel, a smaller, but no less awe-inspiring, dragon also came to land, with its thick claws digging into the rock. The dazzling young dragon was called Ilargo. His scales had a lighter shade of green and golden specks that twinkled in the dying light. Gideon recognised him from the arena in Malaysai, when Ilargo had been freed with another dragon called Bravog.

Without warning, both Gideon and Galanör were overcome with the feeling of being insulted, as if Adriel had just shouted at them in *their* home. The feeling only lasted for a few seconds but it was enough to convey Rainael's irritation. They both took a breath - now, they knew what it felt like to be spoken to by a dragon.

"I'm afraid we cannot help you," Adriel said. "You saw it yourself when Malliath dropped into the arena. The Darkakin captured and imprisoned Ilargo and Bravog over a month ago, before they were rescued upon your arrival in these lands. We attempted to reclaim them but almost lost more dragons in the process."

"How did the Darkakin capture two dragons?" Gideon asked. "They don't even use magic."

"Even with magic it is hard to bring down a dragon," Adriel explained. "But with anti-magic, it is quite easy..."

"What's anti-magic?" Gideon looked to Galanör, who appeared similarly confused.

"I had never heard of it either during my time in Illian, but Rainael and Galandavax told me of it..." Adriel adopted a grave tone. "Crissalith, it is called. They knew it from another age, before even the elves walked the earth.

"The Darkakin must have discovered the stones, though I know not where. They appear as green crystals, but their beauty is deadly. Ilargo and Bravog were out hunting when the Darkakin sprang their trap. In the presence of Crissalith, the dragons grow weak until they cannot even fly or breathe fire. The Darkakin sharpen them and affix them to spears for their hunts."

"You won't help us free Adilandra because you're afraid of some *rocks*?" Galanör's tone was becoming aggressive again.

Rainael took in a sharp breath and looked to Adriel. The two shared a moment of what appeared to be silence, before the emerald dragon spread her wings and dropped off the side of the floating boulder. She continued to drop until, at the last moment, she glided over the tops of the trees, ducking and weaving between the floating rocks.

Ilargo remained behind and padded along, behind Adriel, always watching Gideon as he did. The mage felt scrutinised by those intense blue eyes, as if the dragon was looking into him.

"Dragons are the fiercest, most noble and honourable of all creatures," Adriel said in the wake of Rainael's dramatic departure. "But with nobility and honour comes sensitivity. The first rule of living among dragons: stay on their good side." Adriel smiled and rose to his feet.

Ilargo dipped his horned head affectionately into the elf's shoulder, his stunning eyes always on Gideon.

"Should you wish to return to Illian, Galandavax will take you both as far as The Black Road, in the north. From there you can journey to wherever our people have settled in Ayda. I'm sure they will see you returned to the west safely, Gideon Thorn."

"The Black Road?" Gideon had seen the name on the map he had stolen from the pyramid in Malaysai. The mage pulled the parchment out of his satchel and unravelled it with both hands.

Galanör remained focused on Adriel. "Our people live south of The Crystal Sea, in The Amara. The city is called Elandril, you may have heard the name..."

Adriel tilted his head, guarding his expression. "Named for the first Dragorn."

"His lineage is followed by *our* king, Elym Sevari, whose wife, our queen, is a prisoner in Malaysai!"

Adriel's calm demeanour was obviously irritating Galanör, and Gideon could feel the awkward tension building between the two elves.

Gideon cleared his throat. "The Black Road is beneath a desert by the looks of this." The mage held up the map for the others to see.

"The Q'ol," Galanör grimly replied. "It's two hundred and fifty miles of sand. If we made it to the northern edge, it's *another* two hundred miles until the nearest river. It's a death sentence."

"Queen Adilandra made the journey..." Adriel pointed out.

"You're just afraid we'll tell others of this place." Galanör was like a dog with a bone. "You've lived in this paradise for so long that you have forgotten the rest of the world! All of Verda is about to be plunged into a war to end all wars, and you're living with the very creatures that could tip the scales! We need to free the queen, warn the Illians and somehow find a way to ally them with King Elym. Three Darkakin armies are marching into Illian as we speak!"

"The answer is still no, I'm afraid."

Galanör snarled in a very un-elf like way. "The Dragorn I read about were warriors all! They rode their dragons into battle and knew no fear. It should be you leading us against Valanis's forces!"

"You have been greatly misinformed about the Dragorn." Adriel strolled to the edge of the boulder, calm as ever. "The Dragorn were peacekeepers where needed, but it was never enforced through violence, only wisdom. And you don't ride a dragon; *no one* rides a dragon..." Adriel stepped off the boulder without warning and dropped from sight.

Gideon gasped and ran for the edge with Galanör. The pair jumped back in surprise when Galandavax's hulking form soared into the sky, past the floating boulder, with Adriel sat at the base of his thick neck. The two were perfectly in sync, always aware of the other and what they were thinking. Gideon could only look on in amazement, unlike Galanör.

"Then *we* will go!" the elf shouted at the shrinking image of Galandavax. He reached down and collected his scimitars from the ground. "I will not let her rot inside that city."

Before Gideon could offer any advice, the elf hopped off the side and half climbed, half slid down the boulder with incredible speed.

The mage sighed. "I only just got up here..."

A guttural, yet apparently questioning, sound reverberated inside Ilargo's meaty throat. The blue-eyed dragon was off to the side, looking at Gideon with his head tilted like an inquisitive dog.

"Nice dragon..."

The mage slowly stepped back, hoping to all the gods that Ilargo had already eaten.

~

Galanör strode through the central meadow that sat under the canopy of the dozen floating boulders. The sights and sounds around him were serene and calming, yet they did nothing to sooth his mood.

How could Adriel be so passive? How could creatures with so much power sit back and hide in their crater?

As the sun dropped below The Red Mountains, the shadows of the flying dragons ceased to glide across the ground. A cool night air settled on the valley and the elf wrapped his cloak a little tighter around his arms.

Galanör was drawn to the waterfall that poured out of the protruding mountain. He circumnavigated the giant pool at its base and climbed the smaller rocks until he found a way into the cave, behind the waterfall.

It was dark but oddly warm, offering comfort in his dour mood. Galanör sat in the middle of the cave, facing the wall of rushing water. The roar was hypnotic and helped to calm him. As an elf, his emotions had the potential to control him, forcing him to take action he might later regret.

The elf dropped his head and sighed, trying desperately not to think about the horrors Adilandra would be experiencing in Malaysai...

He thought about what else might be going on in the world. What would King Elym do now that Malliath hadn't been returned to him? Would they still invade? Would it affect the timescale of the war? Then, he thought about his betrothed, Reyna. The princess had been promised to him by the king when he agreed to bring back Malliath. Would the wedding be off now that he had failed? It was a trivial detail in the madness of everything else, but it didn't stop him from wondering.

The diviner on the back of his belt weighed heavy on his mind. He could, if he wished, contact Mörygan or even the king to discover the answers to his questions. Galanör didn't feel he had the energy to converse with the king, even to inform him that Adilandra was a prisoner of the Darkakin. He knew he was a coward for that, but he still hoped to save her, and by saving the queen there was always the chance that the king would forgive him for failing on the mages' island of Korkanath.

There was that voice again; the voice of his duty-bound conscience finding a solution that allowed him to keep his honour and stay in favour with the king and the highborn families.

Galanör had promised himself that when the opportunity arose, he would seek out some kind of new freedom and life in the world. A life where he didn't need to pick up his blades and make decisions that ended the life of another. A part of him still wanted that life and despaired at the thought of the fighting he would have to endure in order to achieve it.

Galanör couldn't walk away from the fact that all the land was about to be plunged into war, and that shadowy figures were manipulating everything from behind the scenes. He didn't want to witness the genocide of mankind at the hands of his own kin, though he didn't mind the idea of wiping out the Darkakin and *their* evil ways.

He wasn't stupid enough to believe that the war could be averted with words. Peace would only come after a bloody fight. The dragons, however, would bring a swift end to any conflict. Adilandra had birthed that vision and been right about where to find them. It was almost enough to give the elf faith and trust in the Echoes of Fate.

He lacked the conviction that Adilandra wore on her sleeve. If anyone could convince Adriel and the dragons to help, it would be her. How he would save her without the dragons was currently beyond his comprehension. He had no crystals to help him open a portal and he had no idea how to climb out of the crater. There was a reason Adriel had named it Dragons' Reach, after all.

Galanör was tired and out of answers...

Without really thinking about it, the elf reached around his back and removed the diviner orb from its pouch. The black sphere sat in the palm of his hand, almost weightless. Galanör decided he would have some answers, even if it was just for peace of mind.

Pouring his magical aura into the orb, Galanör called for Mörygan's own diviner to receive his consciousness. In the dark of the cave, the only light from the waterfall, the elf waited for a response.

It took some time, but eventually Galanör felt himself being pulled into another realm where only shades could exist. He couldn't hide his surprise when he saw the ethereal form of a female elf instead of Mörygan. It was impossible to discern any great detail while in this plane of existence, but Galanör still recognised her, but he couldn't place her name.

"I know you..."

"I am Faylen of house Haldör," the elf replied with a curt smile.

Galanör remembered where he had seen her: Faylen had always been present in court and never far behind Princess Reyna.

"I am—"

"Galanör of house Reveeri," Faylen finished on his behalf. "I know who you are *and* the nature of your mission." She had an air of desperation about her now. "Tell me everything, Galanör. Where is Malliath?"

Galanör hadn't quite got over the shock of seeing someone other than Mörygan. He also didn't like the way Faylen demanded answers.

"What's wrong?" he asked. "Has something happened? Where's Princess Reyna? Where's Mörygan?"

Faylen's ethereal face looked away for a moment. "Mörygan is dead. He was killed by what we suspect to be a member of the Hand."

Before Galanör could question her more on that most shocking statement, his physical body detected another presence in the cave. The elf paused, becoming detached from the conversation, as he considered who else could be inside the cave... or *what* else.

That fighter instinct that never went away, told him to prepare for violence. He disengaged from the diviner immediately and without warning to Faylen. A second later, Galanör's consciousness was back in the dark cave and he was up on his feet.

Two startling purple eyes appeared in the dark, followed by a giant black head which took shape in the shadows. Malliath's breath blew Galanör's chestnut hair out behind him and threatened to overwhelm his elven nose. The dragon's low growl continued to rise in pitch and aggression, his four, well-muscled, legs bringing him ever closer.

Galanör hadn't been around dragons for very long, but he could see the rage in those purple eyes, and he was thankful that Malliath wasn't pushing those emotions onto him. Instead, that fighter instinct kicked in. It was very clear in its decision that running away was his only option.

Using every ounce of his honed reflexes, Galanör turned on the spot and dashed for the waterfall. Malliath's roar filled the cave and four booming legs ran after him, forcing the elf to dive through the wall of water and plunge into the pool below. The cold water hit Galanör like a fist to the chest, but the threat of Malliath allowed him to ignore it and push on for the shore. He had barely taken his first breath when the black dragon burst forth from the waterfall and plummeted towards him, claws outstretched.

At the last second, when Galanör was sure his life was about to come to an end, a green blur slammed into Malliath and sent the black dragon flying into the trees, beyond the pool.

Galanör steadied himself in the water and watched as Rainael the emerald star batted Malliath's claws away and held him down. Their mighty tails swung from side to side, crushing and snapping trees like twigs, uprooting ancient rocks with ease. Rainael entwined Malliath's tail in her own and clamped both of them down to the ground, launching a wave of dirt high into the air. Malliath thrashed under her weight and snapped at her neck with his powerful jaws, but Rainael managed to evade every bite.

The sound of giant wings soared overhead, followed by Galandavax, who swooped out of the night's sky and landed beside the struggling dragons. With an ear-piercing roar, Galandavax dropped his heavy front claw onto Malliath's head and kept it there, as if the black dragon was caught in a vice. Malliath roared and continued to struggle until another dragon dropped out of the sky. The red scales gave his identity away as Dolvosari the storm maker. Together they held Malliath in place and waited for him to calm down.

Adriel appeared by Galanör's side after he emerged from the pool. "It will be some time before we break through the years of imprisonment he suffered under the human mages."

"He's angry..." Galanör observed.

Both elves could only look on, with the dragons struggling to contain the giant Malliath.

"And yet we cannot blame the humans," Adriel continued. "They do only what is in their nature."

"Dragons live just as long as elves?" Galanör said, baiting Adriel.

"Longer perhaps," Adriel replied.

Galanör turned away from the spectacle of dragons and looked at Adriel. "The mages kept him as a prisoner for nearly a thousand years, and now he's broken, an echo of his former glory. Adilandra could live just as long, except instead of human mages who pay her no heed, she will be tortured by the Darkakin. Seeing Malliath now, don't you wish you could have done something all those years ago to save him?"

Adriel looked to reply but his jaw clamped shut. Galanör knew he wouldn't change Adriel's mind so easily, and didn't expect to after one conversation. Instead, he turned away and left the ancient elf to think on his words.

As the cold water ran down his face, Galanör slipped between the trees as a new idea began to surface in his mind. Perhaps there was a way he could save Adilandra after all...

Before he could fully form the new idea, Galanör's thoughts flew to the west, to Illian. The elf reached around his back in search of his diviner, only to be alarmed by its absence. He must have left it in the cave or dropped it in the pool!

"Galanör you fool..." the elf berated himself.

CHAPTER 7
THE HOUSE OF OWLS

An ocean of stars hung over the city of Karath, its flat rooftops illuminated under the stark light of the full moon. The daytime heat of The Arid Lands had been replaced with its usual icy chill.

Like a bird of prey, Tauren son-of-none crouched low over the corner of a warehouse, located at the edge of the city. The district was usually quiet at this time of night, with most of the inhabitants either sleeping or drawn to Karath's entertainment district in the heart of the city.

At least that's how it used to be...

Now, the city was overflowing with violent retribution. In the distance Tauren could make out a range of fires that worked to burn down temples and grand houses - the smoke rising to block out the stars on the horizon.

The capital of The Arid Lands had reached its tipping point seven years ago, when the slaves outnumbered the privileged free peoples. It had barely taken a nudge to plunge the city into chaos. Now, almost a decade later, the slaves were taking back their years of forced servitude at the end of a blade.

PHILIP C. QUAINTRELL

Initially, the emperor's forces had pushed back, and severely. Many slaves were made an example of, with public executions and floggings from dawn till dusk. Their efforts had only helped to fuel Tauren's rage.

Now, at twenty-four, the young man had spent his adult life fighting for the freedom his parents never had. Like all those he had grown up with, his parents had only two options available to them when their child was born: offer him to their masters, who could do with the babe as they saw fit, or whisk the infant away in secret, risking all of their lives in the process.

But, that was before Mother Madakii.

The elderly ex-priestess of Fimir, the god of wisdom, took in every stray and slave child she could find. Her orphanage was run in the shadows and kept away from the masters. It was there that Tauren found an education and opportunities he would never have received as a slave.

Of course, Mother Madakii's orphanage had only ever been known as the house, until Tauren came up with a new name, a name the grand families would come to fear.

Tauren looked away from the effects of the very war he had incited, and fixed his gaze firmly on the adjacent warehouse, where he counted every armed guard he could see. There was once a time when the slavers of the southern lands would flaunt their power and boast to their friends. They would openly trade in lives, as if they were trinkets on a market stand, and laugh as their wealth grew off the misery of others.

For seven years, Tauren had worked tirelessly to turn the orphanage of would-be-slaves into a force to be reckoned with. Now, the guards were quiet and wary of what terrors the night brought. They transported the slaves across The Arid Lands in the middle of the day and with as much secrecy as possible. The slaves were moved a lot and the locations always changed at the last minute.

This particular group of slaves were owned by Orfad Val-Agad, a grossly overweight man with ties to the great families that ran the city and now controlled their young emperor. Trading in lives was only one of Orfad's services to the people of Karath; he also expedited the transport of minerals and supplies from Namdhor, the capital in the north. Such minerals were used in the production of armour and weapons for the emperor's armies.

This was a fact that gave Tauren pause.

The guards were numerous and all well-armed with fine weapons, but Tauren couldn't pass up the opportunity in front of him. Not only could he free these slaves, but the information that came by his *owls* informed him that Orfad Val-Agad was also present inside the warehouse. Apparently, this particular group of slaves were being transported to Ameeraska at dawn, and Orfad wanted to see the transport off himself.

"Everyone is in position, Tauren," Braigo son-of-none announced from behind.

"Excellent. Make certain they know their place in all this; they are to follow only. Anyone who gets out of that building did so because I wanted them to. Let us see where the rats run to when the fat man is dead."

Tauren stood to his full height at six-feet and turned to greet Braigo, his oldest and most loyal friend. Despite giving Braigo the instructions, Tauren knew that his friend had already taken care of the details.

"Are you sure I cannot accompany you?" Braigo asked, as he always did.

"We all have our gifts, and the House of Owls uses them all," Tauren assured. "This strike must be surgical if the slaves are to be freed *and* Orfad slain." Tauren would never doubt Braigo's fighting ability, or that of any of his owls, since he had been the one to teach them all, following his own instruction, but the skills required for tonight were specific to Tauren alone.

"Mother Madakii will be displeased if we aren't back by dawn," Braigo added with a smirk.

"By dawn, Mother Madakii will have over a dozen new sons and daughters." Tauren matched his friend's smile and the two gripped each other's forearms, as they always did, before death was given its next opportunity to claim them.

"See you on the other side, brother." Braigo handed over the white helmet that Tauren had crafted on his nineteenth birthday, five years ago.

Though covered in scratches and the odd deep cut, the visage was still plain to see. Tauren placed the mask and helmet over his head and knew that Braigo now looked upon the face of The White Owl. The facial features of the encompassing helmet were simple in craftsmanship, but undoubtedly that of an owl. Only his eyes could be seen through the large owl-shaped sockets - a fact that pleased Tauren. He had heard it said that the window to the soul lay in the eyes and he hoped it to be true, for when his enemies saw his own they would witness nothing but rage and fury.

The White Owl threw the black cloak over his brown, leather shoulder pads and pulled the hood over his painted helmet. From head-to-toe he was adorned in daggers, short-swords, hidden blades, smoke pellets and a simple four-armed hook and rope that hung from the side of his belt. He was walking death, as he had been trained to be.

Turning back to the edge, Tauren swept the area in search of his owls, but was glad that he couldn't spot a single one. He had trained them well.

Having already planned his entry, Tauren leaped from the top of the warehouse and flung his hook across the street, where it snagged against the lip of the roof. The White Owl swung between the buildings, until he could drop onto a platform, built from scaffolding, that was still attached to the side of the building. He was careful to shift his weight as he landed, ensuring his stealthy approach. A practised flick of the wrist brought his hook back to him in a flash.

"I'm just saying, we could have some fun with the pretty one before we see them off," a bald guard wielding a wide scimitar offered to his friend.

The other was a typical Karathan, with thick, dark hair and tanned skin, wielding a double edged axe.

"Orfad would know," the axe-man replied. "He doesn't like the merchandise damaged."

"Then we'll be *careful*," the bald one added, slyly.

"Then you'll be *dead*," Tauren interrupted, with an acrobatic flip off the scaffolding.

The White Owl landed in between the surprised guards, who couldn't even lift their weapons before Tauren buried a dagger in each of their foreheads. They died instantly without a sound, but he was careful to lower them both to the ground, using the buried blades to leverage their weight.

Tauren left the bodies and proceeded to climb back up the scaffolding, having had no intentions of entering the warehouse via the main door. He just needed to ensure that those inside would have no help from the men outside.

Back on the rooftop, Tauren made for the double doors, built on a slant, which led into the building. He quickly picked the lock and slowly opened one of the doors to avoid it *creaking*.

The White Owl dropped down on the balls of his feet and rolled forward to absorb the landing. With a dagger already in hand, Tauren came out of his roll ready for a fight, but there was none to be had. Light shone through the floorboards from the room beneath him, where deep voices drifted up to greet him.

Tauren moved swiftly down the only set of stairs and dashed up the wall so that he could use the wooden beams to observe his prey. The four-storey warehouse was now sprawled out below him, its secrets laid bare.

The room from which he had heard voices was to his right, where he could now see the plump Orfad Val-Agad talking to his thugs. Tauren moved silently along the beams, until he could see through the window and get a better look at what the men were crowding round. There looked to be a map of some kind on the table, but

Tauren was too far away to see the details. Whatever it was, Orfad was very animated in his instructions.

"They must be ready by then!" the fat man spat. "Any delay will see our heads mounted on Syla's Gate! This is to be the last transport out of the city. After tonight, all slaves are to be sent to the forges, understand?"

Tauren's interest was piqued, but he had to focus on the slaves below. If he killed Orfad too soon, he ran the risk that the others would be alerted and the slaves be put in jeopardy.

Prioritise...

The voice of his old mentor, Salim Al-Anan, rang clearly in his mind. If he was to make an impact on the great families he would have to be smart about it; he couldn't crush an empire and bring about a revolution by marching an army and swinging his sword at every slaver, even though he wanted to. He had to bring them down in the eyes of the people, give the slaves hope and the possibility of a better life. But, most of all, Tauren wanted them to feel the same fear his parents had felt, the fear every slave lived with.

The slaves were easy to spot on the ground floor. Two columns of cages, either side of a large wagon, were both filled to bursting point with men, women and children. Torches lined the four floors, illuminating the many guards that wandered up and down, mostly pretending to pay attention.

Tauren couldn't see a single slaver that didn't look dead on his feet. It had been too long since the owls' last raid. The slavers had forgotten the bite of his blades and the deadly accuracy with which he could throw them.

The White Owl took a moment to single out the ones he wouldn't kill. They were the ones that he would simply allow to run away. The cowards would spread his legend as well as lead him to the next slave house.

Tauren came to a stop in the centre of the beam and gathered his black cape out behind him, noting the frayed edges and holes that marred the thick material. He would have to ask Mother Madakii to repair it for him, as she often did.

For just a moment, Tauren was taken back to his teenage years, when his mentor, Salim, would take him out on such expeditions. As one of the emperor's personal guards, Salim was among the best of all the warriors in Illian. Tauren would watch as the older man showed him the best way to take down multiple targets in a single, fluid movement, for speed was the key. Salim had always planned every step of his attack before moving a muscle, and so too did Tauren.

The dagger slipped from the sheath at the base of his back with perfect ease. The balance felt right in his hand as he turned it end-over-end. Tauren held the knife out, tip down, and steadied his arm, waiting for the perfect moment. He took a deep breath from within his armoured helmet, and released the blade from his grip.

Before the dagger dropped all four floors, and plunged into the passing slaver's head, Tauren had already attached his hook to the beam and swung down to the second floor, where another slaver was strolling by. In perfect synchronicity, the dagger dived into the ground-floor slaver's head, as Tauren flew into the second-floor guard.

The White Owl drove one of his many daggers into the man's heart, before swivelling on the spot and throwing it at the slaver on the opposite side of the second-floor. The blade spun across the expanse and ended its journey in the slaver's eye.

In five seconds he had killed three of the guards.

Tauren had no intention of stopping there; he was already jumping over the railing, and on top of the wagon, before the dagger impacted the third guard's eyeball.

In the same way that many animals changed their shape to appear threatening, so too could Tauren. He flipped backwards off the wagon and held his cape out wide like the wings of an owl, blocking the light from above and scaring the guards beside the wagon. As predicted, one of the slavers screamed and ran for the nearest door, while the other fancied his chances at making a name for himself.

Tauren kept his blades in their scabbards and evaded the guard's swing until he presented the perfect opportunity. Slipping under his wide swing was easy, almost as easy as grabbing the slaver's arm and breaking the bone. A swift fist to the face shattered his nose and sent the man stumbling from the building with a wobbly arm.

The sound of rushing feet and calls for help could be heard above. Tauren stepped over the guard with a dagger buried in the top of his head, pausing only to retrieve the blade, and made for his new prey.

The slaves called out from within their cages, begging to be set free, their arms outstretched through the square gaps in the bars. Tauren was only too happy to oblige and removed one of the two short-swords strapped to his back, positioned so that the hilts were always facing downwards. A strong swing saw the meaty padlocks broken and the slaves flooded out.

"Through there!" Tauren directed them to the correct exit. "Follow the owls." On the other side of the double doors, three of his trusted owls were waiting, each wearing a white mask, similar to his own.

Two slavers descended the stairs and dropped onto the ground floor, brandishing a mace and a sword. Tauren replaced his short-sword with a pair of daggers from his hips. The first one to come at him appeared fresh off the street with an obvious lack of tattoos or scars. He had no idea what was about to happen to him. With one blade, Tauren batted the slaver's sword away and rushed forward, bringing his other dagger to bear horizontally. In a flash of steel, he was standing between the slaver wielding a mace and the now dead swordsman, whose throat gushed blood over the floor.

The mace-wielder lunged with his weapon held high and an expression somewhere between terror and rage. It didn't matter. Tauren threw one of his daggers into the man's chest and laid him low in an instant. Without missing a beat, The White Owl caught the mace in mid-air and flung it at the next guard, rushing down the stairs. The heavy weapon cracked his knee and forced the man to roll down the steps in a heap. Tauren dropped to one knee and drove his knife into the slaver's heart, before jumping back up and flicking the same blade at the guard at the top of the stairs. He too collapsed in a heap and came crashing down the steps, dead.

The cries of the slaves on the other side of the wagon stopped Tauren from continuing up the stairs and killing the rest. Once again, he used one of his short-swords to cut the padlock in half. The slaves thanked him and reached out to touch their hero - a proven distraction. Tauren only saw the arrow after it had flown by his head, skimmed the lip of his dark hood and dug deep into the chest of an old man.

His attention refocused; the *creaking* of more bowstrings had The White Owl spinning away, hoping to take their aim away from the slaves. He raised the black cloak across his body to hide his true size, forcing the second archer to miscalculate and fire his arrow through the material. Tauren responded with one of his heavier throwing knives and launched it up to the second floor, where the blade ended its journey in the archer's head.

"Run!" Tauren hurried the slaves out as the next archer nocked an arrow.

"For too long have you been a thorn in my enterprise!" Orfad shouted down from the top floor, his fat head leering over the railing. "Whoever brings me his head can *live* in my whorehouse!"

More feet resounded from above as the slavers took up the challenge. Tauren used his youth and agility to jump on top of the wagon, between the slave cages. The arrow *thudded* into the wood, only an inch beneath his rising foot. He continued to run across the wagon and jump up to the first floor, where he swiped the legs of an oncoming slaver. Once on his back, Tauren crouched over the top of him and dropped his reinforced mask into the guard's head, breaking his nose and rendering him unconscious. He would have quite the story to tell when he awoke.

Another arrow whistled through the air and dug into the wooden beam beside Tauren's arm. The White Owl made for the stairs and threw a small bag of Talo spices across the gap, his aim perfect. The bag of spices flew into the mounted torch, behind the archer, and exploded in a flash of blinding light. Tauren's helmet muted some of the sound, allowing him to keep his senses, unlike the archer, who dropped his bow and covered his bleeding ears, as he stumbled around without his sight.

Tauren ran round the warehouse, ascending every stairwell and throwing his blades at every angle. Slavers dropped and fell over the railings on every floor. Those who evaded his throws experienced a crueller death, after Tauren unleashed his hand-to-hand combat and shattered bones.

It wasn't long before Tauren found himself back on the top floor, standing before Orfad's office. Sixteen men lay dead behind him, and the seventeenth was already sweating and praying to the gods. Tauren kicked the door in so hard it broke the top hinges and deformed the wood. Orfad yelped and jumped back with a bundle of scrolls and parchments screwed up in his arms.

The White Owl slowly drew his favourite dagger from the strap across his chest, making certain that Orfad saw every inch of the blade that was going to end his life. The hilt of the dagger was sculpted into the shape of an owl, its head forming the pommel.

Seeing no way of escaping his fate, Orfad's fear turned to anger. "You have changed nothing, White Owl! Long after your body is dust, men like me will continue to trade in the lives of the weak!" Orfad laughed nervously. "You have no idea what's coming. The House of Owls will crumble under Valanis!"

Tauren had heard enough. All he could see was red. The White Owl launched over the table and pinned the fat slaver to the wall. The blade was too clean a kill for this monster, and Tauren's rage had reached its crescendo. With Orfad's head gripped between Tauren's hands, he thrust his own head into the slaver's, again and again. He head-butted Orfad over and over until the white of his mask was dripping red with blood. By the time he released the head, the fat man was unrecognisable. He was also very dead...

It took several minutes before Tauren regained his breath and calmed down enough to focus on the scrolls Orfad had clung to. He removed the folded parchments and took note of the heavy ring on the slaver's finger. He had seen identical rings on previous targets, each one always embellished with the image of a sun and a black diamond in the centre.

The New Dawn...

Tauren had been trying to root out every member of the shadowy cult who, from what he had already discovered, had secretly ruled the south for decades, possibly even longer.

He wiped the blood from his faceplate with one of Orfad's expensive handkerchiefs and unravelled the parchments across the desk.

"What is this?" Tauren looked over records and drawings of various pieces of armour.

It was a receipt of some kind, with an order in the thousands!

Tauren continued to unravel more parchment and pour over the information. Orfad had been procuring tons of material and ore from the north to make armour and weapons for an army larger than any in The Arid Lands. And who was this Valanis he mentioned? Another slaver perhaps? Or another member of The New Dawn?

The White Owl took the scrolls and the map and descended the warehouse, trying futilely to put the pieces of the puzzle together. The archer, stunned by the Talo spices, was still staggering around the second floor when Tauren walked by. He thought about leaving him, another witness to his devastating skills, when he remembered the old man the archer had killed. Tauren shoved his favourite dagger up into the man's jaw until it pierced his brain and killed him, instantly. It seemed a shame for the blade to have seen no blood, after all.

Tauren strolled outside without fear, ever aware that he was the most dangerous man on the streets. The sound of fighting and swords clashing were never too far away these days, as slaves and sympathisers took up arms against their oppressors. He knew that his owls weren't among the distant combatants, as he had them organised in other parts of the city. The White Owl always knew where they were and what goals he had assigned them.

For just a moment, he feared what chaos he had inspired. How many slaves would die picking up his cause without ever even meeting him, or stepping foot in the House of Owls? How many were dying right now because of his anger?

The sound of approaching hooves returned him to the moment in an instant. The White Owl dashed for the shadows of the alley and waited. Four black horses galloped down the dark street and came to an abrupt stop outside Orfad's warehouse. Tauren knew these men to be members of the city guard and soldiers in the emperor's army. Three of the riders wore their traditional silver and gold armour, with their helmets concealing their faces. The fourth rider, however, wore a long blue cloak over the top of his armour and didn't bother with a helmet; his authority came from recognition.

"Check inside," the helmet-less commander ordered.

All four dismounted and the three soldiers entered the warehouse with their swords drawn. The commander waited outside and looked around the empty streets and dark alleys, his hand always resting on the pommel of his sword.

"Halion Al-Anan..." Tauren called softly from the alley.

The commander didn't flinch at the sound of his name, the seasoned warrior no doubt expecting such a call. Halion's olive skin and wavy dark hair were cast in shadows as he entered the alley, unafraid. Tauren stepped out and made himself known, his hands hidden within his black cape. Still, Halion walked towards him with his gloved hand squeezing the hilt of his sword. Tauren knew how fast Halion could remove that blade and plunge it into his opponent.

At the point at which both men could strike the other down, Halion smiled and Tauren offered the commander his arm, who instead embraced The White Owl and pulled him in for a tight hug.

"Good to see you, brother!" Tauren's voice was distorted by his mask.

"And you." Halion's smile turned sour at the sight of the blood streaked across Tauren's white mask. "Are you hurt?"

"Of course not!" Tauren pulled away and removed his helmet and hood. "Your father taught me better than that."

Halion's expression of relief quickly faded at the mention of his father, and Tauren regretted his words instantly. For Tauren, Salim Al-Anan's exile from The Arid Lands was hard to deal with and his loss weighed heavy on The White Owl's heart but, for Halion, the loss had been tenfold. Not only had the young warrior had to watch his father be stripped of his rank, humiliated and then exiled to the bitter north, but Halion had been forced to remain and carry his father's shame.

Publicly acknowledging his father's mistakes had been the only way to distance himself from Salim and rise through the ranks. Halion's climb to second in command of the emperor's army hadn't been an easy one, but a necessary one.

"My father's lessons were instructive," Halion replied. "I only wish he had taken better heed of them himself."

Tauren had never stopped thinking about that night, the night Emperor Kolosi and his wife had been slaughtered in their private chambers, under Salim's very nose.

Noise from the warehouse stopped Tauren from dwelling on Salim, his adoptive father, and focus on the present. He looked beyond Halion to make certain that the soldiers weren't exiting the building and searching for their commander.

"Don't worry," Halion bade. "They are trusted men."

That didn't completely convince Tauren. "How can you be sure they aren't loyal to Rorsarsh?"

Just thinking about the supreme commander of the emperor's forces made The White Owl's blood boil. Rorsarsh was an avid supporter of slavery and was most definitely a member of The New Dawn. Unfortunately, he was also Halion's direct commander.

"I started separating my men from his men a long time ago, brother." Halion made a cursory glance over the surrounding rooftops and Tauren knew he was searching for any other owls.

"You need to kill him and be done with it," Tauren said.

"Slavery is an ancient evil that I wholeheartedly agree needs eradicating, but Rorsarsh will die at the right time. You talk of my father's training; did he not teach you patience? The tide is still turning and I'm not sure we would win in an all-out war right now."

"Well, I think that's what *they're* preparing for." Tauren handed over the stolen scrolls from Orfad's office.

Halion looked over the parchment in confusion. "This... this can't be right. The order is too large. We don't even need this much armour or weapons."

"Exactly, so who do they think is going to be wearing it all?" Tauren pressed.

"Who are *they*?"

"The New Dawn, of course!" Tauren threw up his hands, exasperated. "The same cult that runs this country."

"That still doesn't answer why they have ordered so much material." Halion, ever the calm one, rolled up the scroll and handed it back to Tauren. "I will investigate."

"No, *I* will look into it," Tauren quickly replied. "You will only appear suspicious if you go poking your nose into The New Dawn's business any more than you already have. It's a miracle of the gods that they haven't already tried to indoctrinate you."

Halion smiled. "That's a big word for an alley-rat."

Tauren smiled at the nick-name his adoptive brother had given him all those years ago, when Salim had first saved him from a beating in the streets, and seen something in Tauren that no one had before.

"Continue to sway more soldiers to our cause." Tauren replaced his mask and hood. "*I* will look into this new development."

"Be safe, little brother." Halion was on his own in moments, as Tauren slipped into the shadows and disappeared.

CHAPTER 8
THE RANGERS

The Evermoore surrounded them on their journey north, the natural sounds of the forest filling Reyna's ears and reminding her of home. If she closed her eyes, and ignored the clopping of hooves, the princess could pretend she was back in The Amara.

The mighty forest surrounded her home, Elandril, and was easily her favourite place in all of Ayda. Though she didn't mind the smell of the human hubbub, she was appreciative of nature's scents, as was Ölli, who flew above them, following their trail.

Alas, her mind could not find peace, even in the quiet of the wilds. Reyna could only think of Faylen's shocking news earlier this morning. Her mentor had spoken with Galanör!

"He didn't say anything else?" the princess asked again.

Faylen's sigh was not so subtle. "For the third time, no. And I couldn't get back in touch with him after he disconnected."

"Was he in distress?" Reyna pressed.

"It's hard to say. Diviners aren't the best way to hold a conversation."

Faylen's body language suggested she thought the worst of Galanör's situation, but only Reyna could detect such subtleties.

Nathaniel trotted up beside them. "So we don't know if he's with Malliath?"

"We have to assume not, since King Elym was not aware of Galanör's whereabouts," Faylen replied through tight lips.

Now, it was Reyna's turn to sigh. The young elf had met Galanör several times, before she left for Illian's shores, in an effort to get to know her future husband. They had little in common. Galanör was a warrior, and one of the greatest at that, but he would make a terrible partner. The son of house Reveeri was devoted to the invasion plan and set on seeing his family elevated.

Only once had Reyna seen a glimmer of another elf behind Galanör's facade. She had seen it in his eyes during one of their escorted walks in The Amara. He would look at the distant lands with wonder in his heart, as Reyna so often had. But, like her, Galanör was trapped within the plans of those around him.

The princess looked back in her saddle for any sign of the ranger. Asher had told them to press on towards Lirian, situated in the centre of The Evermoore, while he retrieved Hector, his horse. The Selk Road, however, remained devoid of any travellers behind them. Reyna was confident that Asher would find them before they reached the capital of Felgarn.

Not long after the sun had set did the three travellers make camp. Faylen had wanted to stay close to The Selk Road, so that Asher might see their camp fire, but Nathaniel assured her that the ranger could find them anywhere, and so they settled a little deeper into the forest.

Reyna sat on the same log as Nathaniel and rested her head on the knight's shoulder. The princess could feel Faylen's judging gaze on her, but continued to enjoy the closeness all the same. The two had yet to rekindle any passion that lay between them since before the battle of West Fellion. Elaith's death had hit them all hard, but no one more than Nathaniel. Only in the last day or so had she seen a difference in the knight, but there was still a gap she didn't know how to cross.

The young elf distracted herself and examined her new bow, marvelling at the craftsmanship in the firelight. The black coating sparkled between the ancient gold runes that lined the limbs.

As an elf, Reyna was more attuned to the world of magic than other reasoning beings, and so she could feel the power of the weapon humming in her hand. A part of her didn't want to use the bow, knowing how many innocent lives it had taken in the hands of its previous owner, Adellum Bövö. Since she had been the one to finally end the dark elf's life, and with his own bow no less, it was only right that she claim it.

The bow certainly couldn't be allowed to fall into the wrong hands and end up in the clutches of Valanis's generals again. In some way, she thought, the bow went perfectly with her quiver, enchanted to never run out of arrows.

Reyna's pointed ears picked up the sound of hooves before Nathaniel's did. Asher strolled into the clearing, guiding Hector by the reins in his hand. It was troubling to know that Asher had the skills to enter their camp undetected if he wished, though she held no fear of the ranger, but rather the assassins who possessed similar talents.

"Any trouble?" Nathaniel asked, eyeing the short-swords strapped across Asher's back in the shape of an X. The only way anyone was claiming Alidyr's sword would be to prise it from Asher's dead body.

"They won't know he's gone until morning," Asher replied casually, wrapping the reins around the branch of a tree.

"Then get some rest," Faylen bade. "We ride for Lirian at dawn."

Reyna's eyes met with Nathaniel's and held a silent conversation. Emotions, new to both, were swirling around their minds. She didn't love him, or at least she didn't think it was love - this was all too new for her. The princess's frustration was quick to tip her emotions over the edge, her elven urges rising to the surface.

A part of her wanted to forget her self-proclaimed mission to destroy Valanis and bring peace to Verda, and instead run away with Nathaniel to some quiet place and be happy.

That train of thought took her to the logical conclusion that she would inevitably out-live Nathaniel. The thought made her stomach lurch and she broke eye contact and moved away from the knight, much to his surprise. He questioned her with a look, but the princess only smiled in return and lay beside Faylen.

As the sun reached its apex the next day, the four companions broke free of The Evermoore canopy and rode into the city of Lirian.

Asher patted Hector on the neck, happy to have his trusted steed back. The new saddle would take some getting used to but the ranger didn't mind - he was more irritated at losing his goods from the previous saddle.

"It's beautiful!" Reyna exclaimed, taking in the forest city.

The bulk of Lirian was located at the base of a small mountain, with its pointed roofs and elven-styled spires wrapping around the sides. The streets were a mix of cobble and mud, lined with shops and taverns that bustled with activity.

The main street that branched off from The Selk Road ran through the middle of the city and continued up the slope of the small mountain. Asher watched the princess follow the path upwards, until she saw the palace and grand houses that lay nestled between giant pine trees.

"That's where Queen Isabella Harg lives," Nathaniel said, also watching the princess. "She rules—"

"Oh, I know my Illian history," Reyna interjected. "It was once a great elven city, before The Dark War. My parents grew up in this forest. Now, Queen Isabella rules all of Felgarn, the region that surrounds The Evermoore. The towns of Woodvale and Vangarth are loyal to her, the house of the stag. Felgarn has stood between Alborn and The Ice Vales for centuries, a geographical deterrent to war between Velia and Grey Stone."

It was quite the report, but Asher had to agree with her assessment. If not for Felgarn, in the heart of Illian's landscape, the ranger was sure there would be nothing standing between King Rengar of Velia going to war with King Gregorn of Grey Stone. Theirs was a battle that had started hundreds of years before either were born.

Though not before Asher was born...

"I suppose that information would help if you were here to find our weaknesses," Nathaniel replied without looking at Reyna's hurt expression.

Asher could see the new friction between the two, but he couldn't find the cause. Offering advice to two young lovers was not something he was comfortable with and, even if he was, the ranger had no clue as to what he would say. Theirs was a love destined to end in tragedy, if not by their mission, then by their heritage.

"Where to, Ranger?" Faylen asked, no doubt sensing the same unease between the two.

"Follow me." Asher steered Hector away from the main road and into the centre of the eastern district of Lirian.

Asher and Nathaniel took no precautions in regard to their appearance, but the elves continued to keep the wide hoods over their heads in a bid to conceal their pointed ears. Seeing armed people within the city limits was no shocking sight to the Lirians, who had long been hunters. Still, Asher felt the enchanted shortsword on his back drew attention.

In truth, the ranger was uncomfortable having twin swords on his back again. The Arakesh had always fought with twin shortswords strapped to their backs, and it was the first thing Asher changed when he exiled himself.

It wasn't long before Asher found himself outside the only place that he had ever let his guard down. The tavern was unassuming and crammed between a row of shops and houses, with a simple sign hanging over the door.

"The *Pick-Axe?*" Faylen inspected the exterior with a critical eye.

"We just call it the Axe." Asher hopped off his saddle and walked Hector to the post outside the tavern.

"Who's *we?*" Reyna asked, sceptically.

"You'll see..." the ranger replied with a coy smile.

The others tied off their horses' reins and walked up the short steps. The raucous noise from inside was surprising for the time of day, but Asher knew the tavern's popularity had continued to grow since he rescued Queen Isabella, all those years ago. His ties to the tavern had caught the attention of many wanting to hear tales of the rangers that patrolled the land.

"Is that a *warthog?*" Nathaniel asked incredulously. "With a *saddle?*"

Indeed, there was a warthog with a saddle strapped to its back, though it was no saddle a human would fit into. The animal's thick curling tusks were decorated with golden bands to match the gold-laden saddle.

Its light brown fur bristled as the hog snorted and pulled against its reins rebelliously. The familiar sight only made Asher smile all the more, and he realised that it had been too long since his last visit.

The Pick-Axe was certainly teeming with patrons, laughter erupting from every corner and tankards *clanking* in merriment. The companions weren't given a moment's notice from the drinkers when they walked up to the bar, avoiding the buxom maid carrying a tray of beers and the drunkards staggering away from their barstools.

Nathaniel had visited Lirian before, but had never seen this particular tavern. The knight noticed Asher's attention drift over to the gruff, but dramatic, voice by the far right wall, the tone often more a growl than any known speech. Though the speaker couldn't be seen through the throng of on-lookers, he yelled above the others what sounded like an interesting tale about Gobbers, a gangly and vicious race of monsters.

Nathaniel's defences came up when the companions were halted in front of the bar by a solid wall of a man. Asher managed to stop before he walked straight into the hulking barbarian, who looked down on the ranger as if he were a bug. Wearing barely any armour, the man's bare chest and arms rippled with muscles and thick veins that protruded like worms on his taut skin.

"Don't mind him," a stern voice said from behind the barbarian, who walked away, disappearing through a door, beyond the bar. "He's from The Iron Valley. You know what them northerners are like..."

Nathaniel saw a surprising smile light up Asher's face. The man behind the bar was wiping tankards with a cloth, whilst smiling from ear to ear. The ranger strode over to the barkeeper and the two embraced forearms.

Even though Nathaniel guessed the barkeeper to be older than Asher, the man's arms were well formed and tight around his muscles, suggesting the simple barkeeper kept in better shape than the ranger, or even Nathaniel. With razored grey hair, thick broad shoulders and the singular scar that ran up from the top of his left eye and cut through his hairline, the Axe's owner appeared an unusual breed.

"Russell Maybury..." Asher looked over the barkeeper and Nathaniel followed his gaze to the pick-axe mounted on the wall. The wooden shaft was decorated with several dozen notches from end-to-end.

A very unusual breed...

"Asher! You're not travelling alone?" Russell asked with disbelief in his tone, his unnatural yellow eyes flickering across the companions' faces.

"It hasn't been an easy road that's led us here..." Asher replied seriously.

Russell looked at the ranger and lingered over his sword belt, bereft of an actual sword, and the many cuts and gashes that marred his leather armour. That was apparently enough to spur the barkeeper into action.

Russell made for the end of the bar. "Follow me."

"BY GRARFATH'S BALLS!" the overly-gruff voice from the other side of the tavern roared. "Step aside, step aside! Ah, shut it! I'll finish the tale tomorrow!"

Asher quietly chuckled at Nathaniel's confused expression. From their vantage, all Nathaniel and the elves could see was an angry crowd of men and women being pushed aside by some invisible force. The small mob jeered and groaned in protest, until the group burst apart to reveal a well-armoured *dwarf*.

Only his hands and face could be seen, the rest of his stout body protected by plated armour of black and gold. His long blond hair was pulled tight at the back of his head, where it flowed over his shoulders and mixed with a beard that ran down to his waist and ended in a tidy braid.

"I knew it was ye!" the dwarf exclaimed, as he stomped over towards the companions and punched Asher in the leg.

Nathaniel moved his hand within his cloak, keeping his sword within easy reach. The knight had never met a dwarf before and he couldn't be sure of his feelings towards Asher.

"Heavybelly!" Russell Maybury scolded the dwarf from the end of the bar.

"What?" the dwarf replied with his hands held high. The smaller warrior looked from Russell to Asher to the three companions that stood to the side. "Are they with *ye*?" Asher nodded with a hint of annoyance on his face. "Seriously?" the dwarf asked again.

"Yes."

"Well then..." The dwarf stood back and hooked his thumbs into the armoured plates on his chest. "I am Doran, son of Dorain, of clan Heavybelly, at ye service!"

Nathaniel couldn't help staring at the dwarf, an unusual sight south of Vengora, the mountain range in the north that divided Illian from Dhenaheim, the dwarven realm. Faylen took it in her stride, like most things, and Reyna simply beamed at Doran, always excited to see new things.

"Introductions can wait, Heavybelly." Russell ushered them all, Doran included, through a door beyond the bar.

"Thank ye youn' lady!" Doran licked his whiskers and scooped up a tray of beers set down by the barmaid.

Asher reassured Nathaniel and the others with a look, as they descended the staircase that led under the tavern. His show of ease and trust towards these people was enough for Nathaniel and Reyna, but Faylen remained ever vigilant.

The private tavern beneath the Axe was a cosy chamber, devoid of windows and lit with torches and candles, with a stone fireplace set against the far wall. A small bar was situated in the corner, surrounded by a sheer wall of stacked beer kegs. A long table occupied the other side of the room, while comfy chairs and rugs were situated in front of the fireplace. The stone walls were lined with weapons, both old and new, as well as the mounted heads of a Gobber, a Troll and even a Sandstalker.

The Pick-Axe was becoming the strangest tavern Nathaniel had ever seen.

A light melody was being played on a tanbur by an olive-skinned man, sat atop the long table, his foot resting casually on the bench. He stopped playing the tune the instant he locked eyes with Asher. He wasn't the only one who stopped what they were doing, Nathaniel noticed.

An older looking man with a bushy grey beard and tattered mage's robes put his steaming drink down by the fireplace and stood up, along with a young woman with long dark braided hair. The barbarian Asher had almost walked into upstairs was sitting at a small round table in the corner, but he paid no attention to their entrance. Another man with his back to them was sitting with his head hung low over the bar in the opposite corner, oblivious to them all.

"That was a long stretch, old-timer..." The eloquent voice came from the right of the stairs, where a man with dark skin and a bald head rested against a wooden beam. His white moustache and goatee lifted into a smile as his brown eyes took in the sight of the ranger.

"Too long," Asher agreed, embracing the man's forearm.

"Do my eyes deceive me?" the bald man asked, looking over Nathaniel and the elves.

"Yes they're with *me*," the ranger announced, clearly growing tired of the assumptions.

The bald man looked over the companions with a grave expression and bade them to take a seat by the fire. Russell closed the door leading to the tavern upstairs and locked it with a key.

"Asher..." Faylen whispered, touching his elbow.

"We can trust these people," the ranger replied, placing his hand lightly over the top of hers.

"Indeed you can, miss," the bald man said warmly. "We are rangers all, like your friend Asher here."

Asher moved to the fire and Nathaniel joined him, keeping close to Reyna, who was still mesmerised by the sight of Doran Heavybelly.

The bald man placed a hand over his chest and smiled. "I am Jonus Glaide, but everyone just calls me Glaide. This is Hadavad and his newest apprentice, Atharia Danell." Glaide gestured to the bearded man in old mage's robes and the young woman close to his side.

Still wary, Nathaniel observed Asher's nod to the olive-skinned man walking towards him, but the two embraced as old friends.

"This is Salim Al-Anan..." Glaide held out his hand when the southerner, Salim, stepped back from Asher.

Salim cut a lean figure with long black hair and a well-trimmed beard. He wore black robes that touched the floor and a wide red piece of cloth that wrapped around his waist. A white ornate dagger with a curved tip was tucked into the makeshift belt, above several leather pouches. Nathaniel knew a trained soldier when he saw one. It was obvious by the way Salim carried himself, though the young knight couldn't discern the man's history.

"You've already had the pleasure of meeting Doran," Glaide continued, looking down at the dwarf who was inhaling a tray full of beer.

"What is this place?" Nathaniel asked, glancing at a previously unseen head of a Gorgon - its eyes gouged out.

"This is The Pick-Axe," Glaide smiled. "Mr. Maybury over there is the proprietor of this fine establishment. It's more of a home away from home for us wayward types, and Russ is content for us to help pay our way through tales of the road." Glaide pointed to the tavern above. "It brings in the customers. Though I doubt it's *our* tales the people of Lirian crave." Everyone's eyes rested on Asher. "There isn't a ranger here who can't say they owe their life to Asher..."

The barbarian's chair dragged across the stone floor until it toppled over. "So you the famous *Asher*." The huge man slowly walked over towards the gathered group, his eyes fixed on the ranger.

"Bale..." Russell Maybury's tone was unmistakably threatening.

The barbarian continued his determined stride. Nathaniel gripped his sword firmly now, ready to strike if he must. Having grown up in Longdale, in the north, Nathaniel had met many of the barbarian's type as they travelled south, out of The Iron Valley, to trade. Though they weren't as wild and unpredictable as the Outlanders from the mysterious Wild Moores, the barbarians were still brutish thugs with a warped sense of honour and glory.

Bale's accent was thick and his use of the common tongue was basic. "I have travelled world in search of contest. A good death cannot be found in Iron Valley. South of Vengora, all I hear are whispers of ranger, assassin, great warrior they say. I would know truth..."

"You know the rules of my house." Maybury unfolded his thick arms.

They always talk, Nathaniel thought. The knight had already assessed the man-mountain while he spoke. For all the barbarian's muscles and sheer bulk, he was still vulnerable in the throat and the knees, the same as everyone else. His nerve clusters were all in the same places and easily manipulated by the well-trained knight, and his size simply made him a massive target that couldn't be missed by a well-placed throwing knife. With his spare hand, Nathaniel made certain that the two daggers were resting in the small of his back.

I'm starting to think like Asher! he thought with a pinch of amusement.

Before it could come to blows, however, Glaide stepped between Bale and Maybury, the apparent voice of wisdom in the Axe.

Glaide's words were soft but bold. "Bale, son of Hyil, of the Oakbreaker tribe... Have you ever known me to lie?" The barbarian looked down at the older man with suspicion and slowly shook his head. "Have you ever known me to exaggerate?" Again, Bale could only shake his head. "Then listen to me when I tell you that fighting Asher will not grant you a *good* death, just a *messy* one."

The barbarian looked from Glaide to Asher, quizzically. After another moment's thought, Bale snorted his amusement and returned to his little table.

Nathaniel released the white-knuckled grip on the hilt of his sword.

"Bah! Always gettin' in the way o' some fun!" Doran Heavybelly practically spat his words at Glaide, who only chuckled at the dwarf's response.

"Tell us a tale, Asher." Salim rested against the mantelpiece as Hadavad and Atharia sat cross-legged on the floor.

"Perhaps some introductions..." Hadavad said, his grey eyes fixed curiously on Reyna and Faylen.

Nathaniel knew what surprise awaited the rangers of the Axe. They had already spoken of how their mission and very survival would depend upon secrecy. The revelation of the elves' existence would put all of that in jeopardy. Yet, Nathaniel, and the elves to some extent, trusted Asher's judgement.

"I am Nathaniel Galfrey," the knight announced, prolonging the elves' introduction in case a lie was being constructed.

"Galfrey?" The questioning voice came from the small bar in the corner. The unknown man, whose head had been slumped between his shoulders, stepped off his stool and joined them in the firelight, along with the man's alcoholic odour. "As in, Tobin Galfrey?"

He was older than Asher, but perhaps a little younger than Glaide, with short but unkempt white hair and a thick white moustache against a stubbled face. Cold blue eyes and angular features told of a hard life on the road, but his build was wiry and strong and, like Salim, the man carried himself as a soldier.

A long, well-worn and dirty coat hung to his calves in tatters. Most of it was covered in armour and straps, except none of it appeared to match: his pauldrons had each come from a difference suit of armour. One knee pad was layered in flat cylindrical spikes while the other was leather. He wore only one vambrace on his forearm - the other had to make do with bound strips of blue fabric. The sword hanging from his waist was the most telling of all, however, for Nathaniel had an identical one sheathed on his own waist.

"He was my father," Nathaniel replied.

The legendary Graycoat that had been his father would forever cast a shadow over any of his deeds. It was his father's love for his mother, however, that cast Nathaniel in a bad light. The order had always seen Nathaniel as a walking monument to their greatest warrior's singular failure, in breaking his oath to never sire a child. To Nathaniel, he had just been the father he loved and missed.

"I knew him..." The dishevelled man looked into the fire as if he was seeing into the past.

"You are a Graycoat," Nathaniel stated.

Glaide gestured to the drunk. "This is Kaleb Jordain, *formerly* of the Graycoats."

"I don't need *you* to introduce me, Glaide," Kaleb snapped, with unfocused eyes struggling to settle on the ranger. "I am Kaleb Jordain. And apparently not the only disgraced Graycoat in this establishment..." The old ranger looked over Nathaniel's attire.

"I have left the order of my own volition," Nathaniel firmly replied. This wasn't a conversation he wanted to get into.

"So did I... right after they told me to get out," Kaleb added quietly. "The price of love."

Glaide held up his hand to stop the ranger from continuing his story, but Kaleb ignored him.

"I left thinking I had a good woman and a baby to raise." The ranger stopped mid-sentence to burp. "Until it turned out the baby wasn't mine and..." The drunkard twirled his finger in the air as if that explained the rest of his sad tale.

"Why don't you have a seat, Kaleb?" Russell Maybury put another tankard of ale into his chest and rested a meaty hand on the ranger's shoulder.

"Don't mind if I do," Kaleb replied with a simple smile, dropping into the comfy armchair.

An awkward moment hung between the group while they waited to see if Kaleb would continue his rant.

Hadavad, the old wizard, spoke up first. "I am sure that your tale is a good one Mr. Galfrey, but perhaps first we could learn of your companions?" Hadavad looked at the elves with that same curious expression. "I can *feel* the magic that surrounds you both." Atharia Danell nodded absently in agreement with her mentor.

Faylen and Reyna looked to one another, before meeting Asher's reassuring nod. The elves removed their hoods with both hands and allowed the ensemble of rangers to look upon their fair features. Nathaniel could see their pointed ears between their long hair, and so too could the rest.

Reyna stepped forward and announced, "I am Princess Reyna Sevari of the elven nation, and this is my mentor and protector, Faylen Haldör."

As expected, there was a stunned silence that followed. Even Doran Heavybelly looked at the elves in silence, with beer dripping down his yellow beard as it flowed out of the tankard. Nathaniel looked to Asher, who was leaning against the wall with a bemused smile on his face.

"There are rumours coming out of Velia that elves have returned to Illian..." Glaide said, his dark eyes fixed on the elves' unusual ears.

"Bah! If that's an elf then I'm a bearded goat!" Doran slammed his now empty tankard down. "Elves left a thousand years ago for pastures better than these. Why would ye return now?"

"That is a long story, Master Dwarf," Reyna replied with a sad smile, while looking to Asher and Nathaniel.

"We will need to stay here while we prepare for our journey south," Asher explained to the elf. "Tell the tale and earn our keep." The ranger made for the door.

"Where are you going?" Faylen asked.

"To get us some money for our supplies and find a caravan travelling south." Asher looked from Nathaniel to Reyna, silently indicating for the Graycoat to remain behind.

"I have supplies aplenty for any journey, Asher. You're welcome to them," Russell offered.

"Thank you, but our journey will be long and more supplies required along the way." Asher continued for the door.

"You're travelling south?" Glaide asked, tearing his eyes from the elves.

"Sit awhile and listen to their tale," Asher bade. "I promise you it's a good one."

"Well we best get some more ale then, eh..." Doran looked to Russell with a raised eyebrow.

CHAPTER 9
IN THE SERVICE OF
THE GODS

King Merkaris strode through the maze of dark tunnels that formed the foundation of his keep. Originally built by his ancestor, King Gal Tion, the first human king in Illian, the elaborate tunnels had been built as a last resort in case of a siege. The enemy would be forced to pursue them into the labyrinth, where a series of traps and ambushes could be fought on the Tion's terms.

Most of the tunnels were abandoned now, and the separate rooms had been knocked together to form a chamber big enough to store Namdhor's records.

The two guards standing outside the tall, double doors had their backs to the king. He could sense the fear on them as they stared at the black doors with trepidation. They had been ordered to ensure Valanis's privacy, but news had filtered up to the king regarding some apparent distress from within the archives.

Merkaris was silent in his approach, listening to the sounds from within. The sound of tables being upturned and chairs broken apart echoed from inside. A roar that would halt the bravest of souls erupted from the other side of the door.

"Leave," he commanded.

The guards jumped back at the sudden order from their king. They bowed sharply and left at once, both wise enough not to question the king of Namdhor.

Merkaris hesitated as he rested his hands against the cool metal of the doorknobs. He had only ever been in the presence of Valanis in the caverns behind Kaliban, deep in the mountains of Vengora. Seeing the dark elf in his personal chamber had been exciting... but also terrifying. Even as a human, Merkaris could feel the magical aura that surrounded Valanis, cocooning him in power. Hearing his master's rage only made him feel as powerful as an insect.

The king pushed through into the Namdhorian archives. Book shelves higher than most houses stood in rows that stretched back for fifty metres. The central aisle was usually decorated with long tables and chairs, with low-hanging chandeliers above each one. But now, the chamber was a mess.

Scrolls covered the floor, some burnt and shredded while others were left in frozen pieces. The tables and chairs were naught but piles of splinters and spikes, strewn throughout the shelves and central aisle. Three of the large shelves at the back of the chamber had been toppled over like dominoes.

"WHERE IS IT?" the other-worldly voice roared.

Merkaris cautiously moved through the tattered papers and scrolls, searching for his master amidst the records.

Valanis appeared, as if from nowhere, and picked the king up with one hand, his iron grip wrapped around Merkaris's throat. Calculating purple eyes stared back at him from behind that menacing mask. The dark elf's breathing filled the chamber, overpowering the king's desperate spluttering.

Valanis eventually sighed and casually released Merkaris to fall to the floor, joining the pile of scrolls. The king massaged his throat and gasped.

"Forgive me, Merkaris..." The dark elf pulled back his hood and removed the helmet.

King Merkaris forgot his plight in an instant, gazing upon the beauty of his master. Valanis truly was a god. His long blond hair flowed down his back with two pointed ears protruding at the sides. The dark elf's features were fair but strong, set against those dazzling purple eyes. The chamber was granted more light when Valanis's skin literally glowed from within. Veins became visible across his face and neck, glowing like the sun.

"I should not punish such a loyal servant of the gods," Valanis continued.

"Every breath I take is in service to the gods, my Lord... and you!" Merkaris added with as much enthusiasm as his sore throat would allow.

"After The Dark War... after the Amber Spell, the world continued on without me. The elves stood aside as man rose to power and forged war with the dragons, a war they won no less. I have spent forty years catching up on a thousand years of history that should never have been allowed to happen."

"My Lord?" Merkaris knew he wasn't wise enough to understand the musings of his master.

Valanis looked away, as if he could see or hear something that Merkaris could not. For a moment the dark elf was completely distracted, apparently enthralled in another conversation.

"History would have you believe that I started a civil war for no more than simple power. The truth is such an elusive concept. I only wanted to unite the elves so that we might wage war against the dragons." Valanis spoke so casually of world domination until he laughed to himself. "But, it appears such an army wasn't needed. Mankind achieved this end all by themselves. Your kind is not to be underestimated, it seems."

Merkaris couldn't grasp what his master was referring to. "Why did you want war with the dragons, my Lord?" He stayed on the floor, resting on his knees.

"Why would the *gods* have me wage war with the dragons? That is a better question, good king. Alas, the truth of the gods and their needs are beyond your comprehension. You need only concern your-self with *my* needs."

Merkaris bowed, fully aware that he would never be privy to Valanis's ultimate plan. All that mattered was where he would stand in all this. When the war was over, mankind would bow at his feet, as Valanis put him in charge of their entire race.

"At the end of The Dragon War," Valanis purred, "who else plundered The Lifeless Isles, besides your ancestors?"

There were many paintings and tapestries devoted to telling the story of The Dragon War. The archipelago that drifted down from the larger island of Dragorn had been home to the dragons for thousands of years.

When King Tion finally breached its shores and wiped the great beasts out, the Tion kingdom had already begun to fracture into what were now six kingdoms. Merkaris knew well of the other figureheads, whose descendants now shared the land with himself.

"The isles were plundered by all," Merkaris told him. "But, the bulk of its secrets were kept by the now four ruling families of Dragorn; the Fenrigs, the Yarls, the Danathors and the Trigorns. It was the treasures they found that elevated them to rulers.

"My ancestor, Gal Tion, thought that war with the dragons would unite our kind, but it only gave them the opportunity to rebel."

Merkaris looked hard at his master and wondered what treasure the dragons had been hiding. It must be something of great value if Valanis was personally hunting for it through ancient archives.

"I have heard of these people." Valanis replaced his mask and hood, concealing the supernatural light. "They do not crown themselves kings and queens, but they rule Dragorn none-the-less." The dark elf looked upon Merkaris, his expression hidden beneath the mask. "Have you been to Dragorn?" The king nodded. "You have visited these would-be kings and queens?" Again, Merkaris nodded. "Picture it in your mind, as if you were standing there..." Valanis slowly approached the king and reached out to cup Merkaris's face in his gloved hand.

Merkaris did as he was asked and pictured the grand compound and lush gardens that housed the mighty Trigorn family.

As Valanis touched his face, the king felt an intrusion into his mind, something Alidyr had trained him to detect years ago. There was nothing he could, however, do to keep Valanis out. The dark elf penetrated his mind and took what he wanted, stealing the images and sounds that Merkaris dragged from his memory. The mental intrusion intensified until the king lost his sight and any sense of what was around him.

The overwhelming presence vanished as quickly as it had appeared. Only now, Merkaris was lying on his back, atop a pile of discarded scrolls and very much alone. Valanis was gone.

Valanis stepped through the portal, leaving the semi-conscious king and dusty archives, and into the fading light of the sun, as it set over Dragorn.

The dark elf stumbled after his first step, feeling the weight of his magic take its toll. He had transported himself twelve hundred miles in a single step and without the use of a crystal. Naius's power gave him unimaginable strength, but its price was becoming steep. Valanis could feel the threat of a seizure. His left hand twitched uncontrollably and his mouth was filled with a tangy taste.

The shard from Paldora's gem offered him its strength, but it wasn't enough to keep him on his feet. It was for this reason that Valanis had chosen the rooftop adjacent to the Trigorn's luxurious mansion. No one was around to see him drop to his knees and ball his fists in the struggle to take back control. It took every bit of his considerable strength to keep the seizure at bay – something he could not have done a thousand years ago without the gem, even if it was only a shard.

FOCUS... PATIENCE...

The voice filled Valanis's head, drowning out the thundering of blood in his ears. He recognised it as Ikaldir, the god of the hunt. As always, the gods offered him their wisdom as well as strength. Valanis trusted in Paldora's gem to sustain him and he relaxed, sitting cross-legged on the rooftop. He would meditate until the moon replaced the sun.

Then he would hunt...

As the stars formed a canopy over the world, Valanis opened his eyes again. The crescent moon was high in the sky, casting a pale glow across the city.

The dark elf rose to his feet and took in a deep breath, making certain that any chance of a seizure was past him. Dragorn and The Lifeless Isles that trailed off from the main island were a place of ancient and raw magic. Thousands of dragons had once called this place home and the echo of their magical auras continued to resonate throughout. Valanis basked in those echoes for a moment, soaking up its strength.

The city was not as he remembered it. Of course, it had been well over a thousand years since he had stepped foot on the island. His father had brought him and his sister when they were no more than ten years old. They had come to say goodbye to their mother, who had been chosen as one of the Dragorn. She was to live the rest of her life out on this island with her precious dragons and fellow peace-keepers.

His mother had fallen during The Dark War, though Valanis could barely remember the day. He had felt nothing when he saw her body strewn across the battlefield. It had been much harder to kill his father and sister after he discovered the pools of Naius, but the gods had demanded a sacrifice to prove his devotion. At least they had died for something, unlike his mother.

Now, Dragorn was a vast city and overpopulated with humans. The city stank of their kind. The scent was carried in the warm breeze that drifted off The Adean; there was no escaping it.

Looking over the lip of the rooftop, Valanis observed the square grounds that protected the Trigorns. A ten-foot wall encompassed the mansion and its gardens and pools. The house itself was far grander than the other mansions that filled the neighbourhood.

This particular vantage granted Valanis a view over the wall, where a multitude of guards patrolled the grounds. They were a mix of warriors and mages. Some wielded spears, axes and swords, while others walked around with staffs or wands holstered on their hip.

FIND IT!

The voice of Atilan, the king of the gods, was impossible to ignore. The powerful voice rang throughout his mind, reminding the dark elf that he had their strength and blessing.

Valanis took one last look at the mansion, before stepping off the top of the building. The ground cracked under his feet as his muscles filled with the strength of Krayt, the god of war. The peasants and drunks in the street jumped and scuttled into the nearest alley to escape his horrifying image. The black cloak, which hung loose from his waist down, flapped around his great strides.

The wide, heavy doors to the Trigorn compound were at the end of the street, where three guards stood sentry. Valanis's approaching presence demanded their attention. Even though they had no idea who he was, it was clear from their expressions that they understood the threat he posed. They formed into an arrowhead position, the leader wielding a hooked spear, ready to strike.

Valanis struck first.

The dark elf whipped his hand out and sent a concussive wave so powerful, it took all three men through the heavy door, splintering it into a thousand pieces. The dead guards flew into the grounds amid the debris and wrought iron. The thunder-clap would certainly alert the rest of the Trigorns' soldiers, but it didn't matter now.

ENJOY IT...

The god of war's voice was always the sweetest.

Valanis marched into the grounds and made for the main entrance to the mansion. A bell was ringing and guards began to appear from everywhere, some even pouring out of the buildings surrounding the compound. Their numbers would do them no good.

The first to attack him were the mages; both stood before him with their staffs held high, but their spells were for naught. Valanis held up his hand and used a shield of pure blue energy to absorb the first magical attack. The second spell he merely cast aside with the wave of a hand. The spell rebounded into the gardens and exploded, killing three approaching swordsmen. With fire and ice he killed them both, skewering one with an icicle and the other a flaming ball of fire.

As he ascended the steps of the veranda, a guard lashed out with a sword, his aim perfect for slicing Valanis's head in two. The dark elf caught the sword in one gloved hand and froze the steel until the blade shattered. The man looked in dismay from his broken sword to the menacing mask that looked back at him. Valanis punched his arm out and cast an explosive spell that sent the guard flying off the veranda and through the trellis. His sharp elven ears heard all the bones in his body break.

A fireball blew the mansion doors off their hinges and broke the protective spells that lined the framework. Another mage appeared from the hallway to his left and fired off a spell from his wand. Valanis simply shifted his shoulders and evaded the magical attack, which continued past the dark elf and into an emerging axe-man. The axe-man burst apart like a sack filled with too much wine. The explosive blood splatter blinded the guard following Valanis into the house, who was then picked up by the dark elf and used as a shield against the next spell. An icicle shot through the man's chest and threatened to impale them both.

Valanis smiled under his mask as he unleashed a staccato of purple lightning from his palm. The destructive magic streaked through the hallway until it engulfed the mage, killing him in seconds.

The herald of the gods killed indiscriminately as he made his way up to the master bedroom. The expensive decorations and ornaments that lined the halls and walls were covered in blood or destroyed all together.

A small fire had been started in the lavish foyer, where a burning corpse had set the material of a sofa to flames. The men shouted from all around the compound as confusion and chaos took over. They didn't know who was attacking them or how many there were.

Valanis was deep inside the mansion now, using his magical sense to find the traps set by the Trigorns' mages. It was the complexity of these traps that ultimately guided him to the master bedroom.

The cluster of guards standing outside the room were among the biggest Valanis had seen. Even their swords and hammers appeared to be heavier than the average human. The dark elf smiled behind his mask. He decided he would kill them with his bare hands and give his magic a rest for the moment. The group charged and roared, hoping to simply stampede Valanis to death, as his elven form was far slighter than theirs.

A side-step and a shift in his shoulders allowed Valanis to dodge the first two swings, putting him right in the middle of the group. With godly strength, Valanis kicked the man to his left, sending him straight through the nearest window and out into the night.

Blades and fists came at him then from every angle with fierce abandon. Valanis lashed out with his limbs, breaking bones, bursting organs and laying waste to the Trigorn soldiers.

The enchantments around the door to the master bedroom practically sang of their secrets to Valanis. He could tell that the spell was designed to repel and incinerate any who tried to enter without permission.

The dark elf waved his hand across the doorframe and used the power of Naius, the god of magic, to wipe the enchantments from existence, reducing most of the wooden frame to dust. After that, it was merely a flick of the finger to blow open the doors, eliciting a small yelp from the woman inside.

Valanis stalked across the sumptuous room, taking note of the naked, young olive-skinned man, clinging to the headboard for his life. The tattoo on his arm suggested he wasn't the head of the Trigorn family, but rather a lover for hire. That led Valanis to examine the naked woman beside him, her knuckles white from holding onto the bed sheets.

The dark elf estimated her age to be around forty, but human ages were just as hard to judge as elven ages in his eyes. She didn't look as terrified as the man, but her fear was undeniable. Her skin was in perfect condition, with clean, perfumed black hair and expensive jewellery around her neck and adorning her fingers. This was the head of the Trigorn family.

"What do you want?" Her voice was barely a whisper.

FIND IT!

"The treasures your ancestors plundered from these isles..." Valanis enjoyed the effect his altered voice had on the woman. "I would see all that you have and any records of the ones you sold or gave away."

"That... That was a thousand years ago," the woman replied, desperately trying to gain some composure in the face of the one who had slaughtered her private army.

Valanis whipped his arm out and snapped the naked man's neck with telekinesis. His body jerked and slumped off the side of the bed, startling the Trigorn woman.

"The... The vaults are shared between the four houses." The woman didn't even look at her dead lover. "It's lo... located in the central district, fronted as a brothel. Any of the artefacts or treasures that remain are kept underground. But, the security there is tenfold what you encountered here." The Trigorn woman was trying to ignite a little fire in her belly. "You should just walk away from this now, and I will *forget* your trespasses this day."

At that moment, five more guards came rushing into the room with their weapons raised. Valanis swivelled around and unleashed a torrent of fire that engulfed them all, burning them until they resembled the bark of a tree. Through it all the woman screamed and retreated further into her bed.

Valanis slowly turned back to her. "Fear not - you will never forget this day..."

There were more screams to come.

PART TWO

CHAPTER 10

MOURNBLADE

Gideon strolled through the oasis of Dragons' Reach, enjoying the sights and scented smells of the trees and flowers. He wished Abigail could have seen this. She would have been more excited than he was to have found the home of the dragons, not to mention actually living among them.

The mage's hand naturally drifted to the wand on his hip. Her wand...

Gideon wanted to scream and shout and cry at her loss, to hit the world for taking her from him. But now, surrounded by so much beauty and mystery, he realised it was his duty to live *for* her.

The sound of melodic singing brought him from his reverie and steered him to the left. Through the trees and past a cluster of boulders that formed a small hillock, Gideon came across yet another magnificent sight since his arrival in the giant crater.

Adriel, the last of the Dragorn, was singing to a tree, which continued to grow in front of the mage's very eyes. Its roots dug deep into the ground, as the trunk expanded and stretched high into the canopy above. Branches extended from the bark and sprouted lush green leaves.

Then, Adriel finally stopped singing. The tree stood silent, its leaves gently blowing in the breeze. The elf placed his palm against the bark and smiled warmly at his work.

"How did you do that?"

Adriel smiled all the more, but made no motion to face the mage as he continued to check over the new roots. Gideon walked over and placed a tentative hand over the bark as if it was some illusion.

"The elves have always sung to the trees," Adriel explained. "'Tis a gift we are born with, as the woodland folk, though I fear my people have abandoned those ways in favour of *war*. Galanör could do as I just did, if he wished, but he was trained to take life, not grant it."

Gideon looked past the new tree, to the broken stumps and fallen logs that littered the forest ground. This was the spot where Malliath had been brought down by the other dragons a couple of nights ago. Adriel was truly the caretaker of Dragons' Reach, healing the trees and plants that suffered under the feet of such large creatures.

Again, as the elf moved about, the grass and flowers, even some of the low-hanging branches, subtly moved towards him, as if pulled in by some unseen force. The forest loved Adriel just as much as he loved the forest.

"Where's Galandavax?" Gideon asked, changing the subject from Galanör.

Adriel looked to the north. "Keeping a close eye on Malliath."

Gideon didn't doubt that the elf knew exactly where his oldest friend was. "I feel ashamed for my part in his captivity..." Gideon had tried not to dwell on it, but living among the dragons made it impossible.

"It was not you who placed those enchantments upon his scales." Adriel bade Gideon to follow him, as they left the scene of devastation and headed deeper into the Reach. "You cannot take the blame for your ancestors failings any more than you can take the credit for their achievements."

"I don't think Malliath sees it that way," Gideon replied solemnly.

"He requires time, something dragons have in abundance." Adriel smiled, trying to alleviate Gideon's guilt. "He will find all that he needs here, in time."

"What about what the world needs?" Gideon asked pointedly. "The world needs dragons now more than ever, especially the Dragorn. If peace is to be had it will require one such as yourself to broker it between our people."

"Your approach is far more diplomatic than that of Galanör's, I shall give you that." Adriel continued through the trees and made a sudden left.

"Perhaps asking you to fight the Darkakin is too much," Gideon went on, "but, you could certainly help to prevent a war between the elves and man. Their alliance will be needed to repel the Darkakin."

Adriel remained silent and showed the mage into a small clearing with a single smooth rock in the centre. It wasn't particularly big, coming up to Gideon's waist, but the rock itself was not what captured the mage's attention...

Buried halfway into the stone was an exquisite elven scimitar, majestic in its appearance as the light of the sun pierced the canopy and reflected off the blade and the hilt. Gideon was drawn to it. He had never fought with a sword before, always favouring his staff and magic, but something about this blade felt...

Before he knew it, Gideon was standing right in front of it with his arm outstretched towards the hilt. The mage caught himself and looked to Adriel for answers, who could only look back at Gideon with a curious expression.

"I don't understand." Gideon pulled his hand back, almost afraid to touch the ornate sword.

"Before your kind left The Wild Moores and The Dark War ravaged Illian's lands, the Dragorn were a peacekeeping force to be reckoned with. Elandril, the first of my order, was the greatest warrior. The greatest of all elf kind. He fell in one of the oldest wars in elven history."

Gideon's attention was fully arrested by Adriel's history lesson. He knew that Elandril was also the name of the new elven city in northern Ayda, but he knew nothing of its namesake or any ancient wars beyond the fabled Dark War.

"How did he die?" the mage asked.

"Against the *orc*..." Adriel replied bitterly.

"Orc? I've never heard of them."

"And you never will. Elandril united the elves and the dwarves and drove the foul beasts south of Syla's Gate, into The Undying Mountains, where their numbers dwindled until death finally claimed them.

"But his sword, *Mournblade*, has been passed down through the order, as a reminder of what war begets. The Dragorn turned away from the sword and offered wisdom in its place." Adriel turned to the magnificent scimitar. "We carried them as a symbol rather than a weapon, but I lost mine in the final days of The Dragon War."

Gideon looked back at the blade, realising that if Adriel had lost his own sword then this one must have belonged to Elandril!

"I was able to retrieve Elandril's sword before we fled The Lifeless Isles. I placed it in the stone and had Galandavax breathe a special enchantment over it. Only when the Dragorn are truly needed again can Mournblade be pulled free." Adriel reached out and gripped the red hilt that glistened with minute crystals and golden script. With strength that Gideon knew was quite considerable, Adriel tried to heave the blade free of the stone. It didn't budge. "You see; our time has passed, Gideon."

As with all humans, Gideon felt the need to touch the ancient blade, as if that physical connection would cement its existence in his mind. The mage went for the hilt but stopped short when he heard a *snapping* twig behind them. Ilargo, in all his emerald magnificence, was standing in the clearing, having used his hunting skills to follow them silently. The dragon stared at Gideon and tilted his head.

"It seems you have an admirer..." Adriel said with his typical smile. "Ilargo has never met a human that didn't want to kill him before. You are something of a spectacle to him."

"*I'm* a spectacle to *him*?" Gideon asked incredulously. "There is no greater spectacle than him." The mage was truly taken with their kind.

"Indeed, we are of the same mind in that regard." Adriel walked over to Ilargo and affectionately rubbed the scales on his neck.

The green dragon continued to observe Gideon, as if he were the only thing in the clearing.

The mage was suddenly overcome with Ilargo's emotions when the dragon attempted to communicate with him. Gideon felt the need to know Ilargo as much as the dragon apparently wanted to know him. Was this the dragon's way of asking him to be friends?

An echo resounded in Gideon's mind, as if he could hear someone calling to him from far away. The feeling of anticipation filled the mage to the point of bursting, until Adriel stepped between him and Ilargo.

"Is everything alright, Gideon?" the elf asked, concerned with Gideon's distant expression.

The connection between man and dragon was severed, leaving Gideon to his own emotions. It left the mage a little disorientated and confused. He had no idea why Ilargo was feeling so expectant or why he had decided to communicate it, but Gideon quickly found himself craving that connection again. Communing with a dragon made him feel whole in a way he had never experienced.

"I'm fine," Gideon replied. "It just takes some getting used to."

Adriel laughed softly. "Over a thousand years have passed, but I still remember the first time a dragon decided to speak to me. It can be overwhelming in the beginning. After Galandavax chose me, and I embraced the ways of the Dragorn, I found it much easier sharing actual words than raw emotions all the time."

Gideon still couldn't believe that Adriel, and hundreds of Dragorn before him, could actually speak to dragons in the same way they were now speaking.

Ilargo shrugged his mighty wings and turned to leave, glancing at Gideon for a moment before he took off into the sky. The mage watched him fly into the ocean of blue and join his mother, Rainael the emerald star.

~

In the heart of Dragons' Reach, Galanör climbed to the top of the highest floating boulder with the grace and speed typical of his kind.

Today, he needed the vantage point to find his prey. From atop the boulder he could see the entire expanse of Dragons' Reach in every direction. It was the most beautiful prison he had ever seen, but a prison all the same. The elf needed to get out of the crater and save Adilandra, and every second he spent in paradise was a second she spent in hell.

The elven warrior was already annoyed with himself for losing the diviner. For two days he had searched the small lake and the cave hidden behind the waterfall. It was only as the sun set the day before that he found the shards crunched into the cave floor. There wasn't much that could withstand the weight of Malliath.

He found himself craving more information after his few words with Faylen, and now he was completely in the dark. Everything outside of Dragons' Reach was a mystery.

From his high vantage, however, Galanör could easily spot what he was looking for. In the distance, and some miles away, the elf's fine eyes could see smoke rising from the top of the trees. The area around the smoke was surrounded by an unusual concentration of dragons, and big ones at that.

That's where they were keeping Malliath.

Every now and then, Galanör caught sight of flames breaching the canopy, until one of the dragons swooped by and put it out with a breath of ice. It was an incredible sight on its own, since little was mentioned in history about dragons' breath beyond fire, but Adriel had confirmed that they actually use both ice and fire. It was just another reason to stay on a dragon's good side.

Galanör took a breath and steadied his heart. Just thinking about what he was going to do next made his chest feel as if it might burst. It was the only way and he knew it, though.

For the second time in his life, Galanör was going to attempt to steal a dragon...

Adilandra blinked hard in an effort to clear the haze from her sight. The queen of the elves was barely aware of the chains that shackled her wrists together, tying her to the ceiling. Her toes wiggled in search of the floor but could only brush the cold surface. Featureless faces continued to appear from the blurry surroundings and examine her body.

All the while, she could hear rhythmic music being played in the background, underscoring the laughter and general din of a party.

"You can get closer..." a familiar voice purred from out of sight. "She won't bite... *hard*."

The wavy features of a stranger's face came into view before her eyes. The man was heavily tattooed with piercings dotted around his face and bald head. The elf wanted to recoil when he licked his lips, but found her muscles sluggish. The last thing she remembered clearly was being in her cell, deep in the heart of the great pyramid. They must have drugged her food this time; they always found a way.

"She is my favourite play-thing..." The Goddess came into view like a snake slithering around its prey.

As the effects of the drugs began to wear off, the elven queen could see the wicked glee that illuminated The Goddess's face. The wicked ruler of the Darkakin took much pleasure in showing off her prisoner.

The Goddess reached out and took a cup of wine from a passing slave. "When my army is finished with wiping out the Illians and the elves, I will march into my ancestors' lands and show you what's left of your kind."

Adilandra could see them all now. The elf was the centre piece of a party. She had been brought to the central throne chamber, where Ederön had been thrown from the balcony. That seemed like a life-time ago now...

Adilandra wasn't even sure how long it had been since she saw Galanör and Gideon. This had become her life now. By night she was the personal play-thing of The Goddess, suitable only for entertain-ment. Most days she was forced to fight in the arena, though that was an easy task since the better fighters had been sent along with the armies to Illian. The Darkakin were ever cautious of her enhanced strength and speed, however, always drugging her to transport her from place to place.

The Goddess stepped aside to greet another of her guests and Adilandra saw the green crystal, mounted on a pedestal. There were three more around her, just as they were in the arena and in The Goddess's chamber.

The elven queen had never seen them before her time in the southern lands of Ayda, but she knew what the crystals were here for. When in their presence, she couldn't use magic to help her fight her opponents or even resist the drugs. It was only in the brief moments she had in the bath house, before she was presented to The Goddess at night, when Adilandra could use some of her innate power. As always, the queen used her spells to see through the eyes of Ölli, her daughter's owl.

She had almost welcomed the drugs on the night it was revealed that Valanis was free. Reyna and Faylen had been speaking with the ranger she now knew to be called Asher, and the Graycoat, Nathaniel. Not only had the dark elf been freed of his prison, but he had been free for forty years. Despair had almost crippled Adilandra that night. The only happiness to be found was in the extraordinary relationship forming between her daughter and the human knight.

"Excellent!" The Goddess exclaimed, after speaking to one of her soldiers. "Overlord Kett sends word of their progress!" The guests and soldiers stopped and listened to their ruler. "They have crossed Drowners Run and made camp on Illian's shores. At dawn they march to Syla's Gate!" Everyone cheered and howled before continuing with their drinking and merriment.

"You will never... breach those gates," Adilandra said through gritted teeth.

The Goddess swivelled on the elf with a face of fury. It slowly turned into a cruel smile, as the sadistic ruler turned to the stranger who had been enjoying the sight of Adilandra.

"She is yours for the night, Lord Xix. I will have a chamber prepared for you both."

The man flashed a broad smile of yellow, sharpened teeth. Adilandra blinked slowly and kept her expression one of stone. She would give The Goddess no pleasure in her reaction.

Lord Xix and The Goddess walked away to enjoy other aspects of the party, leaving Adilandra to her thoughts alone. She did her best to ignore the others that passed by and inspected every inch of her body. They had a particular interest in her ears and often pulled on them.

The lone tear that streaked down her pale face couldn't be helped in the end. She was utterly alone and the world was coming to an end around her. The queen was helpless to make any kind of difference.

Only the dragons could alter the fate of Verda now...

CHAPTER II

LEGENDARY

Alidyr strode through the palace of Karath as if he owned it, paying no heed to the soldiers and their curious looks. None would dare stop him, or the assassin that walked beside him.

Ro Dosarn had arrived that day, as ordered, having brought with him the feared Arakesh. The capital city of The Arid Lands was now under the watchful eye of the most dangerous killers in human history.

Having spent so many centuries living in Nightfall, Alidyr was accustomed to the heat and humidity that was typical of Illian's southern lands. The elf reflected on the fact that the city was only a day's journey west from their secret school for assassins. How many had tried to find it over the millennia and given up Nightfall as myth and legend?

Of course, the city was not what it used to be. Upon his last visit, Karath had been a place of order, with severe punishments for those who stepped out of line. Now, the slaves had risen up and created chaos when Valanis's plans so desperately needed compliance.

It wouldn't be long before the armies of the Darkakin arrived and the city would need to feed and house them while they were supplied with stronger weapons and armour. Though vicious creatures, the Darkakin were impulsive and would be no match for the elven army. Thankfully, measures had been taken a long time ago to correct this imbalance; the elves would be greeted by the largest army to ever walk the earth.

Small fires and columns of smoke could be seen through every window in the palace. The city had turned on itself thanks to the so-called House of Owls. Alidyr smiled to himself, knowing that, even now, his warriors would be combing Karath and seeking the owls out. He would bring order where his brother, Nakir, had failed.

Two golden doors were swung open for them, revealing a long room filled with the heads of the great houses and the personal advisers to the boy-emperor Faros.

Alidyr could feel Nakir's presence before he saw him, standing at the head of the opulent table that occupied the room. Behind the elf was a large square banner, decorated with the symbol of The New Dawn. Nakir had stylised it himself centuries ago, when he first had the idea to take over The Arid Lands from within. A white circle, with rays of light surrounding it, sat against the red material with a white diamond shape in the centre. Everyone in the room had a golden ring with the same emblem engraved into it.

Nakir moved to greet his brother, putting the others at ease. Their elven heritage was known to these few, as was their swift wrath to any who couldn't keep a secret. It probably didn't help that an Arakesh stood beside him with his red blindfold tied around his eyes. The sight of any such assassin would be enough to make the bravest of souls lose control of their bladder, let alone Ro Dosarn, the current Father of Nightfall.

"Allow me to introduce you, brother." Nakir turned with an outstretched hand to the two approaching soldiers.

Alidyr had met the predecessors of those present, decades ago, and knew none of the current roster that formed the upper echelon of The New Dawn.

"This is Supreme Commander Rorsarsh, the leader of Karath's army."

Alidyr looked upon the rotund human and wondered how long it had been since he actually used the sword on his hip. The large man bowed his head in respect and swept his cloak aside for dramatic effect. He was more politician than warrior.

"It is the honour of my life to meet the head of the Hand." Rorsarsh spoke in basic Illian, rather than his native tongue of Kilanti. "This is my second-in-command, Halion Al-Anan." The elf looked upon what was clearly a warrior with a strong jaw and a physique to match. "Like you, my Lord, this is Halion's first time within the sanctuary."

"I was attending these meetings before your father was born." Alidyr walked away with Ro Dosarn trailing him.

Both Rorsarsh and Halion took a step back to give the assassin more room.

"Shall we begin?" Alidyr looked to Nakir, who nodded resentfully.

It was obvious his brother didn't want him here, but the will of Valanis was not to be questioned.

Everyone except the elves and Ro took their seats along the table. Most wore expressions of fear. They were all weak in Alidyr's eyes. Nakir had taken control of the city, and the three others that dotted The Arid Lands, but looking around the table now, Alidyr couldn't imagine how. Perhaps his brother was owed more credit for his work in the desert.

"Praise Valanis, the new dawn is here!" Nakir announced over the room. They repeated his words with less enthusiasm, looking nervously to Alidyr and Ro instead. "The work of your grandfathers and their grandfathers is about to bear fruit. Soon—"

"You have all failed." Alidyr stated flatly, interrupting his brother.

Nakir, whose bald, tattooed head was exposed without his hood, looked to Alidyr with contempt.

"Valanis has sent me *because* of your failure." The idea of a direct order from the herald of the gods drained the colour from most. "Days from now, the Darkakin will arrive at Syla's Gate and be greeted by *chaos*. This city is in ruin under your leadership."

Alidyr paced the table, meeting every one of their eyes. He noted the look of surprise on the young commander's face, clearly hearing the news of the Darkakin for the first time. "You can't even keep your slaves under control. What hope do you have of supplying Valanis's forces and marching on the rest of Illian? Can a group of slave orphans really topple this city?"

"They are many, my Lord!" one of the advisers blurted from the other side of the table. "They have spies in every house and killers on every corner!"

Ro Dosarn, who had remained on the other side of the table, stepped forward and plunged a small blade into the top of the advisor's skull. It had been executed with such speed, that the man's expression remained the same as he fell onto the table with a *thud*. The others around the table recoiled from the body and the running pool of blood that spread across the flat surface.

"They conquer you with fear." Alidyr continued as if nothing had happened. "But, I have brought something worse..." The room followed the elf's gaze to Ro Dosarn. "As we speak, your city is being flooded with Arakesh."

Supreme Commander Rorsarsh sat back in his chair in shock and looked to Nakir, who said nothing.

"Your army is to stand by and ensure the Darkakin have the room to make camp. Have the forges manned day and night and the armour made ready. Once the Darkakin have been supplied, the combined forces will march to Tregaran in the north of the desert. There we will be met by any soldiers stationed at Ameeraska and Calmardra."

Alidyr could see it beautifully in his mind. From the deep south, the Darkakin and the Karathan army would march north, to the edge of The Arid Lands, and bring order to the city of Tregaran, as well as resupplying and adding to their forces. Then, the soldiers from the east and west of the desert would join them before marching into the green pastures of the north.

First, they would sack Galosha, the most southern town in Alborn, before marching east to the coast. There, they would ravage Barrosh and resupply like a hungry plague of locusts. Then, it was only a few hundred miles up The Shining Coast to Velia, the capital of Alborn and home to King Rengar.

The armies of the north, under the command of King Merkaris, would march south and sweep through Grey Stone and Lirian. The armies of Grey Stone and Lirian would join them or die with King Gregorn and Queen Isabella.

Moving east, their combined forces would devastate Palios and Whistle Town before joining the Darkakin and the Karathan army in Velia, sealing Alborn's fate. From Velia, the largest army Illian had ever seen would greet the white sails of the elven army.

All of that, however, hinged on the next few days. If the Darkakin army couldn't get through the gates and be resupplied with new armour, the Karathan army would be hard pressed to beat the forces of Alborn.

"How will we open the gate?" Rorsarsh's deep voice asked, though his eyes glanced nervously at Ro.

"Leave that to us," Nakir replied, looking to Alidyr.

Indeed, it would probably take all of their considerable strength to open Syla's Gate. They had been magically sealed over a thousand years ago, and would demand equal magic to open them again. Alidyr was confident that with the power of Naius, granted to them by Valanis, the gate would bend to their will.

Another hour went by as the heads of Karath's industry gave their reports. Alidyr continued to interrupt his brother and give the supreme commander and the advisers new orders. He would have them earn their place in the new world.

Eventually, the room was dismissed and the elves were left alone with Ro Dosarn, a dark sentinel in the corner.

"Why are you here?" Nakir hissed.

Alidyr signalled to Ro and the assassin left them to it. "I am here because the master wills it."

"I was told that the Darkakin were mine to command. *I* am to lead the march north!" Nakir came to stand by his brother.

"And so you will, brother," Alidyr replied calmly. "But, if the Darkakin are met with resistance before they can march out of The Arid Lands, the other kingdoms will learn of the invasion and rally to Karath's aid. I have been sent to ensure that Karath falls in line. Once we fully control the capital, the other cities in this gods-forsaken land will follow suit."

"Karath is the anvil, *I* am the hammer!" There was no soothing Nakir's pride.

That mattered little to Alidyr who, as the head of the Hand, always had other options.

"*You* are the hammer; *I* am the hand that wields it. Do not forget your place, Nakir." Alidyr fixed his golden eyes upon those of Nakir's until his brother looked away, submitting. "Now," Alidyr checked that the doors were closed, "how serious a threat is this *House of Owls*?"

Nakir took a breath, bringing his temper under control. "Their leader is quickly becoming legend."

"The White Owl..." Alidyr had already heard the name from his assassins.

"He is well trained by all accounts. Some of the city watch have reported that he fights like that of an honour guard."

Alidyr had heard of the prowess of the emperor's royal guards. They were said to rival any warrior in all of Illian, even the famous Graycoats. Of course, they were children in the eyes of an Arakesh.

"These accounts can be trusted?" the elf asked.

"He always leaves one or two alive, to tell of his skills." Nakir looked out across the city vista, as if he might see The White Owl stalking across the rooftops.

"He uses fear as a weapon..." Alidyr was quickly coming to respect this slave.

"He has inspired the slave population," Nakir continued. "Not only in Karath, but in Ameeraska and Tregaran. I fear that times are changing in the south, and at the wrong time no less."

"How so?" Alidyr asked, curious to his brother's insight. The Arid Lands had been akin to a child to Nakir. He had guided them and moulded them over the centuries.

"The slavers continue their work diligently, but the soldiers, the city watch... they are beginning to sympathise with the slaves, looking to the other kingdoms' way of doing things. They continue to follow their orders, but I sense defiance."

"Rorsarsh doesn't appear to have that attitude," Alidyr offered.

"He garners less respect every day. The men look to his second-in-command, Halion. Despite his father's failings in the royal guard, he has risen through the ranks on the merits of his own deeds."

"His father?"

"I forget his name; these humans are all the same to me. He was exiled from The Arid Lands after failing to protect the emperor and his wife from assassination." Nakir had a wicked smile stretching his cheeks.

"Would that be the same assassination *you* orchestrated?" Alidyr remembered some of the details, but had been more interested in the results at the time.

"Indeed. I killed the spineless pair myself. I made it appear as though the House of Owls were responsible."

"I fear you may have only added strength to their spreading cause, brother. Though controlling the boy-emperor is far easier, I will concede." Alidyr made for the door. He had been travelling almost constantly since leaving Valanis in Namdhor, and was in need of sleep.

"Don't worry brother; soon Karath will be under the lash of your whip once more. In the meantime, you should consider getting some rest. Soon we will be expected to open Syla's Gate, a feat far greater than we expect, I'm sure."

Tauren son-of-none crept through the upper walkways of the great forges. Beneath him, hundreds of blacksmiths and armourers worked tirelessly by their anvils and forges to produce swords, helmets, spears and breastplates, each glowing orange under their relentless hammering.

Walking between the smiths were Karathan guards, keeping a close eye on their work. Except for the orange light of the molten steel, the massive warehouse was cast in darkness on the edge of the city.

The White Owl hopped over the railing and climbed down a wooden beam, until he was among the many tables laden with fresh works. Keeping an eye on the guards' patrolling pattern, Tauren swiped a piece of armour off the table and examined it from within his mask. It was a helmet of sorts, though the faceplate was shaped like that of a hawk, with a long sloping mouthpiece that ended in a sharp point. It was well crafted and made from strong metal. How long had the north been supplying them with minerals? Were they planning on replacing all the armour in Karath's army? Tauren could see no reason why they would, especially with the cost of it all!

The White Owl moved silently between the forges, though his footfalls were entirely removed by the constant hammering. The guards crossed each other's path and completely missed Tauren, who had timed his steps perfectly.

On the other side of the warehouse, the son-of-none examined some of the weapons being boxed and loaded onto carts. Spears, swords, axes, bows and even clubs were being prepared. There were already owls waiting outside, ready to follow the carts and discover their destination.

Tauren reached out to handle one of the swords when he detected the slightest of movement out of the corner of his eye. It was as if the shadows themselves came to life, when the dark edges of the forge gave birth to any warrior's nightmare.

Tauren flung his body backwards, in what would have normally been considered lightning reflexes but, on this occasion, the flying knife skimmed against his owl-shaped mask in an explosion of sparks. The helmet alone saved his life as he turned his evasion into a backwards flip. When he came back up, The White Owl was holding a dagger in each hand.

His resolve faltered, dampening his usual rage, when he looked upon the sight of three Arakesh. Tauren had never seen the deadly assassins before, but the red cloth that covered their eyes was enough to identify them. It was also enough to remind him what fear felt like. For the first time in a long time, The White Owl considered running from a fight.

The smiths stopped hammering and stared at the four warriors in terror. The guards came rushing over, weaving between the many forges and anvils, their swords drawn. All three Arakesh acted as one body and threw a jagged knife, each one slaying a guard before they could interfere with their fight.

Chaos erupted as the smiths dropped their tools and half-forged materials and ran for the doors, leaving sparks to shoot into the air when the heated metals found their resting place on the floor.

Tauren didn't wait for an invitation but lunged at the closest assassin. It was immediately apparent that he was fighting a foe with skills superior to any he had fought before. The Arakesh evaded every swipe and slash of his daggers, not bothering to draw the twin-swords on his back.

When the opening didn't present itself, the assassin made one and flung Tauren's arm away, bringing his knee up into The White Owl's stomach. The blow pushed him back into a wooden pillar, where another Arakesh was waiting by his side. The owl-shaped helmet took most of the swift punch, but the force of it was still enough to knock Tauren to the ground.

Get up! Salim's voice resounded in his mind from years past.

From all fours, Tauren silently removed a hand-sized blade from his belt and launched it behind him without looking. His black cape disguised most of the dagger's flight until, at the last moment, it plunged into the assassin's shoulder, driving him back into the pillar. It wasn't enough to slow him down, however, and the blindfolded man pulled the blade free of his flesh without so much as a grimace.

The White Owl had no intention of letting these men live. Tauren quickly grabbed one of the fallen hammers and threw it end-over-end into the assassin's hand. The hammer slammed into the top of the dagger's hilt, where it drove the blade back into the assassin's heart with his own hand wrapped around it. The Arakesh gasped and slid down the pillar and into the murky depths of the afterlife, a place Tauren was hoping to avoid this night.

The two remaining Arakesh didn't appear to be angered by the death of their kin, but both launched as one, their short-swords raised. Tauren had no time to celebrate his defeat over an Arakesh, forced, instead, to use his youthful agility to evade and dodge their attacks.

The White Owl came up running, intending to change the environment in which they fought. He stopped and swivelled on the spot when the glowing forges and anvils surrounded him. Now, the assassins would have to take care or suffer the devastating heat of molten metal.

Worryingly, only one of the Arakesh chased him across the warehouse. The other had slipped back into the shadows.

As the short-sword dived for his head, Tauren tilted to the left and unclipped the hook and rope from his waist. The Arakesh brought his next blade down, cutting a neat line across Tauren's leather armour. The White Owl used the taut rope in his hands to stop the next attack by catching the thrust at the assassin's wrist. A quick punch knocked the Arakesh off balance, allowing Tauren the opportunity to wrap the rope around his wrist, until the four-pronged hook was driven into the assassin's arm. Despite the killer's scream, he managed to keep a tight hold of his short-sword.

That was when the other Arakesh made himself known.

Leaping from behind a forge, the assassin lunged for Tauren, who simply kicked the other sword arm of his captive Arakesh, forcing it to flick up and slow the approaching assassin. In the same seamless movement, Tauren pulled down on the rope and forced the assassin's hand onto the steaming black surface of an anvil. The skin sizzled and burnt as the Arakesh thrashed about. He soon yielded his sword, which fell to the floor, and lashed out at The White Owl with abandon. Tauren was forced to kick him back into the other Arakesh.

They stood their ground before him, one with both swords ready to tear Tauren apart, the other cracking the knuckles of his burnt hand, now more than happy to simply beat Tauren to death if necessary.

The White Owl breathed heavily inside his mask. He had finally found a fight where his rage had no place. They weren't slavers or whip-masters. This opponent would require guile and cunning if Tauren was to fight another day.

Salim Al-Anan had spent years trying to teach him patience in order to master an inner-peace. This calm, but furious, heart was the core of all warriors, Salim had said to him. Without it he was just an animal lashing out in the dark.

With all that in mind, Tauren had already taken steps to ensure his survival this night.

His width, and that of his cape, hid the burning anvil behind him. The Arakesh both lunged as one, closing the gap in the blink of an eye.

Tauren had only to drop to one knee.

The bag containing the Talo spices had finally burnt through atop the anvil, and the explosion of light and sound overwhelmed the Arakesh. They both staggered backwards with expressions of horror and agony.

Keeping his rage in check, The White Owl pushed off the ground with a dagger in each hand. Having already assessed their armour, Tauren thrust the blades into the gaps behind their chest plates and stepped back. Both men dropped to their knees when blood began to fill their lungs. Tauren removed his finest blade, with the hilt of an owl, and dropped once more to one knee and slashed across both of their throats in one swipe.

After they fell to floor, dead, Tauren stumbled to his feet and sheathed the blade across his chest. He looked down at his work in amazement, the realisation slowly hitting home.

He had killed three Arakesh!

They were said to be the greatest fighters in all of Illian. Tauren owed everything to Salim and his training. Without the old warrior's devotion to a lost and savage slave boy, Tauren would have been killed a hundred times over before this night.

Before leaving the forges, he stooped low to pick up the hawk-like helmet. He would show this to Halion as soon as possible. They had much to discuss, especially the reason why the forges had been under the secret guard of the Arakesh.

CHAPTER 12
OUT FOR A STROLL

Asher stood on the corner of the crossroad in the heart of Lirian. One way would lead him north and out of the city, the other would take him back to The Pick-Axe. The ranger had a bag of gold on his belt and a sword on his back; he didn't need much more than that to get by.

He wasn't sure how long he had been standing there, contemplating his next step. A part of his mind tried to convince him that he would be of no use to Reyna and the others, or even worse, he would lead them all to a certain death in the pit. But fighting was all he knew. It was the only life he understood anymore and he wouldn't be finding a new one any time soon. War was unavoidable.

Fighting aside, thinking of them as friends was still foreign to him, but keeping the elves and Nathaniel alive had started to feel more important to him than *getting by*. Ignoring his training and the instinct to survive came down to putting one foot in front of the other until the tavern was in front of him again.

By the time Asher returned to the Axe, the streets of Lirian had been deserted by its daytime inhabitants. Taverns across the town came to life as their regular patrons drank into the night, preparing to stumble home under the canopy of the stars.

The Axe was by far the easiest tavern to find in the whole city, with the general hubbub of noise breaching the walls and spilling into the street. The ranger stopped briefly to pat Hector across the neck and make sure the horses had plenty to eat and drink. Despite his often cowardly nature, Asher had grown fond of the steed.

The ranger made his way downstairs, to the private bar, and found a most captive audience. Even Bale the barbarian was sat around the fire, listening intently, as Reyna told them of recent events, as well as a few ancient ones. Kaleb Jordain, who should have been residing in a drunken stupor by now, was focused on the elf's every word. Glaide turned to look at Asher with wide eyes and an expression of wonder the ranger had never seen on him before.

"I know I call you an old man, but..." Glaide looked Asher up and down as if seeing him for the first time.

"How 'ave ye of all people wound up in this mess?" Doran bellowed, surrounded by empty beer cups.

Salim walked up to Asher and patted him on the arm. "For a man over a thousand years old, you don't look a day over *sixty*!"

The rangers erupted in laughter, as did Nathaniel and Reyna. Asher simply nodded with the merriment and noticed Faylen's serious gaze. Jokes about longevity were clearly not amusing to an immortal.

"I have coin." Asher placed the satchel of bits onto the table. "And I've found a caravan leaving in three days. They were more than happy to have us on the road with them."

"Three days?" Faylen echoed with disbelief.

Hadavad, the mage, rose from the floor. "You really mean to destroy Valanis?"

"We do," Nathaniel replied for them all.

The old mage looked away in contemplation for a moment, stroking the beard around his mouth. "I think I shall retire for the evening. Good night to you all, and thank you for sharing perhaps the most spellbinding of tales, Princess Reyna." Hadavad bowed and Atharia stood up to follow her mentor.

"I shall retire also." Faylen stood up to leave.

The elf tried to get the attention of the princess, but Reyna avoided her gaze, eager to remain with the eclectic bunch of rogues. Faylen simply rolled her eyes and retired to her room, beyond the private bar. Asher wanted to follow her and discover the cause for her true alarm, though he suspected it was the delayed travel time.

After another hour of questions from the adventurous rangers, Nathaniel and Reyna left together. Asher could see that they had some things to work out, as well as a few other things to get out of their system.

Bale and Salim took up a small table and fell into conversation about the prowess of the Arakesh versus that of the Graycoats. Having seen these two forces collide firsthand, however, the ranger was more than happy to join Glaide and Doran by the fire, ale in hand.

"Elves, dragons, assassins, epic battles and an ancient prophecy to boot..." Glaide eyed Asher over his tankard. "You *have* been busy, Outlander."

"Thankfully, I'm yet to cross paths with a dragon," Asher commented.

"*Yet...*" Doran replied before belching. "Seems to me that there's a whole lot goin' on out there that we don' know abou'!" The dwarf downed another ale. "An' how dare ye be older than me ye haggard old shit! I'm supposed to be the old wise one in these parts!"

Asher and Glaide laughed as they had years ago. "I was asleep for most of it. You're still *older*..." The rangers laughed again, Doran included.

The ominous, high-pitched squeal of a pig resounded from the floor above them, along with the shattering of glasses and screams from the maids. The wooden beams above them shook and dust rained down from one end of the room to the other.

"HEAVYBELLY!" Russell shouted down the stairs. Doran was

already laughing. "I told you to keep that hog under control! He's drinking more than you!"

"He's just for a bit o' fun!" Doran shouted back between fits of laughter.

"Get your fat arse up here before I mount his head on my wall!"

Their merriment continued for the rest of the long night, old friends reunited with new stories and plenty of drink.

Reyna collapsed into Nathaniel's bare chest and moved with the rise and fall of his heavy breathing. Everything about his body was different to that of an elf. From the hair on his face and chest to the scars that crisscrossed his skin, Nathaniel was the most exquisite creature she had ever seen.

The princess kissed him and looked into his eyes, feeling a pit opening in her stomach. She didn't want to see those eyes grow old and finally close once and for all. And yet he was fated to.

"What's wrong?" the knight asked. "You gave me the same look yesterday, on the road to Lirian."

"It's nothing." Reyna shook her head and kissed him again.

Nathaniel rolled over and took the elf with him, until they were side-by-side, Reyna encompassed in his thick arms.

"Talk to me," he said.

Reyna hesitated. "I have become fond of you..."

Nathaniel glanced at their entwined bodies with a child-like grin. "Oh, good."

The knight had sensed those weren't the words she had intended and Reyna knew it. "I am afraid to lose you," the elf replied more honestly.

Nathaniel stroked her jaw and turned Reyna's face to see his own. "We will fight by each other's side, always keeping the other safe."

"There is no fighting *time...*" The princess dipped her head into his chest again, avoiding his look of surprise.

"I thought immortals lived in the present, with no fear of the future." Nathaniel stroked the curve of her ear and kissed her cheek softly.

Reyna rolled out of his embrace. "Even if your mortality wasn't certain, I am a princess, an *elven* princess, and you are..."

"Just a man."

Reyna met his eyes once more and knew that she looked upon more than *just a man*. She cupped his stubbled cheek in one delicate hand and kissed him passionately.

"Nathaniel Galfrey will never be just a man."

"And you are so much more than a princess, or even an elf. They do not define you. You can choose who you want to be... who you want to be with. Meeting you has shown me that. I defined myself as a knight, a Graycoat, but before any of that I am simply a man who loves a woman, an elf." Nathaniel smiled and Reyna couldn't help the tear that streaked across her cheek.

Neither of them had talked about their love for the other before. In her heart she knew that she loved this man but, in her head, Reyna knew that the odds were stacked against them. If the forces of Valanis didn't kill them first, her father surely would before he allowed her to marry any human.

"You won't lose me..." Nathaniel whispered into her ear as he pulled her close.

Reyna held him tight, as if time itself couldn't take him from her.

Asher awoke to the sharp sound of someone clearing their throat. He was still in the same chair he had been laughing and drinking in all night, only now Glaide and Doran were gone and Faylen was standing over him with a scornful expression. Despite her incredible beauty, the elf could look mighty fearsome when she wished to.

"Morning..." Asher's throat was hoarse and the word broke in his mouth.

"It's dawn."

"Hence the greeting." Asher looked away, trying to shake off the spinning feeling in his head. He was relatively immune to the effects of alcohol, but Doran's own brew was potent, even to an old Arakesh.

"Dare I ask how much sleep you have acquired?" Faylen presented the ranger with a glass of cold water.

"Enough for a day of gathering supplies." *Don't be sick*, Asher thought over and over.

"That is not what we are doing today." Faylen had the hint of a smile on her face.

Asher gladly took the water and mirrored her expression. "And what are we doing today?" The water was a soothing balm as it ran down his throat.

"Scouting."

Asher cocked an eyebrow. "What are we scouting exactly?"

"The Tower of Gadavance..." Faylen turned away, missing Asher's confused expression.

"And why are we scouting The Tower of Gadavance?" In truth, Asher was enjoying their little exchange.

"Because we're not waiting around here for three days to then embark on a journey that will take the better part of a week, probably even more if we travel with a caravan." The elf donned her cloak and scimitar.

"How will The Tower of Gadavance help matters?" Asher could see he wasn't going to have a choice, and so strapped his quiver and folded bow to his back, as well as his rune short-sword. He held Alidyr's blade for just a moment before strapping it to his back as well.

Faylen smiled knowingly. "It is a school for magic, yes? Then it stands to reason that they will be in possession of crystals. I can use the magic stored within them to open a portal and transport us most of the distance. We just need to... how do you humans say it? *Burgle* them."

Asher couldn't help his mirthless laugh. "I'm a ranger, not a burglar."

"You were an assassin and an Outlander before that, were you not? I'm sure you will adapt." Faylen stepped over the, previously concealed, sleeping form of Doran son of Dorain, and made for the door to the tavern above.

The Tower of Gadavance was easy to find amid the hybrid elven architecture. Lirian's sleek and curving buildings were interrupted here and there with man-made structures and refurbishments, but the tower had been built around five hundred years ago, if Asher's memory served. The crooked tower was three times the height of those around it and constructed entirely of grey stone slabs. A ten-foot wall surrounded it with a simple wooden gate that opened onto a busy street, which curved around the wall. Its pointed top was decorated with a broken weather vane; all in all, it wasn't much to look at.

"They teach magic in there?" Faylen asked sceptically.

"It's no Korkanath, but it tends to take in those who they reject," Asher offered.

A familiar voice spoke to them from behind. "Gadavance was himself a reject of Korkanath." Hadavad, the old mage, and his apprentice, Atharia, were standing on the corner of the street, observing the pair.

Asher looked around to check that no one was paying them extra attention. It wouldn't be long before King Rengar sent someone to find them after word got back that he had accessed his account at Stowhold.

Hadavad continued, "He appealed to Lirian's king at the time and convinced him that the school would bring good fortune to the region. Some believe he used a spell to sway the king..."

"Hadavad." Asher bowed his head. "What are you doing here?"

"What are *you* doing here?" The mage countered with a tilted head. His sparkling blue eyes bored into the ranger's.

"Just out for a stroll," Asher replied with a coy smile.

The mage leaned on his wooden staff, carved into two entwining snakes whose heads met at the top. Between the two heads was a medium sized crystal, perfectly wedged in the mouths of the snakes. He looked to Faylen, who remained mostly hidden within her hood, and then past her to the tower.

Hadavad was not one to easily fool. "Had I any crystals to give I certainly would."

Asher wasn't surprised that the mage had seen straight into the heart of their 'stroll'.

"Your errand is a grave one." Hadavad sighed and glanced at his apprentice. "S we shall help you in this most perilous of tasks."

"You will help us acquire the crystals?" Faylen asked, surprised.

"Of course," Hadavad replied. "And then we will help you defeat Valanis."

The statement took Asher back. Hadavad and Atharia were willingly going to put themselves in the middle of a war. He thought of Reyna and her tenacity, her resolve to vanquish the dark elf and bring peace to Verda. It was hard to meet the princess and not get swept up in her self-appointed mission.

"You know where we're going..." Asher said.

"Indeed. You mean to go into the harshest desert in Illian, cross paths with the slavers of The Arid Lands and sneak into a place that has never been seen before, except by you, of course." Hadavad looked to his apprentice.

"Sounds like fun!" Atharia's reply was exaggerated by her eager grin.

"You and I have a different idea about fun," Asher quipped.

Hadavad laughed to himself. "Atharia has fallen into some trouble seeking *fun!*" The mage beckoned for them to follow him as he made for the tower. "Now, walking through the gates is not a wise choice for entry. Much like Korkanath, only those who have been invited can pass through them, though instead of a dragon there are two stone gargoyles that will flatten you on the other side. Scaling the walls is also out of the question. The stone will ooze a viscous oil, making it impossible to climb."

Asher gave the mage a sideways look. "You know an awful lot about Gadavance's protective spells."

"I should think so," Hadavad harrumphed. "I helped him to design them."

Asher laughed quietly to himself and took the extraordinary information in his stride, unlike Faylen who stopped walking and looked upon Hadavad with new eyes.

"I thought this tower was constructed *five hundred* years ago?" The elf hurried to catch up again.

"Indeed it was my elven friend!" The mage continued to circum-navigate the wall.

"Keep your voice down," Faylen hissed, looking around for any keen-eared humans.

"Fear not, Lady Faylen." Hadavad tapped the side of his staff. "No one can hear us."

Asher examined his staff and looked around them, expecting to see some evidence of the spell Hadavad spoke of. If there was any, the ranger could not detect it, leaving him to feel vulnerable for the first time without his ring. Paldora's gem had always connected him to the magical world and granted him a sixth sense into that strange realm. Now it was gone.

"I thought my skin was tingling." Faylen inspected the back of her hand, apparently impressed with the human mage. "That doesn't explain your earlier statement."

"I suppose it doesn't..." Hadavad continued to walk through the streets, avoiding the many horses and carts, as well as the playing children.

Asher could only smile at Faylen's frustrated expression.

"Now, even if you had a crystal, you would be unable to open a portal inside the grounds. Though humans have never possessed such magic, we have always known of its existence and taken precautions to counter it. Once inside, however, it should be relatively easy to move about undetected. The school has only ever catered for around twenty pupils."

"It doesn't look like we'll be getting inside to find out," Asher said, moving his cloak aside to allow a small boy to run past him.

"I'm getting to that." Hadavad finally stopped on the far side of the tower. "If you wish to enter the grounds without setting off any spells or traps, you'll have to jump off *that* rooftop and land directly inside the wall. Don't touch the wall!"

Asher looked up at the slated rooftop and did a quick calculation. "That's an impossible jump. Even if I made the distance the fall would break both of my legs."

"Life's hard when you can't heal broken bones with a simple thought, eh?" Hadavad nudged the ranger's arm, as if aware of the thoughts passing through his mind.

"An elf could make that jump," Faylen announced.

Hadavad smiled, as if his words had been spoken for him. "Atharia will accompany you."

"That won't be necessary—"

"Hold on," Asher interrupted. "We should put some more planning into this." He didn't doubt Faylen's capability, or even that of Atharia's; he just didn't want them in harm's way, not when he had been trained for so long to accomplish such a mission.

"I'm afraid there isn't much more you can plan beyond the wall," Hadavad explained. "However, I must insist that Atharia accompanies you, Lady Faylen. Her training demands it."

Faylen ran a critical eye over the young woman. "If she must."

"Excellent. Then I suggest you finish acquiring the supplies you require and get some rest. Tonight should provide plenty of *fun!*" Hadavad appeared almost giddy.

CHAPTER 13
STOWHOLD

V alanis stood in the opulent foyer of the central vaults, situated in the heart of Dragorn. The dark elf was surrounded by dead bodies, strewn and contorted into horrific and unnatural shapes. Blood decorated the marble columns and white floor, snaking between the tiles.

The tall double doors before him continued to shake under the rhythmic impacts of the battering ram. Valanis had already plundered the vaults, easily disabling their magical wards and primitive traps. They held nothing but trinkets. The relic he so desperately sought would be easily detectable amid even the most valuable of treasures.

The agonising screams of those he had *questioned* had been hard to miss, however, and their distress had been reported to the city watch. It mattered not. Valanis had sealed the doors with magic. It would be hours before their pitiful ram knocked the doors through.

WHERE IS IT?

The gods hissed in his ear as if they were standing beside him. The pressure almost made him recoil, but Valanis had come to embrace their presence, even if they were displeased.

FIND IT!

Their rage spilled over into his mind and Valanis hurled a ball of burning pure energy into the farthest pillar. The marble exploded and obliterated the surrounding pattern. The column buckled, but remained in place.

If the ruling families of Dragorn *had* come into possession of the relic, there was only one other place they could be hiding it. Like many of the royals in the human kingdoms, the Trigorns would have more vaults inside Stowhold. The central bank was located in the north-east of Illian, off the shores of The Shining Coast. The island was said to be impregnable.

He would put that to the test.

Valanis soaked up more of the magical aura that permeated Dragorn. After a deep breath from within his mask, the dark elf opened another portal and stepped into Stowhold.

Tai'garn, the eldest of the elders, breathed in the sea air and smiled as the sun blanketed him with its rays. He used his powerful sense of balance to remain upright while sailing over the larger waves. The Adean was a far wilder ocean than The Crystal Sea, north of Ayda.

The elf looked to the north, off the starboard bow, and recognised the island from the many maps he had studied over the years; in fact, he had helped to draw many of them. The island was dark and appeared treacherous by its very nature. Even from this distance, his elven eyes could make out the faintest of structures in the haze.

"They call it Stowhold," Ezeric offered. The tall elf had the lean but toned build of a warrior. His blond hair whipped about behind him as he stood with his hands clasped behind his back, oblivious to the rocking of the ship.

"I know. When we lived in Illian it was known as Suraura." In truth, Tai'garn had precious few memories of Illian he could call fond. He had been in his seventies when they abandoned the land, and most of those decades had been marred by bloodshed and war.

Ezeric scrutinised the sails and looked west, to Illian. "We should reach The Shining Coast by nightfall. The town of Darkwell isn't much farther from there."

Tai'garn looked to the upper deck, behind them. He could see Alwyn magically controlling the sails and guiding the ship; they had made excellent time under his sailing skills. Indeed, all of Tai'garn's companions served some advantage to their mission. Ezeric was one of the greatest trackers, Alwyn an outstanding sailor and unparalleled in the art of stealth, Nalmar, who was below deck, was said to have such sensitivity to magical auras, that he could find anyone or thing that used magic for miles.

Tai'garn looked to the port side of the ship, where Hela hung poised over the railing, her hand tight around one of the sheets. She was an elf whose spirit was as fiery as her hair. Hela's skills could be found at the end of a sword, or a bow for that matter. They were all capable warriors and killers, but Varö had assured Tai'garn that Hela was something else. She had studied the art of fighting with two swords, alongside Galanör Reveeri, the only other elf that could better her.

"We know that they landed in the mouth of The Unmar," Ezeric continued. "We can resupply in Darkwell and travel south to find their tracks from there."

"There's no need," Tai'garn replied. "Their last conversation with the king puts them in Vangarth, in the south of The Evermoore." Tai'garn pondered for a moment how it would feel to once again walk in those woods. "We will journey west, into The White Vale and from there south, into The Evermoore itself."

"As you say, Elder." Ezeric bowed in respect.

Despite all of their combined skills, Tai'garn was the oldest and often considered the wisest of all elves, though his most youthful of looks were deceiving. Of course, his magical talents could not be compared to those aboard the ship, either.

Tai'garn was left by Ezeric to muse on the meaning of wise. Was he wise as they all said? The elf simply believed that he looked upon the world and those around him with more detailed and experienced eyes, as his king did.

A flash of light to the north pulled Tai'garn from his reverie. The elf narrowed his sharp eyes and focused on the sporadic flashes of multi-coloured light beyond the walls of Stowhold. It was certainly magic and powerful at that, since it was enough to bring Nalmar to his side from below decks.

"You can feel it?" Tai'garn asked.

"Yes..." Nalmar tied his dark hair into a tight knot at the back of his head, while his emerald eyes gazed upon Stowhold.

"The humans have made great advances in the magical arts since our departure," Tai'garn observed.

Nalmar continued to stare at the island in silence, leading Tai'garn to ponder the meaning behind the magical display. Their reports suggested the island was some kind of reservoir for the treasures of the six kingdoms. There were, no doubt, a lot of magical barriers and protective spells around Stowhold, but that didn't explain what they were seeing, or what Nalmar was feeling.

Tai'garn knew there would be fighting to come. It was simply unavoidable with the humans, whether it came to war or not. The elder looked to the west and sighed heavily at the coming conflict.

The elf took no pleasure in the planned genocide, holding fast to his belief that magic was meant for more than simple destruction. His king would have him burn the world of man to the ground with magic, but the elder's loyalty had always swayed to his queen rather than his king. Lady Adilandra was ever the voice of reason in Tai'garn's mind.

Of course, King Elym could never know of their secret meetings in the dead of night. If Elym ever discovered that it was in fact Tai'garn who had assisted in the queen's departure from Elandril, he would call for his head.

The Echoes of Fate continued to play over and over in his mind.

The elder believed, as Adilandra had, that the queen was the one who perceived the time they would fall. The prophecy was certainly clear on the alliance required of both shores, but Tai'garn found it hard to believe that any trust could be fostered between man and elf.

Time, something Tai'garn had an abundance of, would tell of any alliance.

Valanis had been unable to teleport inside the smooth black walls of the central bank. He silently cursed only having a shard of Paldora's gem. If he had possessed the gem in its entirety there would be no stopping him, but he could feel the edges of a seizure threatening to overcome him if he pushed too hard.

That particular protective spell had only prevented him from entering Stowhold for a moment, however. The main path that led from the shore into the compound was interrupted by a ravine that ran deep into the rocky island. Visitors would typically have to wait until the drawbridge was lowered and the gate lifted. Valanis had waited long enough.

A warning was bellowed from atop the walls, but the dark elf balled his hands and broke the drawbridge's chains from thirty-feet away. The bridge fell into place before him as the guards atop the black walls opened fire. The arrows were easily pushed aside by the field erected around his body. The projectiles were flung in every direction in sparks of blue and red, unable to prevent his advance across the drawbridge.

A wave of his gloved hand super-heated the metal gate until the orange, molten bars rained across the ground and *sizzled*.

Inside, he came under attack once again as multiple hex-traps exploded to life around him. Monsters of every variety, large and small, poured out of the portals, etched into the ground. Valanis raised his open palm before the rushing horde and used a form of ancient magic known only to the gods. The insidious waves of unseen energy washed over the beasts and overcame their senses, repurposing their instincts. The monsters came to a halt inches from his dark robes and took in his scent, examining Valanis from head-to-toe.

"Eat..." Valanis's order was met with eager obedience, and the creatures immediately dispersed.

The sounds of men screaming and monsters feasting could be heard in every direction. Basilisks and Gorgons slithered across every surface at incredible speed, while Sandstalkers speared the guards to the walls with their sharpened legs.

The dark elf strode through most of the grounds before he was stopped again, this time by a group of mages. Bolts of lightning and balls of fire were hurled towards him with abandon. Valanis stopped them with the wave of his hand.

The dark elf considered what spell to kill them with, until he sensed an overbearing presence from atop the wall, to their right. A seven-headed Hydra half slithered, half crawled, down the black wall and thundered into the mages. Each of its maws ensnared one of the wizards and shook them about, until their bodies were in ragged pieces. Valanis waited patiently until the Hydra dashed off to kill more of Stowhold's guards.

The picturesque gardens, which led to the main keep, were shredded by the arrows and spells that had been aimed at the elf.

Valanis used his enhanced speed to move between the trees and hedges as if he were nothing more than a dark blur. At the edge of the garden, he hurtled into a guard with enough speed to drive the man into the black stone, shattering his spine with a satisfying *crunch*. The wild swing of a sword almost caught his head, but Valanis tilted at the last second and back-handed the man, breaking his neck with a single blow.

The monsters weren't far behind, having eaten and mauled all the guards and mages by the entrance. Creatures that crawled, slithered, rolled and flew descended on the gardens and the main keep.

The arrows and spells soon found new targets as Valanis made for the main doors.

The heavy black doors that barred his way were covered in powerful wards designed to keep them shut. It would take hours to undo them all, and Valanis had no intention of being on the island for that long.

The dark elf inspected the door and its framework closely, sensing the other spells cast over it that couldn't be seen by the eye. Indeed the doors would remain closed to him, but that would not stop him entering the building and vaults within.

The herald of the gods extended both of his hands and used destructive magic to eat into the stonework around the doorframe. The ordinary stone cracked and split, a slave to the earthquake that erupted from within the walls. The stone was quickly reduced to crumbling rubble that ran down the doors like a waterfall. Valanis dropped his arms and stood aside before the double doors fell towards him. A cloud of dust was kicked into the air when the heavy metal slammed into the ground, inches from his feet.

Valanis confidently walked into the dimly lit foyer, ready for whatever they threw at him next. Instead of another monster or spell, an old man, by human standards, was standing between him and the next set of doors. Judging by his fine clothes and arrogant posture, Valanis assumed this to be the bank's overseer.

The dark elf extended his magical aura, to feel out any hidden spells, and found the man to be standing on a barely-visible circle of ancient glyphs. It was no doubt some form of shielding magic or the pathetic human wouldn't be standing before him.

"You are not a customer of this establishment. What do you want?" the haughty man asked plainly.

"I have been asked that question by hundreds over the years," Valanis mused, "but no one ever seems to grasp the truth." The dark elf slowly approached the human, a shark circling its prey.

"And what is the truth?"

Valanis stopped inches from the edge of the circle. "*I've* never wanted anything."

The elf extended his hand to the man's throat and pushed through the now-visible barrier. The shield *fizzed* and sparked under his immense pressure, but his dominance was inevitable.

With his gloved hand around the human's throat, he pulled him close. "I am the herald of the gods, nothing more." Valanis flicked his wrist and broke the man's neck as if he were no more than a bird.

Striding through the lavish corridors, the elf couldn't help but enjoy his every step. It felt exhilarating to be free of the pools and able to unleash his power, however diminished it was without the whole gem.

After slaying a few more monsters and disabling a dozen more traps, both magical and mechanical, Valanis threw the last human body aside and finally entered the vaults.

Their method of transporting money and goods was commendable for their meagre knowledge of magic. Giant alcoves, stored high with coins and jewels, lined the caverns beneath the main keep, with the names of different banks and cities written on signs above the entrances. Behind the bars, inside the alcoves, were a series of chests the staff would use to 'transport' the coin from Stowhold to the specific branch. After placing the coin in the chest, it could then be accessed by a similarly enchanted chest located in the individual branches. It was perfect for security reasons, allowing the transport of coin without delay or chance of being robbed in transit.

Valanis, however, had no interest in coin or jewels.

The elf descended deeper into the caverns, relying mostly on his elven eyes to help him navigate the dim surroundings. The sound of water dripping in the distance was soon lost in the snarl of a large monster. A fearsome guard was a good sign as far as Valanis was concerned, and the snarl was quickly followed by ground-shaking footsteps as a form began to take shape in the gloom.

"Who that then?" The deep gravelly voice of a Cave Troll preceded its giant girth.

Valanis looked upon the simple creature and sighed. The Cave Troll was at least seven times his height and width, and carried with it a tree-like club. A thick manacle and heavy chain was fixed to his other wrist and disappeared off into the darkness, behind his mighty form. Most of its body looked to be made from rock with a soft belly and chest, covered in moles and scars. Its small head was testament to its intelligence, though Valanis had always thought it a miracle that their species had mastered language at all.

The herald of the gods raised his arm and dropped it with dramatic effect, bringing down one of the sharp stalactites from the cave ceiling. The spear of rock plunged into the Troll's head and didn't stop until the bulk of its length was buried in the monster's gut. Valanis was already walking past the creature when it fell over, shaking the cave and the coins therein.

Without warning, the elf's left hand spasmed and retracted into itself, creating a ball of solid muscle. The reaction threatened to creep up his arm and claim his entire body, throwing him into a seizure right there and then.

Valanis dropped to his knee, feeling his energy waning and the power of Paldora's gem leaving him. With his right hand, the dark elf tore off his mask and threw back his hood, illuminating the cave with his golden pallor.

It has been tainted...

Paldora's seductive voice was sweet in his ear, but her words left him with a bitter taste in his mouth. The goddess of the stars felt so close he could actually feel her breath on his ear.

"Paldora... give me strength," Valanis cried.

I gave you a gift from my heavens. It is not my fault you allowed it to slip through your grasp, Herald. The gem now belongs to another...

Valanis snapped his head to attention, his eyes wide. "The ranger."

A thousand years entwined with a boy, leaving you naught but a shell. It no longer favours you, it seems. Perhaps we should have entrusted another with your task.

Valanis clamped his jaw shut and fought through the pain emanating from his left arm. He couldn't help the groans and grunts that escaped his lips.

"I live only to see you returned to these lands..." The tears in his eyes glistened in the light of his skin.

Then serve. Use the magic of Naius and find it. Find The Veil...

With that, he felt Paldora's ethereal presence disappear as if she were no more than fog in the breeze.

Valanis called on the shard, set into the ring, and used it to funnel the power of Naius, preventing the limitless well of magic from consuming him. It was another minute before he could stand again and retrieve his mask and conceal his supernatural appearance.

With no more time to lose, the herald of the gods continued through the cave tunnels until he found the hidden vaults, deep beneath Stowhold. The circular door to the vaults was made of pure silvyr. The rare metal must have been sourced from the dwarves centuries ago and specially crafted by the legendary blacksmiths for a handsome fee.

Valanis placed the flat of his hand on the door and knew it to be thicker than his chest. This door could keep an army of mountain giants out.

He hadn't come this far to be stopped by something as simple as a door.

Valanis pressed his hand into the cool metal and exerted his indomitable will upon it. The effect was something close to the eruption of a volcano, causing the silvyr to glow, turning from red to orange, spreading in waves out from his hand. The door inevitably melted around his hand and Valanis walked through the gap, unharmed.

He entered the personal vaults of the six kingdoms of man. Valanis could feel the gods' anticipation rising at the thought of retrieving the oldest of all relics.

The Veil would be his...

CHAPTER 14

THIEVES IN THE NIGHT

It took Galanör most of the day to traverse the oasis within Dragons' Reach, but the lush canopy and long branches offered much needed shelter from the relentless sun. The elf was starting to wonder if he would ever grow accustomed to the endless heat, as Adriel had.

With the older elf in mind, Galanör looked around to ensure he wasn't being followed. Every so often a shadow would sweep across the grass when a dragon flew overhead. Their eyes were that of a hunter's and the best in the land, forcing Galanör to seek cover whenever his keen ears heard the beating of wings.

He hadn't been told that he couldn't walk through this part of the land, but he knew Adriel wouldn't want him near Malliath. There was a good chance that anything on two legs would upset the great dragon after being held against his will by humans for a thousand years.

That thought only led Galanör to feel better about what he was going to do. After they had rescued or discovered the fate of Adilandra, the elf could watch Malliath the voiceless fly away, truly free for the first time since The Dragon War. Of course, all of that was dependent on Malliath agreeing to take him to Malaysai and the two of them leaving Dragons' Reach without being stopped.

That task didn't seem so impossible when Galanör found the clearing in which Malliath resided. Seeing him so close to other dragons only served to show off his incredible size, with Malliath's bulk dwarfing many around him. His black scales sparkled under the direct sunlight while he lay in the middle of the giant clearing.

The open space was littered with fallen trees and stumps, with tough roots protruding from the ground. It seemed it had become a daily battle for the other dragons to contain Malliath's destructive rage. That was exactly what Galanör wanted to unleash on the Darkakin.

Three large dragons glided overhead in slow circles, there to ensure Malliath was intercepted if he took off. Between Galanör and Malliath were four more dragons, three of which were just larger than Ilargo, while the one farthest away appeared to be around the same size as Galandavax. Again, the thought made Galanör look around for any sign of the brown dragon and his rider. That was when he heard it, the soft crunch of moss under-foot, somewhere behind him.

Galanör dashed behind a tall bush and then slipped behind a tree, keeping one eye on the dragons. The elf waited a moment, listening. A small bush rustled on the other side of his tree before a twig snapped. It was then that Galanör realised it couldn't be Adriel; the elf would have been far stealthier in his approach. That only left one other.

"What are *you* doing here?" Galanör hissed at a startled Gideon.

"What are *you* doing here?" The mage looked at the elf with accusing eyes.

"You followed me?" Galanör grabbed the mage by the arm and pulled him farther into the forest, away from the sensitive hearing of dragons.

"You can't mean to do what I think, surely?" Gideon pulled his arm free and turned on the elf. "Didn't you learn anything at Korkanath?"

Indeed, Galanör remembered the events well and would never forget them. Aside from the fact that he freed the angriest dragon who ever lived and failed to communicate with Malliath, many innocent lives had been taken that day. Galanör now walked a different path, his duty replaced with a sense of honour he was still trying to understand.

"I remember..." Galanör replied, also aware that Gideon's closest friend, Abigail Rose had died that same day. Though he hadn't wielded the magic that killed the girl, the elf still felt responsible.

"You won't get two words out before Malliath reduces you to cinders, and that's *if* you get to him." Gideon looked up as if he could see the dragons above the canopy.

"I have to try, Gideon!" Galanör clamped his jaw shut and searched the area for any dragons that may have heard his hushed outburst. "I have to try..." he repeated in softer tones. "Adilandra isn't just the queen, she's the only one who could convince the dragons, and maybe even Adriel, that action is needed. When King Elym attacks Illian, Adilandra will be the only one who can rightfully stand against him. Imagine her influence if she had dragons standing beside her. Just their presence alone could avert war."

"We can't force them to get involved in our wars," Gideon replied.

"There wouldn't be a war if they acted." Galanör could feel his temper rising.

"The Darkakin are marching into Illian as we speak, your people will set sail for The Shining Coast soon and the alliance between the six kingdoms has ever been on a knife's edge; there *will* be a war, Galanör. You and I both know it will be the biggest war Verda has ever seen, one that even the dragons cannot prevent." Gideon stood defiant before the elf.

Galanör was taken aback by mage's wisdom. For a human, and a young one at that, Gideon was looking at the world with the eyes of an old elf. It was the type of wisdom Galanör should have been using with four centuries on the mage.

The elf dropped his head in defeat and sat on a nearby rock, flicking his cloak over the top as he did. He was starting to sound like Adilandra. Her hope had apparently rubbed off on him, or perhaps he had taken it on himself as the price for leaving her behind. Galanör knew not, but he did know that there was no way Adilandra would be left to rot in Malaysai.

"Regardless of what happens after, I am going to rescue her." Galanör stood up again, his resolve returning. "And I need Malliath to do it." The elf swept his cloak about him and walked away to continue observing the dragons.

Gideon walked off into the forest with conflicting thoughts. He agreed that rescuing Adilandra was of the utmost importance, but using a mentally unstable dragon to do it was beyond risky. Malliath was as likely to kill Galanör and Adilandra before flying away again, and who knew what would be left of Malaysai when he was done.

Of course, there was Adriel to consider. The ancient elf certainly wasn't the dragons' keeper, but he was Dragorn, and that title alone offered him more respect than he had been given by Galanör.

Frustrated, Gideon took no care of his path and continued into the oasis. Should he tell Adriel of Galanör's plan? His thoughts were tumultuous as he considered the danger the elf was walking into. If he didn't act there was a very good chance he wouldn't survive to see the next dawn, not to mention the danger he would be in should Malliath actually take him to Malaysai.

Should he then help Galanör? Could they pull off such a dangerous plan if they instead worked together? All the while, Adilandra's life was in the balance, if she was indeed alive.

Without intending to, Gideon had walked all day, lost to his thoughts. Looking around, he recognised the area he had wandered into as the small clearing where Mournblade rested. Any tempestuous thoughts were forgotten as he gazed at the exquisite blade. How of all places had he ended up here? Dragons' Reach was massive in size and yet he had found himself standing before the sword once more.

Excitement and anticipation suddenly filled his mind, the feelings coming from nowhere, and it took the mage a moment to realise they weren't his emotions. Gideon turned around to see a familiar green dragon staring at him. Ilargo was certainly getting better at sneaking.

The dragon's feelings began to build and Gideon could feel them threatening to overwhelm his senses. The mage stumbled backwards as the world grew eerily silent and a buzz filled his ears. He could feel his heart pounding in his chest, as if desperate to part from his body.

Take the sword...

Those three words put Gideon on his knees and brought tears to his eyes. Ilargo's excitement reached a crescendo, completely overwhelming Gideon, until the edges of his vision blurred and became dark. It was too much for the young mage, who quickly passed out under the shadow of Mournblade.

Gideon...

That same voice filled his mind, calling him from the ether of his deep sleep. This time the voice wasn't so deafening, but instead had the lighter tone of a teenage boy.

Gideon...

"Gideon?" A new, deeper voice brought Gideon from his slumber.

The mage felt the cool grass under his face as the world returned. Adriel was crouching by his head with a concerned expression marring his elegant features. Ilargo was lurching over both of them with his long green neck craning to see past the elf. The mage was finally able to stand with some help from Adriel.

"What happened?" Gideon asked, looking for the sun in the sky to discern the passing of time.

"Ilargo takes the blame," Adriel replied with a smile. "He explained his error in sharing too much emotion with you. I think he was interested to see how much a human could handle." Adriel cocked an eyebrow at the young dragon.

Gideon looked into Ilargo's blue eyes and lost himself for a minute. He instinctively knew that the dragon didn't want Gideon to divulge the extent of *what* they had shared. Now that Gideon thought about it, he wasn't exactly sure what they had shared. Had he heard actual words from the dragon? It was an impossible thought since he wasn't an elf or a Dragorn.

"Let's get you something to eat." Adriel guided the confused mage away from Mournblade.

The sun had set by the time Gideon's thoughts returned to Galanör and his secret schemes. The mage had instead spent most of the afternoon going over the events surrounding Ilargo. Though he was desperate to get to the bottom of the mystery, Gideon began to fear for Galanör's life again.

On the other side of the small lake, that fed from the central waterfall, Adriel sat against the heaving side of Galandavax, sleeping under the starlight. Ilargo lay close by, casually watching Gideon, but the dragon had yet to share any more emotions.

Gideon slowly stood up and replaced his shortened staff in its sheath, across his back. Adriel remained sleeping and Galandavax never stirred, as the mage crept into the woods beyond the shore. Ilargo watched him disappear but made no attempt to follow him.

When Gideon thought he was far enough away from listening ears, he bolted through the trees. It would take most of the night to reach the clearing where Malliath was being guarded, but he would be damned if he let the foolish elf get himself killed.

At least not without him.

Faylen practically floated up to the rooftop, beside Gadavance's Tower, as she gracefully scaled the building. Much to her surprise, Atharia Danell was only a second behind her, with her elegant staff strapped to her back and brown hair braided down her spine. Indeed, it seemed the apprentice was as mysterious as the master.

Looking over the lip of the tiled roof, Faylen could see Asher, Reyna and Nathaniel in the darkened alleyway across the street. The princess had wanted to accompany her, but Faylen tried wherever possible to keep her out of harm's way. She had failed at that continuously since they arrived in Illian. Hopefully, by retrieving some crystals from the tower, the companions could bypass The Moonlit Plains and avoid the threat of Centaurs and bandits. Of course, the threat of a few Centaurs and slavers in The Arid Lands were nothing compared to their final destination.

The elf blinked slowly and pushed the distractions from her mind. Right now, she had to concentrate on making the jump and surviving the fall. Faylen had boasted that an elf could make such a feat but, in truth, it was a long way down. She looked at Atharia and wondered how the fragile human would ever survive the next few minutes.

"Are you ready?" Atharia asked, limbering up.

Faylen raised an eyebrow. "Are *you*?"

Atharia contorted her body into all kinds of shapes while stretching her muscles. "There's a chance that the tower's wards have been upgraded since my master installed them."

Faylen still found the whole thing unbelievable. "And just how is it that your master was around five centuries ago?"

Atharia stood straight and met Faylen's questioning gaze. "I thought elves knew everything."

"So did I..." Faylen had indeed been humbled since their arrival in Illian. Valanis's entire plan had blindsided her, as it had the rest of her kin in Ayda.

Before any further exchange, Atharia whipped her staff about and began to chant in the ancient language under her breath. Faylen felt the hum of magic against her skin, before the wind picked up with supernatural force. Fallen leaves were spun into miniature tornados about them, until Atharia was lifted from the tiles and carried through the air atop the currents. Faylen watched, impressed, as the young human landed softly onto a patch of grass on the other side of Gadavance's wall.

The elf thought about using similar magic to transport herself, but the superior grin on Atharia's face needed wiping away. Elven magic would always impress the humans, but their natural strength and speed would better shock them.

She exhaled a sharp breath and ran for the edge of the roof. Her jump was true and she easily cleared the wall, but the drop was considerable. Faylen braced her legs, ready to drop into the landing and absorb the blow. By the time she stood up, Atharia's smug expression had disappeared, replaced with respect.

Faylen ignored the pain in her knees and adjusted her clothes, having left her hooded robe behind and strapped her scimitar to her back, instead of her hip. The grounds within the wall were simple aesthetically, with a couple of sheds and what looked to be an archery range, though the elf suspected the students weren't learning to fire arrows at the straw dummies.

As Hadavad had warned, there were two stone gargoyles, wielding a mace each, either side of the main gate. Neither statue moved in their presence, proving the mage right in his suggestion to jump the wall.

As they approached the doors, at the base of the crooked tower, Atharia yelped in pain behind Faylen. The elf turned about to the see slender roots wrapping around the apprentice's legs and arms. Before she could act, another root snaked through the grass and claimed Atharia's staff. The root dropped the staff and retreated back into the large oak tree in the corner of the grounds.

Faylen reached for the scimitar on her back when a thick root coiled around her own ankle and dragged her to the ground. The elf could only watch as more roots ensnared Atharia and drew them both slowly towards the oak tree.

Gideon dropped to his knees, exhausted, by the edge of the clearing. He unbuttoned his leather jacket, which appeared brown instead of its usual dark red under the moonless night.

After catching his breath, the mage surveyed the line of trees to his right and left, searching for Galanör. When there appeared to be no sign of the elf, Gideon focused his eyes on the clearing of tree stumps and fallen logs, spread out before him.

The patrolling dragons had been replaced by larger wyrms, though Malliath's sleeping black silhouette was still easy to spot in the centre of the clearing. After several minutes of scanning the ground for Galanör, Gideon pulled Abigail's wand from its holster on his thigh and touched his temple with the tip. The spell changed the structure of his eyes, causing a moment of irritation, and allowed the mage to see vibrant colours in the dark.

"Oh no..." Gideon spotted Galanör lying flat on his stomach behind a fallen log. The elf was creeping towards Malliath's sleeping bulk, but he was only a few feet away from an enormous golden dragon.

There was no way Gideon could reach Galanör before the elf found his way to Malliath. The mage was more than aware that, as a human, he didn't possess the natural skills to be as covert as Galanör; the dragons would hear him blundering through the clearing within moments. A spell of invisibility wouldn't hide his noise, and if he coupled it with another spell to conceal the sound, Gideon would be drained by the magic in minutes and left a spluttering mess at the mercy of Malliath.

Every second he delayed, Galanör reached ever closer to the black dragon. The mage crouched next to a tree and riffled through his enchanted satchel. His entire arm sank into the bag until his shoulder disappeared within its bottomless depths.

"Where are you?" Gideon knew there was only one way he could reach Galanör.

In his early years at Korkanath, the young mage had mastered the art of getting into trouble. Eventually, Gideon came up with the idea of having an escape plan to ensure he was never caught where he shouldn't be. His hands finally wrapped around the small sphere and he silently thanked the gods for his fortune.

Gideon dashed off into the forest and planted the small sphere between two large roots. Using Abigail's wand again, the mage ignited it, allowing the flames to burn through the wrapping that encased the flammable ingredients within.

He didn't have long. Gideon sprinted back through the woods until he was by the edge of the clearing again. Galanör hadn't moved from behind the fallen log yet, though Gideon could see why; the golden dragon rested one of its mighty legs atop the log as it surveyed the land.

The silence was instantly cut when the small explosion erupted in the forest behind Gideon. The sparks could be seen through the branches and the sound of wood snapping seemed to echo for miles.

As planned, the golden dragon and two of the others took flight and headed straight for the source of the explosion. Gideon remained hidden until they flew past him. There was still another dragon on the far side of the clearing, remaining behind to watch Malliath, whose purple eyes were now open. The black dragon stirred, but made no attempt to fly away or start a fight.

Gideon remained low and scrambled over the fallen logs and scattered stumps. It was fortunate that he tripped and fell behind a log, just as Malliath turned his horned head to investigate the ruckus. The mage remained flat and did his best to imitate a dead person. Galanör was only a few feet away, behind another log, closer to Malliath.

A sharp snort told Gideon that the dragon had turned away, and he dared to steal a glance over the fallen tree. He was now hidden from the other dragon by Malliath's bulk, but that offered little comfort to Gideon.

Slipping over the broken log, Gideon clambered across the dead tree to see Galanör rising into a crouch, ready to walk up to Malliath.

"What are you doing here?" Galanör mouthed silently, alarm spreading across his face.

"Stopping you from getting yourself killed," Gideon mouthed back, but he wasn't sure how much the elf could read.

"Go back to the—" Galanör's mouth fell open and he slowly looked up, over Gideon's head.

The mage could feel a dragon's breath on the back of his neck.

Faylen twisted her body, as she was dragged across the tower's grounds, and pulled free her scimitar. The blade cut through the monstrous root in a single, clean swipe.

The elf turned her momentum into a forward roll and ran for Atharia, who was being yanked up into the tree. The apprentice's mouth had been covered by a root and her staff was being absorbed into the trunk.

Of all the spells, fire would deliver the most damage to the tree, but it would also attract the attention of every person in Lirian. Instead, Faylen pushed her hand out and expelled a torrent of ice and bitter frost. The spell froze the staff in place, stopping it from being completely absorbed and becoming a part of the tree. Atharia, on the other hand, was starting to lose the ability to even struggle, as her limbs continued to be strapped to her body. Faylen was reluctant to use the ice spell over Atharia, in case it permanently damaged her skin.

Using her extraordinary sense of balance, Faylen skipped and jumped up the tree, until she could cut the roots attached to Atharia. The apprentice fell back to the ground, still tangled in roots and branches, but unharmed. The elf dropped lightly to the ground and continued to slice the attacking roots, while Atharia wriggled and shrugged off the dead branches.

"Get back!" Faylen pulled the apprentice to a safe distance and the roots slithered back into the tree, defeated. With an extended hand, Faylen commanded the staff to break free of its bonds and fly into her grasp.

"Thank you..." Atharia took her staff back through laboured breaths.

"Let us be done with this place." Faylen replaced her scimitar on her back and made for the tower doors.

Surprisingly, and to Faylen's relief, the doors held no wards or protective spells. Those set around the grounds were obviously considered enough to repel intruders.

The interior was dim, illuminated by torches on the walls and the occasional candle. Portraits lined the walls between the torches, each of a previous teacher, now long dead.

Atharia opened the door at the end of the foyer and gasped at the size of the room that greeted them. It was a library of sorts, at least twenty floors in height, but its width was impossible; the crooked tower simply wasn't as wide as the space before them.

"A pocket-dimension..." Faylen whispered. "I didn't think humans had mastered this kind of magic."

"Only on simple items such as bags or chests." Atharia looked on, amazed. "Hadavad has spoken of this before, but I've never seen it on such a scale. Do elves use this form of magic?"

"Yes. It allows for more space without having to take over too much forest." Faylen found herself instinctively reaching for her scimitar. Something didn't feel right about the tower. "Dark magic fuels this place..." Judging by Atharia's expression, Faylen could see that the apprentice wasn't surprised. "You know of what I speak?"

Atharia looked the elf in the eyes. "Yes. Well, we suspected."

"And you kept this to yourself?" Faylen hissed, retrieving her sword completely.

"There are still crystals here you can take, but Hadavad wishes to cleanse Lirian, as well as testing me in the process. I have to be ready..." Atharia gripped her staff in both hands.

"Ready for *what*? What is he testing you for?" There was too much mystery behind the old mage and it was starting to aggravate the elf.

Frantic whispers began to fill the spiral-shaped chamber. The voices started at the top of the library and quickly descended until it sounded as if they were surrounded.

Atharia dashed around the tables and picked up a discarded empty cup, which she proceeded to fill with water from a small skin on her belt. Faylen walked over to observe the apprentice drop a fine piece of iron filament into the water. It was a crude detection spell, but effective in small spaces. Atharia walked around the tables, following the flickers of the iron filament as it turned in different directions at the bottom of the cup.

"Through there." Atharia pointed at the door situated in the far corner. "You'll find crystals through there."

"What are *you* doing?" Faylen asked, concerned with the ominous whispering.

"I'm going to fight."

The elf looked around. "Fight who exactly? What evil controls this tower?"

"*The Black Hand*," Atharia said with disgust. "They are a group of mages who practice the ancient dark arts and necromancy. They were formed centuries ago, before Hadavad's time even. Korkanath has tried to root them out, but to no avail. Hadavad made it a personal mission of his, a long time ago, to destroy their foul order once and for all."

Faylen looked at the door leading to the crystals and back to Atharia again. "That doesn't seem like something an *apprentice* can handle on her own."

"And yet I must," Atharia replied defiantly.

Shadowed figures darted around the balconies and walkways above. They were incredibly outnumbered.

"Foolish girl!" Faylen abandoned the crystals and braced herself for the fight. "This *cause* is not worthy of your death. One day you will find a battle worth fighting, a cause worth dying for, but this is not it!"

The shadows gave birth to cloaked men and women wielding staffs and wands, while some even held daggers in their free hand. Atharia reacted with speed akin to an elf, once again impressing Faylen, as she flipped onto a table and dropped into a crouch. Her staff shot out and swept across the air horizontally, expelling a stream of fire that engulfed three of the dark mages. One of the hooded figures was able to raise a shield at the last moment, but the other two dropped to the floor, writhing in burning agony. The apprentice flicked the end of her staff out and caught the surviving mage across the jaw.

Faylen was forced to roll out of the way of two fire spells and an explosion of lightning that instead tore a table and chair apart. Amid the shower of splinters and flames, she jumped up and hurled a ball of fire into the nearest dark mage, before launching an armour-piercing icicle at the other. Both mages were dead before they hit the floor.

The elf brought her blade up in a flurry of attacks that removed limbs, while she remained ever on the move, evading incoming spells. A quick glance showed more figures emerging from rooms on the upper levels.

"There's too many!" Faylen shouted over the din.

Atharia broke bones with her staff and fired destructive spells in every direction. Books were blown off shelves in shreds of parchment and others simply caught fire, spreading to other shelves above.

"Get the crystals!" the apprentice screamed, whipping her staff into the neck of a charging female mage. "Go!"

Faylen was torn and she hated it. Never would she have considered the life of a human when measured against their mission, or

Reyna. Her time with their kind was changing her in ways she wasn't sure she liked. Still, without those crystals they would be forced to travel a dangerous road and be delayed in reaching Nightfall.

The elf growled, "Stay alive!" She dashed for the door, cutting down four more mages as she did. The last of the hooded figures was used as a battering ram to open the desired door.

Following her magical senses, Faylen moved quickly and quietly through the maze of corridors until her skin hummed in the presence of the crystals. Beyond a set of ornate doors, she found her prize, and then some. Dozens of crystals lined the walls of the windowless room, each one shining as if they contained a star.

Her gaze was entirely stolen, however, by the larger crystal in the centre of the room, fixed atop a small podium. It was just smaller than an average fist, but the power contained within was more telling of its purpose. This was the source of the magic that allowed for the pocket-dimension to exist.

After a few seconds of marvelling at the crystal, Faylen had an idea she thought Asher would be proud of. With Atharia's life in the balance, Faylen quickly scooped up a handful of crystals and stored them away on her belt, then moved to place one hand over the larger crystal. The elf drew on her power and unleashed a barrage of lightning upon the gem, focusing on one point. The light contained inside began to flicker as the shell cracked. That was all she needed to destabilise it.

A minute later, she was diving back into the library with her scimitar flashing. She loosed a couple of explosive spells to keep the dark mages at bay, before landing at Atharia's side, who had collected a multitude of cuts, bruises and burns.

"We need to leave, *now!*" They fought in tangent, evading each other's attacks while cutting the horde of mages down. "The tower is going to collapse on itself!"

Atharia stopped fighting for a fraction and stared at Faylen in disbelief. One look at the elf's expression told the apprentice how serious she was.

"Run!" Atharia used a spell to turn over a table and fling it at the oncoming mages.

Both human and elf turned about and sprinted to the door as the tower began to shake. Books from the upper levels fell free of their shelves and rained down with deadly effect. The stone walls cracked and entire slabs came free, shattering at their feet and expelling plumes of dust into the air.

"Run!" Faylen shouted over the destruction. She wanted to unleash her speed and run as fast as her elven legs would allow, but she wouldn't leave Atharia behind.

By the time they ran into the grounds, The Tower of Gadavance was falling apart. The weather vane plunged into the soft grass where it remained standing, impaled. A great cloud of dust followed them out of the doors, along with the screams of dying mages. The ground beneath their feet cracked and erupted around them while they made for the gate.

Atharia pushed her staff out and hit the gate with a concussive blow that forced them out wide, bending and snapping their hinges. The two gargoyles came to life and dropped to the floor, but they were too late. Faylen and Atharia dived through the entrance and into the street, just as the tower collapsed on itself, bringing the perimeter wall down with it and destroying the gargoyles.

The plume of dust and rubble swept through the streets in every direction. Faylen coughed and stumbled to her feet when strong arms gripped her waist and elbow. Through the haze she could make out Asher's grizzly features as he pulled her to her feet.

"Back to the Axe." The ranger directed his instruction to Reyna and Nathaniel, who were helping Atharia to her feet.

Hadavad stood in the middle of the street, watching The Tower of Gadavance crumble with a satiated smile pushing his wrinkles together.

Malliath's vibrant, purple eyes bored into Gideon as he fell backwards, beside Galanör. A low rumble echoed inside the dragon's throat and he slowly moved his wings, shifting his entire body to face them. It was impossible to decipher Malliath's expression, as he always appeared fierce with his spiralling horns and razor-sharp teeth.

Gideon wanted to look around for the other dragons, but didn't dare make any sudden movements. For a moment he wondered if he should even be looking the dragon in the eyes, aware that there were some creatures who took it as an insult or a challenge.

Galanör slowly stood up before genuflecting with his head bowed in respect. Whether Malliath interpreted it as respect was another matter. Gideon felt the dragon's eyes shift to him, so he copied Galanör's actions and bowed slowly.

"The queen of the elves is being held prisoner in Malaysai, the city where the younglings were being forced to fight." Galanör clearly didn't know where to start or how much time they would have. "If you could fly me out of here, we could go there together and free her as well as destroying—"

Galanör's next word was lost in Malliath's roar. Both human and elf were instantly covered in hot dragon saliva and driven backwards by the sheer force of his roar. Everything happened at once after that.

Gideon felt a strong elven arm push him several feet to his right, before Galanör himself dived to the left, over the log. Malliath exhaled a jet of fire that scorched the ground where they had been standing and cut a line through the field.

Gideon rolled to his feet, only to dive back to the ground again when Malliath's powerful tail whipped over his head. The ground shook and kicked up Gideon's weight in dirt when the spike-covered tail hammered down. At least he got the tail end, he thought; Galanör had the fire-breathing end to deal with.

More fire lit up the dark night as Malliath followed Galanör on foot, across the clearing. The elf was forced to leap, roll and dive in every direction to avoid being burned alive. There was no magic or weapon that could get him out of this one. But, perhaps Malliath's attention could be split?

With his staff in hand, Gideon fired a destructive spell at the ground, beside Malliath's head. The explosive force aggravated the dragon and made him turnabout in search of the cause.

"Oh..."

Malliath's purple eyes flared, narrowing on Gideon. His tail whipped around and the dragon charged for the mage, who was frozen in place, wondering what shielding spell could stand up to a charging dragon.

"Run!" Galanör shouted from the distance. His cloak was smoking with small flames licking the bottom of the material.

Malliath's mighty feet thundered across the clearing and Gideon could see the other dragons were too far away to do anything. That was his fault! The mage raised his staff, ready to plant it into the ground and raise a globe of shielding around him - the only option left to him.

As Malliath's open maw descended on Gideon, a green blur exploded from the left and intercepted the black dragon. Gideon was forced to jump aside in an attempt to avoid the combined bulk of both wyrms, tumbling and rolling across the ground. Their roars filled his ears, though one was definitely quieter than the other...

"Ilargo!" Gideon saw the green dragon snapping at Malliath's neck and clawing desperately at his thick scales.

Even though Ilargo was less than half the size of Malliath, his charge had been enough to knock the mighty dragon aside, saving the mage's life.

Malliath roared in defiance and smashed his considerable head into Ilargo's, knocking the smaller dragon to the ground. Malliath dipped his head and bit Ilargo's back leg with enough force to break the scales and draw blood.

"NO!" Gideon cried. He could feel the dragon's pain as if it were his own; even his leg began to hurt and the mage felt warm blood trickling down to his ankle.

Without a sound, Malliath was set upon by three massive dragons. Gideon recognised Emenar the golden one and Beldroga the
great hunter, but the largest by far was Vorgraf the mountain child.
Vorgraf was the only living offspring of the legendary Garganafan,
the old king of the dragons, who gave his life to trap Valanis within
the Amber Spell. Vorgraf matched Malliath in size but there were
none who could match the black dragon's rage and ferocity.

Thankfully, their assault was enough to give Ilargo time to limp
away from the brawl. The green dragon came to a stop by Gideon's
side and the mage felt a wave of relief flow out from Ilargo. The
dragon was happy that Gideon survived, but his nostrils flared when
the fresh blood began to fill the mage's boot.

"Are you hurt?" Galanör appeared on the other side of the
dragon, covered in ash and sweat.

Any answer from the mage was drowned out by the roars of all
four dragons. Vorgraf had gripped Malliath's head between his front
claws and moved him about viciously in an attempt to bite his neck.
Beldroga the great hunter had practically mounted the black dragon,
to pin his wings in place, while Emenar the golden one wrapped
their tails together and pinned them both to the ground.

The sound of giant wings battered the air before Galandavax and
Rainael dropped out of the sky. Adriel deftly slipped off the side of
the brown dragon and made for Gideon and Galanör.

Rainael the emerald star strode over to Malliath's struggling
mass and simply stared at him. The look was intense, but Gideon
could feel a great sense of calm emanating from the queen of the
dragons. After a few moments of continued struggling, Malliath
relented under their combined efforts and dropped to his belly.

"Adriel..." Gideon began before the ancient elf held up a hand.

"I already know what has transpired." Adriel glanced at the
massive dragons behind him. "You are not to come here again."
There was a hint of irritation in the usually calm elf.

"Adriel—" Galanör was cut off.

"Do you understand?"

Gideon had never seen Adriel wear such a grave expression. Both of them nodded solemnly and turned for the woods, their heads sunk with guilt. Gideon had a last look back at Ilargo and tried to hide his own limp as they left the clearing.

"That went well," Gideon jested, still in shock. "Considering..."

CHAPTER 15
THE JOURNEY TO WAR

T auren ignored the fresh cuts and bruises that the Arakesh had left him with, and continued to run under the growing heat of the rising sun. The son-of-none had already completed one lap of Karath's circumference, as he did every morning, and was half way around on his second lap.

Flashes of the fight with the assassins played over and over in his mind. Tauren had come closer to death that night than any other, at least since before Salim found and tutored him.

He wanted to push himself, he *needed* to push himself.

With every minute, the heat of The Arid Lands increased, threatening to dehydrate Tauren before he reached Mother Madakii's home, his home, and that of a hundred others with no parents.

With the high wall to his left, Tauren looked out to his right where Syla's Gate stood, a relic of the old world, a time when the elves walked in Illian. The massive gates were fixed in the mouth of the valley, barring the path into The Undying Mountains that decorated the south of Illian.

No human had seen the other side of those gates in centuries. Tauren couldn't even remember which emperor had dismissed the last of those who stood guard, no longer required to keep watch over the empty pass.

The sound of a dozen running feet and just as many grumbles brought Tauren from his reverie. He was moments from lapping a group of new recruits to the House of Owls. Just as Salim had instructed Tauren to run around Karath every morning, so too did he instruct the owls.

This particular group were relatively new and their stamina was untested. In less than a month they would each be able to keep up with him, and those who could not would be found a different role within the house.

"The last through Mother Madakii's door has to retrieve a sword from the northern barracks..." Tauren smiled when their sighs quickly changed to expressions of determination. The only thing they would want to do is eat when they finished, not go sneaking around the soldiers' barracks.

With a last glance at Syla's Gate, Tauren ran on until he passed through the main gates in the north of Karath. Weaving through the streets and the vendors setting up for market, The White Owl quickly found his way back to Mother Madakii's orphanage. The building was humble in appearance and in need of much repair, but Tauren liked it that way; no one looked twice at the decrepit place, let alone suspect it of being the headquarters to the House of Owls.

As always, Tauren found Mother Madakii, a woman of great age, teaching a group of children, as well as being assisted by the older ones to hand out bowls of food. Some things would never change, he thought. He stopped for just a moment to look upon the children and remember why he put on that mask every night. If granting them their freedom required his life, he would gladly give it.

Once inside his own room, Tauren removed his shirt with great difficulty. His torso was glistening with sweat running over his fresh wounds. He didn't like the others to see him in pain, or the toll this life had taken on his body. Every muscle heaved with his laboured breaths, revealing a patchwork of old scars and new - too many for one of his young age. Acquiring the skills necessary to defeat an Arakesh, however, had required a lifetime of beatings.

A familiar knock on the door brought a smile to his face.

"Come in, Braigo."

His oldest friend walked in without his usual smile. "He's here."

Tauren's own smile faded. "Where is he?"

"On the roof. He arrived not long before you."

Tauren looked up to the ceiling as if he could see his brother, Halion Al-Anan standing there. "Make sure the last—"

"Retrieves a sword from the barracks," Braigo finished for him. "I know."

The roof of the orphanage was flat but for the large dome that occupied the centre. The sun continued to rise, casting long shadows over the tops of Karath's rooftops. Tauren marched over to the corner where Halion stood, wrapped in a long cloak and shroud to conceal his head. The White Owl ignored his brother's attempts to embrace and instead threw the hawk-like helmet at the commander's feet.

"What is this?" Halion asked as he bent to pick it up.

"Where have you been?" Tauren demanded, his usual anger rising to the surface. "I have been trying to reach you for two days!"

Halion held up a calming hand. "There have been developments..."

"You mean like the Arakesh?" Tauren could see the surprise on Halion's face, but not for the right reason.

"They have attacked you?" Halion scanned Tauren's body with a critical eye.

"They stalk my owls from the shadows, myself included. Though I see their *presence* doesn't surprise you." Tauren added the latter with accusatory venom. "I've had to pull back half of our nightly patrols."

Halion sighed. "They have been instructed to patrol the city in secret. Their orders are simple; find owls and kill them." The commander was about to turn away before he added, "And don't think they only hunt at night, Tauren. The Arakesh have been trained to blend in to all cultures, day or night."

"How can you know these things?" Tauren asked.

"I did it, brother..." Halion pulled one of his gloves off and held up his hand, where a familiar silver ring sat on his middle finger. "I have been brought into the inner circle of The New Dawn."

Tauren quickly reached out and held Halion's finger in place, so that he might better inspect the ring.

"Tell me everything."

The sun had risen a hand's length in the sky before Halion was finished telling his tale. Tauren sat on the edge of the dome, his expression frozen in disbelief.

"Elves... Darkakin..." The White Owl echoed, as if saying it out loud would make it more believable.

"They call him Nakir," Halion explained, "though I got the distinct impression that the other one was in charge."

"Ali..."

"Alidyr Yalathanil. He was the one who brought the Arakesh." Halion sat opposite his brother on the edge of the rooftop.

"Elves have been controlling The New Dawn?" Tauren was still struggling with the idea of elves even being in Illian, let alone the thought of them being so wicked.

"They serve Valanis," Halion continued. "That is who The New Dawn has been working for all these years."

"I have heard that name before." Tauren stood up and began pacing while he told Halion of Orfad's last words.

"Since being brought into the inner circle, Rorsarsh has had me followed, but I managed to get some time in the palace library. I have been looking through the old tomes for any information. I thought it was some kind of elven god, but then I found this..." Halion removed a scroll from within his robes and laid it out for Tauren to see. "He wasn't a god. He was some mad elf that started a civil war a thousand years ago."

The scroll was old, but it clearly showed the account of something called The Dark War, though the scroll had been scribed by a human and not an elf, so it was most likely inaccurate, as so many legends were after passing through the generations.

Tauren took it from Halion's hands and inspected every inch of the parchment, paying close attention to the names throughout the text. Alidyr and Nakir were mentioned at least twice as being generals during the war.

"I don't understand any of this..." Tauren handed the scroll back to Halion, deflated.

Not only were they fighting against the empire and the slavers, but now they were pitted against ancient elves, deadly assassins and an army of Darkakin, another legend come to life; all of which appeared to be involved in some conspiracy to invade Illian.

This was much larger than just The Arid Lands and freeing the slaves. If The New Dawn succeeded in opening Syla's Gate, the Darkakin would make slaves of all of Illian, a fate worse than death, if the old stories of their kind were true.

"The arrival of the Arakesh is proof that we've become more than a thorn in their side," Halion offered. "But more than that, it is rallying more of the men to our way of thinking. Everyday more of the soldiers complain of the assassins' overbearing presence, not to mention a few casualties. Rorsarsh is losing his grip on the army, and when they see that he is working to open our city to the Darkakin—"

"It will be too late by then!" Tauren paced over the hot rooftop. "If the Darkakin breach those gates it will all be over. If the amount of armour being made is any indication, we're outnumbered..."

Halion said nothing for a moment, his dark eyes glazed over in contemplation. "Then we act now."

Tauren looked up at his brother's face and saw the hard resolve that he wore like armour. "It's too soon to act, Halion. We planned on having more years before taking—"

"You said it yourself; it will be too late by then. The Darkakin are marching towards our home this very moment! Do you have owls in the other cities?" Halion appeared desperate for the answer.

"Of course..."

"Send word, Tauren. Bring them all back to Karath, every owl you have."

"We cannot abandon those cities, brother. Every day they work to free new slaves." Tauren was glad to see Halion finally thinking on an attacking foot, but this time frame was not as they had always planned.

"If we control the head," Halion said as he swept his arm across Karath's vista, "we control the body! One sweeping attack to take the palace! Only then will the army listen to me; once Rorsarsh is dead and the boy-emperor dethroned. The soldiers will fight for us, I know it. They have wives, children and parents in this city. They don't want the Darkakin anywhere near their families."

Tauren looked away, out over the city he thought of as home and a prison all in one. Making a move against the palace now was risky with their numbers, but the added trouble of potentially fighting the Arakesh made the decision all the harder. He didn't even want to think about fighting the elves.

If it went wrong, the House of Owls would be crippled in a single night, Halion would be executed and everything they had worked towards for so many years would be for nothing. The alternative was far worse when Tauren considered it; to do nothing now would spell not only Karath's doom, but all the free people of Illian.

"Gather those in your ranks who are most faithful to our cause," Tauren instructed Halion with the same expression of determination. "I will see to the owls."

Halion smiled. "So... we're really doing it then? We're going to war."

Tauren couldn't find his own smile. "I fear war is coming to us, brother." The White Owl looked to the south, where Syla's Gate stood forebodingly in the middle of The Undying Mountains.

CHAPTER 16
SAYING FAREWELL

Nathaniel ascended the stairwell and entered the hubbub of The Pick-Axe, leaving Reyna and Faylen to meditate in peace. The elves required more time for their magic to coalesce and store inside the crystals stolen from The Tower of Gadavance.

The entire heist had become far more dramatic than originally planned, with the whole tower crumbling into the streets. Thankfully, they had been able to flee the area before the city watch arrived.

The knight had heard of the magical cult known as The Black Hand, but he had never come across them on his patrols, a fact that he was thankful for having heard Faylen's tale.

The early afternoon saw the tavern filled with patrons and visitors from other lands. Doran and Glaide were sat on the far side, surrounded by a gathering of wide-eyed drinkers listening to tales of their joint adventures.

Nathaniel looked around for familiar faces and wondered where Hadavad and Atharia had disappeared off to. After stealing the crystals, the mages had mysteriously vanished, no doubt discussing The Black Hand. Asher had told of their offer to assist them in retrieving Paldora's gem and defeating Valanis: a bold offer. Nathaniel was more than happy to have some more magic users on their side, providing they returned from wherever they were.

"Mr. Galfrey..." Russell Maybury's yellow eyes flashed from behind the bar, as he placed a tankard of ale down for the knight.

Nathaniel gladly took the stool beside Asher and tentatively held the frothing ale. "It's a little early for me."

Russell stared blankly at the knight before walking farther down the bar to serve another customer. Nathaniel had faced many monsters in his time on the road, but Russell's unnatural yellow eyes still managed to make the hairs on his neck freeze.

"Don't worry," Asher said with a coy smile, "he has that effect on everyone."

"What is he?" Nathaniel asked quietly. He wasn't novice enough to miss the supernatural aura that Russell gave off.

"You can't tell?" Asher replied through a stifled laugh. "What were they teaching you at West Fellion?"

Nathaniel refused to rise to the jest. "I have my suspicions..."

Asher finished the last of his ale and dragged Nathaniel's tankard over. "What are you Russell?" the ranger asked in a hushed tone.

Before Nathaniel could ask why the ranger had whispered the question into his drink, Russell Maybury walked back up the bar to stand before them, his yellow eyes boring into Nathaniel.

"I'm a *wolf*." The barkeeper took Asher's empty tankard and wandered off.

Nathaniel tried to keep his expression neutral, but could feel himself going red. He had never met a werewolf he hadn't been forced to kill. Three nights of the month they were among the deadliest of creatures to stalk the night but, even in their human form, people afflicted with lycanthropy were violent and prone to episodes of wild aggression.

"He has a good ear," the knight commented, unable to think of anything else to say. "How is he so...?"

"Human?" Asher offered. "I took a job in Kelp Town, years ago. A werewolf had been seen dragging the local butcher into the woods; typical job. By the time I tracked the beastie down the full moon had passed, leaving Russell behind. Found him covered in blood, trying to hang himself. I thought, *great, I'll still get paid either way.* But, I wasn't the only one to track him down..."

Asher looked down the bar, to Russell. "A small mob came across him in the woods and decided a hanging was too easy. Rus pleaded with them to leave him alone, but when they attacked... instincts kicked in. With his bare hands he beat them back until it was just the two of us."

"You didn't kill him," Nathaniel stated.

"I thought his strength could be put to better use." Asher nodded with his chin to the notched pickaxe, mounted on the wall. "It took a while, but we managed to find a few techniques that helped to keep his aggression in check."

"What about during a full moon?"

Asher licked the froth from his top lip. "There's nothing to keep that in check..."

"You travelled together?" Nathaniel asked, surprised.

"For a while. I've travelled with most of them for some time or another." Asher turned around to look at Glaide and Doran.

"I bet there are a few stories there," Nathaniel replied, eager to hear any of them.

"I suppose there is..." Asher stood up from his stool, distracted.

Nathaniel followed his gaze to the corner of the tavern, where the southerner, Salim Al-Anan, was sitting, sipping hot tea.

"What is it?" the knight asked before the ranger could walk away.

"Where we're going, it wouldn't be such a bad thing to have a native on our side, especially one who knows his way around a sword."

"You mean to have him join us as well?" Nathaniel eyed the mysterious black-clad warrior with new interest.

"I'm going to try..." Asher didn't look very hopeful as he walked away.

Nathaniel remained at the bar, tugging at his cloak to get comfortable. He reminded himself to get rid of the ridiculous cape as soon as he could. The knight didn't understand how Asher could live with one on his back, let alone fight in it.

After convincing Russell to serve him some water, Nathaniel began his search anew. There had been one particular ranger that he wanted to talk to.

"Russell," he called. "Where is Kaleb Jordain?"

"By this hour?" Russell surveyed the tavern. "If he's not passed out in a ditch he'll be in the locker."

"Locker?"

"Downstairs, beyond all the rooms." Russell's thick arms pumped as he dried tankard after tankard.

"I still don't follow..." Nathaniel said.

Russell's laugh was closer to a snort, though it quickly turned to anger when the high-pitched squeal of a notorious warthog burst into the tavern. The pig knocked one of the patrons over and immediately went for his tankard of ale.

"Doran!" Russell yelled at the dwarf.

Nathaniel slipped away amid the chaos and descended back into the secret chambers beneath The Pick-Axe. As directed, the knight continued past the doors of the sleeping chambers and through the door at the end of the stone corridor. With no windows, everywhere under the tavern was illuminated by mounted torches and small hearths.

A partially opened door, leading to a room he had never seen before, caught Nathaniel's attention. He hesitated but found his curiosity overwhelming, as he opened the door and peered inside. The chamber was bare, with a single cage situated in the centre. The bars of the cage were thick and covered in scratches, along with the stone floor inside. Here and there, some of the bars were bent, as if something had tried to push between them.

It didn't take long for Nathaniel to realise what the room had been designed for. Russell Maybury spent three nights of every month inside that cage. The knight closed the door behind him and tried not to think about the werewolf and his subconscious desire to slay the monster.

As Nathaniel approached the so-called locker, he could hear the clean swipes of a sword, cutting rhythmically through the air. As quietly as he could, Nathaniel opened the door and crept into the new room. It only took a cursory glance around the chamber to realise what it really was, and it was certainly one of the better armouries he had seen, and he had grown up in West Fellion.

All four walls of the rectangular room were lined with swords of all sizes, axes, both single and double bladed, clubs, spears, daggers, staffs and shields. Some appeared to be antiques, while others looked newly forged and polished. Padded mats filled the majority of the floor, with thick wooden mannequins situated in the corners, all lined with scars.

Kaleb Jordain was adorned in his usual tattered long coat and mismatched armour and his bristly cheeks were in danger of catching up with his bushy white moustache. Nathaniel could smell the alcohol mixing in the air with his sweat as he hefted his sword through familiar techniques. The knight recognised most of his movements, though it appeared Kaleb had adjusted a few swings as he got older.

"Come to see your future have you, boy?" Kaleb didn't stop his routine to talk.

"Not quite..." Nathaniel walked farther into the armoury to see a small annexe built into the wall.

The alcove was home to a variety of armour and clothes. The knight resisted the urge to look through it all and focused on the old Graycoat. Kaleb ended his routine with a strong swipe that left his sword buried in the side of a mannequin. He finished with a few sips from a small flask on his belt.

"You think that old age is just something that *happens* in our line of work?" Kaleb held his arms out. "If you haven't got my skill, boy, you're going to need a whole bucket of luck!"

"You have good form." Nathaniel nodded along, agreeing with the grumpy ranger rather than starting an argument. "And your swing is strong too." Kaleb's sword wobbled in the wooden mannequin.

"Don't butter my arse, *knight!*" Kaleb shook the flask in his hand. "I might have a little in me, but I can still see that arrogant face of yours. You think you can best me..." The ranger held his arms out, inviting Nathaniel to take a shot.

"I didn't come down here to start a fight." Nathaniel held up his hands. "I don't doubt your skill; I know too well where you were trained."

"You mean you know who I trained alongside..." Kaleb replied knowingly.

Nathaniel had assumed that was how Kaleb knew his father. They would have been roughly the same age, had he still been alive. In a way he envied people like Kaleb for having clearer memories of the man. With every year, his childhood memories faded.

"So what did you come down here for?" Kaleb retrieved his sword and took a seat on one of the low benches, where he proceeded to clean the blade.

"I'm not even sure I know where *here* is. I thought I was in a tavern, then I found out there was a tavern within the tavern, and now there's an armoury to boot..."

"They call it the locker, the other rangers. I wasn't acquainted with the establishment back then, but I hear this was his locker, Asher's that is. Russell allowed him to keep weapons and supplies here, but as you can see, the other rangers had ideas of their own."

Nathaniel nodded along and glanced back at the alcove, realising that the line of swords in the corner were all double-handed and adorned with a spiked pommel, each identical to the one Asher had lost in the battle of West Fellion. Beside them was a rack lined with dark green cloaks; it appeared Asher was a creature of habit.

"So..." Kaleb continued to clean his sword. "What do you want, boy?"

Nathaniel threw a small bag of coins taken from the Stowhold pouch. Kaleb stopped cleaning and surprisingly caught the bag mid-air.

"To remind you of the old oaths you once took. And to offer you a job."

As the warthog dashed by with a triumphant squeal and an empty tankard hanging off one of its tusks, Asher sat back in his chair, having laid it all out for Salim and observed the concern spread across the southerner's face.

"You helped me when I needed it most, Asher, and you gave me purpose when I could only see despair. For that, you will always have my sword. But, you know I cannot enter The Arid Lands. I am exiled."

Asher didn't like asking for help and found the whole experience to be very foreign to him, but he continued to think of the dangers that lay ahead of them, and he knew better than most that they would need numbers if they were to survive.

"I'm not asking you to settle down and find a job in *Ameeraska*. When we get to Karath, we're going to need a guide who knows how to get us in and out with fresh supplies and no noise."

Salim didn't look convinced. "You can speak every language in the south, and you are far more accustomed to such..." The foreign ranger struggled to find the correct word. "...sneakiness."

Asher looked around before leaning closer to Salim. "There have been rumours coming out of the south for years, but over the last few months those rumours have quickly become fact. What started as a rebellion has grown into a not-so-secret civil war over slavery."

"What is your point, Asher?"

"War doesn't make a country easier to sneak in and out of. There will be checkpoints at every entrance to Karath, everyone looking for a fight, and foreigners are considered a complication. A former member of the emperor's honour guard could help with that..."

Salim looked away upon hearing his former title. "I am exiled for a reason, Asher. The emperor and his wife were killed on my watch. Not only was I banished for my failure, but the people of Karath consider me a disgrace. There are no... how do you say... palms I can grease to get us in and out of the city, let alone grant you safe passage inside the city walls."

"Then perhaps the son of a former honour guard can help, one who's now the second-in-command of Karath's forces...?" Asher watched the surprise consume Salim's expression. "Don't pretend like you didn't know. You might be exiled but you're sure as hell still keeping an eye out for your boy. How is Halion?"

Salim's look of surprise slid from his face. "It seems *your* ear is never far from the ground, old friend." The southerner's tone turned grave. "Halion fights with his heart amid a nest of vipers. Like me, he has always disagreed with the idea of slavery, but felt called to serve his emperor and people. In truth, I do not know how he fares in the current state.

"I cannot imagine him fighting to keep slaves, but I cannot imagine him standing against his superiors. Alas, it has been a long time since I have embraced him. He could be a very different man by now..." Salim's sombre gaze found Asher. "I am sorry, old friend. I dream of walking in my land again and conversing in my native tongue with my son. But I *am* exiled."

Asher wanted to protest and continue to pressure Salim into joining them, but he could see that it was futile. The old honour guard had made up his mind and there was nothing the ranger could say to change it.

"If I see Halion, I will tell him his father is well and perhaps share one or two of your tales." With a strong pat on Salim's shoulder, Asher stood up and left.

~

Kaleb Jordain rocked back on his heels with laughter until it turned into a coughing fit.

"Now why would I want to go and do a thing like that?" the ranger finally managed after hearing Nathaniel's proposition.

"You made an oath—"

Kaleb waved away Nathaniel's attempts to inspire honour. "The Graycoats branded me an oath-breaker when they banished me from the order!"

"That's why I brought the coin." Nathaniel nodded at the bag of coins in Kaleb's hand.

"Hmm. It is a *nice* bag of coins," the old Graycoat mused, "but it's not a *great* bag of coins!"

Nathaniel blinked slowly, starting to wonder if he'd made a mistake. "I will give you more upon completion of the task."

Kaleb laughed again. "I might have been drunk but I still heard your master plan. There's no way any of you are returning from that! This here bag of coins is all I'll ever see from you, unless I go looking for your corpse."

Nathaniel sighed at his error in judgement and made for the door.

"Wait..." Kaleb called out. "You know why *I'm* not interested, but why do *you* care?"

Nathaniel considered his answer. "For peace of mind."

Kaleb laughed again. "Peace of mind? What could you possibly worry about? West Fellion got hit pretty hard but *hundreds* of Graycoats are gathering in Darkwell. You think the Arakesh will attack them again?"

"I want you to go and keep an eye on them, that's all. I have an uneasy feeling about King Merkaris's invitation. The men who attacked us in Velia had been seen in his escort out of Namdhor. I'm paying you to go to Darkwell and ensure that nothing is going on behind the scenes. The Graycoats won't be looking for trouble; *you* will. If you discover anything: report it."

"But why?" Kaleb asked again.

Nathaniel looked at the sword on Kaleb's hip and knew there was a part of the ranger that clung to the order. "You and I might not be Graycoats anymore, but those are still good men and women who stand up for the realm, not the *kingdoms*. I don't want to see an Illian without them." Nathaniel could see the old ranger's expression softening as he took in his words. "It'll be the easiest coin you ever make."

"Do you know how many times I've heard that?" Kaleb stood up, fingering the individual coins in the bag as he considered the job. "Fine. Consider the job accepted, though I expect another bag of coins when we next meet."

Nathaniel had no choice but to accept the terms and worry about the second payment later, should he live long enough to give it thought. They clasped forearms, marking the job as accepted.

"I will leave at once." Kaleb made for the door, only stopping to help himself to a new curved dagger off the wall. "That'll do..." the ranger said, inspecting the edge of the blade.

Nathaniel was left wondering what the arrangement was regarding the weapons and armour. With a last look at the alcove, the knight returned to the tavern above.

The rest of the day slowly drifted by and Nathaniel found himself becoming restless. He wanted to check on Reyna and Faylen but didn't want to disturb them. Faylen had stressed how much energy would be required to transport them all through one portal and over such a distance. It was easy to forget how old the young-looking elf was, and the wisdom that accompanied such age. Nathaniel trusted her judgment and left the elves to their meditation.

Asher had sat with Glaide for most of the afternoon, talking about old times on the road together. Nathaniel was content to sit and eat and drink as Doran and Salim took turns telling of their adventures and hunts. Most of Doran's brought Nathaniel to tears with laughter, while Salim's accent made for intriguing story-telling of the kind he could sit and listen to all day. When the big man, Bale, stood up to regale his time on the road, Nathaniel often found himself put off his food by the gruesome details.

When dusk settled over Lirian and the tops of The Evermoore took on an orange hue, Hadavad and Atharia returned to the Axe. Nathaniel picked up his drink and joined them at their table.

"Well met..." the knight greeted them.

"Mr. Galfrey." Hadavad nodded with a warm smile. Atharia remained as passive as ever.

"We missed you today," Nathaniel commented.

"Forgive our absence," Hadavad replied, placing his staff against the wall. "We have been in council with Queen Isabella. I felt it prudent to inform her of The Black Hand's presence, as well as apologise for the tower's untimely destruction."

"You have counselled the queen?" Nathaniel echoed with concern.

"The Evermoore has always felt like home to me, and so for five hundred years I have counselled all the kings and queens who have ruled over the region of Felgarn. But fear not, Mr. Galfrey, I made no mention of you or your companions."

Asher had told Nathaniel of the mage's mysterious age, though neither knew the truth of the matter. The knight was just relieved to hear that their presence remained a secret, for now.

"Reyna and Faylen have been storing magic in the crystals all day," Nathaniel explained. "They should be ready soon."

"We are ready to travel." Hadavad glanced at Atharia, who nodded her agreement.

"We're grateful for your company. I think a great deal of magic will be required if we're to survive The Arid Lands, never mind getting in and out of Nightfall." Nathaniel didn't want to think about that last part.

"The honour will be ours to assist in such a quest." Hadavad called over one of the waitresses to order food.

"I will leave you to eat in peace."

"Please, stay," Hadavad pleaded. "It would be nice to hear a tale or two of the Graycoats. Kaleb Jordain has a way of forgetting the details..."

Nathaniel just hoped the old Graycoat could stay sober long enough to reach Darkwell.

When the sky was filled with stars, Reyna and Faylen emerged from their room, exhausted. They told of their need to rest and the companions prepared to leave at dawn.

In truth, Nathaniel was glad of the extra night of comfort, surrounded by new friends. For just a moment, he glimpsed a life where he didn't patrol the land for months on end, searching for monsters and bandits. Instead, he imagined a life with a house he could call his own, and a wife and children to dote on... A life where he didn't have to think about where the next fight was coming from.

When the dawn greeted the land, Nathaniel awoke in the rangers' tavern beneath the Axe. His cloak had been removed and placed over the top of him as he slept in the worn armchair. The knight looked around to see Asher, Glaide and Doran in similar positions, all sat around the fire with empty tankards at their feet. Bale lay sprawled across the table with his large legs and heavy head hanging over the edge.

Nathaniel sat up and rubbed his eyes, regretting the amount of ale the dwarf had convinced him to drink. They had drunk long into the night with little thought of the journey ahead of them. At least the rangers could sleep it off, the knight thought, whereas Asher and he would have The Arid Lands to contend with if the portal worked.

"Perhaps we should have stopped a little earlier..." Nathaniel commented.

"Wait for it." Salim wore an amused smile.

Before Nathaniel could ask what he was talking about, the door burst open with a *crack* that threatened to open his skull. Asher and Glaide jumped in their chairs, while Bale fell off the table with an almighty *thump*. Doran continued to snore.

"Wakey, wakey!" Russell Maybury strode into the room with a tray of shot glasses filled with yellow liquid.

Glaide shoved a heavy elbow into the dwarf's shoulder. "Doran!"

The dwarf awoke with a start, yelling curses. "What are ye abou'?"

"Wake up, Heavybelly!" Russell placed the tray down on a small table between them all. "Take your medicine."

Nathaniel picked up the shot glass and inspected the luminous liquid. "What is it?" he asked with a groggy voice.

"Better not to ask." Asher downed his shot and winced as he swallowed.

The others all followed suit and made the same face, even the mighty Bale looking pained by the taste.

"Bah!" Doran spat. "Always tastes like hogs' piss!"

"Unless you want that headache to last all day..." Asher bade Nathaniel to drink the shot.

Nathaniel downed the shot in one, and for just a moment the taste almost sent his nausea over the edge, until it suddenly subsided, taking his headache with it.

"That was disgusting." Nathaniel wiped his mouth and returned the shot glass.

"Humans..." Faylen was standing behind Russell with a judging look.

Reyna met Nathaniel's eyes and smiled, amused with his previous disposition. Both elves, however, appeared to have recovered from a whole day of collecting and storing magical energy.

"We should be leaving," Faylen observed, tactful as ever.

Russell held out his hand. "I couldn't have you leave in such a way, and especially with a task such as yours. You have coin for supplies, but I offer you supplies you won't readily find in a market."

The group followed Russell through the underground corridors until they found the armoury Nathaniel had visited the previous day. Bale had to duck to enter the chamber, but the room's contents held no surprises for the rangers.

"I regret that I cannot accompany you. You may take anything you wish. I hope that it serves you well and brings you back to The Axe."

Asher raised an eyebrow. "Anything I like? This is *my* locker..."

Glaide patted the old assassin on the back. "Well, after you stocked it so poorly all these years, I, *we* felt it could be something more."

"I bet that hip of yours is feeling mighty light!" Russell eyed the gap on Asher's left hip and guided him to the alcove lined with identical blades.

Reyna inspected the row of green cloaks and broadswords. "This is very you..."

"I know what I like and I like what I know." Asher proceeded to replace his cloak and choose a new sword.

"And for you, Lady Faylen?" Russell gestured across the room.

Faylen touched the light sack on her back. "I have everything I require, but thank you."

Quite impossibly, that sack housed a large chest with various supplies, though having seen Faylen in a fight, Nathaniel knew well that the only thing the elf needed was the scimitar on her hip.

Nathaniel went straight into the alcove, eager to be rid of his flowing cloak. The knight went for the tough, brown leather jacket with gaps around the shoulders and the elbows; perfect for an archer. The edges of the leather were engraved with a swirling pattern that looked better suited to an elf than a human.

"Good choice," Glaide observed. "That jacket will stop a blade."

"But not an arrow," Asher added, sliding his new broadsword into the scabbard on his hip.

Nathaniel put the jacket on and fitted a pair of hardened

vambraces over the sleeves, offering extra protection for up-close fighting.

Glaide continued, "You're going to find life a little harder without that famous coat of yours." The bald ranger handed over two straps lined with short daggers. "Strap these to your legs. They'll get you out of a pinch..."

With some finger-less gloves and a new quiver for his back, Nathaniel felt right at home among the rangers.

Reyna, like Faylen, remained by the door, more than happy with her elven attire and weapons. Nathaniel had often marvelled at the craftsmanship during their time together and could see how resilient their intricate leather was.

"That's quite the bow on your back..." Glaide observed over Reyna's shoulder.

Hadavad tilted his head with his eyes fixed on the black bow. "It has power."

"I claimed it after I used it to kill Adellum Bövö." Reyna twisted her head to see the top of the weapon on her back. "And it is definitely powerful."

Asher joined them with his hand resting under the spiked pommel of his sword and a fresh, green cloak over his shoulders. Along with the two short-swords on his back, the ranger cut quite the fierce figure, and that was without knowing that the blades on his back were among the most unique in all of Illian.

"Are we ready?" Faylen was growing impatient. "We will need the horses for our journey: a secluded place in The Evermoore would be ideal for opening the portal." The elf looked to Asher for any ideas, but it was Glaide who replied.

"We can show you a good place," the old ranger stated with a smile. "We know all the good places."

To Nathaniel's surprise, the entire group of rangers accompanied them beyond the tree-line, even Bale son of Hyil. The companions received many looks on their way out of Lirian, though Nathaniel noticed that most were staring at Doran, riding atop his warthog.

The knight was more comfortable with the city behind them and the thick wood of trees quickly surrounding them. He wondered how far Kaleb had travelled by now. Was he close to Darkwell? Was he lying in a ditch somewhere, drunk into a stupor? Nathaniel put the thought aside and focused on the journey ahead of them. He had done all he could to look out for the surviving Graycoats; he had his own journey to worry about.

"This will do," Faylen announced after half an hour of trotting into the forest.

They had come across a small clearing, littered with man-sized boulders and covered in green moss. The leaves were already raining down around them as winter loomed ever closer. Winter, however, would be a distant memory after a few days in The Arid Lands. Their winter was still hotter than any summer in the north of Illian.

"You best be makin' that portal big enough for me hog, elf!" Doran said with a big grin.

"Excuse me?" Faylen looked to Asher again.

Glaide cleared his throat. "What Doran is trying to say is: we have decided to accompany you. *All* of us..."

Asher looked to Salim with a hint of surprise in his expression.

"I would not have you tell my son of my story, and remain absent from what is perhaps the most important quest in history." Salim looked to Reyna with a warm smile.

"And I would not have name left *out* of story." Bale's thick accent wasn't easy to understand, but his intentions were clear enough.

"An' I'm comin' because me blade's been clean for too long!" Doran laughed to himself, his whole body shaking inside his black and golden armour.

Nathaniel noted that Glaide offered no explanation, just a simple nod to Asher. Out of them all, it appeared the pair had most history.

Before Faylen could protest, Reyna stepped forward. "You do not have the gratitude of your people yet, but when our actions bring peace to all of Verda, your names and courage will be sung throughout history." The elven princess beamed. "For who could stand against us?"

Indeed, Nathaniel thought. Despite Russell staying behind, those standing in the clearing were among the most skilled and deadliest in the land. Perhaps they *could* survive The Arid Lands and the Arakesh; the knight still didn't want to think about the nightmarish creatures that Asher told of inside the pit.

Faylen protested, "I cannot transport us all through the same portal to Karath. It will cause too much stress on the portal and I don't have the strength to open more than one this day."

"We will do it together," Reyna replied with confidence.

"You have never succeeded in opening a portal... in the right place."

"Then at least use my strength." Reyna wasn't taking no for an answer.

"Very well. Is everyone ready?" the elf asked.

Hadavad moved forward atop his horse of pure black with a giddy expression.

Russell Maybury stepped away from the horses. "I'll have a tankard of ale waiting for all of you. Make sure you return to drink it, eh?"

Asher looked to the owner of The Pick-Axe with what passed for a thank you from the ranger.

"We must be quick." Faylen removed a crystal from the pouch on her belt. The light broke through the gaps in her fingers as if the elf held a star in her hand.

Faylen flicked her wrist and launched the crystal out in front of the group. With a deafening *crack* and a brilliant flash of every colour, the crystal exploded and expanded into a black abyss, lined with silent bolts of lightning.

Hadavad was the first to gallop ahead, eager to experience this new form of magic. The remaining nine spurred their horses, and hog, through the portal with all haste. Nathaniel had travelled through one before, but it didn't stop the dizzying wave wash over him when reality reformed around his galloping horse.

The brief moment of shadow was obliterated by the startling blue sky and brilliant sunshine. Nathaniel blinked hard to adjust his eyes and brought his horse to stop alongside the others.

When his eyes found the faces of the rangers, Nathaniel felt his stomach drop at their expressions, like wild cats with their hackles up. The knight turned in his saddle and followed their gaze across the endless green fields of The Moonlit Plains.

The portal was already gone, allowing for a clear vision of the Centaurs three hundred yards away.

"We're not in The Arid Lands," Glaide observed, never taking his eyes off the Centaurs, who were all equally staring at the companions.

"We're in The Moonlit Plains..." Nathaniel replied, unable to count the number of Centaurs amassing in front of them.

"I couldn't..." Faylen slid from her horse, only to be caught by Asher mid-fall. The elf appeared exhausted and paler than usual.

That was all the Centaurs needed apparently, as the team burst into a gallop with their bows raised and stolen swords at the ready. Their howls and cheers were beyond what any man could achieve, and only served to put a chill down Nathaniel's spine.

"Ride south!" Glaide shouted.

Asher heaved Faylen's limp form over his saddle and threw her horse's reins to Atharia, who ushered it to run alongside her own. With the added weight, Hector galloped at the back of the group, with Asher's determined look showing no signs of fear.

It was only a few seconds later when the first arrows began to whistle past their heads. Nathaniel looked ahead, surprised with the speed of Doran's hog, which sprinted and weaved between the horses' powerful legs. Reyna led from the front, her blonde hair flying out behind her and Adellum's bow glistening under the sun. Nathaniel wanted to ride beside her so that he could ensure her safety, a responsibility he felt tenfold since Faylen's collapse.

The ground thundered under the stampede of hooves. Every time Nathaniel looked back it appeared as if the Centaurs had swelled in size. The plains were predominantly flat, dotted with small forests and ancient rocks, but the Centaurs dashed out from behind every cover until they were charging at the companions from all sides. One arrow flew between Asher and Nathaniel and skimmed the edge of the knight's new jacket.

"Stay low!" Asher commanded. "They won't risk hitting the horses!"

"How do they feel abou' hogs?" Doran shouted back as his unusual mount dashed between falling arrows.

The small woods ahead of them exploded with life when dozens of Centaurs leapt onto the plains. The companions' collective speed instantly slowed as they were quickly surrounded.

Nathaniel kept looking to Hadavad and Atharia who, among the group, were the most qualified to get them out of the trap, but the mages slowed with the others and came to a complete stop.

The companions were herded into a tight circle, until the green of the plains was hidden behind a wall of Centaurs.

Nathaniel couldn't help staring at them all, having never seen one this close before. Everything below the navel was that of a horse, but their torsos were quite distinctive. Every one of them was well muscled and covered in thick tribal tattoos of varying colours. Their heads were human in appearance, with hard lines and scraggy beards, but their ears were pointed like that of an elf. Instead of a mane, the Centaurs had long braids that ran down their human backs.

The Centaur with the broadest chest and longest braid stepped forward with a bow in hand. His mouth opened as if to speak, when his dark eyes flicked to Reyna and fixed his gaze. For a moment, Nathaniel didn't know what to do. The princess was on the other side of the circle and if the giant Centaur attacked her he wouldn't be able to help.

"El'shenae..." the Centaur whispered, before bending one of his powerful legs and stretching out the other to bow. All the other Centaurs whispered the same word and bowed as one.

"What's this abou'?" Doran said out of the corner of his mouth.

The head Centaur looked up at Reyna. "You are El'shenae... an elf."

Doran son of Dorain looked around quizzically. "Does this mean we're not goin' to die?"

The void collapsed behind him and Valanis dropped into the shadows of Kaliban's caves. The herald of the gods had once loved these caves, when they were full of wonder and power. Then, they became his prison for forty years, the only place he could exist without being consumed.

The pools were always warm and welcoming, made entirely of crystals that weren't quite solid yet. Now, Valanis looked upon them with a growing hatred. After decades, he had finally roamed the world again, free and superior... but he wasn't strong enough.

Valanis fell to his knees at the foot of the nearest pool, its light reflecting off his iron mask. He had spent days underground, scouring Stowhold's secret vaults, countering hexes and spellbound doors. The herald of the gods had searched through chamber after chamber of trinkets, ancient coins and treasures that only a human could ever value. The occasional guard would venture down when they had plucked up the courage to pursue him, but all had found their resting place in those cold tombs.

Day and night, the gods had ceaselessly bombarded him with their demands to find the only treasure that really mattered. The weight of the pantheon was taking its toll without the entirety of Paldora's gem to keep his mind and body intact. He looked up to the glittering stalactites and cursed Alidyr, the head of his trusted Hand.

"Alidyr!" he screamed into the caves. "Where is it? I need the gem..." Valanis scraped the mask from his glowing face and looked up, as if the gods were standing before him. "Without the gem, I cannot retrieve The Veil. I am failing you..."

Find the ranger...

Find the gem...

FIND THE VEIL...

Atilan's voice dominated that of Paldora's and Naius's. The king of the gods demanded The Veil be found and so it must be. But without the gem, Valanis knew the magic would consume him.

Find the ranger...

Paldora's sweet voice whispered in his ear. The herald cursed the Outlander, wondering how a savage from The Wild Moores could be so entwined with his own fate.

"Master!" Thallan, sovereign of the sword, ran through the tunnel. His emerald blade, gifted to him by Valanis, was resting on his hip, as always.

"Thallan..." Valanis took his subject's hand and pulled himself to his feet. "Help me into the pools."

Thallan helped his master to remove his robes before Valanis fell into the sparkling pool. The relief was instantaneous. The dark elf stayed under the magical waters for a moment, allowing his strength to return and any risk of seizure die away. When he finally rose above the surface, Thallan was waiting eagerly by the edge, his pale features marred with concern.

"Has there been any word from Alidyr?" Valanis rasped.

"No, Master." There was some joy in Thallan's response. "The ranger's fate remains unknown to him. He has met with the council in Karath; both he and Nakir are preparing to open Syla's Gate."

Valanis sighed. "They will not be able to open those gates; I see that now. Even I have not the power to undo the spells cast over it."

Thallan hesitated. "But then... how will the Darkakin enter The Arid Lands?"

Valanis smiled. "I believe the gods have already answered that question, Thallan. You, however, will just have to have faith."

It was clear that Thallan had more questions, but the elf remained silent, trusting in his master.

As the general made to leave, he turned back to the pools and asked, "Master, what have you been searching for? I could feel you in Dragorn and then in Stowhold."

Valanis began to sink back into the pool. "Faith, Thallan. You must have faith..."

CHAPTER 17

UPON THE EDGE OF A BLADE

T auren skulked on the landing, leaning over the dusty rail, as he looked down at the orphans being herded together and counted by the older children. They had been escorted from the orphanage in groups, like this one, for the last two days and taken to secret places of refuge elsewhere in the city.

As the children departed, the owls arrived from across The Arid Lands in similar groups to avoid arousing suspicion. Tregaran, the most northerly city in the desert was the only place that hadn't yet been completely emptied of his agents, but they would soon arrive. Then, they would go to war in earnest.

He met the eyes of every owl, each as young as him, and nodded his thanks. They had all grown accustomed to the cities Tauren had sent them to, and it was asking a lot for them to abandon any plans and ride for Karath at a moment's notice.

They were loyal, he thought proudly. Every one of them was loyal and not just to the cause, but to him personally. Tauren had used Salim's techniques to train all of them, ensuring they could each do more than just defend themselves. He had turned them all into killers and he didn't regret it for a single second. His only regret was the size of his force.

Tauren looked at their faces and wondered which of them wouldn't make it through this. This part of his plan had always involved more owls and several more years of preparation. These were his brothers and sisters, people he had grown up with on the streets, people he had survived with.

Mother Madakii came to stand by the railing. "You look troubled, my boy..."

Most of her body was hidden beneath robes and a colourful head scarf, revealing only her wrinkled face and welcoming brown eyes. Her years in the desert had hardened her skin and Tauren knew that was the truth in more ways than one.

"I'm asking a lot of them."

"You think they aren't ready?" Mother Madakii asked, sceptically.

Tauren thought about the approaching Darkakin army and the unbelievable appearance of the elves. "I'm not sure any of us are ready for what's coming. What do you think, Mother?" He had valued her opinion for as long as he could remember.

Mother Madakii thought for a moment. "I think they have been freeing slaves every day since you trained them, and I *know* you trained them well."

Tauren glanced at the Mother, aware of the disapproval in her voice, though not with him, but rather with Salim Al-Anan for training him in the first place. The two had never quite agreed on Salim taking Tauren under his wing as a teenager, and Mother Madakii had made that quite clear to the older warrior on more than one occasion.

"However..." Mother Madakii continued with a sombre tone, "if what Halion says is true and history is accurate; the Darkakin will make the slavers irrelevant. There will be no free people left to fight when they are finished with our land."

Tauren digested her wise words. "So you think we should do this? You think we should take the palace?"

"I think the House of Owls stands on the edge of a blade. You will either take the palace and our ranks will swell until all are free. Or you will fail, and the House of Owls will be wiped from history by The New Dawn. It's going to be quite the night..." Mother Madakii added some levity and a smile to her serious speech.

Despite his sour mood, Tauren couldn't help but be infected by that smile. Mother Madakii rested her head on his shoulder and wrapped her hands around his arm. They enjoyed a moment together, mother and adopted son. In truth, she was closer in age to be his grandmother but, even to this day, Tauren had never met his parents or discovered which grand family they belonged to.

"I will be going with the last group of children," Mother Madakii commented as she moved away. "Try not to get my house too dirty." She stopped on the landing and looked back. "You *must* return to me, Tauren." The Mother's expression and tone suggested she wasn't to be argued with. "And make sure everyone wipes their feet on the way in!" Tauren could only see the back of her when she made her last remark, but it still made him smile.

A sharp whistle from below caught Tauren's attention. Braigo was standing in the middle of the hall with alarm spreading across his face.

"The lookouts have spotted a lone soldier walking this way."

A curious thing.

"On his own?" Tauren's question was met with a nod. "Stop the last group of children from leaving and hide their bags. Keep the owls in the back and—"

"He's got a white band around his arm." Braigo interrupted, aware of the fabric's significance.

Halion and Tauren had come up with several methods of contacting each another over the years; one of which was a soldier he trusted with a white cloth around his arm. This was unexpected though. Halion himself was supposed to be coming at sunset, to finalise the details of the attack.

"Divert him through the back. Have the lookouts retrace his steps and make certain he wasn't followed." Tauren dashed to the other side of the orphanage, leaving Braigo to carry out his orders.

A few minutes later, the soldier was being bundled through a back door and surrounded by Tauren and three armed owls. In the tussle, one of the owls slid the soldier's sword from its scabbard and pushed him against the wall. They weren't taking any chances with so many of their forces in one place.

"A nice day for a walk..." Tauren said. If the soldier didn't give the correct response he would never see home again.

"I was hoping for rain..." the soldier replied with some trepidation.

Tauren let his shoulders relax and he dismissed the owls, giving Braigo a nod in the doorway. The soldier realised that he wasn't about to die and removed his short-pointed helmet, inspecting the surroundings.

"Not what you expected?" Tauren looked around the cramped room, full of junk collected over the decades.

"I can't believe you've nearly toppled an empire from inside... *this*. I thought it was—"

"Why has Halion sent you?" Tauren didn't have time for long-winded observations.

The soldier stood a little straighter, not used to being spoken to in this manner, and especially by someone out of uniform. Tauren tried to appear less tense and remember that it was a miracle that there were any soldiers who disagreed with slavery. He should be thankful that Halion had even got through to as many as he had. Tauren wanted to free the slaves; he didn't want to cripple the country by eradicating its forces and killing the people's husbands, brothers and sons. The Arid Lands only stood a chance of thriving in the new regime if there were people left to live in it.

"Forgive me." Tauren held up a hand. "My responsibilities have increased today. My name is Tauren son-of-none."

The soldier bowed slightly, as if accepting his apology. "My name is Argo Nor-Valen. Commander Halion has sent me with his regrets. He cannot attend tonight's... meeting."

"Why not?" Tauren asked immediately.

"Supreme Commander Rorsarsh has invited him to dinner in the palace. He has sent *me* with the details you require to take the palace." Argo revealed a rolled-up scroll inside his breastplate.

"So, while we fight for our lives he's going to enjoy some fine dining?" Tauren's temper was rising again. This was just typical of his brother!

"He would fall under suspicion if he were to decline." Argo rose to his commander's defence, as any owl would do for Tauren. "Emperor Faro will be present for the meal..."

Was that Halion's game? While they secured the palace, he would secure the boy-emperor? More likely he would enjoy the meal and wait for Tauren to do all the hard work!

"So he sends you in his place, in the middle of the day and dressed in full armour no-less." Tauren looked Argo up and down, still a slave to his temper.

"I wasn't followed."

"*We* will determine that," Tauren snapped. "There are still those among your ranks who believe slavery is a natural way of life. They might find it suspicious in a time of rebellion, for one of their own to go for a stroll on his own in a neighbourhood where entire battalions don't dare tread."

"I *wasn't* followed," Argo replied firmly.

"Tauren..." Braigo was standing in the doorway again. "Every owl from Hervona and Ameeraska is accounted for."

Tauren took a breath to calm himself. "What of Tregaran?"

"Most of them will be here by sunset." Braigo glanced at Argo with a critical eye.

Tauren bade Argo to follow him and Braigo into the hall where the children usually had their meals. Now it was filled to burst with just over four hundred owls.

The White Owl turned to the soldier. "Perhaps, we should go over these... *details*."

~

The Centaurs had led the group of rangers and elves across The Moonlit Plains to a hidden clearing within one of the smaller forests. The Centaurs had built humble shelters, filled mostly with straw and gathered food.

Despite all the horrible things humans said about the blood-thirsty creatures, Reyna could only see vegetables and fruit dotted around the camp. The centre of the site was occupied by a large pyre that made most hearths look relatively inadequate by comparison.

The sun was on its way down when the princess felt she could leave Faylen in the hands of the Centaurs. Reyna had spent most of the day keeping watch over her and using magic where she could to restore Faylen's energy, but her magical talents had always fared better on physical wounds.

Two Centaurs crowded around Faylen and applied their herbal medicines to her skin and offered prayers to the gods for restoration. Dark rings marred her mentor's eyes and her pale complexion had turned almost ghostly now. Opening a portal to transport so many had been too taxing, even with Reyna's combined efforts.

Reyna was angry with herself for not taking more time to prac-tise the art of magic. The princess had always taken to her bow or a sword, allowing her natural magic ability to fall by the wayside.

"It's not your fault." Surprisingly, it was Asher and not Nathaniel waiting for her outside the hut. "Don't blame yourself."

The ranger's cool blue eyes put Reyna at ease as they strolled across the camp together. "If only you still had your ring." Reyna looked at Asher's hand, noticeably absent of Paldora's gem. "You could have restored her with no effort at all, or even opened a portal all the way to Nightfall."

"Even with the shard, I was still a novice in the ways of magic." Asher was among the hardest of humans to read, giving little expression to his words. "I think it would still have been safer to allow Faylen to open the portals, even if she needs time to recover."

"She likes you, you know..." Reyna didn't know exactly why she said that. "She enjoys your company, that is. She doesn't show it - she's almost as hard to read as you are, but she does like you."

Their conversation came to an end when they reached the others, who had all huddled together so that they might better observe the wild Centaurs that trotted around the camp.

Doran had already started a small fire and was busy preparing a spit, when Hadavad advised him to put it away in favour of eating something that had never required a heartbeat. The dwarf was about to protest when a pair of Centaurs walked by and eyed the spit with disgust.

The broad-chested Centaur, who had introduced himself as Xastus, and met them on the plains, stepped in front of Reyna and Asher.

"Princess Reyna," the Centaur said, in a voice that was deep and rich, "my people are preparing a feast tonight, in honour of the El'shenae's return to these lands. Your... *friends* are welcome to partake."

There was clearly a lot of distrust and bloody history between the Centaurs and humanity. Reyna decided that would be one of the first matters she attended to when the war was averted and peace finally reigned over Illian and Ayda.

"Thank you, Xastus. The honour will be ours, I assure you." Reyna bowed her head and watched with real wonder as the chief Centaur walked away. They were truly magnificent creatures.

Asher observed, "For all the trouble you're going to be in with your own people, you do make a good princess, Princess..."

Reyna smiled at the compliment. "I learned from my mother that leading is just another word for serving. My father is more concerned with words such as rule and control, but he sees the world through different eyes." The latter brought a sadness to her tone.

"Perhaps he has simply seen too much over his long lifetime. Ageing around bloodshed has a way of narrowing one's view."

Reyna smiled briefly. "You speak too eloquently for a simple ranger, you know; it gives away your prior training."

Asher matched her smile. "It adds to the mystery."

Reyna's laugh was mirthless as she considered her father. "My father has indeed seen a lot, especially living through The Dark War. I can't help but feel, however, that new eyes are required for a new time. He is living in the past where all the violence and wars should have stayed."

"Would you take his place?" Asher inquired.

Reyna had asked herself that same question many times over the years. "Elven hierarchy is somewhat violent - another addition implemented by my father. If he were to die or abdicate, my mother, Adilandra, would take the throne. If they both abdicated or died, I would no doubt be assassinated and replaced by one of the highborn families. I have long been considered too weak for elven society..."

"It seems to me you are more elf than any other. Without having lived it, you alone remember the old ways of your people. I have lived around violence my whole life and seen what it has to offer. The road you would choose for your people may be the only one that sees us find some semblance of peace. Or at least learn to tolerate each other..."

"You mean as I tolerate you?" Reyna jested with the hint of a smile turning up her cheeks. The ranger played along and pretended to be hurt, but the princess placed an affectionate hand on his arm. "Never have I had more hope in my heart than when I met you and Nathaniel. Together, we have the chance to make real change... but tonight, we have a feast among new friends, under the stars no less!"

"I hope you weren't planning on anything too civilised." Asher looked to the rangers with a coy smile.

Indeed, Asher had been right, for as the sun dropped below the horizon and the grass beneath their feet glowed under its ancient enchantment, the group of rangers introduced the Centaurs to alcohol.

For the first time in centuries, the Centaurs enjoyed their time with the 'two-legs' and shared food and drink alike. Reyna returned to Faylen regularly to check on her condition, though the princess knew she needed sleep more than anything.

As the moon rose higher and its glow further illuminated the grass, the Centaurs took up a dance around the pyre to celebrate the elves. Reyna couldn't help but smile and laugh under the canopy of stars. For just a moment, she felt as if she was back in Ayda, celebrating at one of the festivals in The Amara Forest.

Nathaniel appeared from nowhere and gripped her with both hands, pulling the princess into the dance with the Centaurs. They laughed and danced together as if there was nothing else going on in the world.

Off to the side of the dance, the barbarian, Bale, was sat opposite a crouching Centaur, as the two contested each other's strength with an arm wrestle. The barbarian cried to the gods for strength, but the Centaur slowly pushed the man's arm down with casual ease. Doran spat out his ale in laughter and dropped to his behind, which wasn't so far from the ground to begin with.

Asher and Glaide sat with Salim, still in control of their senses and deep in discussion by the looks of it. For Reyna, the whole world was spinning as she danced with Nathaniel. The princess caught glimpses of Hadavad and Atharia closer to the pyre, talking to Xastus with great interest.

It was some hours before the dancing was broken up by the mad dash of a notorious warthog. The animal ran between the Centaurs, squealing with glee and a shining coat of ale over its face and tusks.

"Hey!" Nathaniel shouted, lifting his leg in time to avoid the hog. "Doran! What do you call it?"

The dwarf stopped laughing with a confounded expression. "What do a' call it?"

Nathaniel laughed. "Yes, the warthog's name..."

"Bah! I see no warthog! This is a *Warhog*! Bred in Dhenaheim for... well, war!"

Reyna couldn't contain her amusement. "The poor creature has no name?"

Doran Heavybelly shrugged. "Well, aye, it does. I jus' call it Pig!" The dwarf swigged his ale. "Sometimes I jus' whistle..."

The companions fell into fits of laughter before returning to the feast.

It was much later by the time Reyna retired for the night. The Centaurs had left Faylen to rest when Nathaniel joined her in sitting beside her mentor and keeping watch.

The princess didn't know if it was the ale Doran had kept pouring into her cup or not, but the elf looked at Nathaniel and, for the first time, she didn't think about their differences. She didn't care about their different life spans or the fact that she was falling for a human instead of an elf, never mind the fact that he wasn't even royalty. Reyna looked at his strong, stubbled jaw and dark eyes and knew that what she felt was in fact love.

These moments of peace and enjoyment were going to be few and far between after tonight. They had found some luck with the Centaurs' change of heart today, but there would be no such luck once they entered the desert. A part of Reyna was looking forward to seeing the southern kingdom, and observing how the humans had thrived in a land the elves naturally avoided. But, there was a part of her that wanted to run away with Nathaniel into The Evermoore and never look back.

Reyna looked at Faylen and drew some strength from her mentor's resolve. After all, they were not the only ones fighting to keep the peace. The princess thought of her mother, who was somewhere in the south of Ayda, a world away. Her mother had sacrificed much to find the dragons, leaving her home behind and all the comforts that befit a queen; an inspiration to all elves.

Reyna knew that the life she wanted with Nathaniel was worth fighting for, even if she didn't know what that looked like yet. First, they would fight to bring an end to Valanis's machinations. Then, they would strike an accord between man and elf so that peace might reign again. Reyna fell asleep in Nathaniel's arms and dreamed about what could be.

CHAPTER 18
INSURRECTION

Midnight had come and gone by the time Tauren son-of-none was in position outside the palace. After finalising the plan and going over the details of the patrols and the layout inside the fortress-like palace with Argo, Tauren had ordered the owls into various positions throughout the day, to avoid suspicion; after all, four hundred rebel slaves walking through the streets would draw the entire army out of their barracks.

Every hour, the owls had left the orphanage in small groups and waited patiently for the day they had all been training for.

Tauren looked over the edge of the building to see Argo striding through the main gate, the only way in and out through the surrounding wall that protected the palace. The soldier had assured him that the men on the gate were loyal to Halion but, as an added measure, he also had owls on all sides of the wall with grappling equipment.

The plan was simple, he reminded himself. First, they take the grounds and replace the guards, armour and all. The guards at the front seal the gates after the owls go in to ensure the rest of the barracks don't come with any aid if an alarm is raised. Then, while the bulk of the force works their way up through the towering palace, taking each floor at a time, Tauren scales the outside wall until he reaches the royal chambers. There, he meets up with Halion, kills the wretch Rorsarsh and secures the boy-emperor, though, in truth, he had no idea what they were going to do with the child.

Braigo asked, "What do we do about the elves? Or the Arakesh?"

Tauren had left out telling the owls about the elves as he didn't want to complicate matters, but everyone knew the assassins were lurking in the shadows. The White Owl had told them to overwhelm the assassins if confronted. Superior numbers was the only way they could beat the legendary warriors.

"Once we take the palace and hold the emperor hostage, they will be forced to flee."

The main gate remained partially open after Argo walked through. That was the signal. If the gates had closed completely then there was something wrong and the guards had changed. Braigo cupped his hands together and imitated the call of an owl. The reaction was immediate, with the surrounding buildings, lining the edge of the palace walls, coming to life. Owls dashed out from their hiding places and made for the wall with their grappling equipment, while Tauren made his way down into the alley and headed for the main gate.

Karath was silent but for the light footfalls of the running owls. No one yelled in defiance and no horns were blown in alarm, as the owls quickly made their way over the wall and into the palace gardens. Tauren looked through the holes in his mask and examined the expressions of the guards on the gate, searching for any sign of betrayal. As ordered, the guards closed the gates and barred the massive doors behind him. It would require many hours of battering to open the gate from the outside.

No talking was needed when the owls descended upon the royal estate. Their years on the streets had gifted them many skills; chief among them was the ability to move unseen and unheard. Those natural talents, combined with the training he had passed on from

Salim, made them a deadly opponent. Tauren ran through the gardens, between the palm trees and thick hedges, with a throwing knife in each hand, ready to silence any guards that were off their patrol routes.

A pair of soldiers dropped in the distance without a sound, as a group of owls ambushed them on the path. Tauren paid them little attention and instead began his climb up the palace walls. Braigo gave him an affirming nod from below and disappeared into the palace with the owls at his back. So far everything had gone according to plan and with no loss of life on their side. Tauren pushed any thoughts from his mind and focused on the climb. He was well accomplished in scaling almost every surface, but he had never attempted anything as tall as the palace; then again, he had never seen anything outside of Karath.

It took just over half an hour to reach the balcony belonging to one of the state rooms. Relieved, Tauren hopped over the edge and rubbed his sore forearms and flexed his fingers. The plush chamber held nothing of interest to The White Owl, and he crept into the hall in search of stairs - there was still some climbing to go.

Argo's information continued to prove accurate, as he turned the corner and found the spiral staircase used by the palace's slaves. He took heart in the thought that the first few floors would already be under their control.

Tauren stopped halfway up the staircase and held his breath. The sound of *clinking* armour and heavy footsteps echoed from above, descending towards him. The White Owl crept back the way he had come and flattened himself to the wall at the base of the staircase. There weren't supposed to be any patrols in this wing, but the two guards were pleasantly chatting about their next meal. Tauren couldn't tell which soldiers were sympathetic to the cause, and so he left his blades in their sheaths. Steel wasn't required to subdue a pair of ordinary guards, though he would never tell Halion such a thing.

As they took their last step off the staircase, Tauren swung his arm into the nearest guard with the edge of his flattened hand. The side of his knuckle connected with the man's throat and launched him back up the staircase in a choking mess. The second guard jumped in surprise; a crucial moment in which he might otherwise have put up a fight. Tauren however, was already dropping to one knee and, in the same fluid motion, he pushed his elbow into the man's knee, bringing them both to the same level. The White Owl jumped back to his feet, while simultaneously removing the guard's helmet, where he could thrust the man's exposed head into the spiral bannister. He was unconscious before he hit the floor, unlike the first guard who was rolling around the stairs in a desperate bid to suck some air into his lungs. Tauren grabbed him roughly by the collar and similarly removed his helmet so he wouldn't break his knuckles on the man's nose.

To give him as much time as possible before any alarm was raised, Tauren dragged the bodies into the empty room and closed the door. He paused on the stairwell and tilted his head to listen for any commotion above or below. It seemed his owls were performing well, just as he had trained them.

As he moved deeper into the palace, Tauren took stealthier measures to remain hidden from the increasing number of guards. By the time he was reaching the upper level he had but to simply follow his nose. Growing up on the streets gave him a particular affinity for sniffing out food, especially when it had been cooked by the royal chefs.

At the final corridor he came face-to-face with the door that separated him from the Supreme Commander and the boy-emperor.

Something wasn't right...

The corridor should be lined with honour guards, as Salim had once stood, ready to give their life for the emperor. The smell of the cooked meat told Tauren that the feast was definitely beyond the door, but there was no talk on the other side.

Something was definitely wrong.

Tauren knew he should find the nearest window and blow a clear note on the horn he carried on his belt. That would alert the owls that the plan was to be immediately abandoned and they should meet back up at dawn, in the south of the city. But he didn't. Tauren had come this far and curiosity had wormed its way into his mind.

Checking every alcove and shadow, Tauren slowly approached the double-doors with the lightest of feet. With his ear pressed to the door, he was sure he could hear the sound of Rorsarsh's greedy mouthfuls. He had to know. The White Owl steadied his breathing and tried to recall some words of wisdom from Salim's teachings, but nothing came to mind. He just wanted to kill and tear and destroy the lives of those who inflicted so much misery on The Arid Lands. The son-of-none thrust open the door with two throwing knives balanced in one hand, ready to throw at whoever attacked him first.

Tauren lost all heart at the sight that greeted him, his bloodlust immediately dispirited. Through dark, swollen eyes, Halion lifted his battered head and looked upon his brother with despair.

"I'm sorry..." Halion croaked with watery, bloodshot eyes.

His brother was strapped to an expensive looking chair in the middle of the chamber, with his hands bound behind his back. His armour and clothes had been stripped and tossed aside so that he sat naked, covered from head-to-toe in blood, both fresh and dry. Halion had been sat in that chair for some time. His face was barely recognisable after all the blows he had received, and his flesh was marred with burns and gaping wounds. His bare feet slipped around atop the puddle of blood beneath his chair.

Tauren dragged his sight from Halion and looked at the man in white, standing beside him. Next to him was another man with broad shoulders and a thick jaw. He was an Arakesh by the looks of him, but he didn't have the red cloth around his eyes, only the blades on his back.

Off to the side, Rorsarsh gorged himself on a large piece of meat, his appetite unaffected by the smell of blood and piss. Emperor Faro was nowhere to be seen, he noted.

"*You* must be The White Owl I keep hearing about." The man in flowing, white robes flashed a confident smile his way. "I applaud your skill young warrior, for not just anyone can slay an Arakesh, let alone three." The man swept his robes behind his back and slowly walked behind Halion. "This must come as a bit of a surprise, I'm sure. You were expecting to take this palace and reset the order of things in Karath, nay the entire Arid Lands." There was a note of respect in his tone, if a hint of mockery. "Where are my manners? My name is Alidyr Yalathanil, this is Ro Dosarn, your brother's personal torturer, and of course I'm sure you know Supreme Commander Rorsarsh over there."

Tauren wanted to respond to the elf, but his rage kept his lips sealed and his muscles tensed.

"Run..." Halion strained against his bonds. "Run..."

"Will that be all, Father?" The familiar voice came from behind Tauren, in the doorway.

The White Owl swivelled round to see Argo standing perfectly at ease. How had he approached Tauren without being heard?

"Thank you Argo," Alidyr replied. "Find the others and kill them all."

Argo nodded and removed his helmet, only to replace it with a strip of red cloth across his eyes. Tauren felt his knees go weak at the revelation. An Arakesh had walked freely through the orphanage, telling them what they wanted to hear via secrets gained from Halion's bloody lips. The entire plan was unravelling before him and there was nothing he could do to stop it.

The House of Owls was going to fall.

The elf in white lost his smile. "Unlike my kin across The Adean, I have borne witness to the rise and fall of your various kingdoms over the last millennium. I have seen firsthand the treachery and deceit your kind are capable of. I was there when King Gal Tion, the first of his name, rallied mankind and forced the elves out of Illian. I was there when he declared war on the dragons. I was there when his most trusted turned *against* him. You might say I have a unique insight into humanity." Alidyr pulled Halion's head back by his thick hair. "I know a rat when I see one..."

226

"You will die for this!" Tauren replied through gritted teeth.

Alidyr gave a short laugh. "It has been a long time since I entertained the thought of my death. I see no reason why I should consider it today."

Rorsarsh finally stopped eating. "Your rebellion is at an end, little owl. The New Dawn will rule these lands for all time!"

Tauren's hand twitched and one of the throwing knives took flight. The blade found its end deep inside the Supreme Commander's throat. He gargled and dropped to his knees with fresh blood pouring from his mouth. The fat man's face quickly turned red, then purple before he finally collapsed on the floor, dead.

"Well that saves me a job," Ro Dosarn commented.

Tauren let fly his second blade with another casual throw, aimed to strike the assassin in the head. At the last moment, Alidyr stepped in and amazingly caught the knife mid-throw, inches from Ro's face. Elven speed was a wonder to watch, if terrifying.

Alidyr examined the small blade. "You have but this one chance to live, and maybe even save your brother's life. Lead the Karathan forces and put your skills to good use. The Darkakin *are* coming through those gates; at least this way you will maintain a measure of control and keep your city from being reduced to ash under their heel." Before The White Owl could respond, Alidyr spoke again. "Take a care, Tauren son-of-none. Your next words might well be your last."

Tauren looked at Halion, bloody and battered with tears cut lines across his swollen cheeks. Even now, his owls were being hunted down inside the palace and slaughtered by the assassins. Should he take the offer and save Halion's life at least? He didn't care about his own life, but he couldn't bear to see his brother lose another drop of blood.

The thought of giving up now was crippling, however. Tauren had been fighting for as long as he could remember and not just for the sake of fighting, like so many did on the streets. He had been fighting for a cause greater than himself, or any of the owls for that matter. It was a cause even greater than his adoptive brother.

With one hand concealed behind his dark cloak, Tauren gripped the coiled rope and felt for the four-pronged hook. He wanted to say something, anything that would leave them with a lasting impression of the atrocities Tauren would unleash upon them when next they met, or at least assure Halion that he would return to save him. But Salim's teachings were ever present in his mind, and warned him of such foolishness. His best chance of escape was over the open balcony, to his left.

Giving no indication, Tauren dashed to his left, his cape blowing out behind him. That was when the shadowed figure stepped out of the darkness. Had he been standing there the entire time? How had Tauren not noticed his presence? He had no time to ponder on the questions however, as a whip, which appeared to glow from within its strands, lashed out. The three prongs at the head of the whip caught The White Owl across the mask and sent him flying across the room. The helmet had been cracked from jaw to head and even cut Tauren above the eye. How could a whip cause so much damage?

The shadowy figure stepped into the light and Tauren saw the face that would surely be the death of him. It was another elf, like Alidyr, but bald and very pale, with intricate tattoos arching over his head. His armour was black and gold with similar glyphs to his tattoos, worked into the plating. This had to be Nakir Galvörd.

"You have been an irritation for some time." Nakir coiled his whip and replaced it on his hip. "I hear you have been trained by an Honour Guard..." The elf looked back to Halion, the source of his knowledge. "It was *I* who created the Honour Guard, centuries ago, to protect my interests. My teachings and techniques have been passed down through the ages to keep the emperors safe. What good is a puppet if its strings are cut?" Nakir turned his back on Tauren and walked away. "Let us see what you have learned, *White Owl*."

Tauren placed his hands either side of his head and flipped back onto his feet. The owl mask was broken but he could still see clearly.

More than anything he wanted to head-butt the elf so that the jagged metal might cut into his pale skin. Salim's teachings and words of wisdom abandoned him now. Tauren could only see red.

The White Owl launched into an attack that would confuse, disarm and defeat any soldier in the army. But Nakir was no soldier. He was an elf that had been fighting in wars before The Arid Lands had even been named so.

Nakir moved with the grace of a cat and the supernatural speed of a Basilisk. Their arms and fists connected in a series of blows that was hard to follow, but every attack of Tauren's was either blocked, pushed aside or used against him. Eventually, Nakir pulled Tauren into him and rammed his pale head into the owl mask, before landing a simple punch to his sternum. The combination of blows sent Tauren flying across the room once more. Somehow, Tauren had come off worse from being hit in the head, and was forced to blink several times to correct his vision.

"Your technique shows promise," Nakir's raspy voice commented. "But you haven't been forced to give your all for some time. I suppose killing slavers and running into the occasional patrol doesn't offer much challenge."

Tauren managed to stand up and stretch his back until it cracked. Defeating Nakir wasn't an option right now; he had been surprised and caught off guard. If he was ever to challenge the elf it would need to be on a field of his choosing. The balcony was on the other side of Nakir and it was still his best chance at escape. Alidyr and Ro Dosarn continued to stand by Halion and watch them fight. Had they chosen to get involved, Tauren would have been dead by now.

Relying on his anger to grant him one last burst of energy, Tauren ran at the elf and jumped at the last second to bring his foot up into Nakir's jaw. The elf easily stepped aside and pushed Tauren's foot away, before following up with another series of punches and elbows that forced The White Owl into the wall. Tauren slid to the floor and spat blood into his mask. One of his ribs was definitely broken, as his armour did nothing to soften Nakir's blows.

For all the pain he was actually in, Tauren played heavily on his suffering and made it appear worse than it was. He slowly crawled on all fours and groaned as he attempted to stand, adding in a stumble to his performance.

Nakir laughed. "I'm not sure you could even stand up against an Honour Guard. How you defeated three Arakesh is beyond me."

Tauren sucked in a breath, aware that his next actions would cause considerable pain. Using his cloak to conceal his hands, Tauren quietly removed a blade from his waist as he rose into a crouch. His hand flew out, stretching his chest and pulling at his broken rib, while releasing the blade in Nakir's direction. As expected, the elf caught the knife before it could plunge into his neck, but that had not been the point of the attack. Tauren dashed to the left again and dived cleanly over the railing with his grapple already in hand.

The White Owl allowed himself to fall to the next floor down before throwing the grapple over a smaller, curved balcony. The hook snagged and became taut, but Tauren's injuries proved too much, and his grip loosened under the sharp pinch from his ribs. His halted fall prevented him from breaking anything, after dropping down another floor and landing awkwardly on the next balcony. He was just thankful the state rooms had been built with symmetry.

It took everything he had to climb fully over the railing and onto the balcony floor. He was now two floors below Halion and the elves, but still inside a palace filled with Arakesh. As painful as it was, Tauren drew in a long breath and blew into the curved horn. He could only hope that it carried enough to warn any who had yet to be set upon by the Arakesh.

Tauren tried not to think about Halion, and instead thought of how he would escape the palace. If he could survive this, there was still a chance that he could return and save his brother.

If he could escape...

Tauren ran through the lavish hallways with abandon, all attempts at stealth forgotten. Clashing swords rang out, echoing off the hard walls, along with the sound of his owls crying out in defeat.

The House of Owls was well trained, but they were no match for the Arakesh. The White Owl blew into the horn again and again in hopes of signalling his friends.

Leaving the slave hallways behind, Tauren headed deeper into the palace until he came across a grand staircase. Warriors of his house fought for their lives against the assassins, who pushed them back down the stairs, away from the double doors that led further into the palace. The three Arakesh, one of which was Argo, were all dressed in the garb of Karathan soldiers, but they had replaced their helmets with strips of red cloth.

"Run!" Tauren screamed as he jumped onto the stairwell, attacking the assassins from behind.

The distraction saved the life of a young female owl, who was helped to her feet by the others. They looked at Tauren for guidance but he only screamed at them to run away again. Hesitantly, the group rallied around the injured female warrior and retreated back to the gardens.

The three blind assassins lunged for Tauren as one, working together in harmony. Despite using the weapons of the guards, and not their usual twin blades, the Arakesh fought with grace and deadly precision. Tauren was forced to ignore the pain in his ribs and evade the multitude of strikes that aimed to remove his limbs. The White Owl threw small knives here and there, but the acute senses of the assassins always prevailed, allowing them to easily dodge the flying blades.

A misstep on the stairs put Tauren in the path of a roundhouse kick that connected with his already broken mask. The young fighter went spinning across the landing with a mouthful of blood.

The pain made him angry.

He stood up, all pain forgotten, and swiftly removed the two short-swords concealed upside down on his back. Two lunging moves put the assassins on a retreating foot, but their balance on the stairs was impeccable, and the three killers batted aside his attacks and slowly circled him.

How long could he really keep this up?

Tauren was already injured and outnumbered, and who knew how long it would be before one of the elves showed up to finish him off? It didn't matter, he told himself. He only needed to give the owls more time to escape.

"Tauren!" Braigo came charging into the foyer at the bottom of the staircase with six owls, all armed with bows.

Six *twangs* unleashed the barrage of arrows at the assassins, who either cut the projectiles down or evaded the tips. For Tauren it was his best opening. The White Owl lashed out with both swords and took out the legs of one while bringing the weapons up and into another's chest. The Arakesh who had been cut to his knees succumbed to the next barrage of arrows, leaving only one; Argo. Tauren pulled free his swords from between the plates of armour and watched the bloodied body collapse at the survivor's feet.

"Surrender..." Tauren rasped.

Argo slowly turned his head. "Where you were taught to surrender, I was taught to survive."

The treacherous Arakesh leapt from halfway up the staircase with his sword held high. Braigo and the owls braced themselves and even managed to hit the assassin with two arrows as he descended. Tauren half leapt, half ran down the stairs, but the assassin was already amongst them, cutting through the owls with trained ease. By the time Tauren was within striking distance, Argo had cut through the group and killed four of the seven warriors. The White Owl attacked Argo with a flurry of swordplay, each attack designed to push the assassin back, away from the others.

It made little difference.

Even with two arrows in his shoulder and leg, Argo slipped past Tauren and plunged his sword into Braigo's stomach.

"NO!" Tauren cried, his shock holding him in place as his oldest friend received a mortal wound.

Before he could counter-attack, Argo spun around and kicked

Braigo into Tauren, driving them both to the floor. The surviving owls retrieved their bows and forced Argo to flee through a side door.

"Braigo..." Tauren held his friend in his arms as blood spilled onto the floor. "Quickly," he ordered the owls, "take him! We need to retreat!"

The owls picked Braigo up and dragged him out into the gardens. Tauren blew again and again into his horn and looked around frantically, searching for any more assassins in the shadows. He quickly followed behind the trailing Braigo and looked on in horror as his friend's blood streaked the floor.

They had failed. *He* had failed...

PART THREE

CHAPTER 19
ANTI-MAGIC

Gideon looked on in wonder when the morning sun filled the small clearing and caught the blade of the ancient Dragorn sword. Mournblade's pommel, the sleek head of a dragon, glittered and shimmered in the light. The mage had never been interested in swords, always relying on his magic or the strength of his staff, but something about this blade called to him. He had sat on the soft grass for most of the last two days, simply marvelling at it while his leg got better.

It had been a relatively lonely time, as Galanör often retreated to the higher perches of the floating boulders, and Adriel had avoided them entirely. It was easily done considering the size of Dragons' Reach. Oddly, Gideon had noted more the absence of Ilargo. The green dragon had been injured, saving him from Malliath's rampage, but he was confident the young dragon would heal quickly. That particular confidence came from the fact that Gideon's own injury, in exactly the same place, had already healed.

Before he could truly consider the implications of that connection, Galanör walked into the clearing. The elf had deliberately made some noise to announce his arrival, as he was more than capable of

237

creeping up on Gideon. It was a consideration the elf would have once foregone.

"Why do you continue to stare at that thing?" Galanör asked.

"I honestly don't know. There's magic bound to it... as a mage I suppose I'm naturally drawn to magical items. Isn't it the same with your kind?" Gideon remained on the ground with his legs crossed.

"I can feel it," Galanör admitted, eyeing the sword. "It's from a time before either of ours. Not that I wouldn't like to give it a try." Galanör fixed his grip around the red hilt and pulled. The sword didn't even wobble in the stone.

Gideon quietly chuckled to himself. "I told you about the spell Galandavax placed over it..."

"Just making sure I'm not a Dragorn," Galanör said with jest. "Have you not tried it?"

"The sword? Why would I? I'm not even an elf, let alone a Dragorn!" Gideon had wanted to, but found his attention entirely stolen by its mere appearance.

"Well come on then," Galanör bade, wiggling his arm on the hilt. "What else is there to do?" There was a bitter tone to his question.

Gideon sighed and stood up to face the sword. Its red and gold hilt was of the finest craftsmanship and incredibly cool to the touch. One by one his fingers wrapped around the grip and the magic contained within ran up his arm, promising great power. The mage adjusted his grip at the last second and pulled with all his strength.

Nothing happened.

"I told you it was pointless." Gideon released the sword.

Galanör waved the notion away. "What would you do with a sword anyway? You're as likely to stab yourself as anyone else." The elf laughed, though it was clear he was trying to goad Gideon.

"You want to test your blade against my staff?" Gideon retrieved the staff from his back and mentally commanded it to grow to its full length.

"I feel obliged to remind you that I *choose* to fight with swords. I am still an elf, of four hundred years no less, and therefore still your better in the magical arts."

"Prove it..." Gideon replied with a cocky smile, before running at the elf.

"Don't say I didn't warn you." Galanör began to slowly pull his swords free of their scabbards when a blinding light formed between them, followed by a concussive force strong enough to launch the pair in opposite directions.

When Gideon opened his eyes again he was flat on his back at the foot of the rock containing Mournblade. Galanör was in a similar position on the other side of the clearing, with his chestnut hair covering his angular face. Both of their weapons had been lost in the tumble and now lay at Adriel's bare feet, by the edge of the clearing.

"If you must use your time this way, please do it *elsewhere*." Adriel looked at Mournblade as if it were a religious relic.

"Apologies, Adriel." Gideon stood up and brushed the grass off his trousers.

Adriel watched Galanör rise from the ground. "Your actions against Malliath could have cost not only your life, but that of Gideon's, Ilargo or any of the other dragons keeping watch."

"Keeping watch?" Galanör spat back. "He doesn't need watching Adriel, he needs unleashing! He's got a thousand years of rage trapped inside him. Let him take us to Malaysai and rid the world of the Darkakin once and for all."

"I grow tired of this discussion, Galanör." Adriel moved further into the clearing. "Rage may be something our people now embrace, but it is not the way of the dragons. He will –"

The sun was momentarily blotted out by the descending shadow of Galandavax. His gargantuan size wouldn't fit inside the clearing and so he continued to hover above the trees. Adriel looked up at his companion and appeared lost in thought for a time.

"A scout party of Darkakin have made it past the Sandstalkers," Adriel explained. "I must leave with Galandavax and deal with it."

"Take us with you!" Galanör shouted over the beating of Galandavax's heavy wings.

Adriel looked back at his elven kin with a doubtful eye. "I think it better if you stay here."

"You don't want us to fight here... let us fight out there," Galanör countered, picking up his fallen blades.

Before Adriel could reply, Ilargo came bounding out from between the trees, previously hidden from view. The green dragon roared and met Adriel's questioning gaze with brilliant blue eyes.

Adriel's confusion quickly turned to curiosity. "It seems Ilargo wishes to take you, Gideon."

The sound of Galandavax's wings was the only noise to fill the clearing, as all eyes fell on Gideon, who continued to stare at Ilargo in surprise. The green dragon didn't wait for Adriel to speak, as he did not require the elf's permission, and bowed one of his strong legs and dipped his left wing, exposing his spine. Gideon felt all control abandon him, when he walked over and used Ilargo's wing as if it were a step, and climbed onto his back.

Adriel remained silent, gazing upon them from a distance. His expression was unreadable to Gideon, who struggled to find a comfortable place between Ilargo's spikes. A short roar from Galandavax reminded everyone that action was required. The great ebony dragon dipped his hovering body just enough to allow his powerful tail to drop into the clearing. Adriel moved with centuries of experience and caught a hold on the dragon's thick scales, quickly ascending the tail with the speed and natural grace of a cat, until he found his position at the base of Galandavax's neck.

Gideon's neck craned and his mouth fell open as he observed Adriel. The elf was incredibly comfortable at such a height, and the mage could only wish for such dexterity.

"Wait!" Galanör shouted over Galandavax's wings. "What about me?"

Ilargo exhaled a sharp sigh through his nostrils and dipped his wing again. Galanör cautiously approached the young dragon, his eyes flitting from Ilargo's big blue ones to the space available behind Gideon. Another sharp sigh told the elf to get a move on; the dragon was clearly eager to find the Darkakin scouts. The mage offered his hand but wasn't surprised when Galanör hopped onto the dragon's back with irritating ease.

"I hate this part..." Gideon swallowed hard, remembering his first sickening flight holding onto Malliath's tail and then again in the claws of Rainael after she saved them from the Sandstalkers.

Before Galanör could reply, Ilargo shot into the air as an arrow from a bow. The ground dropped away and the tops of the trees quickly became pinpoints in the distance. Gideon lost sight of the clearing and only caught a glimpse of the lake and waterfall in the heart of the Reach, when Ilargo banked sharply to the right and headed for the surrounding wall of The Red Mountains.

The mountains lay sprawled across the horizon, concealing The Flat Wastes that sat wedged between Dragons' Reach and Malaysai. Gideon looked down briefly but felt his stomach rising into his mouth and turned away. Galanör, on the other hand, appeared completely at ease with their soaring height. Indeed, it was the first time the mage had seen him genuinely smile in many days.

In line with the horizon, Gideon could see Galandavax gliding on the air currents alongside Rainael, whose pale green scales glittered in the desert sunlight as if she were nothing more than a mirage. After a few minutes of flight, the mountains began to open up to flatter ground and sparse trees that offered little shade. Gideon recognised the valley where Galanör and he had been set upon by the Sandstalkers. That day would forever be imprinted on his mind.

Ilargo bowed forward allowing a better view of what they were heading towards. Gideon and Galanör adjusted their grip on the spikes and peered into the bright distance.

"I can't see anything!" Gideon bellowed over the howling wind in his ears.

"It's a Darkakin scouting party," Galanör replied, closer to his ear. "Thirty or so by my eyes!"

Twenty-eight, actually...

Gideon heard the number in his head and had to fight the dizzying wave that threatened to steal his conscious mind. The voice had not been his own, but that of a younger man, a teenager perhaps. The mage blinked his confusion away and kept the dizzying moment to himself. He couldn't explain what was happening to him, but he knew now wasn't the time to examine it.

Galandavax and Rainael dropped into a dive, tucking their wings into their body, and plummeting towards the ground with unbelievable speed.

"Oh no..." Gideon knew what was coming. "No, no, no, no –"

"Hold tight!" Galanör shouted, anticipating the same thing.

Gideon couldn't help but shout at the top of his lungs when Ilargo dropped out of the sky like a stone discarded from the heavens. The mage's howl only faded when he could no longer draw enough air to make a sound. The ground rushed up to meet them and the Darkakin finally took shape against the desert sand. A dozen of them were riding giant lizards while the others walked along the sides. The group bristled with spears and other pointed weapons that had been specially crafted to inflict maximum damage from every angle.

At the last possible second of their dive, Galandavax and Rainael extended their wings and flew over the top of the scouting party, breathing a line of fire either side of the caravan. The Darkakin howled and leapt about to avoid the great beasts, while throwing spears into the air. The projectiles might as well have been moving through treacle when measured against the speed of the dragons.

Ilargo's wings fanned out, dramatically slowing their descent, until the dragon's strong legs were able to take the impact as they set down at the head of the caravan. A jet of fire exploded from Ilargo's mouth and consumed the lead lizard and its rider, reducing them both to cinders. Gideon and Galanör were quick to jump off the dragon's back and retrieve their weapons, ready to battle the Darkakin. Ilargo didn't remain grounded, but instead took off again, pausing only to dip and pick up another lizard with its rider still in the saddle.

"Watch out!" Gideon warned, shoving Galanör aside.

The two dived in opposite directions, narrowly avoiding another torrent of fire expelled from Galandavax's burning throat. The flames incinerated at least ten of the Darkakin and injured many more. Galanör was back on his feet in a blur of motion, with smoke rising off his burnt cloak. Through the fiery haze, the mage caught sight of the giant lizard that Ilargo had picked up. The hulking creature tumbled out of the sky and flattened a distant group of Darkakin, who had been readying their spears to attack Rainael.

Perhaps it was the heat that made Gideon think of something cold, but the first spell he unleashed upon the nearest Darkakin froze him mid-run, until his limbs shattered from the momentum. Galanör was already leaping over lines of fire and running into the fray, eager to take his frustration out on the Darkakin. Gideon moved to join him, watching as the elf's swords shone in the desert sun before they cut through the violent savages.

A giant lizard ran in front of the mage in a desperate attempt to flee the soaring dragons, who continued to drop out of the sky, talons first. In the wake of the fleeing beast, two Darkakin appeared, as if from nowhere, with their serrated blades and spiked clubs swinging at Gideon. The young mage deftly swatted the attacks aside with his staff and countered with a swift hit and a concussive spell. The chaos of the fire, smoke and clouds of sand had Gideon instinctively running to Galanör's side, leaving the Darkakin to roll about the ground in semi-consciousness.

Somehow, without looking, Gideon became aware that Ilargo had landed behind him and finished the two savages off. The mage was sure he could taste their blood in his mouth and actually feel the dragon's talons sink into their flesh. He scrunched his eyes tight and shook the feeling off.

As Galandavax glided overhead, Adriel slipped off his neck and dropped to the ground from a bone-breaking height. The elf however, tucked into a roll and came up without so much as a scratch. The ancient Dragorn was soon at Galanör's side, though he used no weapon to beat back the attacking Darkakin. Using a form of hand-to-hand combat Gideon had never seen before, Adriel twisted their arms and legs, breaking bones and crushing nerve clusters with the tips of his fingers. The elf could wield an open palm as well as a closed one and deliver just as much damage, if not more. Gideon also noticed that the elf never took a life on his journey to Galanör's side.

The young mage forced himself to concentrate on his immediate surroundings. Chaos continued to rule their environment, with the dragons dropping out of the sky and raining fire down upon the Darkakin. The sounds of screams and clashing steel mixed with the yelps of giant lizards and roaring dragons. Gideon added to the clamour and unleashed devastating spells in a bid to keep the scouting party from overwhelming them.

Through the fumes and smoke, Gideon caught sight of one particular Darkakin in the distance. He was running for one of the few remaining lizards in the centre of the fray, ignoring the dragons and the elves.

Gideon immediately felt as if something was wrong.

The Darkakin pulled free a spear from the lizard's saddle and tore the black canvas from the weapon's head. A jagged piece of green crystal adorned the end of the spear, fastened to the wood with leather straps.

Everything stopped.

The sound of the fire and screams disappeared, along with the roar of the dragons. Gideon felt panic rising inside him and knew the feeling originated from Ilargo, not himself. The Darkakin marched into the middle of the chaos and planted the spear into the ground so that the Crissalith pointed to the sky. Adriel's cry was piercing as they watched all three dragons fall from the ocean of blue sky. It was a strange sight to see creatures who flew with such finesse, drop out of the sky with no more grace than a lifeless rock.

Rainael reached out with all four of her claws and managed to ensnare Ilargo, shielding him before their combined bulk hammered the desert. The younger, green dragon rolled out of his mother's embrace and lay limp under the relentless sun.

Everyone had to run from Galandavax's mighty girth.

The ebony dragon had been flying at a higher altitude and hit the ground in front of the scouts. His thick scales kicked up plumes of sand and broken rock as he skidded towards them with considerable speed.

Adriel performed an exceptional feat of magical strength and pushed both of his arms out towards Galandavax. The dragon's momentum gradually slowed down, but not before he buried three Darkakin, who had been too slow to get out of the way. Gideon looked at Adriel with awe, wondering if he would ever be able to muster the magical strength to stop a fully grown dragon with his staff.

Rainael stirred to the left of the group, catching Gideon's eye. His stomach dropped. In all the chaos, they had taken their eyes off the Darkakin wielding the Crissalith. The savage was now standing over Ilargo with the jagged crystal aimed to plunge into the dragon's chest. Both dragons appeared disorientated and looked to be in pain, groaning and struggling to find their footing. They were powerless in the presence of the crystal.

Gideon levelled his staff at the Darkakin, but he was too slow; the savage warrior thrust the spear of anti-magic down at the dragon, but Ilargo found the last of his strength and lifted his front leg, taking the impalement there in place of his heart.

Gideon released his explosive spell and sent the Darkakin careering into the distance. The mage, however, barely noticed the savage's death. His arm had erupted in burning pain, forcing him to let go of his staff and drop to his knees in agony. Pulling the leather sleeve back on his left arm, he stared in disbelief at the elongated hole in his forearm; warm blood streaked down his elbow and soaked his shirt.

Galanör skidded to Gideon's side and joined him on his knees.

The elf gripped both ends of the mage's forearm and examined the wound intently, while Adriel ran by them to reach Ilargo. As the dragon cried out in pain, so too did Gideon. He could feel the healing magic that Galanör was already pouring into him, but the wound refused to knit back together.

"I don't understand..." Galanör stated exasperated.

"Your magic will not work as it should in the presence of the Crissalith." Adriel was trying to navigate Ilargo's thrashing. In one fluid movement, the ancient elf put one foot on the dragon's leg and pulled the spear clean from the wound.

Again, Ilargo and Gideon cried out in unison. Galanör looked upon the green crystal with cautious reverence, as Adriel jogged over to the nearest lizard and tied the spear to its saddle. A quick slap to the hide sent the giant beast running back into The Flat Wastes.

Rainael was the first to recover and find her feet, so that she could once again tower over the bipeds. Galandavax stood up and shook his massive head as if he were trying to correct his vision, while his impressive wing-span flexed into the air, ridding him of the sand.

"Ilargo..." Gideon ignored Galanör's attempts at nursing and ran over to the green dragon with his arm cradled close to his chest.

Ilargo remained on his back and allowed Adriel to examine the wound. The elf turned the thick leg this way and that, but the mage didn't know what he was looking for. Perhaps Adriel was acquainted with dragon physiology?

"I can't see any traces of the Crissalith inside," Adriel stated.

The elf looked from the wound to Rainael and stepped away from Ilargo as his mother dipped her regal head. The breath that she exhaled appeared wavy, like that of the desert heat on the horizon, only this breath was profound in its purpose. The bone healed first, followed by vessels and then strands of muscle and tendon covered it from sight. The skin knitted back together and two dull, green scales grew into place, standing out next to Ilargo's shiny and gold-speckled armour.

"Your arm..." Galanör lifted Gideon's injured arm and marvelled at the new skin and obvious lack of a wound.

Once again, everyone was staring at Gideon. The mage quickly covered his arm and tried to look anywhere but at Adriel, whose inquisitive gaze felt piercing. Galandavax gave a short roar and dipped his head to look upon Gideon more closely. The ebony dragon looked at Adriel and snorted a jet of warm air over the group. What conversation had taken place between them remained a mystery.

"Most curious..." Adriel whispered. "But we must return to Dragons' Reach. This scouting party won't be reporting anything. We'll send out some patrols into the outlying areas around The Red Mountains tonight. We will discuss this further in the safety of the Reach." Adriel looked at Ilargo with concerned eyes. "It would be better if Ilargo flew home unencumbered. Rainael has offered to take you."

Gideon didn't know at what point the queen of the dragons had made such an offer, but it was preferable to walking through the desert. The mighty green dragon took two strides towards them and stood as still as a statue.

"How do we..?" Gideon wasn't sure how to climb onto her back since Rainael refused to dip.

Adriel smiled. "Rainael the emerald star is the queen of dragonkind. You do not get to sit on her back."

Before either man or elf could protest, the magnificent dragon took off from the ground, picking both of them up between her claws.

It wasn't long after they returned to the safety of Dragons' Reach that Adriel caught up with them by the lake, in the centre of the crater. Ilargo walked tentatively by the edge of the water, testing the strength in his healed leg, while Galandavax ascended one of the floating boulders and relaxed, allowing his long tail to hang over the lip. Rainael stood proud before Gideon and Galanör, making it clear that they weren't to stray until Adriel had finished speaking to them.

"Is this the first time you have shared an injury with Ilargo?" Adriel asked pointedly.

Gideon hesitated under the questioning. "No. I hurt my leg when Malliath fought with him. But it healed within a day."

"What else have you shared?" Adriel asked.

Gideon looked to Galanör for support, but the elf appeared just as interested in the answer as Adriel.

"I've heard, I *think* I've heard some... thoughts?" Gideon turned his statement into a question as he felt completely out of his depth.

"Anything else?" Adriel continued.

Gideon thought of the pull he had felt to Mournblade, but he wasn't sure how it could be connected to the strange events of today. His expression betrayed him however, and Adriel could see that there was something else.

"I've never used a sword in battle but..." Gideon wasn't sure how to explain it. "But I am drawn to Mournblade more and more."

Adriel glanced at Rainael for just a moment. "Have you tried to pull it from the stone?" the elf asked, casually.

"Yes, but nothing happened."

Adriel looked away and slowly paced the shoreline, his expression unreadable. A light breeze blew his blond hair and robes out behind him, carrying a sweet scent to Gideon's nose. The elf turned on his heel and met Rainael's vibrant blue eyes as if she had spoken to him.

Adriel asked, "When Malliath was on Korkanath, did you ever experience such connections?"

Gideon thought about it for a moment. "No. Never. I would remember something like this. The first time I heard Ilargo I thought I was going to pass out."

Again, Adriel and Rainael locked eyes and a moment of silence passed between them. Without warning, the green dragon bowed her head until her mouth was only a foot away from Gideon's face.

He could smell the blood and flesh of the giant lizards she had torn apart in the desert, and he changed his breathing to use only his mouth.

"Stay very still..." Adriel warned, sounding alarm bells in Gideon's head.

Rainael inhaled a deep breath, so deep that Gideon feared his skin would be pulled from his face. The dragon exhaled softly and returned to her regal posture without incident.

"There's no elf blood in you," Adriel explained. "If there was any elf in your ancestry, Rainael would know."

"Wait. Are you saying what I think you're saying?" Galanör stepped forward, scrutinising Gideon with new eyes.

Gideon took in every detail of Adriel's silent reply and still couldn't read his expression. Galanör on the other hand appeared to have got stuck somewhere between shock and awe.

"What?" Gideon pleaded.

"You're..." Galanör couldn't find the words. "You're a..."

"Dragorn, Gideon," Adriel said softly. "You are the first human Dragorn."

Gideon's mouth attempted to ask a thousand questions at once, but instead he mustered only stunned silence. Ilargo walked through the shallows and came to stand by his mother on the bank, his beautiful eyes fixed on Gideon.

"I'm not an elf," he finally managed. "Only elves can be Dragorn."

"Only elves have ever *been* Dragorn," Adriel replied with the hint of a smile. "There is an important difference."

"Wait." Galanör held up his hands. "The first human Ilargo ever meets and he happens to be a Dragorn? I don't believe it."

"You are not required to believe it," Adriel said in his usual calm voice. "It is very likely that many humans would qualify to become Dragorn, given the chance. They scuppered that opportunity themselves, however, when Gal Tion went to war with the dragons." The elf looked over the mage as if examining his essence. "Gideon is a relatively empathic person, making him susceptible to a dragon's form of communication, and he's a mage – a magical being by human standards."

Gideon was completely bemused. "I'm a…"

Dragorn!

The familiar voice rang clear in his mind and he knew instantly that it was Ilargo. Once again, the presence inside his mind threatened to rob him of consciousness. Galanör quickly caught him by the arm and steadied him with strong hands.

"Easy," Adriel bade, closing the gap between them in a second. "Much training is required to master even the basics of being a Dragorn."

The elves took Gideon by the arms and helped him to a nearby log, where the mage was convinced he was going to be sick.

"Can you *train* a human?" Galanör asked sceptically.

"It has never been done before." Adriel stood back from Gideon, taking him in. "But that doesn't mean it cannot be done."

It took Gideon a minute to realise the area around the lake and the floating boulders had suddenly filled with dragons of every colour and description. They were all looking at him. What began in the back of his mind as a collection of whispers quickly grew into a chorus of new voices that filled every space in his head, until he could no longer think of a single word himself. The edges of his vision blurred and soon turned to elliptical shadows, masking the details of the world.

"Ilargo..!" Adriel's cry was distant despite his close proximity.

Gideon felt the world gently slip away under the weight of so many voices and memories, which were not his own, pressing into his mind. Another moment and there was only darkness.

CHAPTER 20
EVER SOUTHWARD

Nathaniel stared in wonder at the Centaurs as they prepared the companions' horses for their journey. The older Centaurs combed their manes and sang soft melodies to them, while the younger, smaller Centaurs combed their coats. The saddles and various belongings were adjusted to make it as comfortable as possible for the horses. Indeed, they had paid more attention to their rides than the humans.

The same could not be said of their attention to the elves.

The Centaurs had practically worshipped Reyna and Faylen during their time in the camp. The young knight couldn't blame them either; the elves were certainly captivating. As if their knowledge and wisdom wasn't fascinating enough, their very presence held a magical aura.

With everyone prepared and ready to travel, the group waited at the edge of the camp with all eyes on Faylen's hut. Asher emerged first, looking as fierce as ever with his new double-handed sword adorning his belt. Combined with the short swords on his back and the Arakesh bow attached to his quiver, Nathaniel was thankful to be the ranger's ally and not his enemy. Asher held the leather strips aside to allow Faylen to walk out into the sunshine, closely followed by Reyna and the much taller Xastus.

Nathaniel ran a critical eye over Faylen and was elated to see that she'd recovered well. The care, as well as the medicinal herbs, from the Centaurs had brought the elf back from a sleep from which the knight had feared she might never wake. Asher's proximity to Faylen didn't go unnoticed either, as well as the concern on his usually expressionless face.

Faylen turned to Xastus and the gathering Centaurs. "Thank you for your hospitality. Without your healing I would not be standing before you." The elf took Xastus's hands in her own and squeezed affectionately.

"It has been an honour to receive the El'shenae," Xastus replied warmly. "My ancestors passed down the stories of your great race, and the fruitful times you brought to The Moonlit Plains. We only hope that the El'shenae will return for good."

Oh they're returning alright, Nathaniel thought sarcastically.

"We have sent word to the other tribes," Xastus continued. "You will have no trouble on your journey to The Arid Lands."

"You have the eternal gratitude of the El'shenae." Faylen bowed her head. "But it will not be necessary. I have one crystal left with enough power inside to reach Karath."

Asher stepped into her view with the same concern etched across his scarred face as Reyna. "Are you mad?"

"You have only just recovered from the first portal," Reyna added with a softer tone.

Faylen raised a hand to silence any more protests. "Time is not our ally. We must reach Karath, resupply and journey to Nightfall before Paldora's Star graces daylight sky."

Nathaniel recognised the quote from the Echoes of Fate, as well as the comet's connection with ominous calamity. Despite aspects of the prophecy proving true, the knight couldn't believe that a phenomenon that had only ever been witnessed at night could be reversed.

Xastus towered over the group. "I would find another route to your journey's end. Smoke rises from the southern cities; war has claimed those lands..."

"Our time in the desert must be as short as possible," Asher explained. "Travelling from Karath is our only chance. If we forego civilisation and take the eastern road to Nightfall, we will be exposed to the harsher elements of The Arid Lands."

"We will go to Karath," Faylen continued. "I will have us there in but a few steps." The elf moved in front of the rangers and removed a crystal from her belt.

Hadavad and Atharia broke free of the group and approached Faylen. The old mage rested a hand on her shoulder.

"You have our strength this time," Hadavad offered.

"And mine." Reyna hurried over and placed a hand on Faylen's free shoulder.

Faylen flashed a curt smile and nodded her head, a hint of resignation on her face. Nathaniel guessed the elf wasn't entirely back to health.

Reyna turned to the Centaurs. "Thank you for your hospitality, Xastus. The generosity of your people will not be forgotten by the El'shenae... or the humans."

Xastus bowed his head. "Until our paths cross again, Princess..."

Faylen threw the crystal and opened another portal, large enough to fit the riders and their mounts. Nathaniel covered his eyes when the portal sparked to life, but he took note of the large, red gem that slipped out of Hadavad's tunic. The gem glowed a brilliant ruby red as he offered Faylen his magical strength.

"Ride!" Asher shouted, encouraging the rangers to make for the portal before the magic was drained.

～

Tauren awoke with a start and sharp pains in his ribs. Having succumbed to his injuries and fatigue, he had fallen asleep sometime around dawn. The son-of-none was sitting, curled up, on top of a roof in the heart of Karath. His leather armour and black cloak were covered in splatters of blood, and he knew there wasn't enough of it that belonged to the Arakesh. The owl mask lay at his side, broken and bent out of shape after taking a beating from Nakir. A jagged line cut through the mask from above the left eye, down to the right cheek. Tentatively, he touched his face and felt the identical cut that would forever scar his features. Tauren couldn't bring himself to look at the mask, for the shame threatened to consume him.

The White Owl cautiously shifted his position and felt everything ache. Taking a punch from an elf was not something he could ever have prepared for. Tauren groaned, as if he were an old man rising from his chair, and stood up to take in the city. Karath should be weeping for its loss. The House of Owls had fallen in a single night. The few who stood for freedom and a better way of living had been cut down in the night like animals.

And yet the city went on...

Tauren looked around at the streets below with confusion and heartbreak marring his face. The markets were in full swing with fresh produce and goods being sold as if it were any other day. Further down the street he could hear slaves being sold openly for the first time in months. Karathans walked the streets with their slaves in tow, fearing no reprisals from the owls.

He had been tricked by the elves, by Argo. Tauren felt his rage rising to the surface at the thought of the treacherous assassin. He took a moment to think of all the things he would do to the Arakesh if he ever saw him again. Those bloody images only led him to think about Halion. What tortures was he being exposed to today, if he was even still alive? There was a very good chance the elves had killed his brother by now.

He had to find out and, if he could, rescue him...

The blood on his hands caught his attention and shifted his focus. The blood belonged to Braigo. His brother from the streets had been stabbed by Argo only feet away from him, and yet he had been powerless to stop him. Tauren had failed in so many ways.

Looking out over the rooftops, Tauren focused on the buildings to the south. Before he did anything else, his only course of action should be to see who had survived the night's massacre.

To see if Braigo yet lived...

The White Owl stopped before leaping the gap between the buildings, and looked back at the mask on the floor. He sighed through the pain and bent low to pick it up. The empty eyes of the mask that had become his identity looked back at him. There was nothing in it anymore. The mask no longer filled him with confidence and strength, but only served to remind him of his blind arrogance and worthless rage. As The White Owl he had achieved nothing the elves couldn't undo by the next new moon. Tauren could hear Salim's calming words of patience and he didn't have the strength to shut them out.

Tauren released the mask and turned away, not even bothering to watch it tumble across the rooftop. He was done with it. Instead, he used the breathing techniques Salim had taught him and launched himself across the gap, between the buildings. The pain in his ribs and the ache in his muscles were almost overpowering, but he pushed on, never slowing or giving himself a moment to rest.

At last he found the rooftop he was looking for. At the top of the three storey building, canvases were stretched between poles to provide shelter from the sun. Dozens of owls sat around in the shade, nursing each other's wounds. Tauren felt only shame when he leapt the final gap and landed amongst those he had failed. To his surprise, the men and women he had come to consider family embraced him and thanked the gods that he was still alive. He felt many hands clasp his shoulders and grip his armour in affection. He didn't deserve it. That feeling was compounded when the group dispersed and Tauren saw Braigo for the first time.

"You're late..." Braigo rasped.

Tauren hurried to his brother's side and dropped to one knee, so that he might better take the measure of his wounds. He was sickly in colour and clammy to the touch. His pale skin was cold but sticky with sweat and Tauren could smell the blood. Pulling back the blanket, the son-of-none could see the mortal wound that spelled Braigo's fate. A sword through the belly was a slow death, painful too. It wasn't befitting of a man who had given his best years to fighting for others.

"I had to be sure I wasn't followed," Tauren explained.

He couldn't look Braigo in the eyes for any length of time without finding his own filling with tears. This wasn't how it should have ended. Right now they were supposed to be announcing to the city that the old ways had come to an end. There would be freedom for all with a new and fair hierarchy to rule over The Arid Lands.

"Pesky assassins..." Braigo attempted to laugh but his face contorted into agony.

"Save your strength," Tauren pleaded.

"I sent some of the others to check on Mother Madakii and the children," Braigo spluttered.

Tauren felt more shame overwhelm him. He hadn't thought to check on the woman who saved him from the streets and put a roof over his head. Again, more proof that he wasn't fit to lead the House of Owls. Being trained how to fight by an honour guard wasn't enough to qualify him for the role.

"What became... of Halion?" Braigo asked.

Tauren dabbed the sweat on his brother's forehead. "He was discovered by the *elves*." Tauren couldn't help the venom in his tone. "The assassins tortured him for information."

"Animals..." Braigo scrunched his eyes and strained his neck in pain.

Tauren looked around and did a quick head-count. There were so few left. How many lives had been lost because of his plan? It would take time to calculate that number and learn who had never made it to the rendezvous.

"There are more inside," Braigo explained, following Tauren's gaze. "And more should be arriving from Tregaran later..." The sentence went unfinished as his pain intensified.

"Rest," Tauren ordered.

"What will you do now?" Braigo finally managed.

"I must find a way to free Halion, if he still lives." Tauren looked back out at the city and saw the palace that dominated the cityscape.

"No..." Braigo replied. "Halion has given his life to this cause, as so many others have. The Darkakin are still *coming*. Syla's Gate must not be opened." Braigo's expression of horror focused Tauren. "If the House of Owls does nothing, this city... will fall," he continued, fighting through his pain. "After Karath is theirs, The Arid Lands will fall next, and from there Illian will be..." Again, the pain was too much.

Tauren looked at his dying brother and saw everything he should have been. Braigo saw past the horrors that lay in store for Karath and looked to help the entire realm. How could Tauren continue without him? Without Halion?

Braigo used what little strength he had and gripped Tauren's leather armour. "You must hold the gate, brother." His bloodshot eyes filled with tears. "Take whoever is willing and hold that gate..."

Braigo's eyes appeared to look through Tauren, who could only wait for a breath that never came. The son-of-none shook his oldest friend and called his name with a fool's hope. Only Braigo's glazed expression remained. Tauren fell into his brother's chest and wept for his loss. When his despair gave into denial he thumped Braigo's chest with anger, commanding him to wake up. Through his pleas, the other owls crowded around him and laid their hands on Tauren's shoulders. They offered their strength and shared the grief, relieving Tauren of his anger.

"You were the best of us." Tauren gently closed Braigo's eyes and let his hand fall onto his brother's chest.

The White Owl lost track of time, sitting on the edge of the rooftop, watching the world go by beneath his dangling feet. The others had taken Braigo's body inside and called for Mother Madakii.

257

If she was inside with him now, Tauren didn't know. He looked up and stared out at The Undying Mountains to the south. Syla's Gate was only the size of his thumb from here.

The sun was kissing the horizon when Tauren felt a hand on his shoulder. Mother Madakii looked down at him with red-rimmed eyes and an expression of deep sorrow. She wept for every one of them, not just Braigo. The Mother stepped aside to reveal the crowded roof. He had been so lost in thought that he had shut himself off from his surroundings and missed their arrival.

"There are more downstairs," Mother Madakii explained. Bowing her head, she whispered, "They have come to hear *you*."

Tauren slowly stood up and glanced at the sea of faces before him. He knew them all. At some point or another they had all sparred with him and received one-on-one training. There were so many faces he couldn't see and the thought nearly crippled him.

"I..." He didn't know what to say.

For the first time since he had started this crusade, Tauren had no words of encouragement. The flame that ignited his rage was gone. That rage had driven him ever onwards for as long as he could remember, guiding him and keeping him strong. Now it had brought only grief. Braigo's last words had echoed in his mind for hours, accompanied with the image of his last breath.

"Our brothers and sisters have been taken from us," Tauren began. "I have failed you all." He held up a hand to cut short their protests. "An ancient evil has taken a hold of this city... but something *worse* is coming." Tauren glanced at Syla's Gate. "Any day now, an army of Darkakin will march on those gates and sweep through this city like a plague. Slavery will become a way of life for everyone, not just those of us in the south, but everywhere. The northern kingdoms don't even know they're coming. The line must be drawn *here*."

Tauren looked at Mother Madakii and felt his heart break knowing what his proposal would do to her. She had already lost so many of them over the years and now he was going to march to a

certain death, maybe taking the rest of the owls with him. She would
have to mourn them all before the end.

Mother Madakii lightly gripped his forearm. "You don't have to
fight..."

Her alternative would be to run and hide. Illian was a big place
after all. The Mother didn't care about honour, or doing the right
thing; she just wanted them to live.

"I've been fighting to survive since I was born," Tauren replied
lightly, taking her hand in his own. "Now I'm fighting for everyone
else." The White Owl turned back to the crowd. "I am going to those
gates. I will hold them for as long as I can. I won't ask any of you to
join me."

As one, the entire crowd stepped forward and the sound of feet
rhythmically stamping on floorboards resounded from the floor
below. Their courage and loyalty brought tears to his eyes, but he
held onto them.

"We are with you." It was Kali who spoke on everyone's behalf.

The dark haired warrior was a capable fighter and had proven
herself a leader time and time again. Braigo had always spoken
highly of her. Tauren knew he could rely on her as he had his brother.

The White Owl nodded his approval and appreciation. "Kali, find
our best runners and have them get word across the city to any who
will listen. Karath must be ready to flee should we fail to hold the
gate. We leave at high moon."

"Tauren! Tauren!" The call came from the adjacent roof, where
two owls could be seen running towards them.

The crowd made space for the runners to leap onto their roof.
They were exhausted and desperate for breath, but their look of
dread and despair had Tauren searching the cityscape for assassins.

"Brothers..." The White Owl crouched by their side.

"The palace!" the first exclaimed.

"Halion..." the other whispered.

Tauren's eyes filled with tears when he understood the expressions on their faces. Without a word he jumped between the build-

ings and ran for the heart of Karath. His feet pounded relentlessly against the dusty rooftops, drowning out the sound of the city below. The son-of-none didn't stop until he found himself panting for breath opposite the palace slave markets.

He dropped to his knees at the sight.

There were other owls behind him, but he hadn't noticed them following him. They were all just as stunned by the sight of Halion, hanging from one of the lower balconies with his hands and feet bound. His body was just as beaten and broken as Tauren remembered, with streaks of blood dripping to his toes.

Tauren didn't have enough energy to feel rage. He had lost Braigo and so many owls... now Halion was gone. So many thoughts rushed through his head, but the numbness that overtook him could not be penetrated. The gravity of what had happened, of the loss, was slow to sink in. Tauren's stomach flipped when he thought of Salim, Halion's father. Exiled from these lands, Salim would never know of his son's fate, and yet Tauren felt a responsibility to tell him. But he hadn't seen his old mentor for years and wouldn't even know where to start searching for him.

"Look..." Kali gazed down at the base of the palace.

Tauren followed her sight and found a group of Karathan soldiers huddled within the grounds, staring up at Halion's lifeless body. Looking around, the son-of-none discovered more soldiers outside the grounds, forsaking their duties and simply staring at Halion.

"Kali," Tauren called without taking his eyes off Halion. "Have word find its way into their ranks." A single tear reached his lips, leaving a salty taste in his mouth. "Let the soldiers know that Syla's Gate has been manned once again."

"Is that wise, Tauren?"

"Halion spent years convincing his men of our cause. We will see the strength of their mettle." The son-of-none knew he should get up and make straight for Syla's Gate, but he couldn't tear himself away. He would have to keep looking at Halion until he believed it was real...

Nathaniel stood at the top of the rise, with his hands resting on his sword belt, as he looked out on The Arid Lands. Karath, the capital in the south, sat on the horizon, its high walls too small to hide the rising smoke in the moonlight. War had certainly plagued the city, though Nathaniel found the war to be a worthy one. Slaves fighting for the right to live under the Illian sky as free people was a battle he would have gladly joined, had he still been a fully fledged Graycoat.

It seemed life outside of that vocation was just as dangerous, if not more so. The knight gripped his sword tight at the thought of entering Nightfall's dark halls, not to mention the pit.

"First time in the desert?" Asher came from nowhere, as he always did.

Nathaniel tried not to show his alarm. "I've had the misfortune of visiting The Arid Lands several times, actually. There are monsters a plenty in these parts."

The ranger sighed and inspected the walls of Karath. "It's the monsters inside the city that bother me."

"So shouldn't we be finding a way in now, then? While it's dark."

The lightest of smiles pulled at Asher's lips. "You're still thinking like a knight. You're not wearing that coat anymore. If we approach Karath's gate at night, we'll have arrows raining down on our heads before we state our business. We wait until day; everyone is less suspicious under a blue sky. Besides, Faylen will need the night to recover."

Nathaniel trusted the ranger's expertise in the matter. As a student of Nightfall, Asher had come to understand the way people think and especially their perceptions, since these were the very things he had to manipulate. In some ways, the knight felt sorry for the older man, having lived so long with such an outlook.

"How is she faring?" Nathaniel asked.

"The spell was less taxing, thanks to Hadavad and the others, but she still needs to rest. Surviving on the other side of those walls isn't easy..."

"You were an assassin of Nightfall; can't you just sneak in?" Nathaniel asked with a jesting tone.

"Oh *I* could sneak in, sure," Asher replied, playing along. "But sneaking nine more people in is beyond my skill. I kill monsters these days, I'm not a magician."

Nathaniel chuckled. "I'm sure even the Magikar of Korkanath couldn't figure out how to sneak Doran Heavybelly into Karath."

Both men shared a laugh and continued to stare at the forbidding city under the dome of stars above. In the quiet that followed, Nathaniel found some of his curiosities rising to the surface.

"You having real friends in the world aside, and we will circle back to that, what's the truth behind Hadavad? I can't believe he's as old as his tales would claim."

Asher was massaging his index finger, where Paldora's gem had once sat. "Why not? I'm over a thousand years old."

"And I wouldn't have believed *that* had there not been an explanation," Nathaniel countered. "He certainly looks old, just not five hundred years old."

"I've learned not to ask. Hadavad is very guarded."

Nathaniel inspected Asher's features and was sure he could see a crack in the ranger's usually impenetrable expressions. "What are you not saying?"

"You have nothing to worry about, Nathaniel. Hadavad's motivations have always been virtuous, more so than any other I've met."

"I understand them all in some way, but there's too much mystery surrounding him. Almost as much as there was around you. Have you seen the gem around his neck? The ruby one? It's like no crystal I've ever come across."

"I've seen the gem," was Asher's only reply.

Nathaniel sighed, resigned to the fact that the ranger would give nothing more away.

After another moment of silence, Asher spoke without ever

taking his eyes off Karath. "When I first met Hadavad, I was still an Arakesh. I was young then, hunting one of my earliest targets in Kelp Town."

"Did he appear as old as he does now?" Nathaniel asked.

"It wasn't his age that I found so striking, though he was certainly younger." Asher turned to the knight. "It was the colour of his skin."

It took Nathaniel another moment to truly understand what Asher was trying to say. "He was... somebody else?"

"He *looked* like somebody else." The ranger waved his hand. "Like I said; I've learned not to ask."

The sound of Doran's armour preceded his stout appearance. "Are ye two requirin' a moment, or are ye joinin' us for an ale and a tale?" The dwarf laughed deep in his belly, as he always did, and trotted off back to the group.

Asher placed a heavy hand on Nathaniel's shoulder. "I can provide the ale if you can provide a tale."

Nathaniel smiled, happy to see a lighter side to Asher, a side the other rangers appeared to force out of him. "Life as a Graycoat never leaves one without a tale or two." The two began to walk back to the group. "I'm still not satisfied with your answers."

"Neither am I..." the ranger casually replied, leaving the knight to ponder on the mystery that was Hadavad.

Nathaniel found camping with the rangers to be far more enjoyable than when it had simply been the four of them. The fire was bigger, the laughs came from the belly and the food was better. Doran was very particular about his meat and the way it had to be cooked, while Hadavad and Atharia ensured the fire never died.

They were awash in the glow of the moon and enjoying each other's company for most of the night. Faylen was wrapped in blankets and sat close to the fire, under the watchful eye of Asher. Nathaniel smiled, with a full stomach, and watched Reyna beside him as she examined her bow. The knight had noticed the princess inspecting Adellum's magical bow several times since she had taken ownership. He knew the elf was loath to wield a weapon that had been used to kill so many. It was just another reason he was so drawn to her.

"Asher..." Salim announced in the firelight. "It has been too long since I tested my skills against a worthy opponent. It would be an honour."

Doran's head swivelled round in offence. "He sparred with me not five days ago..." he spat.

Asher stifled his laugh and looked over Faylen with a critical eye, but the elf nodded him on and even offered a brief smile.

"The honour would be mine, Salim," Asher replied curtly.

Glaide shuffled over and sat next to Nathaniel and Reyna by the tree. His dark, bald head reflected the firelight.

"You're in for a treat," Glaide said in hushed tones.

"I saw Asher in the battle of West Fellion," Nathaniel explained. "He held back hundreds of Arakesh..."

"That was battle, war, survival even," Glaide continued. "This will be closer to a dance. Art in its own way, really. The honour guards of Karath might be the only warriors in Illian that can match an Arakesh."

Nathaniel took offence and gave the ranger a hard stare.

"No offence intended," Glaide smiled warmly. "The Graycoats are a force to be reckoned with, but they are peacekeepers. Your training is too broad and diplomatic. Honour guards are trained to attack and kill with swift efficiency, like that of an assassin; only they use those skills to protect their emperor."

The ranger's explanation didn't completely redeem him, but Nathaniel's interest was certainly piqued. He turned his attention to Salim as he removed his sword from its scabbard and tossed the sheath aside. The blade was thin and of moderate length, but the guard was black and sloped down toward his hand, providing cover from stray blows that might relieve him of any fingers. The southerner stood very still and waited for Asher.

The old ranger removed his cloak and left the short silvyr and magical blades with Faylen. His new double-handed sword made a satisfying sound when it came free of its scabbard. Asher stood as still as Salim with his sword-tip resting on the ground.

Nathaniel looked around the camp and noted everyone's attention was on the two fighters. He was sure that Doran and Bale were placing bets between themselves. Even Reyna put down her bow and watched closely.

The two warriors lunged at each other at exactly the same moment. Their clash of swords was momentary and brief, as both danced around the other with feigning attacks and stances designed to put the other off. Salim's sword worked more like that of a spear, jabbing and thrusting, forcing Asher to evade or push the weapon away. In the blink of an eye, Salim was inside Asher's arm and brought his elbow to bear. The ranger was knocked backwards with enough force to take him off his feet, but at the last second Asher turned it into a roll and came back up with his sword ready.

"Not used to the weight..." Asher grunted, hefting his new sword.

"I believe it is identical to your old one," Salim countered with a sly smile.

After a couple of twirls to get a feel for the blade, Asher lunged forward and executed a series of moves that Nathaniel found hard to follow. Luckily for Asher, so did Salim. The old honour guard dashed about with incredible reflexes, but it wasn't enough to hold off the ex-assassin. Asher performed an intricate spin of his sword, while locked against Salim's, and sent the smaller blade flying into the air. The ranger held his sword at Salim's throat for just a moment before stepping away, allowing the southerner to catch his sword before it hit the ground.

Glaide chuckled to himself. "I never get tired of watching those two fight. I once had the pleasure of rooting out a nest of Hydras with them both, many years ago now. They fight each other with incredible skill, but *together* they are a force to be reckoned with."

Nathaniel felt jealous in that moment and he didn't know exactly why. He had fought alongside Asher many times now and considered them to be quite the pair. It was a silly and petty thing to feel a qualm over. Nathaniel hadn't known Asher nearly as long as any of the rangers, especially Glaide, yet he felt the bond between them was stronger.

The knight turned to Glaide. "How is it you and Asher came to know one another?"

Glaide looked down at his chest with a furrowed brow. "He stopped me from doing something foolish..." The ranger looked into the roaring fire and stroked his white moustache. "In your days as a Graycoat, did you ever come across a Vorska?"

Nathaniel had indeed come across the wretches, but only during his training and with a more experienced Graycoat by his side. Unlike most of the monsters that lurked in the shadows, Vorska had the ability to appear human at night. Their true, hideous, form was only revealed in the light of day, forcing them to live in caves on the outskirts of towns or cities. After the sun had set they would hunt their prey openly, in the very streets in which they lived. The worst aspect of the Vorska was their wicked tongue; designed to suck out their victims' blood and leave behind a toxin that transformed the victim into a new Vorska, adding to their clan.

"As a student, I helped to track one down in Dunwich," Nathaniel explained. "Very elusive and extremely hard to catch at night."

"The real trick is finding one and tracking it back to the nest." Glaide rested his head against the tree. "Before I turned to this life I was a tailor; I know it's hard to believe. I had my own shop in Bleak."

Nathaniel was already feeling sorry for him. Nobody wanted to live in Bleak. The town fell within the reach of the cursed land of The Ice Vales, just north of Elethiah and not too far from The Wild Moores. The people who lived there were constantly under threat of being attacked by Outlanders from the Moores.

"I had a beautiful wife and two gorgeous girls..." Glaide took a moment to chew over his next words. "Two Vorska followed them back from the market and... left them in an alley. By the time I found them my wife was already succumbing to their venom. I killed her myself."

Nathaniel felt Reyna's hand squeeze his knee and he looked at her to find fresh tears in her eyes. It was because of stories like this that he became a Graycoat.

"My rage drove me to madness. It was the kind of rage that can only end in self-destruction." Glaide looked over to Asher, who was still fighting Salim. "That's when he found me. Asher had been tracking them as well, and he found the cave before I did, thankfully. I was about to enter their lair and die taking as many as I could. Could you imagine how well that would have gone? I'd have been dead in seconds."

"How did he stop you?" Reyna asked.

"The same way he stops everything. He hit me really hard!" Glaide laughed to himself. "When I woke up he convinced me that there was a better way to kill monsters like that. He took the time to teach me and show me a few of his tricks."

"What happened to the Vorska?" Nathaniel asked.

"We killed them all, together. It took some time and some planning but when we returned to that cave..." Glaide had a faraway look on his face. "I put my rage away and embraced a new life." There was a pause before the ranger spoke again. "You should ask Doran how he came to be in Asher's debt. Now there's a story!"

The fighters came to an abrupt stop with Salim down on one knee and Asher standing over him with his broadsword pointing down at the southerner's head.

"Ha!" Doran yelled into the night. "I told ye he'd get tha' better o' him! Pay up laddy." The dwarf held his hand out to Bale, who begrudgingly dropped four coins into it.

Glaide cleared his throat and pointed at the fighters, drawing the group's attention to Salim's sword, which was currently angled up towards Asher's chest. The barbarian snatched the coins back from the dwarf with a smug grin.

"Bah! Always ruinin' me fun!" Doran shot at Glaide.

Glaide laughed, along with the mages and even Asher. Nathaniel didn't quite believe that Asher had drawn with Salim, especially after seeing him fight at West Fellion. The knight kept the thought to himself, not wanting to insult Salim, however.

The two fighters embraced forearms and complimented the other's talents. Asher was quick to return to the fire and check on Faylen, who had watched silently from within her blanket. Nathaniel looked from the pair to Reyna with a questioning look, but the princess could only offer a shrug in response. The knight was about to comment how odd they were together, before a moment of introspection warned him of being a hypocrite.

"We should rest now." Hadavad was standing at the edge of the light, leaning on his staff. "Evil stirs in the south." His vision was fixed on the darkness, towards Syla's Gate. "Our journey to Nightfall will not be easy."

Nathaniel looked at Reyna and hated the fact that they were knowingly walking into danger. They would all have to fight for their lives before any of this was over.

CHAPTER 21

AN APPROACHING STORM

U nder an ocean of stars, the elven king walked up and down the beach of The Opal Coast. Between the moonlight and the torches planted in the sand, Elym was able to survey his fleet of ships, currently under construction. Therö of house Velanii had been overseeing the work taking place day and night to ensure the ships were ready for the invasion. The larger pieces of wood, which made up the framework, were lifted from the ground with magic and put into place, to be secured with manual labour afterwards.

Up and down the shore, Elym's keen ears heard the sound of orders being given and received in perfect harmony. With their strength and magical talents, the elves could have themselves an entire fleet in weeks. Normally, that thought would have been cause for celebration, but Elym couldn't even bring himself to smile. His days had been filled with dark thoughts and crippling doubt since Faylen had revealed the truth about Valanis.

The original plan had been simple, in his mind. Reyna was to act as an ambassador and retrieve valuable information about the king-doms of men, while Galanör and his companions broke Malliath free

269

from Korkanath. Allied with the dragon, Elym could finally unlock the secrets of Mount Garganafan and breed an army of dragons to invade Illian. This would have greatly reduced any fatalities in the elven army. They were to start by taking Velia, on Illian's eastern coast, and attack outwards from there.

Valanis was supposed to be trapped in the Amber Spell in Elethiah. From there, he could be easily destroyed for good, ridding all of Verda of his threat. The timing of everything was still suspicious to the king. It fuelled his doubt day and night, haunting his dreams and robbing him of sleep. For forty years Valanis had been free and no doubt scheming to spread his twisted evil across the entire realm.

It couldn't be a coincidence that the elves had been planning to invade Illian for that exact amount of time. Members of his own council had put those thoughts of invasion in his mind and convinced him it was the right thing to do. A council that had been loyal for a thousand years!

If the worst was true, then Elym, and the entire elven nation, was playing into Valanis's plans. But what could Valanis gain from having the elves take back Illian? Did he want the destruction of mankind? To what end? Humanity would be far easier for the dark elf to conquer than the elves. Perhaps he merely wished for chaos to rule over the land, as it had during The Dark War.

Trying to understand Valanis was a fruitless exercise. The dark elf was notoriously mad, having always claimed that he could *hear* the gods.

He didn't even want to think about Reyna. Even though she had only been in his life for a fraction of his time on Verda's earth, his daughter had made quite the impression. Creating any offspring had been his way of showing that he too was making efforts to rebuild their society, as Adilandra and he had taken much criticism over the centuries for not practising what they preached. In truth, Elym had cared little whether it was a boy or girl, prince or princess – for that was all they could ever be. As an immortal he could rule for ever, and he intended to.

It was only in their absence, both Reyna and Adilandra, that the king had felt the sting. He missed them and he hated it. There wasn't time for these *feelings*. An entire country had to be invaded, a race of people defeated and a mad elf dealt with. That thought only served to make him think of where Reyna was right now.

Elym focused solely on an elf in the distance, hammering on a metal bar, by the orange glow of a forge. After a moment, it sharpened his mind and brought him back to the present. High Guardian Varö was by his side, dressed in full armour and cloak. The warrior gave his king a concerned look, no doubt having noticed his attention wander during Therö's tour of the beach.

The patriarch of the Velanii house stepped into view. "My Lord..."

Elym realised he had been asked a question but he knew not a word of it.

To save his king embarrassment, Varö gripped the hilt of his sword and stepped forward. "How many can they hold?" the elf asked.

Elym's attention was split as he heard the sound of boots breaking through the treeline, beyond the beach. A warrior, whose name escaped him, sprinted across the soft sand in full armour without a hint of exertion. She stopped in front of the group and bowed before whispering into Varö's ear. There was always a hierarchy to observe.

The High Guardian ignored Therö's inquisitive expression and moved closer to his king. "Tai'garn has made contact," he whispered.

Elym nodded and swiftly turned to Therö. "Continue the hard work Therö and bring honour to the house of Velanii."

Therö bowed deeply, but the king was already in the process of throwing a crystal into the air. The magic-imbued stone exploded in a brilliant flash, before leaving behind a black vortex lined with miniature bolts of lightning. Elym strode through the portal and into his palace, closely followed by Varö.

PHILIP C. QUAINTRELL

"The fleet will be ready soon," Varö commented.

Elym wanted to reply with a suggestion that it wasn't fast enough, until that sparked a thought he couldn't ignore. "Could that be his intention?" the king asked out loud.

"My Lord?"

"Valanis..." Elym couldn't quite put the pieces together. "If you wanted chaos, if you wanted two sides to go to war..." The king thought of his daughter. "You're my greatest tactician, Varö. Think as if you were Valanis."

"That would be a dangerous thing, my Lord," Varö quipped.

"He has my daughter attacked with the intention of killing her. But why? He risks revealing himself and the Hand. But what if he hoped that such an attack would enrage the elves of Ayda and press us into invasion before we are ready? We forego the dragons and years of further planning and just attack Illian in retribution."

"You think we aren't ready," Varö stated.

"I'm trying to think a step ahead of an enemy who has been plotting against us for forty years," Elym replied. "Perhaps Valanis thinks that mankind can defeat us if we attack prematurely."

"That would be another reason to have Princess Reyna assassinated," Varö theorised. "Without her information we do not know mankind's true power."

"But what could he possibly gain from any outcome?" Elym was struggling to keep his regal composure. "Valanis may have control of the Arakesh, but their force isn't nearly large enough to take on mankind or ourselves..."

They were missing something vital and it was driving Elym mad. Valanis had yet to reveal his real play in all of this and the king knew it would prove costly.

"Perhaps Tai'garn's presence in Illian will prove valuable." Varö gestured to the double doors.

Elym bowed his head, acknowledging the High Guardian's subtle suggestion. The king entered the room that couldn't be penetrated by any other's magic, ensuring its privacy. With both hands, Elym gripped the diviner in the centre of the room and allowed his consciousness to be pulled into the ether. Sitting in front of the king was the ghost-like image of his oldest advisor and most powerful elder.

"My Lord…" Tai'garn bowed his head.

"You have reached Illian's shores?" Elym was in no mood for pleasantries.

"We are on the edge of a town called Darkwell," Tai'garn explained. "We will gather any supplies there and make for The Evermoore, until we reach Vangarth."

"Make all haste, Tai'garn. I do not think they will stay in the town for much longer." Elym wanted to order Tai'garn to discover as much information as he could while in their ancient land, but he *needed* Reyna to be safe. "Contact me again when you have news."

"Of course."

"Tai'garn, should you hear anything else during your time amongst the humans, inform me immediately. There is more going on than we are aware of, of that I am sure."

Tai'garn bowed. "My Lord…" His ethereal image faded, like smoke in the wind, leaving King Elym to his doubts.

Tai'garn replaced the diviner in his satchel and picked up his staff. He returned to the group, who, in his absence, had been keeping an eye on Darkwell in the distance. Without a word, the elves donned their dark cloaks and hoods and made for the town under the cover of night.

In Tai'garn's eyes, Darkwell wasn't too dissimilar to the earlier towns built by the humans, before the elves left for Ayda. They were certainly bigger and used a great deal more stone than wood, as they had a thousand years ago. There were no structures big enough to rival anything in Elandril however, but Tai'garn silently applauded the humans for their towers and roads.

The five elves crossed the stone bridge and into the streets of Darkwell under much scrutiny. The town appeared to be guarded by an unusual number of soldiers. Their shields and cloaks bore the lion sigil of Namdhor, showing their allegiance to King Merkaris of Orith. The guards watched their every step and slowly walked along the bank to follow the elves into the town. Once they reached the streets, all five elves split up, taking the alleys and different streets to confuse the guards.

In seconds, Tai'garn was on the roof of a nearby house and watching, as the soldiers conversed in furious dialogue before splitting up. They would never find the elves.

"They seem awfully suspicious of visitors..." Ezeric commented.

The lean elf was crouched behind Tai'garn on the sloped roof, his approach as silent as the dead. Using his fingers to speak the silent language, known to all elven warriors, Ezeric signalled for Alwyn and Nalmar, on the other side of the road, to meet them further down the street.

"Where is Hela?" Tai'garn thought about the elf's predilection for violence and began to worry.

Ezeric joined him in his search of the torch-lit streets below. There was a chance Hela had foregone hiding and decided to just kill the soldiers. It wasn't the entrance Tai'garn had in mind.

Thankfully, the red-headed elf stepped out of the shadows and met the group outside a closed butcher's shop. Tai'garn gave her an expressionless look that reminded Hela who was in charge and that violence was not permitted... yet.

Tai'garn wasn't sure yet how he felt about the idea of killing humans. So far he had followed his king's orders and gone along with the invasion plan, but there was still a part of him that remembered how elves used to be. In Tai'garn's mind, he could still see his people a thousand years ago as clearly as he saw them now. They could birth entire forests with their songs and enjoy the delights of nature day and night. Now they were just efficient killers. In truth,

Tai'garn had hoped that, after this new war, the elven nation might return to how they had been.

But at what price..? he thought.

"Why are we sneaking around?" Nalmar asked. "I thought we had the king's authority to announce ourselves as ambassadors."

"It would make things quicker," Alwyn commented.

Tai'garn replied, "We will play that card when it best suits us. For now we will blend in and learn what we can." The elder checked the streets for any more guards. "We should find shelter for now and gather supplies in the morning."

The elves stuck together and moved through the streets of Darkwell in search of an inn. At this time of night the town was quiet and dimly-lit, making it easier to find the taverns. Tai'garn followed Ezeric's lead until they came across a selection of taverns that inhabited the centre of the town, surrounding a large oval-shaped building. These streets were alive with laughter and merriment, as men and women fell out of doorways and staggered into the streets with drinks in hand.

The elves took a moment to observe the patrons through the windows of the various taverns.

"Soldiers?" Hela asked.

Tai'garn used his sharp elven eyes to go over every detail of the men and women dressed in the same long coat. They had identical weapons and they certainly moved like soldiers – at least the ones who weren't intoxicated did. Without any warning, the door swung open and the group sank into the shadows as two men wearing normal attire exited the tavern.

"Damn Graycoats!" the larger of the men exclaimed. "I can't believe King Merkaris has given them refuge here."

"There won't be any ale left in the whole damn town at this rate!" the slighter man replied.

"Well they've already taken over the theatre." The larger man gestured to the oval building in the middle of town.

The two grumpy men walked off into the night and the elves

returned to the window. Tai'garn had heard of these Graycoats from the reports over the last forty years. Their purpose was noble, but their namesake was nothing but a murderer in Tai'garn's eyes.

"These are the greatest warriors in Illian?" Hela asked, critically.

"Among the best," Tai'garn replied. "But do not underestimate the humans, in battle or otherwise."

More of the Graycoats stumbled out of the door, taking no notice of the elves.

"How they defeated the dragons I'll never know," Alwyn commented.

Tai'garn pulled his hood a little closer, feeling the lightest of rain drops. "When given a common cause, humans are capable of a great many things."

Tai'garn had watched their kind emerge from The Wild Moores and build kingdoms. They had mastered speech and even made their own. These mud dwellers and Outlanders had conquered architecture, poetry, art and even magic. Sadly, they had perfected warfare. This particular trait had been used against the noble dragons with terrifying results. Tai'garn had left Illian just after their war began, but the stories of war machines and other such evil contraptions had found Ayda.

"Are we to stay here?" Ezeric asked, incredulously.

"Indeed we are." Tai'garn turned to Alwyn. "I would take advantage of your light feet. Find a way inside that theatre and learn all that you can. Join us later."

Alwyn nodded once and disappeared into the shadows of the alleyway without protest. As an elder on the council, it had been a long time since Tai'garn had heard any protest his word.

Organising rooms to stay in had been relatively easy. A lie here and an extra coin there kept the questions at bay, but the stench of the place could not be bribed away. Humans had a distinctive smell at the best of times, but squashed together, drunk, in a tavern, added new aromas the elves found hard to stand. When they reached their sparse rooms on the top floor, Tai'garn found the other three elves whispering among themselves.

"Something perplexes you all?" the elder asked.

The elves hesitated, but Ezeric answered on their behalf. "We've just never seen..." The elf made a gesture with an open hand over his strong jaw.

Tai'garn chuckled. "You've never seen a beard!"

"A what?" Nalmar scrunched his face at the word.

"Human males can grow hair on their face," he explained with an amused smile.

"I thought that was just in stories." Ezeric appeared disgusted at the thought.

"I *liked* it..." Hela added, coyly.

The night went on for a couple of hours before Alwyn returned from his private errand. The elf removed his sodden cloak and balanced himself on the window sill. Tai'garn had noted, on their journey across The Adean, the young warrior was never content to sit normally, or stay still for any length of time for that matter.

"What news do you bring?" the elder inquired.

"Graycoats from all over Illian are coming here. Their leader, Lord Marshal Horvarth, is inside the theatre. They have taken over every room behind the stage, as well as many of the local inns. Apparently, the king of Orith has offered them sanctuary for a time. There were many talking about the events that led to their current state."

"Did they mention the princess or the ranger?" Tai'garn asked, urgently.

"Only in the context of the battle," Alwyn quickly replied. "They don't seem to know about their presence in Vangarth from what I could gather. But the Lord Marshal appears to have been in recent contact with the king of Velia, judging by his conversation with his second-in-command."

This changed everything. Though Tai'garn had struggled with his faith, it was hard not to believe that the gods were guiding them.

They had arrived in a town with potential sources of information that could not be ignored.

"I'm never getting this smell out of my clothes," Hela commented with disdain and the agreement of her companions.

Tai'garn ignored the interruption and fell back into deep thought. The presence of the Graycoats didn't offer any problems, but he wondered if they could be used to gain any advantage. If the Lord Marshal had been in touch with King Rengar of Velia, there might be valuable information to garner. The kings in these lands would no doubt have their spies, and it stood to reason that Rengar would be searching for Princess Reyna, as they were.

Alwyn swept his wet hair over his head. "Did any of you see the man behind the bar? He had hair on his *face!*"

Tai'garn allowed the others their laughter before interrupting. "I'm afraid rest will have to wait." The elder thought of his king's urgency. "I would speak with this Lord Marshal and gather what details there are to have."

The elder could see the protest marring their elegant features, but no words escaped their lips. His word was final and born of experience gained from a lifetime longer than all of their ages combined.

The five elves made their way back through the streets of Darkwell, their identities concealed by their extensive hoods. The town was somewhat quieter now, with many of the taverns closing for the night. Even with their cloaks and hoods, Tai'garn was aware that the group stood out. The way they carried themselves was simply different and, though subtle, it was detectable.

"Which part of exiled did you not understand?" a voice bellowed from inside the theatre.

The elves came to an abrupt stop outside the double doors, moments before they burst open and a man tumbled to the ground. The man slipped in the mud and stumbled to his feet with a glazed expression. He was older by human standards, with a white moustache and unkempt hair to match.

"Fennick..." The man said the name as if it were dirt. "You always were a little slow to the words finding your ears." The older man wiped mud from his face and adjusted the sword on his belt, which hung between a scruffy, long coat and mismatched armour.

"Kaleb Jordain..." A younger man, though not by much, walked out of the theatre in typical Graycoat attire. "I suppose a man who couldn't learn to keep it in his pants could never learn when to keep his words in his mouth!"

The wide-set Graycoat was quickly followed by a small mob of knights, each appearing eager to lay into the older man. Seeing them all together, Tai'garn noticed the similarities between the mob and Kaleb Jordain. Despite the intrigue behind the event, the elder did not have time for it.

"Darius," Fennick called to a knight with blond hair and hard jaw. "See to it that Kaleb here is *escorted* from the town and sent on his merry way. Go piss your life away someplace else, you drunk!"

Tai'garn stepped forward and his elven companions moved with him. Without a breeze, their cloaks hung over them as shrouds, concealing most of their weapons, as well as their heritage.

Fennick looked from one face to the next, bemused. "This is Graycoat business. On your way."

Tai'garn removed his hood and the others followed suit. "I am High Elder Tai'garn, of the elven council to King Elym Sevari. I would speak with your Lord Marshal."

The mob were stunned into silence, none daring to move under the elf's gaze. It was not surprise at seeing an elf however - the difference subtle but observable to Tai'garn's keen eyes. These men had seen elves before, just not so many. Kaleb Jordain simply rolled his head, stretching his neck and blinking hard.

"Then perhaps you had better come in," a voice replied from inside the doorway. A man strode out with an air of command about him. "I am Lord Marshal Horvarth."

"We have much to discuss and very little time, Lord Marshal. We are searching for Princess Reyna, who I believe you have already met."

Horvarth hesitated, clearly wanting the discussion to take place inside. "Yes, I have had the pleasure of meeting your princess. Indeed her actions at West Fellion saved many lives. Perhaps we should go inside, away from prying eyes..." The Lord Marshal glanced at Kaleb Jordain.

If it sped things along, the elder was happy to accompany the Graycoat.

"I know where she is..." the dishevelled knight announced.

All eyes fell on him, with Horvarth swivelling on his heel to face the drunk. "Ned," he glanced at the wide-set Fennick, "if he utters another poisonous word you have my permission to run him through."

Tai'garn raised his hand to halt the sword already being drawn from Fennick's scabbard. "If this man has knowledge I seek then I would hear him out."

"He is drunk, my Lord," Horvarth came to stand between elf and man. "He would say whatever he must to find a warm bed and shelter for the night."

The drunk straightened his back. "They were in Vangarth."

Kaleb's words arrested Tai'garn's immediate attention. This was knowledge passed on to King Elym by Faylen Haldör herself. The elven elder moved past Horvarth and faced the apparently disgraced knight.

"From there they travelled into the heart of The Evermoore, to Lirian."

"How do you know this?" Tai'garn asked.

"They were brought to us by Asher. He's a..." Kaleb hiccuped. "Well he's actually quite complicated as it turns out."

There was another name the elder had recently come by. The Outlander who had been in possession of Paldora's gem and trapped in the Amber Spell for a thousand years. Indeed his was a story Tai'-garn would like to hear someday.

"Whose *us*?" Horvarth interjected.

"Rangers, like myself." Kaleb tugged on his tattered coat. "Wait...

I'm not sure if I'm supposed to be telling you this part." The ranger scratched his head and frowned.

"*This part?*" Tai'garn echoed. "It seems we have much more to discuss than I believed." The elder looked from Horvarth to the interior of the theatre expectantly.

The Lord Marshal clenched his jaw and stared at Kaleb. "Let us get to the bottom of this together, my Lord."

Tai'garn smiled and gestured for the old knight to accompany them inside.

"Elder..." Nalmar came up close on Tai'garn's side and whispered, "I can feel magic. Something approaches from... the north I think."

The ancient elf had come to trust Nalmar's abilities. "The same thing you felt as we passed Stowhold?"

"No, not as powerful, but it must be strong for me to feel it approaching. Whoever it is, their magic has been drawn from a powerful well."

Tai'garn nodded along. "Remain vigilant. If this man proves true, we will leave at dawn."

CHAPTER 22
THE CALL OF A DRAGON

G
ideon fell through his dreams, until his conscious mind became fully aware that he was falling through fog. This unique blend of reality and dream was dizzying and disorientating, but his confusion soon passed when he realised, with no small amount of terror, that he was actually falling through clouds. The constant rush of air in his ears gave way to the sound of a battle, and a large one at that.

His body broke through the clouds to reveal a land he didn't recognise; at least not from the sky. A giant city dominated the landscape, surrounded by an army he had never seen before. Dragons flew in every direction, delivering death by fire and ice, while evading the giant projectiles fired from inside the city grounds.

Gideon blinked and he was no longer falling, but standing on the battlefield instead. The mage knew he must be dreaming, but he had never been so aware before. Everything felt so real, from the breeze on his face to the ground under his feet.

The sky became dark with unnatural speed and filled with storm clouds that rumbled like angry gods. The heavens *cracked* and lightning erupted from every cloud with malicious intent. Gideon's heart sank when those same bolts struck the soaring dragons.

The ground thundered under his feet and Gideon looked towards the foreign city to see an army of thousands running at him. The mage held out his hands in panic, but the screaming army ran past him without notice. He didn't recognise any of their armour or the sigil they bore. The army didn't appear to be charging at another army, but they all had their eyes firmly fixed on the sky. That was when he saw it. Every twenty-foot there was a soldier with a tall spear, held upright, with a large green sphere attached to the top.

"Crissalith..." Gideon whispered under his breath.

A torrent of fire tore through the ranks only a hundred-feet away, as a mighty green dragon swooped over the top. Gideon followed the dragon's flight and recognised Rainael the emerald star immediately, though she was smaller than he knew her to be.

The smell of burning clothes and melted flesh reached the mage's nose and he cringed. Giant spears and enormous rocks were hurled from somewhere inside the city walls, creating chaos amid the dragons' flight patterns. The ground shook every time a dragon was struck and fell to the battlefield, crushing dozens of soldiers.

An ear-splitting roar had Gideon spinning about, to where a large, black dragon was on all four legs and being overrun by soldiers with Crissalith spears.

"Malliath!" Gideon yelled over the battle cries.

The black dragon's head dipped as the anti-magic took effect, weakening him, while Gideon could only watch as the soldiers closed in with their deadly spears. A stream of ice came from nowhere and froze the soldiers in place, killing them instantly. The biggest dragon Gideon had ever seen dropped from the sky, in front of Malliath, and crushed the ice-figures with his bulk. The dragon inhaled again and a jet of fire spread across the battlefield, taking the lives of at least a hundred men.

"Garganafan..." Gideon didn't know where the name came from, but he was certain that was the identity of the dragon before him. "Where am I?" the mage screamed above the raging battle.

Chaos surrounded him and he realised the question should be *when am I*, as Garganafan had been killed a thousand years ago in Elethiah, before The Dragon War. Was he witnessing a battle from The Dark War? Gideon had no clue, but his surroundings made it hard to think straight.

Lightning continued to light up the sky, every bolt searching for a dragon. Using a storm as a weapon was an incredible feat of magic, in Gideon's mind. He looked around him for the caster but instead he saw a soldier running directly at him. The mage stumbled backwards, seeing the spear of Crissalith aimed at his belly. He was defenceless. He had no staff and Abigail's wand wasn't attached to his thigh.

"NO!" Gideon's cry blew the vivid dream away and he awoke, sitting bolt upright.

The mage was sitting on the grass in front of Mournblade. Rays of moonlight pierced the branches, bathing the magnificent blade in soft light. A heavy sigh, Gideon had come to recognise as a dragon's, came from behind him. Ilargo was lying close by with his wings tucked into his sides, as if he too had been sleeping. The dragon's long neck stretched high, bringing his elongated head to tower over Gideon's.

"What was that?" the mage asked, referring to his nightmare.

Ilargo tilted his head as if considering an answer.

"What was what?" Adriel walked into the clearing.

"I..." Gideon didn't know where to begin.

The mage stood up and straightened his clothes, taking in the serene surroundings. Galanör was close behind Adriel as they entered the clearing; both elves, regal in their approach, with perfect posture and handsome features. How was it that he, a human, could ever be a Dragorn, he wondered?

"You have been asleep since yesterday," Adriel said. "I'm sure it all feels very confusing."

"And then some..." Gideon added, rubbing his eyes.

"How's the arm?" Galanör gestured to Gideon's left forearm.

The mage examined the healed skin and nodded absently, trying to fix himself in reality again. The dream had been so vivid with its sights, sounds and smells. What was happening to him?

"What happened yesterday?" Gideon finally asked.

Adriel replied, "You were mentally connected to Ilargo at the time. Through his mind you were then connected to every dragon in the Reach. That many voices and minds must have been overwhelming. Some of the earliest Dragorn experienced the same thing before we developed the training. You will need training, Gideon."

The mage glanced at Galanör before facing Adriel. "I don't have time to be trained. We need to return to Malaysai and free Adilandra. Then we need to find a way of getting word to the kingdoms of Illian. They *must* be warned before the Darkakin invade."

"Being a Dragorn is not something to be taken lightly," Adriel countered. "It is not a path you can easily walk away from. The call of a dragon cannot be denied."

"I'm not Dragorn!" Gideon strode over to the only rock in the clearing. "See!" The mage pulled with all his might on the scimitar's hilt.

Adriel smiled and walked over to meet him. "Observe." The elf gripped the red hilt and attempted to lift the stubborn blade. "I told you; Galandavax laid a spell over Mournblade centuries ago. It can only be removed by a Dragorn when they are *needed* again. Even I cannot lift the blade."

Gideon's shoulders sank. Growing up in Korkanath, he had dreamed of a life of adventure and destiny; to have a purpose in life beyond that of normal men had been his only desire. Now he just wanted to have Abigail back.

"Adriel's right," Galanör said. "You should train, Gideon. This is an honour my people have dreamt about for a thousand years. You shouldn't pass it up."

Gideon shared Adriel's expression of surprise. It was the first time Galanör had agreed with the ancient elf instead of protesting to leave.

The mage locked eyes with Ilargo and felt that familiar pull that, he now knew, was a call to connect on another level. The prospect of becoming a Dragorn was indeed exciting, but it also sounded like a long process.

"How long does it take to complete the training?" Gideon asked.

Adriel hesitated. "Longer than a human lifespan..."

"Probably best to start now then," Galanör added, placing a heavy hand on Gideon's shoulder.

Galanör had stayed with the new master and student for as long as he could before boredom set in. He wasn't like his ancestors. Galanör didn't have the patience to sit and watch Adriel teach Gideon the art of *elven* meditation. The elf needed to be doing something, to be on the move. He filled his time with swordplay, moving through his routines and stances. Even after four centuries, practice was required.

It was easy to stop and marvel at the flying dragons however, each more beautiful than the next. Rainael flew overhead and it made Galanör think of his own queen. Adilandra needed saving from that hell. He knew in his heart that she was still alive. He had to believe that or succumb to his guilt.

The elf looked back at the wall of trees that concealed Mournblade, where Gideon was receiving his first lesson. The way Galanör saw it, there were two ways the mage's training could go; either Gideon would come round to Adriel's point of view, and believe that the dragons should stay in the Reach, or he could use his new found connection with Ilargo to help them attack Malaysai.

Galanör couldn't leave it to chance.

The elf climbed atop one of the floating boulders with the need to act pressing on his mind. Who knew how long it would take for

Gideon to master even the most basic of skills needed to be a Dragorn. What he did know was that Adilandra's time would be running out. If she wasn't dead already, the Darkakin's cruelty would force her to find creative ways to kill herself.

Crouched by the lip of the boulder, Galanör scanned the vast crater for any weaknesses he might have missed. His sharp eyes took in every detail of the almost sheer cliff face that wrapped around Dragons' Reach. There were no gaps or valleys to take advantage of. The thought of climbing out of the crater was a futile one and he knew it. Even if he did make it past the vicious Sandstalkers that lived in The Red Mountains, he would surely die of dehydration between there and Malaysai.

Galanör hung his head in defeat.

Everything he had done was for nothing. All the terrible acts on behalf of his people would be with him forever. The faces of the children, taken by the Mer-folk, flashed before his eyes and brought tears with them. The students, children all, in Korkanath who had fallen under his leadership... Tears ran freely down his cheeks and the elf felt despair for the first time in his long life.

Before he could fall any further into his dark reflection, his keen eyes caught movement in the distance. Galanör wiped his eyes and watched as Malliath took off into the sky with an entourage of dragons. They flew in a wide circle before heading out, beyond the Reach. What were they doing?

Galanör practically flew down the boulder and the thick roots that attached it to the ground, when he saw Adriel and Gideon heading for the small lake with Ilargo in tow.

"Malliath's leaving!" Galanör shouted as he closed the gap.

Adriel stopped by the edge of the lake and turned to regard Galanör without a trace of alarm. "He's not leaving. He's *hunting*. A dragon that cannot fly goes mad. Even the mages at Korkanath knew that. Every day he is escorted to the north where he can hunt and enjoy the gift of flight. His freedom will be increased every day as he regains some semblance of himself."

Galanör felt like a fool for rushing over. He looked at Gideon, but the mage was stroking the scaly hide between Ilargo's eyes, oblivious to their conversation. Perhaps he already knew of Malliath's daily jaunts through his connection to Ilargo.

Rather awkwardly, Galanör nodded his understanding and turned to leave. Ever the warrior and tactician, the elf found an idea forming in his mind. Perhaps he could lie in wait during one of Malliath's hunts, hiding within the debris and the mud. Then, when the black dragon returned, he wouldn't have to sneak into the clearing to converse. That thought vanished when he considered Malliath's size and weight. It was more likely that the dragon would return and land on top of him.

Galanör sighed and strode into the forest. The elf could feel desperation creeping into his thoughts, planting schemes that most would consider irrational and dangerous. Desperation was not a good place for Galanör to be...

Adilandra squeezed her hand until the knuckles turned white and her grip was that of a vice. Her elven strength was a magnitude above most humans, proving true in this very moment, as she relieved her latest bedmate of his life. The ugly Darkakin struggled and clawed at her bare arms, but the elven queen continued to look ahead and tighten the vice. Adilandra had to be precise with her grip, ensuring that not a single gurgle could escape his blue lips and alert the guards.

The elf lifted her leg and rolled off the Darkakin after hearing a crack inside his throat. The cold floor found her first as she battled the elixir of drugs still coursing through her veins. Finding the strength to strangle the savage had taken most of her energy.

With her head leaning against the side of the bed, the queen sat there for a moment and focused her resolve. She had to escape. The Goddess had continued to pass her round the richer clans within their twisted society, always drugging her into submission. Adilandra was unsure of how many days and nights she had been fettered now, each day blending into the next, but the elixirs were beginning to lose their bite. It was only the gladiatorial matches that gave her any reprieve from the drugs.

Adilandra brought her hand up to her face and balled it into a fist, testing her strength. Perhaps she was developing an immunity to the concoction of drugs? The elf could only dare to hope. Scrambling for her clothes, the queen was finally able to stand, though her new found freedom was accompanied by overwhelming nausea and dizziness. Adilandra used the edges of the bed to walk around the room and make for the balcony, where the green crystal sat perched on a stand.

She hated those crystals.

In their presence, her magical connection was lost. Her greatest advantage over the humans had been taken from her by nothing more than a rock, and she had no idea how. Between the crystals and the drugs, she had been used time and time again as nothing more than a plaything.

Before Adilandra could reach the crystal, however, the vomit in her stomach demanded attention. The reflex couldn't be helped and the queen vomited her gut's contents across the floor.

The doors were bursting open before she could clear the tears from her eyes. Bare feet padded into the room with the harsh language of the Darkakin shouting unintelligible words at her. It didn't matter; she just had to reach the crystal and launch it from the balcony. With it gone, her powers could return and she could reduce the guards to charred corpses.

On her hands and knees, Adilandra made a dash across the floor, ignoring the vomit beneath her. A swift kick to her ribs had her sprawled over the cold tiles and gasping in pain. A second kick, quickly followed by a third and fourth brought pain and blood, but still the elf crawled across the floor. As her fingers touched the stand, numerous hands grabbed for her and lifted her from the floor. The stand wobbled and the crystal fell to the floor, where it rolled ever closer to the balcony. Adilandra kicked out, trying to stall the inevitable club to the head, while watching the crystal roll towards the gap in the railing.

With a prayer on the edge of her lips she willed the crystal to drop, but a foot came to rest on top as it teetered on the lip. Adilandra followed the foot up an athletic leg, laced in tattoos, until her eyes rested on The Goddess. The elf now found herself within the grip of four Darkakin, who forced her to her knees with rough hands and serrated blades.

"You have saved me the trouble, elf-queen." The Goddess flashed her wicked smile and picked up the crystal. "I was coming to kill Lord Xix myself. He was only to have you for the night, not three. He refused my guards the right to bring you back." The Goddess regarded the corpse of Xix with disgust and pity. "He thought with my armies invading Illian I would be weak. Did your subjects test you so, old one?"

Adilandra surged forwards in an attempt to break free and snap the savage's neck, but eight strong arms coiled around her with python-like strength.

The Goddess didn't flinch, but smiled all the wider. "Are you hollow yet? Have we stripped you down and left you raw?" The savage queen stroked Adilandra's cheek with the back of her hand. "You will be among my legacies. I will hand you down through the generations of my bloodline, each one breaking you again and again. When your gods give you strength and hope musters in your heart, the Darkakin will be there to crush it."

Adilandra wanted to unleash the fury that had been building inside of her. She wanted to curse and spit and make promises of a bloody death to all Darkakin, but that shouldn't be the elven way. Her husband, Elym, would have every elf behave in such a way and prove their superiority, but Adilandra refused to give in; she would be as her ancestors had been and...

The faces of all those who had accompanied her on the

pilgrimage to these lands flashed through her mind. Most were the faces they made upon their death at the hands of the Darkakin. She saw Lörvana have her head removed by Overlord Kett and Fallön slice his own throat under the influence of The Goddess's elixirs. She saw Ederön be thrown from the balcony of the throne room, as if he were nothing but a sack of wheat.

The queen's rage couldn't be denied any longer. "I will kill every last one of you!" Adilandra screamed and pushed against the guards, putting their strength to the test. "This city will be left a smoking ruin! Not a soul will escape Malaysai when I am finished burning it to the ground!"

The Goddess laughed with glee "You're going to be perfect...!" The queen of savages brought the hand-sized crystal down on Adilandra's head, robbing her of thought.

CHAPTER 23
DARK TIDINGS

The elves heard it first, as they would. The thunder of boots falling into the rhythm of a march. The scraping of armour against armour. Had the doors of Darkwell's theatre been open, Tai'garn was sure they would have inhaled their sweaty aroma too. The elves looked at each other, keenly aware of the danger moving through the streets, but it was Nalmar's tortured expression that raised the fine hairs on the back of Tai'garn's neck.

The elven companions were on their feet moments before the doors were forced open and a stampede of soldiers in gold cloaks rushed into the theatre. Their war cry and drawn weapons were clear signs of their intentions, and Ezeric had an arrow flying across the theatre before a single Graycoat had found their sword.

Lord Marshal Horvarth exploded from his chair with Ned Fennick and Darius Devale at his back, but all three were quickly set upon by the soldiers. There was no warning or questions asked by either side; just bloody battle. Ezeric glided around the stage, firing arrows with enviable speed and precision, every projectile delivering a fatal message. Hela and Alwyn waded in with their exquisite scimitars, bringing down the strange soldiers with every swipe and slash.

"Nalmar; with me!" Tai'garn rallied the elf and dropped from the stage with his staff at the ready.

Destructive spells burst forth from the elder's staff and Nalmar's hands. Shields were cracked and swords melted by the magical attacks. Any who found their way past Tai'garn's spells found their doom at the end of his enchanted staff.

"Traitors!" the Graycoats cried over the chaos.

The elder unleashed a concussive spell so powerful it shattered a soldier's shield and blew the man backwards, into three more of his brothers-in-arms. Bones were broken and flesh torn in the throng of limbs.

The ancient elf looked about, between parrying blows and evading stray arrows, to see his kin, each enjoying themselves. Taking human lives was the very thing they had all been trained for and they loved it. They revelled in their superiority over man; their strength and speed unmatched. Hela was even laughing through most of it.

"Die traitor!" The blond Graycoat, known as Darius Devale, jumped in front of the elder and plunged his sword into the belly of a golden warrior, his blade piercing the mail and biting into the soft skin beneath.

"For King Merkaris!" two gold cloaks shouted back, advancing on Darius. "For the north!"

Darius pulled on his sword, but found the blade wedged. Tai'garn stepped between them and swiped his staff across both of their faces, knocking the gold cloaks down. Nalmar appeared from nowhere and finished them with an ice spell, reducing the soldiers to frozen blocks.

"Who are these men?" Nalmar asked, seeing the soldiers flooding the upper levels of the theatre now.

"They are Merkaris Tion's men," Darius replied, tugging his sword free.

Tai'garn loosed another firebolt, wiping a soldier's face clean off. "Was it not King Merkaris who invited you here?"

There was no time for words as more gold cloaks descended on them. Graycoats were starting to be overwhelmed, especially with many of their number still injured from the battle of West Fellion. Tai'garn could see the fight shifting unfavourably. The cramped quarters of the theatre made for terrible battle grounds, offering advantage to the shield bearing northmen. The Graycoats, for all their skill and grace, had no room to manoeuvre; constantly facing the broad shields.

The Lord Marshal and Ned Fennick were being backed into a corner by a group of soldiers. The two men fought fiercely, with venom in their veins, but their righteous anger would not save them from the spears and swords. Tai'garn made his move to help, when a savage cry from the balcony above gave him pause. The drunk, Kaleb Jordain, threw himself from the railing and landed atop the gold cloaks.

The older man stumbled to his feet though, through some miracle, his sword continued to bat away spears and even counter thrusting blades. He might be a drunk and dishonoured knight, but his skill could never be taken from him. Tai'garn commended the ranger and used his staff to launch the remaining soldiers up into the ceiling, breaking their necks.

Horvarth and Fennick eyed the old ranger, neither thanking nor rebuking him. Kaleb didn't help himself by standing up, swiping the nearest tankard of ale and downing it in one.

"Why have we been attacked?" Tai'garn shouted over the ruckus.

"King Merkaris has betrayed us!" Horvarth wiped the blood from his mouth.

"But why?" the elder pressed.

"If Tion wants Graycoat blood he must be planning an invasion. He doesn't want us stepping in. It must be Velia he desires; they have the largest army of all six kingdoms."

Tai'garn flicked his staff upwards and broke the jaw of an advancing soldier. "Why would he attack the kingdom with the largest army? Surely he would seek to conquer the smaller regions first."

"You have never met King Merkaris, my Lord..."

No, Tai'garn mused, but he had met his ancestor, the first of his name. He too had been ambitious and greedy, setting his sights upon the dragons and their treasured Lifeless Isles.

"Merkaris Tion would see Velia as the head of the snake," Horvarth continued, almost every word between a parry or swipe of his sword. "He has but to win the one battle and the other kingdoms will fall into line with Velia under his banner."

Tai'garn's companions had rallied to him now, cutting a bloody path across the theatre. The elder noticed the other soldiers giving them a wide berth, as well as a few Graycoats who now clung to the elves.

Nalmar placed a heavy hand on Tai'garn's shoulder and the elder followed his gaze to the theatre's entrance. Nalmar had felt it first, but the magical aura emanating from the doorway could not be ignored by any of the elves.

A cold pit opened up inside Tai'garn's gut.

A lithe figure, clad in black and gold armour stood as a sentinel, with the light of dawn breaking over her cloaked silhouette. A dark hood covered her head and a stylised veil concealed her mouth and nose. The shadowy figure held a spear upright, each end housing a curved blade with an edge of diamond. Tai'garn had seen that weapon before and the one who wielded it.

Samandriel Zathya was a general in The Dark War and devoted disciple of Valanis. The twisted elf had been a member of the Hand since the beginning and was responsible for the deaths of countless innocents, many of which had been Tai'garn's friends and family.

Samandriel's golden eyes blazed from within her hood and the elder was sure she was trying to delve into his mind. The general sought to plant fear in him, driving him from battle and securing the northerners' victory.

Tai'garn could not be so easily swayed.

The elder made for the dark elf and his companions fell into line behind him, as if the manoeuvre had been practised. More soldiers died at the end of their blades and spells, none strong enough to halt their progress. After Tai'garn had blown the last soldier from his path, the doorway was empty.

"She's outside," Nalmar confirmed.

The elves drew together, leaving the Graycoats to their heated battle. Samandriel was a foe no man could stand against, though Tai'garn was led to dwell on Asher, the elusive ranger. By Faylen's report, both the ranger and another Graycoat had fought against Adellum Bövö and lived. Still, the elder would face the general with his kin at his side.

The light of dawn was cresting the rooftops, casting stark shadows in the early morning. The streets were deserted and for good reason; there was no doubt that the battle inside the theatre had woken the entire town, if not the marching battalion.

The elves naturally fell into formation with their backs to one another; their keen senses taking in the world.

"Was that who I though it was?" Ezeric asked.

"There was only one who wielded a spear of that description," Alwyn offered, referring to the tales of old that all elves were brought up on.

It occurred to Tai'garn then how young these elves were. The Dark War was a story to them, the death toll and bloodshed impossible to truly understand. Fighting for them had been a game... until now.

Without a sound, Samandriel dropped from above the doorway and brought her double-ended spear down vertically. Alwyn died instantly, as the diamond-tipped blade cut a line from the top of his head down to the base of his back, severing his spinal column. The elves reacted immediately and turned on the general, but Samandriel's defences were already up. Tai'garn's super-heated spell exploded against the dark elf's magical shield, erected by an outstretched hand, and blinded the others.

The elder regretted his attack but had no time to dwell upon its failure or indeed the death of Alwyn, for a swift side-kick found his sternum and launched him down the street. Tai'garn tumbled and used what elven grace he had left to land on his feet. Samandriel was a demon among the elves, however. Her spear kept them at bay before coming back down on their blades with deadly intent. Hela flew around the general with both of her scimitars probing for any vulnerability, and more than once her swords found flesh - but nothing could slow the dark elf down.

Tai'garn was old enough to predict some of Samandriel's attacks and see where her spear would fly next, and so the elder dived into action, sprinting down the street, where he intercepted the curved tip of the General's blade before it cut Nalmar in half. His enchanted staff took the blow, jarring his hand and wrist as he struggled to keep it aloft. When Samandriel twirled away, the elf glanced at his staff and tried to hide his surprise at the fresh cut that would forever scar the wood. Tai'garn wasn't aware of any weapon that could damage his staff.

Ezeric and Hela pincered the general between their combined attack, hoping to overwhelm their foe. Samandriel proved the superior opponent and bowed her body, extending the spear ahead of her, while bringing her leg out behind her. The leg caught Ezeric in the gut and forced the air from his lungs, but the spear found its end deep inside Hela's chest. By the time Ezeric had rolled to a stop, Samandriel was already sliding her spear clean from Hela's chest and allowing her limp body to collapse in a heap.

"It has been a long time since I have taken the life of an elf..." Samandriel twirled her spear by her side and stalked around the survivors.

"You would kill your own kin and take pleasure from it?" Tai'garn knew it was folly to barter words, but he could never be rid of that hope that lay inside his soul - a hope for every elf.

Samandriel laughed to herself. "I see no kin of mine." The general looked down at Hela and Alwyn. "You are a thousand years behind the times. You should have embraced your true nature before The Dark War; maybe then we could have cleansed Verda together and embraced the gods upon their return."

"Gods?" Nalmar exclaimed, his anger easy to hear. "Madness has claimed you, just as it did Valanis!"

"Take a care, young one..." Samandriel's eyes were fixed on him.

Tai'garn stepped forward, wishing to regain her attention. "You say return? You believe the gods have already been here?"

Samandriel laughed again. "You will find no answers here. Valanis offered you all a chance to be a part of his vision. You declined and chose war instead." The general adjusted her grip on the magical spear, giving away her intent. "Besides, you are moments from death. The gods will answer your questions personally..."

"I can wait." Tai'garn hadn't been interested in any of Samandriel's words; he simply needed to distract her while his spell took effect.

The dark cloud that had formed from nowhere was now over Samandriel, its presence blocking out the new sun. With one knock of his staff against the ground, the cloud delivered its payload of charged energy. The lightning struck the dark elf with the speed and unbridled ferocity that only nature could muster. Tai'garn shielded his eyes from the flash, only catching a glimpse of Samandriel, who was hurled down the street.

Ezeric joined the elder and Nalmar as they cautiously approached the prone form, draped under a black cloak. Tai'garn put his arms out to stop them from advancing when Samandriel stirred and slowly rose to her feet. Her armour and hood were smoking and burnt, the stylised veil across her mouth ruined.

Still she smiled.

"You do not possess the power or weapon to undo the magic that fuels me."

Tai'garn looked beyond the general, to the doorway of the

theatre. "Perhaps we do not, but I think we have enough blades to pin you down while we find such a weapon..."

Samandriel turned around, pain evident across her face, and looked upon the amassing Graycoats. Lord Marshal Horvarth strolled out with his knights at his back, every one brandishing their one-handed swords, stained with the blood of northmen. Mixed within them was Kaleb Jordain, a sword in one hand and a bottle in the other.

"I do not know who you are," Horvarth spoke boldly, "but you can run back to King Merkaris Tion and tell him this betrayal will be answered for. You tell him that it will take more than a battalion of soldiers to end the Graycoats."

Samandriel stood her spear against the ground. "I do not serve mortals. You can give your message to Merkaris when his army marches over you."

Tai'garn glimpsed the smallest of glimmers within Samandriel's hand. The elder moved to stop her but she was too quick, especially so for someone who had just been struck by lightning. The crystal shot from her hand and exploded into a portal in front of the Graycoats, shocking them into stepping back. Samandriel dashed for the portal of pure black, a clear limp in her left leg. Tai'garn stopped short of the portal and extended his staff with a spell on his lips, drawing more strength into the magic. A fireball erupted from the end and passed through the abyss with the General.

Wherever she was going, he had no doubt that the destructive spell would find her.

The portal collapsed in on itself, leaving a crowd of surprised Graycoats. Only Kaleb Jordain stood unaffected by the display of magic, though it was possible his blink lasted longer than the entire event.

A quiet settled over the group of knights and the elves regarded their dead kin. Hela and Alwyn were drenched in their own blood, as lifeless as the street on which they lay. Ezeric brushed Hela's red hair aside and stroked her cheek, while Nalmar closed Alwyn's eyes and uttered a curse upon Samandriel.

Tai'garn offered a silent prayer on their behalf, his faith ever a secret. He would mourn their passing in time, thankful that he never got to know them on a deeper level. They had journeyed together, but he had only met the group of elves upon High Guardian Varo's introduction. Besides, there were more troubling things to set his mind to.

The elder turned to Ezeric. "Why would Samandriel Zathya be leading a battalion of Tion soldiers?"

"It is as King Elym feared. Valanis has taken control of man's armies."

Valanis was playing a game that Tai'garn was yet to fathom. It troubled the elf beyond words.

"I am sorry for your loss, Master Elf." Horvarth sheathed his sword, his words hollow. "These treacherous bastards have claimed many Graycoats this day. More than our order can take, I fear."

Tai'garn ignored the marshal's comments and addressed Kaleb Jordain. "You say Princess Reyna has gone south, to The Arid Lands?"

Kaleb swigged his bottle and wiped his moustache. "To Karath... I think."

"Show us the way and you will be rewarded," Tai'garn offered.

"I'm already owed a reward." Kaleb took another swig. "Nathaniel Galfrey owes me a bag of coins the size of my fist."

"Galfrey?" Darius Devale asked, his blond hair matted with blood. "He lives?"

"The stupid bugger paid me to come and warn you... keep an eye on you." Kaleb shrugged. "I couldn't tell you why. From what I could gather he wasn't exactly appreciated by you self-righteous bastards. Much like myself."

"If Galfrey is alive he is no longer a Graycoat," Ned Fennick announced. "He sided with the assassin..."

Kaleb snorted. "Well if he hadn't sent me, you and the lordy over there would be dead."

Horvarth reached for his sword again. "You were not -"

Tai'garn stamped his staff into the ground and generated the smallest of sparks between the wood and the ground, adding an ear-piercing crack to his protest.

"A guide through Illian would make our journey swifter." Tai'-garn's gaze continued to rest upon the dead elves at his feet.

Lord Marshal Horvarth stepped into the middle of the street. "Master Elf, our destination should be Velia. You heard the..." The Graycoat struggled to define Samandriel. "Merkaris's forces are on the march; the other kingdoms should be warned. A raven from King Rengar will carry the weight required to convince the other monarchs of Merkaris's betrayal."

Ezeric stood up from Hela's body. "We did not cross The Adean to get involved in your feuds."

Tai'garn held up his hand, sensing the elf's aggravation. "Valanis has a hand in this..." The elder looked through Ezeric, lost in contemplation.

"The swiftest route to The Arid Lands is The Selk Road," Horvarth continued. "Accompany us south and we shall part ways at Velia, though King Rengar would benefit greatly from hearing your account."

Tai'garn could see that Ezeric and Nalmar wanted to go their own way, without the knights who were famous for their part in The Dragon War. The elder could see the benefit in travelling with the small army, however, especially with Valanis's spies in Illian. Ultimately, it was the Echoes of Fate that swayed the elf. If there was to be any hope for the realm, an alliance between their two shores would have to be forged.

"First we cremate the dead," Tai'garn said, "then we travel south, to Velia."

Kaleb Jordain let out an obnoxious burp and threw his bottle aside. "I still get paid though, right..?"

CHAPTER 24
UNWELCOME GUESTS

After the sun rose, Asher approached the gates of Karath on foot and bade the others to follow his lead, each pulling their horse by the reins. The ranger was always thinking ahead, anticipating his target's perception and he knew how intimidating the group appeared without approaching the gates astride their mounts. If the Karathan guards felt vulnerable, they would likely turn hostile and call for reinforcements. Asher knew that avoiding violence in The Arid Lands was impossible, but he at least wanted to be inside the capital first.

The dusty road that led from the main gates was unusually sparse of life. Asher had visited the city many times in his life, and knew the area to be busy with trade - either stalls or moving caravans. The ranger didn't like it.

"Something isn't right..." Salim said close to his ear.

Asher nodded his head in agreement and glanced at Nathaniel and Reyna, a silent warning. They were a group of fighters all, so there was no point in hiding their weapons and concealing their armour; even the dumbest of soldiers would be able to assess the threat they posed.

The ranger cautiously entered through the large gates, left entirely ajar by their keeper. Karath's doors were usually open and so the sight didn't bother Asher too much, but the absence of any guards was alarming. People could be seen milling around, going about their day, but the outer edges of the city were relatively deserted.

"Is there a festival?" Glaide asked.

"No," Salim replied from behind his scarf, pulled up to hide his mouth. "Karathans do not celebrate the harvest of Ymira. This is too quiet."

Asher walked up to the first person who didn't run from the sight of him. "Excuse me," he asked in the language of The Arid Lands. "Where is everyone?"

The young woman hesitated with her answer, dwelling for a moment on the assorted company before her. "Most have gone to the palace. Emperor Faro is addressing the traitor."

"Traitor?" Salim asked first.

Asher turned back to the young woman. "Why are you not there?"

"Because I have heard what is coming. The House of Owls never lies. My family and I are leaving for Tregaran as soon as we have enough supplies. You should all turn around..." With that, the woman bundled her fabrics and goods and disappeared down an alley.

"What was that?" Faylen asked, the language unknown to her ears.

"Something about a traitor..." Asher was trying to put the puzzle together.

"That was not all she said," Salim stated, his body angled for the street that led to the heart of the city.

"Salim," the ranger warned. "We don't have time. We need to get our supplies and move on; use this to our advantage."

It was already too late and Asher could see the fear in Salim's eyes. The old honour guard knew of two traitors inside Karath's walls and both were his sons. Asher had heard him talk of both Halion and Tauren many times over the years, often with pride in his tone. That's why when Salim made a dash down the street, Asher wasn't surprised.

"What's happening?" Reyna pulled her horse forward, leaving Nathaniel behind.

Asher growled, thinking of his knees. "He's getting all of us killed!"

The ranger ran after Salim, pulling Hector along as he did, with the others closely behind, each as confused as the other. The streets became more crowded the further in they ventured, slowing their pursuit with the horses in tow. Asher pushed and shoved at the building crowd and turned down several alleys in the hope of catching up, but Salim knew the city like the back of his hand.

The noise found the ranger's ears first, then the smell, before the real crowd could be seen. It appeared that most of Karath had turned out to hear their boy-emperor and see the traitor. A gap appeared in the wall of bodies and Asher reluctantly took advantage of both his demeanour and Hector's girth. The companions pushed through until they found Salim, who was standing still in front of the palace gates. Instinctively, Asher's eyes were drawn to the guards beyond Salim and the gates. They didn't appear too bothered by the amassing crowds and the lack of security for their approaching emperor. In fact, most weren't even watching the crowd, but instead looking up, at the palace itself.

Then he saw it. The spectacle that had drawn so many.

Asher's hold on Hector's reins became slack and he sighed in despair for his friend. No father should ever live to see their son pass on before them, let alone hung from the palace walls and streaked in blood. The ranger knew a tortured body when he saw one.

"What's this all abou' then?" Doran huffed. "I can't see a bloody thing!"

"Asher." Faylen said his name in a harsh tone over the noisy mob. "What's happening? Who is that?"

The other rangers had crowded round now, almost shutting out the mob as they surrounded Salim from behind. The old honour guard had yet to move, allowing strangers to jostle him in the fight to get a better look.

"Asher?" Nathaniel prompted.

Asher locked eyes with Glaide for just a second; both men aware of what was about to happen next. "It's Halion Al-Anan... Salim's son."

Reyna gasped and covered her mouth, but the others remained silent, the gravity of the situation slowly sinking in. Asher noticed the barbarian, Bale, puff out his chest and adjust the angle of his shoulders, so he could quickly reach for the axes that rested there. Glaide's hand coiled around the slender hilt of his fine sword, while the son of Dorain cracked his knuckles in anticipation. Hadavad was whispering in his apprentice's ear, who quickly retrieved her staff from the side of her horse.

There was a call above the din of the mob and a stilted cheer from the crowd. Emperor Faro was sat in the middle of what appeared to be an oversized throne, carried by four slaves and lined with honour guards. The procession led out from the palace through the gardens between the main entrance and the gates in front of the rangers.

Something about the honour guards didn't look right to Asher.

"Start clearing a way out." The ranger addressed Nathaniel and the elves with urgency. "Glaide..."

The dark-skinned ranger nodded in agreement and rolled his shoulders in preparation. Pulling Salim out of the crowd without bloodshed wasn't going to be easy.

They were too late. The rage that spilled from Salim's mouth was without definition or syllable. It was hate in its purest form, born of the deepest pit that lay dormant in every soul.

Something inside Salim snapped and he shoved those in front of him aside and sprinted for the gates. The rangers yelled his name in protest, but there was no stopping him. Not even elven speed could get in front of him now. With his cutlass drawn already, the old honour guard entered the palace grounds with the fury of a hurricane. The guards who had been too occupied with the sight of Halion were the first to fall, each taking a beating that dropped them hard and fast.

The honour guards formed a wall in front of their emperor and the slaves carrying the boy immediately reversed direction. That was when Asher saw it, the subtleties that made these guards stand out. The way they moved, the way they carried themselves... they were Arakesh!

"Salim!" The ranger's cry fell on deaf ears.

The southern ranger jumped with his cutlass aimed low, ready to skewer the first person to get in his way. The Arakesh were typically fast, however. Salim's sword was deflected and his next three attacks either collided with steel or found naught but air. A solid push-kick had one of the assassins flying over the low hedge, reducing his opponents to five. That was at least two too many when it came to the Arakesh.

With a battle cry of his own, Asher waded into the fray, hoping, if nothing else, to distract the remaining Arakesh. His double-handed broadsword cut the air horizontally and pushed through the defence of one assassin and opened his armour up. The blade had drawn blood, but it wasn't enough to put the assassin out of the fight. A swift backhand however, had his spiked pommel knock the helmet and break the jaw of another Arakesh. Salim twirled and spun like a dancer, quickly finishing the man with a clean swipe across his throat.

More cries of battle preceded the other rangers, who charged up the path with weapons drawn. Doran had left his stubby fat blade attached to his hog, instead opting for the spiked gauntlets that matched his armour. The dwarf darted between the clashing of steel and dived through the air until his momentum and tremendous girth took down an assassin. Without taking a breath, Doran pummelled the man until blood decorated his blond beard and the Arakesh became very still beneath him.

Despite having already been sliced by the assassins' blades in various places, Bale of the Oakbreaker clan moved through the group with his double-sided axes and a smile on his face. Glaide was forced more than once to duck under the barbarian's swing, while simultaneously parrying the blade of an Arakesh. It was only a minute more before the six assassins were lying dead at the rangers' feet. Salim remained crouched over his last victim with his dagger in hand. The ranger repeatedly stabbed the dead body with a rage-filled cry that would give any attacker pause.

Asher pulled his own sword free of his opponent's neck and looked about, assessing their environment through laboured breaths. Like ants hurrying from their nest, guards and Arakesh came from everywhere, running out of the palace and appearing throughout the gardens. A bell rang in the distance, telling Asher that more would be coming from across the city.

"Withdraw!" Glaide shouted. "We need to withdraw!"

Still Salim continued to stab the dead body.

Asher knew they had only seconds to choose their fate. Stay and fight, killing as many as they could and avenging Halion's death, or run back into the city and attempt escape. The ranger didn't need to count the number of enemies to calculate the outcome of a stance. They would certainly reduce the Karathan army by day's end, but their own deaths would be inevitable. Then again, running away didn't hold much hope either. Karath was a maze of alleyways and colourful bazaars, each blending into the next with disorientating effect.

The amassing guards and assassins broke Salim's concentration and he finally replaced his dagger with his cutlass. The look on his face told Asher everything he needed to know; the old honour guard would not be sated until he had killed every last one. Glaide was the first to act, sheathing his fine blade and diving on top of Salim. The men struggled furiously until Asher and Doran intervened, each hooking an arm around the southerner's shoulders and tugging backwards.

"We need to go, Salim!" Glaide shouted in his ear.

Asher could see the nearest assassin bearing down on them. "Bale..."

The big barbarian moved to intercept the Arakesh, but was too slow compared to the actions of an elf. Reyna unleashed an arrow from her powerful bow and launched the assassin back into a group of soldiers. The arrow continued its flight, piercing armour, flesh and bone with ease, until it buried itself in the palace walls and cracked the sandy stone. The elf's barrage was accompanied by Nathaniel's arrows and Faylen's spells. Their combined attack was perfect, with Reyna taking down the assassins, who could evade Nathaniel's arrows, while the knight felled Karathan guards. Faylen was far happier to create chaos with explosive spells.

"Come on!" Asher strained against Salim's pull.

Doran pushed from the front as Glaide and Asher pulled at Salim's arms, but blind rage gave the southerner the strength of ten men. Thankfully, any who survived the arrows, flying between their heads, were tackled by Bale, who was more than happy to add notches to his axes.

"Salim! We need to go!" Glaide had one hand on the ranger's wrist, keeping his sword at bay.

More arrows whistled past their struggling bodies, each finding their mark and littering the palace grounds with bodies. Reyna's arrows never failed to bring down more than one attacker at a time.

"Bale!" Asher met the barbarian's eyes and looked from him to Salim.

The Oakbreaker knew exactly what to do.

Bale's fist connected with Salim's face to devastating effects. The ranger's nose broke instantly and his head snapped back, as his legs gave out beneath him. Asher and Glaide were suddenly holding his entire weight and Doran had both of his hands cupping the southerner's face, searching for signs of life.

"Did ye kill 'im?" the dwarf asked.

"He sleep..." the barbarian replied, before turning about to clothesline a rushing guard.

Asher looked up from Salim and saw death walking out of the palace. Billowing white robes swept around the ancient elf, contrasting with his long, black hair which draped over his back like oil. The ranger's eyes were immediately drawn to Alidyr's short-sword, resting on his hip with a crystallized pommel. Its twin was sitting diagonally across Asher's back, begging to be returned to its master.

The old assassin had every intention of giving it back...

The two locked eyes across the gardens, between the oncoming guards and Arakesh, each aware of their inevitable collision.

"Bale, take Salim!" Asher and Glaide lifted the southerner into the barbarian's hands, who threw him over his shoulder as if he were an empty sack.

"Asher?" Glaide was following the ranger's gaze.

"Don't Asher!" Reyna cried. "We need to go! Now!"

The ranger wasn't sure when it happened, but both of his hands were now holding a sword each. In his right hand was the silvyr short-sword, crafted in a dwarven forge and decorated in the oldest of runes, while in his left he held a blade gifted to Alidyr by Valanis himself. The pommel housed a crystal imbued with the power of Naius, the god of magic. Asher was yet to be convinced of the gods and their power, but he more than believed in his power to shove the jewelled pommel down the elf's throat.

For Elaith...

Asher ignored the warnings and went to work. He didn't care what Alidyr was doing in Karath or what part the Arakesh had to play in everything. They had killed Halion, the son of a friend and a good man, but the elf had taken a life that actually mattered to Asher, a young woman who should have been left to grow old and discover the wonders of the world.

The first Arakesh to get in his way was dead by the ranger's second strike, both blades opening up arteries. A Karathan guard came next, if somewhat hesitantly, and found the pommel of Asher's silvyr sword lodged in his throat, stealing any breath. A swift push-kick launched the man into three more guards, staggering their advance, while the ranger deflected and parried more assassins. One particular Arakesh struck from above with more force than the others; his blade shattered against the elven short-sword. Asher simply dropped to one knee and thrust his silvyr blade into the man's chest.

It had been a while since the ranger had been in the thick of a fight, but the art of killing always returned like an old friend. He was no longer aware of anyone else, the rangers or the elves, but focused instead on carving out a path to Alidyr. Guards and assassins alike dropped around him, as each of his fine blades cut through their armour and defences with the ease of a knife through butter. His green cloak flowed around him, whipped about by the dance of battle, his swords singing the oldest of tunes.

Without warning, small pellets exploded across the gardens and filled the space with thick, grey smoke. Where the ranger had only seen red was now concealed by rising grey fog. As Alidyr's image disappeared, Asher's rage deflated and a reasoned mind took back control.

"Asher!" Nathaniel's voice carried over the chaos.

The ranger turned around and saw Hadavad enter through the gates with Atharia and four men in what appeared to be white owl masks. The men in masks were all wearing light armour and hoods, but they were all throwing pellets.

"I believe these young men intend to help us..." Hadavad called casually.

"This way!" one of the owls beckoned.

Asher could see Bale charging out of the grounds with Salim slung over his shoulder. Glaide and Doran were close behind, but they kept a wary eye on Asher. The ranger knew that if he decided to stay and fight, they would fight with him. Faylen was tugging at

Reyna's arm, who continued to fire arrows, as did Nathaniel, into the wall of smoke.

The old assassin had a final look into the smoke and knew it would only be moments until Alidyr emerged, and with him a small army of assassins and soldiers. Asher would be condemning them all to death if he stayed, just as Salim had done in his blind rage.

Seconds later, his decision made, they were all out of the gates and mounting their horses once again. The crowd had already dispersed, but those left behind dived for cover to avoid the charging steeds. Asher looked over his shoulder, before they turned a corner, and saw Alidyr stride out of the smoky courtyard with his short-sword in hand.

The companions followed the directions of the men in owl masks, each astride one of the ranger's mounts, until they came across the south gate. Three Karathan guards stood duty with spears in hand; the perfect weapon for dismounting a rider. Asher reached for his broadsword, still feeling the rush of the fight coursing through his veins. Oddly, the guards simply nodded at the owls and stepped aside, allowing them all to leave the city unhindered. The ranger inspected their faces as he rode by and saw Halion Al-Anan in all of them.

Soon, the companions were riding out into the desert with a dust cloud steadily rising behind them. The horses were pushed hard and Asher wondered if they would be followed across the flat terrain. Their destination was obvious to any who might be observing from Karath's high walls.

Faylen rode up beside the ranger and shouted over the deafening hooves, "That was Alidyr Yalathanil! Why is he here?"

Asher had no answer for her, but for a simple grimace and a glance at the crystal pommel poking over his shoulder. Indeed, the elf's presence was curious if not maddening.

Syla's Gate stood defiantly before them, wedged between The Undying Mountains as an immovable sentinel. Asher had seen it before, but never had he approached the ancient gate and taken in its true size. It took time, even on horseback, to reach the base and discover the details.

Asher pulled on Hector's reins and had to crane his neck to see it all. The doors were bronze by the ranger's eyes and entirely covered in runes. There wasn't an inch of the gate that didn't have ancient glyphs engraved into the metal. There was a clear divide up the middle, but the whole gate was concave in shape and apparently devoid of any hinges. There were no bolts across the threshold, but the gate was clearly locked in place with magic. On either side stood a complex framework of walkways, stairs and ladders. They reached to the very top and connected with the gate, where Karathans had once kept watch over the southern passage.

"Who are these men?" Faylen came up on his right and looked at the owls who had jumped down from the horses.

"Syla's Gate..." Reyna left no room for answers, coming up on the ranger's left. "I have longed to see this, ever since I was a girl."

"Asher?" Faylen pressed, ever cautious.

The ranger took immediate note of the men and women appearing from behind some of the larger rocks and the framework.

"I think we're about to find out..."

The four owls walked up to the amassing group and addressed the young man in the lead. Asher instinctively took the measure of the man. Adorned with a flowing, if ragged, black cloak and covered from head-to-toe in worn brown leather, the warrior was olive-skinned, like his kinsmen, and carried himself with confidence. Despite his solid appearance, Asher could see the cracks. This was a man who had seen the end of a beating and had felt the sting of a blade more than once. Blades of all sizes were sheathed on his person, with a particularly elegant dagger strapped across his chest.

There was only one person this could be.

"I am Tauren son-of-none," the young man announced with authority. His confidence faltered when his scrutinising gaze found Salim's limp body over Bale's saddle. The son-of-none made to inspect Salim but found his path suddenly blocked.

Asher jumped down from Hector and faced the head of the owls. "We need shelter, Tauren son-of-none." The ranger could see the alarm across the man's face, unsure if he was standing before enemies. "I am Asher, a friend to your father."

"As are we all, laddy," Doran added from atop his Warhog.

Tauren was stunned, if his silence was anything to go by.

Reyna approached from behind Asher, her melodic voice preceding her. "Salim needs somewhere to rest, especially before the midday sun finds us. Do you have shelter?"

Tauren caught himself, instantly taken by Reyna's beauty and calming nature. "Bring him this way. The House of Owls offers shelter to all in need of it."

Asher nodded his appreciation and released his grip on the broadsword within his cloak. His fingers had only sought the weapon when Reyna came between them, a new protective instinct that had apparently awoken within him. Thankfully, Tauren was proving an ally, as Asher would have been ready to cut the young man down had he posed a threat to the princess.

CHAPTER 25
SANCTUARY

Gideon sat with his legs crossed by the edge of the shore, his eyes closed. The view across the central lake was often breathtaking, surrounded by the floating boulders and crowned with a magnificent waterfall, but it had proven a distraction for the young mage. He had to close the world off *amid* distractions, Adriel had said. If Gideon became lost in the flow of conversation between the dragons, it could spell his end if they were flying.

"Focus..." Adriel was slowly circling the young man, his feet lightly crunching against the pebbles. "Know Ilargo's voice as if it were your own."

Gideon could feel Ilargo's presence, both physically and mentally. This connection had magnified over the last couple of days, as if the dragon was pressing upon him on purpose now. The mage could feel Ilargo's scaly exterior against his skin, despite the fact that the green dragon was resting atop one of the lower floating boulders. Their minds were reaching out into the void and merging as one, only this time Gideon was in control of the flow.

Gideon...

Ilargo's voice was soothing and somehow familiar. Gideon had never known his parents, but he imagined hearing their voices would be similar. Ilargo felt like family, a bond that was only strengthened by their mental bleed. The dragon was delving into Gideon's memories, creating the impression that he had been in the mage's life since the beginning. Gideon wanted to push into Ilargo's memories but he hesitated, thinking about his recent dreams.

Look... You must look.

Ilargo's voice was filled with trust and confidence. Gideon felt his physical surroundings melt away, along with the sound of Adriel's pacing. The mage saw the green dragon in his infancy, keeping close to Rainael, his mother. He saw Ilargo's first flight, which amusingly ended with the dragon flying headfirst into one of the floating boulders. The first time he breathed fire was in his sleep, while dreaming. The dragon had woken up in a coughing fit and set the nearest tree ablaze. Gideon could feel himself smiling at the scene, as he watched Rainael breathe ice over the hot bark.

A great sense of vertigo overtook Gideon's senses when he looked at Rainael the emerald star. Her deep blue eyes drew him in and before he could stop himself, the mage was falling through the sky again. Beneath him was the same battle he had witnessed before, with an army of men on the ground and a swarm of dragons above. Gideon still didn't recognise the banners or even the castle that fought off the dragons. What he could see was green crystals being erected along the walls on giant spears. The Crissalith turned the dragons away before they could inflict any damage to the stone.

Gideon...

Ilargo's voice reversed Gideon's fall and the battle blurred into darkness, until the mage was lying under a canopy of stars. Ilargo was there, standing regal against the backdrop of infinity. Soft grass was under them, but the horizon had no end, with only the stars for company.

"Where are we?" he asked.

There was no moon or sun, yet the two were easy to see, their silhouettes blocking out the stars as they moved.

Ilargo looked down at him. *This is our place. A place where dragon and Dragorn may dwell together, regardless of distance or constraint. This is a place where you and I will always meet.*

Gideon's eyes welled with tears at the sound of Ilargo's voice, every syllable resounding inside his mind as if it had come from his own thoughts.

This kind of bond takes most Dragorn decades to master. Most elven Dragorn, that is...

"I don't understand." Gideon was still trying to make sense of all the things he had seen. "I don't... Has there ever been a human Dragorn? And what is that battle I keep seeing? Is it The Dragon War?"

You have a lot of questions, but the answers will have to wait... I'm afraid what is about to happen next is going to be quite jarring.

Before Gideon could ask his next question, the starry surroundings were ripped away with an explosion of sense and pain. The mage was suddenly back on the shore of the lake and falling flat against the pebbled ground. His face stung, specifically his right cheek. Adriel was standing over him in a threatening fashion. Gideon had a question on the edge of his lips when the ancient elf buried his leg in the mage's ribs, sending him across the beach.

The pain brought anger, and the anger had Gideon reaching for his staff. It wasn't on his back. It was resting against a tree thirty-feet away, beyond Adriel, who was quickly advancing on him. The mage drew Abigail's wand from the holster on his thigh and let fly a concussive spell, designed to knock the elf back. Adriel batted the attack away with a defensive spell of his own and countered with roundhouse kick, accurate enough to strike Gideon's wrist, beneath his palm, and send the wand flying away.

"What are you doing?" Gideon managed, just before the elf hammered him with fist, elbow and foot.

When the mage finally found his feet again and the world

regained its sharper edges, Gideon located Adriel coming up behind him. The elf countered every backhand and punch, often following up with an attack that found one of the mage's nerve clusters. Every blow was developed to inflict maximum pain.

In moments, Gideon was once again on the ground, gasping in pain. "Why are you doing this?"

"The Dragorn were the greatest warriors in the realm, even above the High Guardian and his most experienced fighters." Adriel circled Gideon, a predator circling its prey. "You must learn the ways of the Mag'dereth. A martial art known only to the Dragorn."

"You couldn't have waited until after the meditation?" Gideon wiped some blood from his lip.

"In time you will need to learn how to be there and here at the same time. Did Ilargo not warn you of my attack?"

Adriel lunged again and set upon the mage with a flurry of exotic moves. Gideon was successful in blocking some, but the elf always found a way of using his defences against him. The melee ended with Gideon on the ground again.

The mage looked up at Ilargo, perched on the boulder. "He wasn't entirely forthcoming," he groaned.

"You have seen Mournblade," Adriel continued. "All Dragorn carried a sword, but seldom was it required. If our words failed to diffuse a situation, and our opponent was stupid enough to ignore the presence of a dragon, the art of Mag'dereth was enough to disarm or incapacitate them."

Gideon stood up and brushed the dirt off his leather jacket. The mage was only doing it to appear busy, however. Without warning, he launched himself at Adriel. His time in Korkanath had instructed him in many ways of fighting, though without his staff or wand, he was limited.

"Stop." Adriel held up his hand to halt the mage in his tracks. "I can see that some of the basics will need to be addressed."

"I know how to fight," Gideon protested.

"Not like this. Mag'dereth is about control, detachment. Every

317

move is measured and deliberate." The elf stood to the side, facing the lake, and fell into a series of slow movements. His arms and legs created shapes in the air and his robes swept about him.

Gideon came alongside Adriel and began to copy his movements. All the while, Ilargo watched from above. He could feel the dragon's gaze taking in everything the mage did with great interest.

"You must continue to commune with Ilargo while you train. Your connection is the most important thing."

"Every time I connect with Ilargo, I see the same thing..."

"You see the war," Adriel replied without looking, always moving.

"Yes. A great battle, with Rainael and Malliath... even Garganafan is there! Which doesn't make sense; he was already dead when The Dragon War began, wasn't he?"

"Keep up." Adriel insisted, noticing Gideon fall behind with the movements. "You're seeing Rainael's memories, passed on to Ilargo. You see now the weight that lies on your shoulders, on all Dragorn. You can see through the eyes of the oldest beings in Verda. This gift will allow you to see into the past, to see things mortals and immortals were never meant to glimpse."

"But what war am I seeing?" Gideon quickly flung his jacket to the ground and fell back into his movements.

"The First War."

Gideon dropped one of the movements in his confusion. "The First War? There have only ever been two wars worthy of history's note; The Dark War and The Dragon War. I've never heard of any First War?"

"The First War was never recorded, though I suspect if one was brave enough to enter The Wild Moores, you would find something relating to it. Your people have always been avid artists when it comes to history taking; cave drawings and the like..."

"I don't follow," Gideon said. "The Wild Moores? In Illian? What do the Outlanders have to do with The First War?"

"It is a piece of history that should only be told by one who was there. I think Ilargo's memories will suffice."

Gideon looked up at Ilargo, his scales glittering in the falling light. The dragon's long neck craned over the lip of the boulder and the mage could feel their connection becoming tangible. Before any exchange could take place, Rainael the emerald star glided down from the heavens and gracefully landed atop the same boulder, her wingspan easily larger than the rock's width. Gideon wasn't entirely privy to their conversation, but he got a single word from Ilargo and the feeling of excitement.

Hunt!

Mother and son took off from the boulder and flew high into the sky, until they were too small to see. Gideon felt deflated at Ilargo's sudden departure and stopped his movements.

"Never get in the way of a dragon's hunt," Adriel advised. "Your questions will have to wait."

"But Ilargo said that distance was not a concern when we were in our... place." Gideon had no idea how to describe the starry paradise he and Ilargo had occupied.

Now Adriel stopped as well. "You have formed a sanctuary? Interesting..." The elf mused over his thoughts for a moment before standing in front of him. "Again. You will know the movements until your muscles no longer require your mind to perform them."

By the time the moon rose and the lake became a mirror for the stars, Gideon was exhausted. He sat with his back to a rock and enjoyed the comfort of being able to rest his head. Galanör had made a modest fire and caught a pair of rabbits, which were currently cooking over the fire and making Gideon's stomach rumble. Every muscle ached from the practised movements and the sparring in between. Adriel, who never grew tired, had kept the mage going all day, but in truth, Gideon was more aware of Ilargo's absence. It created a void inside of him that hadn't required filling until now.

"So," Galanör began as he stoked the flames, "has Adriel given you any idea what all this training is for?"

Gideon didn't even have the energy to frown. "To be a Dragorn of course."

"Yes, but why? Why have the responsibility of being a Dragorn if you do nothing with it but stay here... in paradise?" Galanör's tone suggested he didn't quite believe that last part. "Dragorn were the peacekeepers, not gardeners."

"Well from the sound of it, I'll be dead before my training is complete anyway. So what does it matter?"

"It matters because we finally have a way out!" Galanör had the expression of a man who had been wronged. "Adilandra is still our priority, is she not?"

Gideon found the energy to lift his head and look at the elf. "Galanör... think about it. Even if she is still alive, our priority is to warn Illian. Darkakin invade from the south and your own people will invade from the east. Adilandra would tell you herself that the dragons are our only hope. We need to convince them that flying to Illian is -"

"She sacrificed herself so we could escape!"

"To find the dragons and stop all of Verda from falling into ruin!" Gideon could feel his appetite fading away as they fell into awkward silence.

Galanör hung his head, his fair features cast in shadow. "I have to do something, Gideon. I have to save someone. All I've ever done is take life and fight and then fight some more. Rescuing Adilandra is the first thing I've ever thought to do that was *right*. She isn't just the queen, she's the ruler my people need. If the elves are left as they are, they will be nothing but killers for eternity..."

Gideon caught a glimpse of a rogue tear running down Galanör's cheek. How fate had toyed with the mage's emotions, that he had gone from wishing the elf dead to wanting nothing more than to help him. Gideon wanted Galanör to have that opportunity at redemption to become the great elf that lay under all those centuries of misguided training.

Adilandra's captivity was also bearing down on the mage, and he desperately wanted to help her, but he wasn't nearly trained enough to march up to Malliath and ask the black dragon if he felt like burning down Malaysai. Without Adriel's blessing, they were stuck in Dragons' Reach for the time being.

"We will find the road we are meant to take, Galanör. Together, we will leave this place, find Adilandra and save the kingdoms of man and elf alike. But we must have patience, just for now..."

Galanör had the hint of a smile in the corner of his mouth. "You're already sounding like a Dragorn."

The two shared a laugh and ate together, until sleep found them both.

Sleep never found Adilandra. After a day of slaughtering Darkakin gladiators in the baking sun, she had been fed and taken straight to the baths. The guards stood watching over her, while two female slaves went through the usual routine of scrubbing her so she could be presented to The Goddess. They had already pricked her with one of the darts before dragging her to the bath and another dose would be administered before the queen was deposited in The Goddess's bed chambers.

This was her only window of opportunity.

There was no green crystal in the bathhouse, as the drugs always kept her docile enough, but the binding spell between herself and Ölli, Reyna's owl, was deeper, instinctual magic that required very little effort. Relaxing into the warm waters and allowing the slaves to clean her gave her the state of mind to fall into the spell.

It was dark and very warm where the owl was. Adilandra could sense that the animal was hunting and becoming frustrated with the lack of prey. A mental suggestion had Ölli return to his master and give up the hunt for now. Adilandra had to control her emotions, lest she give herself away to the guards, as the owl turned about to face a landmark the queen had not seen since she was a child.

Reyna was at Syla's Gate.

The owl glided in, heading towards the scattered campfires and pyres. The princess welcomed Ölli to her side and gave him an affectionate stroke that Adilandra wished she could feel. The owl's big black eyes settled on Reyna and her mother took her in, a sense of pride and fear mixing together in her gut. Her daughter had changed, that was clear to see. Where a naive and unsure girl had once been, there was now a warrior, filled with confidence and serenity.

Reyna was sitting next to Nathaniel, the knight that had accompanied her since arriving in Illian. Adilandra could find no fault in the man and considered her daughter to be an excellent judge of character, but her gaze was stuck on her daughter. Her fine clothes had been replaced with tough leathers and her belt was adorned with an elven scimitar and daggers. Adilandra knew those weapons had come from Faylen, her most trusted friend.

More than anything, Adilandra wanted to embrace her daughter and hear all about her adventures and the incredible feats she had achieved in her absence. But the gods demanded more of her than the responsibilities she held as queen or a mother. The Echoes of Fate could not be denied. The time of their fall was coming and the elf could feel it in her bones. It was this faith that kept her strong in the dark. A faith that would not let her give up yet. She would continue to go through the motions of fighting in the arena and sleeping with whichever Darkakin was required of her to survive the night.

In the end they would all die. She would see to that.

For now Adilandra just wanted to enjoy the sight of her daughter before the drugs took complete hold of her. She could already feel the link with Ölli slipping away and her sense of self becoming numb. The drugs left her susceptible to persuasion, no matter the command and its consequences.

The rage she had let free upon The Goddess previously had now been forged into a quiet fury, as if the sun itself had settled in her chest. Adilandra refused to give in to what her husband called their natural instincts, but the righteous anger that had built up inside of her would never leave her, not until The Goddess and all of Malaysai was ash.

Soon, she thought. She believed in Gideon and Galanör and their ability to find the dragons. After they had saved Illian and the dragons brought an end to Valanis's evil deeds, they would surely return to Ayda's south and rid the land of the Darkakin once and for all. In truth, that future felt a long way away but, before it could overwhelm Adilandra, the drugs finally kicked in and she lost the ability to care about anything.

At least there was some reprieve in that...

CHAPTER 26
SENTINEL

I t was a still night in The Arid Lands, without a cloud in the sky and with a bitter chill in the air. Tauren son-of-none, a Karathan and native to the desert, took no notice of the weather, his attention entirely fixed on Salim. Inside the makeshift barracks, built centuries ago at the base of Syla's Gate, father and son shared the edge of a canvas cot. The two had sat in silence for some time after embracing each other, neither knowing exactly what to say.

"He was brave..." Tauren whispered. "Every day of his life, Halion was brave. He had enough courage and faith for the both of us."

"I should..." Salim had fresh tears flowing down his face. "I should have shown him a different life. One without fighting and bloodshed."

Tauren put an arm around his adoptive father's shoulder and pulled him in. The old honour guard still had the blood of assassins and Karathan guards in his hair. The son-of-none held him for another minute and wept with Salim.

"Tell me everything," Salim finally managed. "I need to know everything."

"As I told your companions, The New Dawn has taken control of Karath's resources."

"The New Dawn?"

"An old religion devoted to an elf called Valanis." Tauren saw the recognition in his father's eyes, as he had with the others. "They have been secretly ruling the empire for centuries. There are two elves in league with the Arakesh who appear to have taken control. They are the ones who killed Halion."

Tauren had visualised killing all of them. They were responsible for Halion's death and the death of so many owls.

"As we speak, an army of Darkakin savages advance on Syla's Gate." Tauren gave Salim a moment to absorb that. "It's part of some plan that would see all of Verda fall under Valanis's fist, not just the empire. We have to hold them here."

"I should never have left." Salim sat up and leant on his knees, burying his head between his legs.

"You had no choice."

"There is always a choice, Tauren. I should have taught Halion that years ago. I should have taught you both. Instead I left you here to *fight*."

"I made a choice," Tauren replied softly, "as did Halion. We chose to fight for what is right. The empire doesn't work; it is built upon the broken backs of slaves. Its foundations are rotten and its hierarchy corrupted. While I fought in the streets, Halion fought where it really mattered. He spent years converting the soldiers to our way of thinking, whilst influencing the highborn families. He didn't always win, but I was there to watch his back and he mine."

Salim looked up at him with glistening eyes, though his voice was full of judgement. "And what choice have you made now? You man the gate and incite open war with the Arakesh? This is a fool's errand! If the plans you speak of are true, those elves will march the entire Karathan army and all of the Arakesh out here to kill everyone. You don't have the numbers."

Tauren could feel his mood switch instantly. "Numbers? This

isn't about numbers or strategy. We stand and fight for the entire realm. It was you who taught me about honour, *honour guard*! Have you lost yours during your time in the wilds of Illian?"

"Yes! I have!" Salim stood up and paced like a caged lion. "I was stripped of my honour and exiled, remember. My time as a ranger has taught me about the importance of *survival*, and the life that can be achieved without some sense of honour! There's no honour in death, Tauren. It's just death..."

"How can you say that?" Tauren was on his feet now. "Your son hangs from the palace walls because he died doing what was right, what was honourable!"

Salim turned away and placed both of his hands against the cool wall. The two men stood in silence, their heavy breathing filling the room. This was not the reunion Tauren had dreamed of for so long.

"Forgive me..." Salim slowly slid down the wall and crumpled to his knees. "Please forgive me..." Through his fresh tears and matted hair, Tauren couldn't tell if he was talking to him or Halion. "I should never have left him."

Tauren couldn't help but weep with his adoptive father; the sight of him defusing any anger that burned inside of him. The son-of-none crouched by his side and the two embraced again, remaining there for some time.

Asher wandered throughout the makeshift camp, his eyes taking in these owls and their weapons. Those who weren't manning the top of the gate or the scaffolding were huddled round small fires, sharing stories and scraps of food. They weren't much to look at and their leathers were light with too many visible gaps to really be called armour. Still, they had apparently attacked the palace and fought Arakesh and Karathan guards alike. Those who were still alive before him deserved some credit.

Looking up, and the ranger had to really crane his neck, he could see the pyres lit atop the gate. They had doomed themselves by lighting them; everyone in Karath would be able to see them. Not that it mattered. Their presence would bring hell down upon them all. Alidyr would no doubt seek an audience with him, wishing to learn the real location of Paldora's gem. Such a relic could not be easily forgotten, even with a shard in Valanis's possession.

The ranger returned to the small fire on the edge of the camp, the furthest point from the gate, where his companions had found rest. They were all discussing the revelations delivered to them by Tauren son-of-none.

"I don't believe it!" Doran snorted. "Darkakin marchin' north? Sounds like bollocks to me..."

"It doesn't matter," Asher interjected. "We need to leave. Nightfall is east of here." The ranger could see Reyna's face falling into protest. "If we stay we're exposed; Karathan soldiers and assassins to the north, Darkakin to the south now. We need to head east before we're trapped here."

"He's right," Nathaniel agreed. "We didn't come here to fight an army of Darkakin, or the Karathans for that matter. We need to reach Nightfall and recover the gem. Win the war, not the battle."

"No." Reyna was standing now. "We can't allow the Darkakin to breach those gates. Their arrival must be Valanis's way of securing war in Illian. There is still hope for our people finding peace, but the Darkakin will bring chaos. How can we stand by and do nothing? The gods have brought us here for a reason."

"Look around, Princess." Asher's tone was harsher than he meant it to be. "If the Darkakin really are coming this way, the gods have delivered us to our deaths. We few cannot fight off an entire army of savages on one side and an army of trained Karathans on the other. It cannot be done."

"It cannot be done?" Reyna echoed incredulously. "I saw you stand in the gates of West Fellion and defy death time and time again."

"That was when I had the ring." Asher couldn't seem to lighten his tone. "Without the gem I die just as easily as everyone else; something you will witness if we linger here."

"I hope to *never* see that..." Reyna's soft, but genuine, tone disarmed Asher immediately.

All eyes fell on the ranger.

"I'm—" Asher's apology never found his lips, for that extra sense, which would forever attune him to the Arakesh, tugged at his attention.

The ranger flicked his head to the right and he scanned the darkness between Syla's Gate and Karath. The elves were the first to catch on, also detecting the intruders. It was Asher's alarm however, which had the other rangers and Nathaniel on their feet in seconds, all weapons drawn. Their combined commotion had the owls on alert and they too came to their feet, every one gazing into the dark.

Without a sound, the shadows gave birth to a single row of Arakesh, twelve by Asher's count. The assassins' approach was slow and their short-swords remained on their backs. Each was blindfolded behind red cloth, though completely aware of their surroundings. They would already know who among them was injured by the taste of the blood in the air, or how many arrows were aimed at them by the sound of the individual bowstrings.

Ro Dosarn stepped in front of the other assassins, his facial scars and square jaw setting him apart from the younger, fresher faces. His grey goatee and razored hair had yet to change over the years. Asher kept his hands relaxed by his side as he too stepped in front of his companions.

"It could have been you standing where I am now," Ro said. "But you didn't have the balls to see this life through, so now you're going to die, alongside your *friends*."

Asher didn't want to waste his breath bartering words with the killer. "You're here to deliver a message, or we wouldn't be talking at all."

Ro smirked, twisting his old scars. "Do you want to know how he died? Nasta Nal-Aket? You were close weren't you? He brought you to Nightfall all those years ago, trained you personally... like a father."

Asher clenched his jaw but he remained in place, Nasta's own training ever present in his life. He wouldn't give Ro the satisfaction of rising to the bait. It was true that, of all people, Nasta had been the closest thing to a father figure, but their relationship was an extraordinary one. The same man who kept him close and protected him, also beat him and subjected him to awful torments all in the name of Nightfall.

"He whimpered and begged like a dog," Ro continued.

The ranger gripped his broadsword but kept it sheathed. Ro chuckled to himself and balled both of his fists, while the other Arakesh tensed, some even reaching for their swords. All but one. Asher noticed the assassin on Ro's left, a young man by his features, who never flinched.

"I bring word from Alidyr Yalathanil," Ro finally announced. "You and the elves come back with us and everyone else gets to live."

Asher could already see how futile that promise was. Alidyr may permit the owls and the others to live, but the Darkakin army would still march right on through and kill them all anyway. The only thing the ranger was considering, was how best to send his rejection back to Alidyr...

"That one." Hadavad stepped forward and pointed his staff at the young assassin to Ro's left.

Everyone turned to regard the old mage, curious as to what he was trying to say. Even the Arakesh appeared somewhat confused. The young assassin did not.

"Hadavad?" Asher inquired, his eyes never leaving Ro.

"That one is not what he seems," the mage continued. "I know possession when I see it."

Despite the blindfold, the young assassin regarded Hadavad with some intensity.

"How astute... for a human." The young assassin stepped further into the firelight and removed his blindfold, abandoning it on the ground.

Ro swivelled on the man. "What are you -"

"Silence!" the young assassin hissed, his voice not quite his own. It was enough to give Ro Dosarn pause. "We meet again, ranger. And you have something that belongs to me..."

Asher followed the young man's gaze to the crystal pommel over his shoulder and instantly drew his broadsword. "Alidyr!"

This was enough to set off the Arakesh, who as one removed their twin short-swords and fell into attacking stances, with Ro in the lead, eager as ever. The unique sound of Reyna's enchanted bow being pulled back was the last noise to resound across the desert.

The possessed assassin held up his hand and smiled in the same eerie way as Alidyr. "Stop. There doesn't have to be blood, not yet anyway. Accompany Ro back to the palace, with the princess, and no one has to die."

"You want the gem," Asher said, as he fought the urge to remove the assassin's head from his body.

"You should have told me the truth in Elethiah; now I will have to extract the information at the expense of considerable pain."

"I'm not unaccustomed to pain..."

Alidyr smiled. "Who said it would be your pain?"

The ranger glanced over his shoulder at Reyna and knew there and then that the night would end in bloodshed.

Faylen said, "You expect us to come with you knowing what you intend? Our legends credited you with more intelligence than this, Alidyr."

Alidyr looked directly at Reyna. "I think if it means the lives of everyone here, you will *run* back to Karath if I command it."

Now Reyna stepped forward, her arrow still nocked as she lowered her aim. "Then you have underestimated us, Alidyr Yalathanil. As you did when I claimed this bow as my own." The magical bow still glittered out of the firelight, as if the stars were trapped inside.

Alidyr's smile was gone now. "Your next words will decide the fate of everyone behind you, Princess Reyna. Choose them well."

Reyna matched his tone perfectly. "We will stand here and show you the difference a few can make. Not a single Darkakin will set foot in these lands."

"You really think you can stop what's coming?"

"If we stand aside, you and your *master* would have Verda become an empire of dirt."

Alidyr laughed to himself and grinned. "And what would be wrong with that? The world is *made* of dirt. Now imagine it without the stain of humanity or even our own kin. A land made clean for the return of the gods!" The young assassin laughed again. "An empire of dirt indeed..."

Doran son of Dorain hefted his thick sword over his shoulder. "Ye have our answer, pisspot." The dwarf snorted and spat on the ground in front of the assassins. "Are we gettin' to it or what?"

"Not tonight, Master Dwarf." Alidyr met Asher's eyes. "Tonight you will need your rest. Tomorrow we will have our war, though I feel slaughter would be a better description."

One by one, the assassins melted back into the dark without a sound. Had Asher not been privy to their talents, he would have sworn it was magic. The last thing he saw was the wide smile on the young assassin's face before the shadows reclaimed him.

It was another moment before the entire camp breathed again. Tauren had emerged with Salim and was already adding extra guard to the perimeter. Salim still appeared to be in a different world to everyone else, unfazed as he was.

Asher turned around and looked upon Reyna with an impressed eye. There were not many who could stand up to Alidyr Yalathanil and even less when he was reinforced with Arakesh. Then again, this was the same princess who had killed one of the Hand, a feat that had never been accomplished before.

Their previous conversation not forgotten, Reyna stood in Asher's way. "Leave if you must, ranger. Go to Nightfall and retrieve

Paldora's gem, but I am staying here." With that, the princess replaced her arrow and walked away.

Asher regretted his harsh words and tone and knew there was still an apology to be given. Seeing the state of the perimeter guard however, the ranger decided it would have to wait.

"Glaide, Doran, take the western watch. Hadavad, Atharia the east. Bale-"

The barbarian put his hand in Asher's face. "I do not take command from little man." The behemoth strode into the camp and started ordering the owls about.

Salim was already walking back into the old barracks. Asher knew to give the man time, even if it had just become a very precious thing. He was bolstered by the knowledge that when the fighting started, Salim could finally be unleashed.

"What shall we do?" Nathaniel asked.

Asher didn't look to the knight, but instead bent down and picked up the discarded blindfold, left behind by the possessed assassin. He still loathed the feel of it in his hands and the memories it invoked, but the Nightseye elixir still coursed through his veins, and it was an advantage he couldn't waste right now.

"Make sure everyone gets some rest and patrols are taken in turns. Work with this Tauren son-of-none; the owls take his command."

Nathaniel raised his eyebrow. "And where are you going?"

Asher proceeded to tie the blindfold around his eyes, until all the light was gone and the world truly came to life in all its unseen detail. His senses were instantly heightened and his heart rate increased as he took it all in.

"I'm going out there." Asher nodded at the dark expanse between the gate and Karath. "Make sure we get some warning in case they come back."

"You think they might return before day break?"

"I think every word out of Alidyr's mouth is a lie." Asher strode out into the night.

CHAPTER 27
STAYING THE COURSE

Alidyr opened his eyes and found himself back in the palace, his spell at an end. He had been sat cross-legged in the middle of the balcony where the emperor would normally have his breakfast and enjoy his position above all others. The view from the palace offered the elf a vista of stars that watched over the city of Karath, now quiet and dimly lit. The atmosphere had changed in the city and Alidyr wondered if Nakir had made a mistake hanging the young Halion from the walls.

Still, the gods had delivered Asher back into his path.

The ancient elf said a prayer to Atilan, the king of the gods, and thanked him for the favour. Now he could accomplish his task and retrieve the whole gem, empowering his master once more. Valanis's private mission was still on Alidyr's mind, however. What had his master been looking for in Namdhor's archives and what was his interest in The Lifeless Isles? He didn't like his master having errands he wasn't aware of. Throughout The Dark War the Hand, and especially Alidyr, had been privy to all of Valanis's plans.

Faith, he had heard his master say. He had to have faith in not only the gods but also Valanis, their herald. He was to oversee the Darkakin's arrival and find Paldora's gem; nothing more.

"I take it they refused?" Nakir strolled onto the balcony.

"Of course."

"Did any of your Arakesh survive the refusal?" Nakir asked with some amusement in his tone.

Alidyr leaned on the railing and looked to the south, where Syla's Gate was now visible thanks to the torches and pyres. "You now control the Karathan army?"

"I always have. The leaders who opposed The New Dawn are dead."

"Then prepare them to march on Syla's Gate." Alidyr was already going through the coming battle. He would not be able to avoid this one.

The elf was sure of his skill and had never backed away from confrontation, but his strengths lay elsewhere. His brothers and sisters ran into battle perfectly, as though they were born for it, but Alidyr preferred to take the battle in from afar and see the bigger picture. That would be impossible with the ranger now. He had to ensure the ranger's survival so he could question him until the gem was in his hands. Alidyr trusted this to no one, not even Nakir, as his brother was often blinded by his desire to fight and the bloodshed that followed.

"The entire army will not be needed to take back the gate," Nakir replied. "They have what, a few hundred men? Some of whom are women."

"Don't let Samandriel hear you say that; she'll have your head." Indeed that was a fight Alidyr would enjoy watching.

"My point, brother, is that we have three thousand men ready to fight. I don't think we need to march all -"

"Three thousand?" Alidyr snapped his head around. "The emperor of The Arid Lands boasts an army of six thousand!"

"The emperor? That child can't count to ten!"

Alidyr was standing before Nakir in the blink of an eye with his finger pressed against his chest. "No, *brother*, as you have pointed out, you are the true ruler of The Arid Lands. Where are your forces?"

"Spread between the four cities -"

"Why are they not here?" Alidyr spat.

"Most are on their way as we speak, but they will not be needed. The soldiers we have here can keep order while the Karathans outfit the Darkakin with their new armour and weapons."

Alidyr was growing tired of Nakir's incompetence. "You underestimate the Darkakin. When they get through those gates they will be more akin to a plague of locusts than men. We need to funnel ten thousand of them through the city, equip them, and move them north to Velia without incident. That cannot be done with three thousand men!"

Nakir clenched his jaw and bowed his head slightly out of respect. "What would you have me do, brother?"

"Have word sent to those travelling here; they must reach Karath before Paldora's Star crosses the night's sky. Tomorrow, both you and I will march what army we have to the gate. Also, you will ensure that every soldier knows of Asher and Princess Reyna. I want both alive."

"As you wish." Nakir bowed again and made to leave, only stopping before he reached the archway. "And what of the emperor? Faro?"

"When the Darkakin arrive it won't matter who rules what. Chaos will reign in Karath after we march north. Kill the boy, or don't... it doesn't really matter."

Alidyr remained outside for a while, looking down on the city. When Valanis was returned to power, he would burn it all down and replace it with a realm fit for the gods. The old elf knew he would see that vision through to its end.

Still, he worried about the herald of the gods...

～

Valanis slowly emerged from the sparkling pool, his head and flowing blond hair as dry as when he entered. The elf stopped before getting out completely and examined the shard of Paldora's Gem on his finger. It would give him moments of reprieve outside of the cavern, but it would never last. The goddess of the stars had intended him to have the gem in its entirety, ensuring his dominance over Naius's magic.

Valanis looked on at Thallan and Samandriel. Samandriel appeared to have been in a fight, though her victory was unclear, with smoke rising from her cloak and a cut across her pale cheek. No human could have struck her so.

"How long was I under?" he asked.

Thallan stood up and genuflected before answering. "Days, Master. Where were you? Alidyr said you went to Namdhor."

Valanis ignored the question and looked at Samandriel, her expression pained. "Have the Graycoats been dealt with?"

Samandriel hesitated. "No, Master. The battalion from Namdhor wasn't enough - the Graycoats were too skilled."

"Not for you!" Valanis half rose from the water, baring his chiselled torso. "You could have killed them all."

"They were assisted by *elves*, Master. One of them commanded powerful magic."

"Elves? In Illian?" Valanis weighed her words. "How many?"

"There are only three now," the general replied with a wicked smile.

"A vanguard then. And you presented them with a common enemy?" Valanis had a tone of disappointment.

He was moments away from punishing her when the pressure changed inside the cavern. Valanis looked from Thallan to Samandriel and saw their mouths moving but there were no words finding his ears. The elf scooped his hand through the magical water and lifted a dozen small crystals from the water, but there was no sound. Valanis ignored his disciples' confused expressions and sank back into the pool, fearing another seizure coming on. They had never affected one of his sense like this before, especially while he was in the pools.

We didn't give you this power so you could take a bath...

Valanis looked about the cavern searching for the source of the familiar voice. There was never any mistaking the voice of Naius, the very god who had gifted him with such magic and left the pools behind.

My pools have restored you, now find The Veil!

Valanis could just make out the dark shadow of a lingering figure beyond the stalactites. "I have searched through the archives in Namdhor, torn through the ruling houses of Dragorn and emptied the vaults of Stowhold, Lord Naius. The Veil is hidden from me!"

I gave you the gem! The seductive voice of Paldora came from above, where the gravity-defying pools sat.

We told you in the beginning, Naius said, *the gem is only a means to an end. The Veil is all that matters!*

Valanis could see that neither Thallan nor Samandriel understood what was happening. They were speaking to each other but still no words could be heard by the herald.

Your kind was made to be strong...

This new voice carried more weight behind it. Paldora and Naius quickly faded away, as if scared by this new presence, but Valanis welcomed the king of the gods, privileged that he was to even hear his mighty voice. Atilan's ethereal form continuously changed shape, keeping his true form hidden. The dark shadow spasmed and flickered between worlds as the greatest of gods hammered through the cavern, until he was at the lip of the pool, towering over Valanis.

I made you to be strong. The ethereal, smoke-like, figure leaned over the glistening pool. *So be strong. I will give you what I can to sustain you with only the shard, but Paldora is sending you another gift, one foretold of a millennium ago.*

Valanis thought immediately of the prophecy. "Paldora's celestial gem graces daylight sky..."

And in its beauty ordains calamity... Atilan's eyes flashed within his ever-changing face. *Finish what you have put in motion. Bring the Darkakin home and lay waste to Illian. When the dust settles, The Veil will be revealed and our return will be assured.*

"My Lord." Valanis bowed his head and watched Atilan dip his finger into the pool. The elf gasped, his breath taken away, as the energy inside the magical waters intensified and the shard within his ring began to glow.

When he at last opened his eyes, the king of the gods had disappeared and the sound of the world had returned.

"Master..?" Thallan was staring at the pool.

Valanis looked down and saw that he was now sitting in a pool of dark stones, the liquid crystals drained of their energy. The elf lifted a handful from the surface and saw that they were as lifeless as any rock, but the ring on his finger continued to glow.

"You were speaking in a language I have never heard." Samandriel had tears in her eyes. "Was it the language of the gods?"

"What happened to the pool?" Thallan examined one of the dead crystals with concern.

Valanis stood up and walked out of the pool, bringing dozens of dull gems with him. "The gods are ever by our side. Their gifts know no bounds." He inspected the shard and its new glow, similar to his own golden aura.

A wave of his hand had the dark robes and armour rising from the floor and adorning his naked body with ease. The menacing facial mask flew into his hand and he placed it over his head and drew the encompassing hood over the top.

"I think it's time Illian witnessed the true power of the gods..."

PART FOUR

CHAPTER 28
TAKING FLIGHT

Gideon looked from Ilargo to Adriel and felt his palms become clammy and hot. Both elf and dragon watched the young mage with expectation and incredible patience. It was another beautiful day in southern Ayda, with a canvas of brilliant blue and not a cloud in sight. That was where they wanted to go...

We will do it together, Gideon.

Flying was not something Gideon had found pleasant to date. It hadn't helped that his dreams often had him falling through the sky, a topic he was determined to return to - if he survived the day's training.

Off to the side, Galanör chuckled softly. "I never thought I'd see the day a Dragorn was afraid of heights..."

Gideon rolled his eyes. "I'm not afraid of heights. I'm afraid of falling!"

"You will be safe with Ilargo," Adriel offered. "Galandavax and I will accompany you also."

Ilargo walked over to Gideon, his long tail skimming the edge of the lake. The dragon simply lowered his head until the mage could place his own in the space between Ilargo's eyes. The two shared a moment and Gideon felt Ilargo's confidence and excitement fill him up as if it were his own. The young mage lifted a hand and stroked under Ilargo's jaw, each scale silky and smooth against his skin.

"Together..." Gideon whispered.

Always...

Gideon grabbed one of the horns above Ilargo's eye and pulled and twisted himself up, until he came to rest between two larger spikes on the dragon's back. The green dragon roared with elation and joy. There was no pause however, as Ilargo sprinted to the edge of the lake and took off, the force of which pulled Gideon closer to his long neck. His knuckles turned white when the dragon banked to the left and weaved between the floating boulders, aiming for the sky.

Are you ready?

Gideon's heart was pounding fast and his focus was entirely on his grip. He wanted to shout *no* at the top of his lungs and feel the ground under his feet once more, but his terror kept his mouth clamped shut. Upon feeling this, Ilargo continued to pour his emotions into the mage, mixing the two together until there was no distinguishing. As the dragon shot through the gap in the boulders and soared into the big blue above, Gideon felt his terror ease and a sense of calm filled him.

The sound of the waterfall died away and Ilargo's beating wings became a soothing reassurance. Gideon's grip loosened and he pulled back slightly to take in the surreal environment. It felt good to fly without fleeing Sandstalkers or attacking Darkakin, but instead just to simply fly. The Red Mountains dropped away and all of Ayda was laid out beneath them.

Freedom. The word reverberated through Ilargo's mind and settled in Gideon's as if it was his thought.

The oasis of Dragons' Reach looked all the more beautiful amid the dry lands of the south and The Flat Wastes to the west; a green gem in the desert.

"I want to go higher!" Gideon yelled over the wind, all fear abandoned now.

You don't have to shout. I can hear you remember...

Gideon closed his eyes for a moment and said in his mind, **I want to go higher!** He could tell that the statement made Ilargo happy.

We cannot go much higher or the heavens will steal you from me.

The mage looked up and saw the faintest of stars looking back at him. Indeed the more he thought about it the more he realised how cold it was becoming and the air felt thinner. He dared to let go of the spike with one hand and reached for Abigail's wand on his thigh. It was a small spell to restore the heat, but the air was another problem altogether.

Ilargo...

I know. And with that, the green dragon dived and levelled out where the air was easier to breathe. The change in direction made Gideon's stomach flip and he gripped the spikes again.

They continued to fly for a while, giving Gideon a chance to adapt to the sudden changes in direction, as well as learning the subtle changes in Ilargo's muscles that would alert the mage to the dragon's intentions. After an hour or so, the pair had drifted away from the Reach and glided over The Flat Wastes, giving them a clear view of the dense jungle known as The Great Maw. Further still, Gideon could make out the city of Malaysai in the heart of it, its pyramids and towers easy to spot.

It would be so easy, he thought. They could swoop in and set the whole city on fire before saving Adilandra.

Is that what you wish to do?

Gideon caught himself. Not having his mind to himself was going to take some getting used to.

I know I want to save Adilandra, and I certainly want to destroy that wretched city...

But...

I would not risk you or the others. You're too important. They have too much Crissalith at their disposal.

There was a curiosity to Ilargo's questions. The dragon did not appear opposed to the idea of attacking Malaysai, as Adriel was.

We are bonded now, Gideon. Our thoughts and wants will begin to align. Adriel shares Galandavax's thoughts and memories, and both have seen more war than they would like.

Are you talking about The First War? Gideon had many questions on the subject.

For Galandavax, yes. Adriel wasn't alive then.

Before Gideon could ask anything else, the elf and his enormous ebony dragon cast them in shadow. The pair soared above for a moment, before gliding down beside them. Adriel appeared regal astride Galandavax's back; completely at ease.

Hello, Gideon. Adriel's voice was inside his mind, just as Ilargo's was. *Through the dragons, all Dragorn share a bond which allows us to communicate.*

It's getting awfully crowded in my mind. Gideon noticed the two dragons flying perfectly together, each always aware of the other's position.

Imagine what it used to be like when there were hundreds of us... Adriel adjusted his position to face Gideon better. *Are you ready for your next lesson?*

Gideon really didn't like the tone of Adriel's question. **No.**

Adriel laughed, though the melodic sound could not be heard. *You must have faith and trust in Ilargo. As long as you are together, the sky is your realm too.*

The elf extended his hand and Gideon realised too late what was about to happen. The concussive force knocked him from the dragon's back and sent him careering over the side. The mage scrambled for the wing, but his grip was for naught. He fell, and this time it wasn't a dream. Gideon flipped end-over-end, with his limbs swinging in every direction, and the view constantly changing from sky to land.

Balance yourself, Ilargo uttered. *Give into the fall and relax; then you will balance.*

Gideon thought about every expletive response he could give, but instead he heard Adriel instructing him to have faith in Ilargo. Despite his plummet, the mage relaxed his muscles and felt for the pull of the earth, until he was finally able to turn in the air, allowing his back to face the sky. With his arms and legs out, Gideon continued to fall, taking in shallow breaths as he did.

The sight of Ilargo was pure relief. The green dragon glided underneath him, the membrane of his wings filled like that of a sail. It took a moment longer for the two to match their speed. Gideon gripped the familiar spikes and pulled himself into place, just as Ilargo flapped his wings and sent them back into the sky. It was only then that Gideon saw just how close they had both come to meeting the ground.

That was fun!

Gideon didn't yet share that particular emotion...

Galanör had started running as soon as Adriel and Galandavax left the ground. The elf knew exactly where he was going and had no intention of stopping until he got there. His unrivalled stamina and strength proved true, allowing him to move through the oasis with grace and ease. His tattered cloak flew out behind him and his dual swords clung tightly to his hips.

There was nothing else to be done.

That thought had rattled around inside his mind for days and it was the only thing that kept him running. The guilt was almost crushing when he launched the first fireball. Using his magic to destroy life, even that of a tree felt inherently wrong. But burn them he did. His stride never faltered and the balls of fire erupted from his hands, each spell finding the heart of a great tree and setting it ablaze. The fire spread quickly, finding the neighbouring trees and bushes.

It wasn't long before the oasis had a burning, black line cutting it in half. Galanör could hear the wood burning and the fire crackling behind him, but still he pushed on. Anything that was lush and green he set on fire. The damage had to be as widespread as possible.

The elf skidded to a stop at the edge of the clearing where Malliath rested; the smoke was already drifting through the trees. As predicted, the other dragons could not ignore the size of the growing blaze. Galanör knew that another distraction wouldn't work, unless it put the entire Reach in jeopardy. Malliath remained low to the ground, appearing entirely ignorant of the fire. Galanör waited another moment for the last of the guarding dragons to disappear overhead before making his move.

The warrior had given his approach much consideration. He didn't want to surprise the dragon, but instead give the great wyrm some notice. Galanör strode into the field of broken logs and fallen trees, balling his fists to keep his nerve.

Malliath's purple eyes found him immediately.

Galanör's foot hesitated before finding the ground, but he thought of Adilandra. The queen had to be saved. As the elf approached, the black dragon shifted his weight and extended his wings in time with his arching neck. Galanör had seen the movement before and knew that a jet of fire was usually what followed.

"Malliath!" The elf kneeled and looked up. "This is our moment. For both of us. We can fly away from this place and be free, free to be unleashed. Take me to Malaysai and we can do what we were both made to do."

He was yet to be consumed in fire and Galanör took this as a good sign. Perhaps his time among the other dragons had begun to work after all. That thought was fleeting when the black dragon bared his numerous teeth and narrowed his eyes. Apparently, Malliath had no intention of burning the elf, but was in fact planning on eating him. The dragon lunged. His mighty head arced high to come down on Galanör. The deadly maw seemed only inches away from the elf when a hulking mountain of ebony scales collided with Malliath's neck.

Galanör rolled across the ground, giving in to his survival instincts, as the two dragons smashed into one another. Fire was spat high into the air and ice sprayed across the ground in the savage battle. Galandavax's claws raked down Malliath's hardened chest, tugging loose scales and cutting the flesh beneath, while the black dragon clamped his jaws around Galandavax's neck.

That was when the largest and oldest dragons arrived.

Rainael the emerald star hit the ground hard with Vorgraf the mountain child and Dolvosari the storm maker by her side. Beldroga the great hunter flanked Malliath while Angala the wise went low for his legs. Emenar the golden one was the last to drop out of the sky, and drop he did. The gold dragon buried Malliath, throwing up dirt and broken logs into the air.

"You will never learn!" Adriel was advancing on Galanör with some speed.

"We need to -"

Galanör's protest was cut dramatically short when Adriel's flat hand thrust out into a nerve cluster in his shoulder. The ancient elf followed it up with three swift, open-palm, attacks that each found a vulnerable place on Galanör's body. The point of Adriel's fingers caused an explosion of pain to ripple through his muscles.

Another flash of pain had Galanör on his knees in the mud. He couldn't quite find the right amount of air to please his lungs or the balance to stand back up. Beyond Adriel, the younger dragons had already started gliding over the treetops and putting the fires out with their ice breath.

Galanör finally looked up at Adriel and saw new wounds appearing across his neck and patches of his robes dripping with blood. Galandavax's wounds were mirrored in the Dragorn's body, though he seemed to barely notice. Instead, Adriel brought his hand down across Galanör's neck like a hammer, robbing him of conscious thought.

Galanör had no clue as to how long he had been unconscious, but the sun was higher than it had been when Adriel unleashed Mag'dereth on him. The air was hot and dry, also. The elf blinked hard and sat up, taking in his new surroundings for the first time.

There was no mistaking The Flat Wastes.

For miles around there was nothing but harsh desert and a wavy horizon. The Red Mountains were small in the distance, the backdrop to Gideon and Adriel, who both stood under the sun watching him. As he found his feet again, both Ilargo and Galandavax dropped down, their claws sinking into the crusted ground. The sound of birds and insects soon found Galanör's ears and he turned around to see that he was standing on the very edge of The Great Maw.

"You are exiled from Dragons' Reach, Galanör." Adriel's grave tone told of his disappointment. "Rainael the emerald star agrees that your freedom is the best thing, though I would point out that your path leads only to death." The elf looked beyond Galanör, to the jungle.

Galanör ignored Adriel for the moment and focused on Gideon. The mage couldn't meet his eyes, choosing to look at the elf's chest. Galanör wanted to ask if he would come with him so that they could rescue Adilandra together, but that would have been selfish; Gideon was born to be a Dragorn, a title that bore responsibility. He decided to make it easy on the mage and address Adriel instead.

"When history looks back on this..." Galanör laughed mirthlessly, withholding the insult that sat on the end of his tongue. "Well, I suppose when all of this is over, you'll be the only one left to write history. Enjoy paradise." The elf turned and strode towards the jungle, hesitating before entering. "And Gideon..." He half-turned to regard the young man. "You're the first of your people to become a Dragorn. Being the first means you get to make the rules. Be the Dragorn *you* want to be..."

Without waiting for a response, the warrior-born entered the jungle and quickly disappeared from sight.

CHAPTER 29
SCHISM

T auren son-of-none leaned against the old iron parapet and looked down at the land below Syla's Gate. On the one side was civilisation and Illian as man knew it and, on the other, a world that hadn't been seen for over a millennium. Illian's southern lands were unknown and as dangerous as, if not more than, The Wild Moores in the north. Tauren widened his vision beyond the valley floor and the encompassing mountains, searching for any sign of the Darkakin horde.

The dust cloud on the horizon opened a pit in his stomach.

"I can't believe they're actually coming..." It was the Graycoat, Nathaniel Galfrey, who made the comment.

Tauren had brought them up at the request of the princess, the elf. That fact alone turned his whole life upside down. There had always been a part of him that considered the elves to be no more than stories, but fighting Nakir, meeting Alidyr and now standing side-by-side with Princess Reyna... Tauren didn't know what to think anymore.

"This gate will bar them," Reyna replied confidently, her lithe hands running along the edge of the parapet.

Faylen turned back to look at the city in the distance, her fair features marred with concern. "If anyone could find a way it would be the Hand of Valanis. We already know that both Nakir and Alidyr are in Karath. Both were blessed by Valanis with a portion of Naius's magic; they shouldn't be underestimated."

Tauren examined the gate under his feet, taking in its incredible width of at least twenty-feet of solid iron. The walkway that formed the top of the gate was interrupted by a single line in the middle, where the two doors were sealed. Most of it was layered in sand and dust after centuries of standing in the desert, but up close the son-of-none could see the intricate work of the elves. Almost every inch of the dark iron was engraved with glyphs Tauren didn't recognise.

"We shouldn't be up here," Nathaniel said, unimpressed with the view.

"We have time," Reyna countered. "If Alidyr marched the Karathan army out of the city we would see them coming."

Nathaniel crossed the walkway and looked out over Karath. "This is a killing field. Open spaces, no cover, a wall to our back and no escape route. They'll cross the desert and pin us against Syla's Gate with arrows before a single Karathan soldier even lifts his sword."

"Are you always so glum?" Tauren said, the hint of a smile on his face. In truth, the man was just happy to have left Salim below, where his grief could not tip his own over the edge. In some ways he welcomed the fight to come, if only so he could give himself over to the mayhem and forget about the deaths that weighed on him.

"You'll get used to him," Reyna said, though her smile spoke of her true feelings for the Graycoat.

"My owls are good fighters. They aren't Arakesh, but they can stand up to any Karathan soldier." Tauren directed his words at Nathaniel, who didn't seem convinced.

"Then let's hope Alidyr decides to leave his greatest weapon inside the city walls." Nathaniel turned away from the vista and locked eyes with Faylen, but Tauren could not decipher the silent conversation.

"The Arakesh are unaccustomed to open warfare," Reyna said. "We saw that at West Fellion. They get in each other's way and they certainly won't get along with the Karathan army."

"And what's left of West Fellion now?" Nathaniel added.

The princess didn't have anything to say to that. Tauren had certainly heard of West Fellion, having narrowly avoided their patrols of Karath, as a child, while they searched for fresh recruits. The battle described to him at their fort was hard to imagine, but something told him that the battle about to take place at Syla's Gate would dwarf it.

The son-of-none looked from north to south, weighing up the events that were taking place around him. Never did he imagine that he would be in the heart of a struggle that held all of Verda in the balance. Though he was young, The White Owl could see where the battle would be fought and where the war would be fought. Valanis was the insidious will that drove the Darkakin north and manipulated the elves to the east. He was the enemy.

"If your task is as grave and important as you claim, you should leave now." Tauren knew he was offering the greatest fighters at his disposal a way out, but his was the battle and theirs was the war. "Go to Nightfall before Karath marches on the gate. Asher said it is north east of here. If you follow The Undying Mountains east until you smell the sea, then turn north, you will avoid any patrols."

Princess Reyna stepped away from the parapet with her magnificent bow in hand. "Your owls are too few, Tauren son-of-none. Every blade and arrow is going to count in the fight to come."

Before Tauren could reply, the sound of a horn blared on each side of the gate, where the look-outs held positions. They all moved swiftly to the north side of the walkway and gazed intently into the distance, where a line of armoured men on horseback could be seen. The riders were charging out of Karath's southern gate in rows of three, their black cloaks draped over their mounts.

"We need to be down there!" Tauren ran for the scaffolding to their right and instructed the two owls to lower them all on the newly roped pulley system.

The group were closed in tight on the way down, the only sound coming from the two men turning the levers above. There were stairs beside them, but the height was dizzying and the energy required to run down so many steps would be gruelling before a battle. They could only watch as the soldiers gradually closed the gap across the strip of desert, each with a spear and a shield emblazoned with the head of a horse.

"Asher..." Reyna whispered.

The ranger was still in the desert, between the gate and Karath. Tauren squinted to see the man stand up and pull his broadsword free of the ground. It was quite the sight, to see his green cloak billowing and his sword shimmering under the sun, as an army of Karathans charged towards him.

"Fool! Why isn't he running?" Faylen asked.

"I don't think he knows how to run..." Nathaniel offered.

"He is an angry man." Tauren's comment had their attention. "I have only known him for a few hours and even I can see the anger that lives inside of him." In truth, Tauren could see his own anger reflected in the ranger. It was a quiet anger that lived just under the surface, always ready to take over and never satisfied. He would recognise it anywhere.

"Angry he may be," Reyna said, "but he would stand before an army if it meant keeping others safe."

The princess's admiration was easy to see and easily shared by the son-of-none.

Tauren hung over the side to see his owls below. They were running about, forming lines and defensive positions with the other rangers running ahead of them to their horses. The big man, Bale, was easy to see, even from this height; he was riding in line with Glaide, Doran and the two mages.

Salim was nowhere to be seen.

"Doesn't this thing go any faster?" Nathaniel asked with irritation.

By the time the lift reached the bottom four flights of stairs, the companions jumped out of the platform and sprinted down the steps. The Karathan horses were lining up now in front of Asher, spreading their size around him in a semi-circle and concealing Karath in the distance. Tauren was new to war, but even to him it seemed a foolish thing to have stopped their charge and simply lined up. With the speed of the horses, the Karathan soldiers could have run through Asher and the lines of owls, cutting them down with ease. In that regard, perhaps being so close to Syla's Gate was a deterrent.

The son-of-none joined the three in mounting a horse and riding out to meet the rangers. He called to his owls to hold their positions before leaving.

The elves showed incredible agility, jumping down from their trotting horses with a bow in hand and an arrow nocked. The rangers had all left their mounts and come to stand behind Asher now. Hadavad, the mage, was whispering into the end of his staff; the spells were just mutterings to Tauren, but he was more than glad that they had some magic at their disposal. Bale of the Oakbreaker clan looked ready to kill anything that moved, with an axe in each hand and a massive grin on his face. Doran appeared more as a bull, squat and ready to charge with his wide sword and spiked gauntlets. Glaide and Asher were of a calmer demeanour, each holding their sword in a casual hold.

The sound of three bow strings being pulled taut beside Tauren had him looking at the elves and the knight, each as focused as the next. They were certainly few, but the son-of-none was sure these few could make a dent in the Karathan army that would be remembered for all time. His own owls were behind him, in the distance, looking out at the riders lined before them.

"Well what are ye waitin' for?" Doran yelled, smashing his fist into his chestplate.

There was only silence that followed.

A single rider left his horse behind and approached the group on foot. He dug his spear into the ground, along with his sword, before slowly removing his helmet to reveal a southerner's face and shoulder-length black hair. Tauren was sure he had seen the soldier before, but he couldn't place him.

"I am Kail An-Agoh. Before you are twelve-hundred of Karath's greatest warriors. Each man here has pledged an oath to protect these lands but, more so, they have sworn to protect its people." Kail looked past Asher and locked eyes with Tauren. "We were taught the true meaning of this oath by our commander, Halion Al-Anan."

The next moment was that of only stunned silence.

"You're not here to fight us?" Tauren asked, incredulously.

"We have come to fight, but we would fight by your side. The Darkakin must not be allowed to breach Syla's Gate; our families depend on it."

Asher commanded Kail's attention. "You would fight your own to this end? Twelve-hundred men do not make up the army of The Arid Lands. Alidyr will march out your brothers to take this gate."

Kail raised his chin. "If our brothers cannot see the evil that has taken a hold of our lands, or do not truly understand what marches on our city, then they will be *re-educated*. At the point of a blade if necessary."

Asher appeared to be assessing those words closely. "How many more remain under Alidyr's command?"

"Around eighteen-hundred," Kail replied grimly.

Tauren wasn't really taking in a lot of what they were saying. Instead, the son-of-none was dazed, examining every Karathan face. These were men who had each spoken with Halion at some point and at great length if they had all come round to a new way of thinking. These soldiers were the ones his brother had been converting for years, convincing them that slavery was not the way forward. These men were the future of Karath, if it had a future.

All these years he had thought his brother had the easier task of the two, with Tauren living a harder life on the streets, fighting slavers. Now he saw that Halion had been completing the much harder task of changing a mindset that had ruled over Karath for a thousand years.

Asher glanced at the old mage. "Hadavad?"

The old man looked about the faces with a scrutinising eye as he leant against his staff. A quick shake of the head was his only reply to the unasked question.

"Where is the rest of the army?" Asher asked. "Why haven't they marched out yet?"

"They will soon," Kail replied. "The shadowed ones, Alidyr and... Nakir. They have sent word to the outlying forces. They are waiting for reinforcements to arrive, but they will certainly march tonight, with or without all of them."

"How do we know this is not a trap?" Faylen lowered her bow, her question directed at Asher.

"There would be no sense in setting a trap," Asher replied, his eyes scanning every soldier. "They already have superior numbers and Alidyr knows it." The ranger turned to Tauren. "Does this make more sense to you?"

The son-of-none nodded his head. "Halion and I have been working together for years; the owls and myself on the streets, Halion on the inside. Our original intention was to take the palace and replace the emperor with a better ruler, thereby ending slavery in The Arid Lands. My brother always said there were those loyal to our cause..."

The ranger sheathed his sword and the others followed.

"Asher..." Faylen said with caution.

"Only alliance and trust between two shores." Asher's words were lost on Tauren. "Isn't that what you keep saying?" The ranger turned and looked at Faylen. "I suppose this will have to be the trust part..."

Glaide announced, "We will need to work fast if we are to be ready for their attack."

"Not just them," Tauren added. "The Darkakin are almost here." That comment had the line of riders muttering amongst themselves; their concern evident.

"You are sure?" Glaide asked.

Nathaniel replaced his arrow and shouldered his bow. "Unless there is a cloudless storm in the south, an army is marching towards us."

"Then there is work to do." Reyna appeared more warrior than princess to Tauren. "Asher?"

"Forgive me, Princess, but it was Tauren son-of-none who led his people to protect the gate. He chose to stand before the Darkakin. I believe this fight is his to command." The ranger half-turned to Kail. "If you would take it."

Kail An-Agoh looked from Asher to Tauren. "An order from The White Owl is an order from Halion Al-Anan."

Tauren wished his brother could have seen this. "We will be ready to defend from the north first. The Darkakin are still a day away and they will struggle to find a way past Syla's Gate, but Alidyr *will* march on us without any obstacle. We have to be ready."

Alidyr could feel his master's disappointed gaze fall over him and he wasn't even in The Arid Lands. Valanis would punish them all severely if they failed to usher the Darkakin through Syla's Gate, and right now the odds were tipping. From the balcony he could see the thousand-strong traitors on horseback, trotting along with their new allies. The battle on this side of the gate would be more evenly pitched now.

The elf was so angry he couldn't even look at Nakir. "What a mess you have made, brother. You were supposed to have The Arid Lands under your control."

"A betrayal in their numbers could not have been foreseen."

"It isn't about foresight, you fool! It's about planning. Our master set this plan in motion decades ago. You have spent too long herding the upper echelons of Karath, when you should have been focusing on those that count." Alidyr pointed at the riders in the distance. "Soldiers, Nakir! Mindless troops who want for nothing but the thrill of killing! *That* was all you were supposed to create."

"We still outnumber them." Nakir was holding his anger back.

"They have a few who count for more. Do not underestimate your enemy, Nakir; that has forever been the downfall of you and the others. You think the power gifted us makes us invincible, but I saw Adellum fall at their hands through his own arrogance."

"Then together we will concentrate on those few. Let the soldiers create a bloody mess of it, while we thin the herd of the strongest."

"We will not be riding out with what's left of our army. That gate must be opened when the Darkakin arrive or our master will have both of our heads." Alidyr had been meditating almost continuously in preparation for opening the gate.

"And how are we to do that with a battle raging around us?"

"Who said we'll be on this side of the gate?" Alidyr held up the glowing crystals he had taken from the pools of Naius. "We will portal to the other side and open it from there. While they are busy fighting Karathan soldiers, the gates will be opened and the Dark-akin will finish off anyone still standing..."

CHAPTER 30
REVELATION

Gideon took blow after blow as he forgot specific movements within Mag'dereth. Every time his arm or leg failed to be in the right place at the right time, Adriel would lash out and hit the mage around the head or jab him in the ribs. They had been going through the routines together for hours on top of the highest boulder, floating above the lake.

"You're not concentrating..."

Adriel's statement was followed by another smack to the side of the head. Gideon rubbed his pain away and moved off instead of falling back into the Mag'dereth.

"The view can be distracting," Adriel commented, "but I don't think that's what's on your mind."

"Galanör was just exiled!" Gideon replied with an irritated tone that he quickly regretted.

"It wasn't that long ago that you wanted him dead for his part in your friend's death."

Gideon blinked slowly; that very thought having crossed his mind more than once since the elf's exile. The mage was standing by the edge now, looking out over the Reach. Smoke was still rising from the forest canopy where Galanör had set the trees on fire. The dragons had halted the flames and brought Malliath back under control, but the oasis was scarred. Adriel had plans to rejuvenate the damaged trees, but emphasised the importance of Gideon's training.

"Galanör will see to his own suffering for the part he played." Gideon sighed and dropped his head. "What am I doing? Why am I training to be a Dragorn? I've already had years of training; I'm a mage, and a good one! I have the power to help Galanör and maybe even rescue Adilandra. Why am I not doing that?" Gideon was pacing now. "I should have gone with him..."

"You need to train."

"For what?" Gideon threw up his hands. "Galanör was right. I'll be dead before I finish my training and what little I learn will never be put to use in Dragons' Reach!"

"You cannot think of yourself anymore; you are Dragorn."

"I'm not thinking of myself! I'm thinking about Galanör and Adilandra. I'm thinking about how I warn Illian of the Darkakin and the elves when I'm stuck here!"

"I was not talking about them." Adriel looked up, beyond Gideon's shoulder.

The mage turned around to see Ilargo flying towards them with magnificent grace.

"Ilargo has bonded with you. You even share a sanctuary. You could not abandon him any more than you could abandon your arm or leg."

I can feel your turmoil.

The words had Gideon following Ilargo's flight path over the boulder and around the lake below. Just watching the dragon glide between the rocks was soothing.

People don't actually say turmoil.

I am not people.

It's hard to argue with that.

You must train, Gideon.

You sound like Adriel...

Adriel is right.

Gideon could feel a rising sense of hope building inside of him. It wasn't his hope. The mage continued to watch the green dragon and realised that Ilargo had invested a great deal in their bond, though his expectations were still beyond him.

"You said it yourself, Adriel; the Dragorn are not needed anymore. Why are we doing this? If it's so we can help the rest of Verda then let's go with the dragons, destroy the Darkakin and broker peace between our people before they go to war! Without the threat of war you could open the Dragon Wall at Mount Garganafan and release the eggs. Their kind could thrive beyond The Red Mountains..."

Adriel turned to the horizon. "The Dragorn harbour a greater responsibility than keeping peace in the realm."

"What could be more important than averting a war so terrible it will consume every race? Or destroying the Darkakin; they're pure evil, Adriel!"

The elf locked eyes with the mage. "You don't know real evil. It's hard to understand from your perspective but, by staying in Dragons' Reach, we are preventing evil from reigning over Verda."

Gideon was more confused. "What are you not saying? What are the Dragorn really supposed to do?"

Adriel was silent, his expression unreadable as he gazed across the Reach. "I would talk with Rainael." Without any warning, the elf stepped off the edge of the boulder and plummeted to the ground, where Galandavax swooped in at the last moment to carry him away.

"I hate it when he does that."

We could do that. I would catch you.

Gideon looked over the edge, his fear of falling not quite expelled. ***I think I'll climb down the old-fashioned way.***

The mage collected his staff, standing rigid on end, and stamped it into the hard rock. The boulder cracked around his feet and lifted away, hovering over the edge. Gideon did his best not to look down as the platform descended back to the lakeside. Ilargo continued to glide overhead, casting shadows over the pebbled beach.

What is Adriel not telling me, Ilargo?

A sense of trepidation swept through Gideon's body, emanating from the green dragon. The feeling was so powerful it made the mage instantly regret asking the question, as he too felt that the subject was somehow forbidden.

Our bond is strong, Gideon. Stronger than I thought it could be. No elf and dragon have ever formed a sanctuary inside of ten years together. It took Adriel and Galandavax fourteen years to share theirs. The memories you have seen through my mother's eyes... you were not expected to see those so soon.

Ilargo came to land elegantly in front of Gideon, with his impressive wingspan outstretched to slow him down. His green scales glittered with the same gold that his mother had and his blue eyes bored into the mage.

You didn't answer my question. I thought we didn't have secrets anymore. Gideon touched the side of his temple, signifying their deeper bond.

Ilargo arched his neck and puffed out his chest. Gideon knew this was the dragon's physical display of contemplation. For just a moment, Ilargo checked the skies above, searching for his kin. Gideon didn't flinch as the dragon's head dipped to his level.

Adriel lied to you. You are not the first human Dragorn...

CHAPTER 31
ATTACK ON SYLA'S GATE

A sher leaned against the scaffolding beside Syla's Gate and scrutinised the new forces. They had spent the day discussing strategy with Tauren son-of-none and Kail of the Karathan army. The ranger had glimpsed victory when the Karathans arrived to help, but he had kept his true thoughts to himself.

They were all going to die...

That particular thought had stuck with him since Vangarth, when they had first decided to retrieve the gem from Nightfall. Asher didn't consider himself a pessimist - he was simply a realist. He had seen too many battles and fought enough foes to know that the victorious underdog was just wishful thinking. The larger force always won in the end.

"You think we're going to lose..."

Asher was getting used to Faylen being able to sneak up on him. "They outnumber us, and that's without the Darkakin at our backs."

Faylen came to rest beside him, her natural perfume as intoxicating as her beauty. "I have been taking the measure of these men. The horses will put us on an equal footing -"

"The horses will create chaos," Asher interrupted. "It's not the kind of battle I'm accustomed to fighting."

Faylen half-smiled. "I thought you thrived in chaos."

Asher turned to the elf. "Have you ever been hit by a charging horse? You don't get up from that. The best thing we can do is let the Karathans fight Karathans out there, away from the gate. When the horses realise what they're in the middle of they'll scatter. That's when we should wade in with the owls."

Faylen nodded, no doubt thinking about Reyna's safety. "I believe they plan to keep their backs to the gate, so the over-whelming forces can't surround them on the battlefield or charge into them with any great speed."

"Then we'll be pinned, and we'll die." Asher was massaging his index finger again, missing the shard of Paldora's gem. He had never liked using magic, even when he had an unlimited supply of it, but it had clearly given him a confidence he was sorely missing now. He could no longer heal himself or use it as a last ditch effort to beat his enemy. He was just like everyone else.

"I have been talking with Hadavad and Atharia. Along with Reyna, we have a considerable magic arsenal. We will break their ranks before they meet us in battle." Faylen's gaze had left the preparations below to look at the forbidding gate.

Asher couldn't help looking at the elf. He wondered how long it had been since he'd lain with a woman and the thought struck him as crude in the presence of someone so... *pure*. The ranger shook his head and thought of anything else. "Nathaniel told me about your conversation up there. You think Alidyr and Nakir can really open this thing?"

Faylen reached out and touched the iron, her fingers tracing the intricate patterns. "The door was sealed by Lady Syla and the elders. I believe the magic binding its seal is impenetrable to any human or elf, but the Hand are blessed by Valanis and the power of Naius. I wasn't alive to see them in battle during The Dark War, but there is a reason those five survived everything. They are strong."

"I don't put much stock in the power of the gods. The pools of Naius? I don't believe it. Valanis, the Hand, they're just more naturally powerful with magic. I'm willing to bet there's nothing they can do that you couldn't with enough practice."

Faylen's exquisite features furrowed. "But you saw Adellum at West Fellion..."

"I saw Adellum *die*. That's good enough for me." In truth, Asher hadn't been able to comprehend those events. Even magic couldn't prevent four impaling swords from delivering death where a single arrow had done the job. Still, the ranger concentrated on the part that mattered; the bow could kill them, and they had the bow.

"The Echoes of Fate cannot be undone..."

Asher rolled his eyes. "Don't start with the prophecy, please. I'm about to take part in a fight that will most likely be my last."

Faylen gripped his hand on the scaffold and squeezed. "Don't you see your own part in the Echoes? It has already come to pass. The immortal man, risen from infamy to playing a significant role in the fate of the world."

"If that's true then my only role was to ensure that Valanis got his hands on Paldora's gem." Asher lifted his ringless hand. "Which he now does..."

"So you do believe."

"That's not what I said ." Asher's next words were drowned out by the sound of blaring horns.

Through the wavy lines on the horizon, Asher and Faylen could see the horses pouring out of the southern gate of Karath. The soldiers and owls below scrambled for their weapons and horses, with Tauren in the middle barking orders. The twelve hundred Karathan soldiers in front of the gate had removed their cloaks in a bid to make it easier to identify friend from foe, but Asher could already see the chaos of this battle.

Faylen gripped his arm. "This isn't going to be like West Fellion. Whatever happens, we stick together."

"I would be more concerned about Reyna going off and doing something heroic than me."

The two set off down the stairs, Faylen skipping over the bannister in most cases. Asher jumped the last flight and came to land on the dusty desert ground with his folded bow in hand. A flick of his thumb had the cogs rolling and the limbs *snapping* to life, pulling the string taut. Thoughts of the coming fight distracted him from the pain in his knees, after the drop.

Both Karathan soldiers and owls were running in every direction to get into position. The ranger shook his head, thinking that the men should have already been in place. It was only after the dust had settled and a quiet took over the field that Asher realised that his judgement was in err. The few hundred owls that remained at the foot of the gate had lined up with Karathan bows, gifted to them by the soldiers. At their feet were dozens of arrows, buried into the desert, waiting to be plucked and fired. Reyna was still running along the edge and pulling handfuls of arrows from her enchanted quiver. For every handful she dug into the ground, ten more took their place on her back.

"Are they charging?" Asher asked Tauren, who was walking back from the horses.

"Not exactly," Tauren replied with a wicked smile. "Kail and I were talking with Nathaniel and we had a different idea. I hope you're good with that bow."

"So you trust this Kail?" Faylen asked, readying her own bow.

Tauren sighed. "I don't believe that every man here wants a world without slavery, but I do believe they want a world for their families to live in. They have all heard the legends of the Darkakin; no man wants those savages in The Arid Lands."

Asher nodded at Glaide and Doran, who were a mixed bag of skills when it came to archery. Glaide wasn't a bad shot, but Doran was simply too small to use any of the bows.

"Pah! When can we get to the real fightin'?" Doran pulled out his wide sword as he trotted up on his hog. "Bows just aren' personal enough."

Glaide rolled his eyes. "Bale is practically salivating in anticipation."

Indeed, the barbarian was hefting his axes around on the far end of the archers, shouting his prayers to Krayt, the god of war. Close by was Hadavad and Atharia, chatting calmly with each other, as if they weren't in a fight for their lives.

"Mages..." Asher muttered to himself.

Something in Karathan was yelled over the top of the amassed forces, but Asher missed it. He assumed Alidyr's army was growing closer and orders were being given by Kail. From their position at the back, none of the rangers or even the elves could see what was happening.

"Positions!" Tauren barked. Every owl nocked an arrow and aimed at the sky, where the sun was about to kiss the horizon.

Fighting in the dark had its advantages, Asher thought.

The old ranger removed the red cloth from his belt and examined it. For fourteen years he had been able to resist its call to give in to his old ways. Since meeting the elves and Nathaniel, Asher had not only worn it twice, but he had needed to wear it to survive. It was an advantage he could no longer ignore.

"Are you ready?" Nathaniel asked, though he was watching Reyna and Faylen attend their positions in the open space between the riders and the owls.

Asher thought about his next words very carefully. "If this doesn't go the way we want it to, find three horses, take Reyna and Faylen and ride east until you hit the coast, then go north, to Velia. King Rengar has the largest army in Illian; you'll be safer there."

Nathaniel raised an eyebrow. "I thought you were going to tell me how to reach Nightfall..."

Asher frowned, reaching for an arrow on his back. "None of you would survive inside Nightfall without me. It's a maze filled with assassins and a basement of monsters. Oh, and there's no light. If this goes the way I think it's going to, ride for Velia and forget about the gem."

Nathaniel smiled at some unsaid joke. "Tauren wondered if you should make some rousing speech to the men, but I deterred him..."

Asher had a sharp retort on the edge of his lips, but the sight of Salim caught his attention. The old honour guard was standing beside the barracks with his sword in hand and a deadpan stare. There was nothing left of him anymore; long gone was the composure and serenity that had always surrounded him. There was nothing but the desire to destroy now. Asher had never lost anything in his life that could be compared to losing a son, but he knew the look of a man who felt he had nothing more to lose.

Glaide leaned into Asher and Nathaniel. "A piece of advice. Stay away from Salim on the battlefield. I fear he won't recognise friend from foe."

Asher nodded in agreement, but he also knew that if he saw Salim in trouble, he would step in.

Another call came over the riders and dust began to rise into the air. They all heard the thunder of hooves before the last line of horses charged away. Hadavad and Atharia strode across the gap and met up with Reyna and Faylen, ahead of the owls. Lost as he was, the ranger was starting to regret walking away from the preparations now.

The riders charged into the desert to meet their enemy, but before any collision, the twelve hundred split down the middle and rode either side of the oncoming soldiers, who were clad with dark cloaks. Asher released some of the grip on his bowstring and watched as the two rows of riders skimmed along the edges of the dark-cloaks. Swords clashed and both men and horses went down in a shower of blood, but attacking them from the sides had other benefits.

"Fire!" Tauren shouted.

It was impossible to miss the dark-cloaks when they had bunched together to avoid the riders on the outside. Asher released his arrow with the others and watched as a few hundred flew high into the orange sky. Before the first wave of arrows found their way back to the earth, the owls had nocked another arrow and fired it into a tight cluster. All but Reyna aimed for the sky, as the elf simply fired her arrow dead-ahead. Adellum's bow was perhaps their greatest weapon in this fight. Asher delayed his third arrow to watch the princess.

"By the gods..." Nathaniel whispered.

The arrows dropped into the charging dark-cloaks, every projectile felling men and horses without missing their marks, but Reyna's arrows knew no limits. The first of her barrage tore through three men before any of them were thrown backwards, relieving their horses of riders. The falling riders then created chaos through the charging ranks and Asher had to wonder just how far her arrow would go.

"Come on ye bastards!" Doran was still astride his hog, desperate to be unleashed.

Tauren fired another arrow and turned to Asher. "The riders will loop round and attack them from behind while we tackle the front!"

Asher released his own arrow and looked to Tauren and the rest of the owls. "We'll be dead by the time they wade through!" The ranger changed his mind about the son-of-none's strategy.

"Halion's allies brought some supplies we have repurposed. Along with your friends," Tauren glanced at Hadavad and the elves, "I think we can hold out."

The dark-cloaks were close now, their shouts mixing with the stampede of hooves. The arrows continued to thin their ranks, littering the desert with dead bodies and horse carcasses, but their numbers were still too great.

"What supplies are you talking about?"

"Watch!" Tauren lifted his chin at Hadavad.

The old mage stepped forward and stamped his staff into the ground once; eliciting a fireball from the top. The molten ball of flames shot into the air, cresting just under the wave of arrows, until it silently fell back to Illian's embrace. The dark-cloaks thundered towards them, riding into Reyna's arrows without hesitation. Only Alidyr could motivate such warriors.

The fireball landed in a small gutter, dug into the ground, that Asher hadn't noticed until now. The fire spread in the blink-of-an-eye, stretching across the battlefield into other gutters that connected to the first. Oil for the lanterns had been poured over the battlefield to great effect. Asher couldn't help but smile, at least for a moment.

"Swords!" Tauren yelled over the sound of the charging horses.

The horses immediately slowed down when faced with several walls of fire. For the most part they continued, jumping and galloping through the flames, but their speed had been reduced. The heat and fire soon had the horses and their riders knocking into each other, however, and in their bid to escape the flames, a few were even set ablaze.

Asher flicked a switch on his bow and collapsed the limbs, so he could tuck it away under his cloak. The ranger lined up with Nathaniel and the owls, his broadsword gripped in both hands. Tauren removed two curved short-swords from his lower back and shaved one against the other.

Asher thought to put on his blindfold when he noticed the elves, still standing in the gap between them and the charging riders. "We need to get to Reyna and Faylen!"

"Leave them to it!" Tauren commanded.

Asher didn't take commands very well.

The ranger dashed across the desert with only a moment before the riders met the elves. Faylen glanced behind her at the old assassin, her expression unreadable at this distance. The elf quickly swivelled on the spot and both the mages and the elves pushed outwards with their hands and staffs. It was the same offensive Asher himself had used at West Fellion, only much more powerful. A wave of energy that could not be seen, but only felt, crashed over the charging horde, sweeping sand, oil and dirt into the air, before finally smashing into the dark-cloaks.

The result was utter devastation.

Men were flung from their horses and the mounts themselves were pushed back in a throng of broken and shattered limbs. The domino effect stretched across the front line and beyond, quickly turning the desert into a graveyard. The centre of their charge had been dented, but the outer edges continued their ride until they were met by the owls.

In the far left, Bale could be heard wading through the first attackers; the barbarian of the north cared little whether his axes found horse or man. Salim was far more surgical in his attack, but no less fierce. The southerner whipped his curved cutlass with clean lines, every swipe removing heads or blocking swords. Asher lost sight of them then, as the centre of the charge caught up, meeting him and the elves in the middle. There were very few horses now, as it had become too dangerous for the riders to charge through, blind as they were through the flames.

"Asher!" Nathaniel screamed, but he too was lost in the rush of dark-cloaks, many of which had caught fire.

The ranger wanted to turn back and fight alongside the Graycoat, but he was closer to the elves now, and surrounded by enemies and smoke. There was nothing elegant about the fight that followed, with Karathan soldiers rushing towards the gate with abandon, swinging their swords at anything not wearing a dark cloak. In the beginning there was no room to even lift a sword, as everyone bashed into each other in a vicious shoving match. Many were brought down before the fighting in the crushing impact.

Asher pushed and kicked until he carved out some space, where he could heft his broadsword in savage arcs, giving them pause and himself some time. In all the chaos he had forgotten to blind his eyes with the red cloth, leaving him to his very ordinary senses.

The blade of his sword caught attack after attack and always followed up with a cleaving swipe or a hammering from his spiked-pommel. Asher fell into the rhythm of the oldest dance known to man, using his elbows, knees and fists to keep his opponents at bay. Everything is a weapon, Nasta used to say. Ignoring the aches and pains in his knees and back, the ranger fought his way through the oncoming soldiers until he glimpsed the blonde hair of an elf.

"Reyna!" Asher could see the dark-cloak that had circled around to attack her from behind, but his call could not be heard over the din.

Two quick slices had the men in front of him reduced to coughing blood and collapsing at his feet. One more swing relieved them of their heads, helmets and all. The ranger ran through the drifting smoke and barrelled into the sneaking foe before he could strike Reyna down. With one hand on the hilt of his broadsword and the other on the blade itself, Asher shoved his sword horizontally into the man's chestplate and pushed him back, into another dark-cloak. The ranger wasted no time dispatching the soldier with a pommel to the jaw and backswing to cut open the man behind him.

Now he was back-to-back with Reyna.

"Where's Faylen?" Asher asked as the next pair came in.

"I don't know!" Reyna ducked and pivoted on her knee with her scimitar held out to the side. One dark-cloak was brought to the ground without his legs and the other split open at the waist.

Asher kicked and swung and never stopped until his opponent was still. There was no end to the horde of soldiers marching on them. The ranger could only hope that Kail's forces were burrowing their way through from the back.

A black and gold blur of motion flashed from left to right and half a dozen dark-cloaks dropped to the ground with missing limbs and cries of agony on their lips. The blur came back from another angle and Asher finally caught a glimpse of Doran Heavybelly racing through astride his armoured hog. His thick sword couldn't be denied, as it easily cut through Karathan armour and bone. The ranger was fairly certain he could hear the dwarf laughing.

A group of three dark-cloaks targeted Asher and tried to

surround him, splitting him up from Reyna. The ranger parried the first two blades and kicked the third man away, using the space to retrieve his silvyr short-sword from his back. The rune-blade was in hand at the just the right moment, as the broadsword impaled the first attacker and became lodged between the man's ribs and chest-plate. Asher spun the short-sword in a quick circle and deflected the second blade before releasing the broadsword and using his free hand to deliver an open-palm strike into the third man's throat. Spinning around to tackle the second dark-cloak, Asher was relieved to see Reyna's scimitar buried in his chest. The ranger gave a nod of appreciation and turned around to spear his silvyr blade into the choking man's face.

The display warded off the next group, giving Asher a moment to pull his broadsword free of the dead dark-cloak. He took a deep breath and felt pain stab at his ribs; there was no blood but the pain was very real. When had he taken the hit? This was why he despised fights such as these.

The sound of magic could not be misheard. Asher headbutted another dark-cloak and blinked the blood out of his eyes to see Hadavad making short work of his enemies. The old mage contorted his staff into every unorthodox position and fired off spell after spell. Any who survived the destructive magic were met with a wooden bat to the head. Watching Atharia fight was more akin to observing a dance, as the younger woman leapt from one attacker to the next, using her powerful legs to push the soldiers away before following up with her staff and a spell. The mage never stopped.

"Faylen!" Asher called over the fire and screams and horses. It was madness.

There was no keeping track of time anymore, but the sun had descended beneath the horizon and the fight continued under the stars. It took Asher a bit longer to realise he was only twenty-feet away from Syla's Gate now; they had been pushed back. The owls were proving their worth and keeping the dark-cloaks working, but there was still no sign of Kail and his riders. Every now and then the ranger would catch a glimpse of Bale singing his way across the battlefield, waving his axes around, or Doran's hog taking legs out. The dwarf was missing now too.

"Asher!" Glaide brought a dark-cloak down with a tackle around the midriff and rolled out to stand at Asher's side.

The two friends fought back-to-back until Reyna glided in with her scimitar. The three of them fell into a pattern that expanded and contracted to dispatch the waves that fell upon them.

"Where is Nathaniel?" Reyna asked, her movements hard to keep track of.

Asher wrestled a soldier off Glaide's back and spun him around, where he thrust his broadsword until the crossguard connected with the dark-cloak's armour.

"Asher!" Reyna parried a stray blade, saving the life of an owl, before beheading the soldier in a single swipe. "Where's Nathaniel?"

"I..." Asher looked around at the falling bodies. "I don't know..."

Nathaniel had completely lost his bearings in the mayhem. When the opportunity became available he could see that Syla's Gate was much further away than where he had started, though much of it was hidden behind a curtain of rising smoke. Some of Kail's riders could be spotted in the distance, cutting their way through and fighting those still atop their mounts. Many had been thrown from their horses or simply abandoned them after injury. There were two or three owls by his side, but the majority of those he would call allies were now cloakless Karathans.

"Watch out!" Tauren shoved Nathaniel to the ground as a riderless horse charged towards them.

The leader of the owls had been a sight to behold amid the chaos of battle. The young warrior was just as skilled with his curved blades as Asher had been with his own. Nathaniel found his feet just as two dark-cloaks came in with their swords aimed at his chest. The

Graycoat could never be called a novice with a sword, and he easily batted the attacks away and followed up with an elven manoeuvre he had picked up from watching Reyna. The two men were dead before they hit the ground.

Tauren was there one second and gone the next, as an exotic flip in the air had an assassin's foot colliding with The White Owl's jaw. The Arakesh took no prisoners and killed three of Kail's soldiers with her twin-blades. The three men were dead before Tauren retrieved his swords and stood up. It was the first woman Nathaniel had seen in the battle and, as out of place as she appeared, the assassin proved that the art of delivering death cared little for gender. Her time in Nightfall had left only a killer behind.

Both Nathaniel and Tauren advanced as one, but the Arakesh jumped into the air and hit them simultaneously with a split kick. They once again found themselves on the dusty ground that had now become wet with blood and piss. Looking up from his back, the knight could only watch as the assassin cut down an owl and two more Karathan soldiers. Tauren recovered faster than Nathaniel and launched himself at the woman, where the two became locked in combat. They occasionally broke from each other to strike down another foe before coming back together.

Not to be left out, the Graycoat carved his way through four soldiers until the Arakesh was before him. A swift punch had Tauren on the back-foot, opening the melee for Nathaniel to wade in. The sound of constant battle distracted the knight from the thundering of hooves, bringing the sound and image into one bloody vision, as Faylen galloped past astride a white mare with her scimitar swinging. The assassin's head was cleaved from her body.

The fighting had become too clustered, preventing the elf from riding much further. Demonstrating her kind's grace and uncanny agility, Faylen back-flipped off the horse and came down fighting. Before she had come out of her crouch, two dark-cloaks had already lost everything below the knees.

Nathaniel fell in beside her without a word and the two went to work fashioning out their territory on the battlefield. Tauren rallied what owls he could and the group grew in size until they were a force to be reckoned with.

"Salim!" The distinct voice of Doran Heavybelly rang clear over the clashing of swords.

The group of fighters, led by Faylen's scimitar, turned and fought their way towards the dwarf. The smaller warrior could not be seen but enemies falling around him were easy to find. The armoured ranger was climbing up a piling mound of bodies when they came across him, scrambling to kill his next opponent with a sword in one hand and a spiked gauntlet covering the other.

"Salim ye fool!" Doran cried, barrelling through the mess of soldiers.

"Doran!" Nathaniel called, rallying the dwarf.

"It's Salim," Doran explained, dragging a dark-cloak to the ground and burying his sword under his exposed chin. "The fool's going for the Arakesh!"

Nathaniel used the pile of bodies to briefly elevate himself above the din. Thirty-feet away, the old honour guard was striding towards a tight group of blindfolded assassins. The Arakesh had stayed near the back of the army, avoiding much of the chaos; Nathaniel wasn't looking forward to this fight and he quickly scanned the carnage for any sign of Asher.

Salim was set upon within seconds by the Arakesh. Tauren broke from the group and ran to his side, his own blades dripping with blood. Nathaniel wasn't nearly agile enough to slip between the melee as Tauren had, forcing him to fight his way through. Together, Faylen and Nathaniel covered each other's blind spots, though for every one that the Graycoat struck down, the elf took two with her fine scimitar.

"Father!" Tauren screamed, using the crumpled body of an allied Karathan to jump high into the air.

With both blades held high, The White Owl fell into the fray with a fury Nathaniel had never seen. This young man was simply angry and in possession of a set of skills that combined to make him a deadly opponent. The knight could see his flaws, however. Nathaniel had no choice but to dash ahead of Faylen and intervene before an assassin's short-sword removed Tauren's head.

The Graycoat took a slash across the waist for his assistance and a kick to the stomach. With all thought of honour fleeting, Nathaniel plunged his one-handed blade into the Arakesh's foot on his way down. From his crouched position, the knight removed a dagger from his belt and thrust upwards, into the assassin's neck.

"You need to be quicker!" Faylen was by his side and batting away two more short-swords before they could find Nathaniel's flesh.

Tauren and Salim were working together in perfect harmony, their blades moving in every direction to keep the Arakesh at bay. Their anger would get them killed. Nathaniel knew of the level head required to engage an assassin of Nightfall in combat.

"Come on!" Doran ran through with his sword taking out legs and opening guts. Any who fell to the ground with a beating heart soon found his spiked gauntlet buried in their skulls.

A great wave of heat burned against Nathaniel's cheek and he shielded his eyes from the flow of fire erupting from Faylen's hand. The torrent lit three of the Arakesh on fire, sending them running into the mass of bodies and creating havoc. With quick thinking, the Graycoat ripped the pouch of Talo spices from his belt and threw them into the stream of fire. The resulting explosion was deafening and blinding, but only for an instant to his eyes. For the Arakesh it was hell.

"Now!" Tauren called, running his blades through the nearest assassin.

Nathaniel wasted no time cutting them down while their senses were overloaded. A part of him hated killing anyone who couldn't defend themselves, but he could see the faces of so many Graycoats that had been murdered by the dark foe.

When the assassins were no longer a threat, Nathaniel couldn't help but drop to one knee and lean heavily on his sword. He was exhausted. Looking around, so many others, both friend and enemy, were doing the same, with some even playing dead. Only Faylen remained upright and able to fight the soldiers that came from the back. The Graycoat could no longer tell what was blood and what was sweat on his face.

Nathaniel grunted and pushed himself up, side-stepping a dark-cloak's swing and spinning about with his sword angled to remove his attacker's head. The resistance in the man's bones jarred against Nathaniel's wrist and forearm, threatening to release his grip on the hilt. The knight had never fought for so long and so hard before. The Graycoats kept the peace, they had never fought in wars.

Salim roared into the night and Tauren screamed in protest. Nathaniel turned about to see the old honour guard stumble to his knees with a hand across his stomach. Tauren jumped between him and the three soldiers who surrounded Salim. It was probably a stupid thing to do on a battlefield as crowded as this, but Nathaniel threw his sword end-over-end into one of the three men, leaving Tauren to dispatch the others. One successfully slashed The White Owl's leg and the other managed to backhand him across the face. They were all becoming too exhausted to fight now.

Nathaniel wanted to help Salim, but in the moment he was numb, as if the ranger hadn't been mortally wounded. He knew he should feel something, anything, at the sight of Salim in peril, but making sense of his feelings in the bloody slaughter was impossible; he could only move forward.

With no sword to hand, Nathaniel barrelled into his next opponent and landed on top of him. The Graycoat dropped his forearm into the man's throat and pressed down until the life left his eyes. When he looked up again, Faylen was launching one of Tauren's attackers into the air with a telekinetic spell and cutting the throat of the other with her scimitar. Nathaniel rolled off the dead body beneath him and prayed to the gods for the strength to stand up again.

It was going to be a long night...

Tauren stumbled to Salim's side and half-fell to the ground. His adoptive father was bleeding to death with a gash across his stomach and another across his chest. The son-of-none ignored the pain in his own leg and instinctively held a hand over Salim's gut, but the blood oozed out relentlessly.

"Father!" Tauren couldn't bear to see the look on Salim's face; a look of resignation.

"Get up!" Faylen called from behind, cutting down two more dark-cloaks.

Tauren ignored the elf and stared at his father. It was the cruellest twist of fate that they should just be brought back together and then ripped apart forever.

"You need... to fight, son." Salim gritted his teeth and squeezed Tauren's arm. "Now!"

The alarm in Salim's eyes had Tauren raising his short-sword to prevent his head from being removed. The White Owl gave into his rage for the briefest of moments and barrelled the soldier to the ground. He stabbed him repeatedly long after he was dead.

"You fight for naught, Son-of-none!" a voice cried over the din.

Tauren slowly stood up, recognising the voice, and looked beyond Salim's prone body. Argo was braced defiantly between a group of Karathan soldiers, his short-swords in hand. The assassin's blindfold covered his eyes and he had now swapped his watch uniform for his real Arakesh armour.

"Fighting for the dead will only see you join them..." Argo glanced at Salim, who was close to death now.

"I will kill you for your part in all this." Tauren's statement was flat, despite his resolve.

Before he could launch himself at the assassin, a pair of horses galloped through and made a bloody mess of things, their riders swinging mercilessly. Kail, the commander of the allied Karathans, leapt from his horse and brought Argo's entourage down in a heap of limbs. Tauren wasted no time in closing the gap, bringing Argo within arm's length. The new limp in his leg was affecting the speed of his attack, making him clumsy and predictable.

"You'll have to do better than that!" Argo spun away and brought the flat of his blade across the back of Tauren's head.

The son-of-none fell into the fray and took a kick to the face, as one of his own owls stumbled past. Kail was already on his feet and back to fighting his own kinsmen, too far away to help now. Tauren crawled over the bodies and through the blood, desperate to get back to Salim's side. There was no hiding from Argo, however; the assassin's heightened senses would find him anywhere.

As Salim came back into sight, two strong hands gripped his head, one under his chin and the other around his temple. Argo was standing over him with a wicked grin on his face. The assassin pulled the son-of-none to his knees and held him in a vice.

"You were so easily tricked," he hissed into his ear. "You led so many to the slaughter, *White Owl*."

Tauren's head was fixed with his gaze over Salim, who continued to cling to life. The son-of-none recognised the grip he was in, having employed it before, and knew he was moments from having his neck snapped. But, in his mind, he was seeing his father bleed to death, seeing Halion tortured and hung, seeing Braigo take his last breath, and his owls dying around him.

He could only see red.

With both hands, Tauren threw his arms up and sank his thumbs into Argo's eyes, pushing through the blindfold. With his elbows, the son-of-none squeezed Argo's hands, preventing him from executing the neck snap. The assassin screamed and Tauren smiled. That was all he wanted to hear.

With the strength he had left, Tauren flipped Argo over his head, bringing the assassin down on his back, hard. The fine blade strapped across Tauren's chest slipped from its scabbard with ease, but it sank into Argo's throat even easier. The Arakesh spat blood, which quickly became a gargle before his body spasmed and went limp.

Tauren roared into the night. Killing Argo did nothing for the rage trapped inside of him, a rage that would see him find his feet and keep fighting. Until the empty embrace of death claimed him, the son-of-none knew he would never stop.

CHAPTER 32
THE FIRST WAR

G ideon strode into the clearing, where Mournblade rested
in the stone. He swivelled on Ilargo, who had followed
him in, his mind racing with questions. The stars were
out now and the moon cast the tranquil setting in a pale glow that
sparkled over the dragon's scales.

What do you mean Adriel has lied to me? Gideon had made for
the clearing at Ilargo's behest before they continued their discussion.

Ilargo looked down at the mage and his narrow pupils expanded.
Gideon could feel the dragon inside his mind, inviting him into their
sanctuary. Giving himself over to the magical pull, the Dragorn, as he
now was, opened his eyes under a different canopy of stars. The
endless fields of green were somehow calming in their infinite depth.
Unlike before, there were tall, lush trees dotted about the fields,
giving the mage some idea of the distances he was looking at. Small
flowers of every colour had sprouted from the ground and the grass
had grown taller in his absence.

Sensing his confusion, Ilargo said, *The sanctuary grows as our bond
does.*

Gideon closed his eyes and shook his head. *You said I'm not the first human Dragorn.*

You are not. There were many more before our bond, before either of us were born.

Are you not supposed to tell me this? Gideon could feel everything Ilargo was feeling. The dragon felt guilty for both keeping this secret and telling it.

You are Dragorn... This secret is yours to guard now.

Tell me, Ilargo. What is it?

I will show you...

The sanctuary was ripped from under him and the familiar feeling of falling through clouds had his gut twisting in knots. As the mage broke through the last bank of clouds, the battle that had plagued his mind was raging below, with dragons weaving and diving between giant spears and hordes of soldiers swarming over the land. Ilargo appeared from nowhere and glided beneath his falling form, until the two came together with Gideon astride his armoured back. Ilargo tucked in his wings and dropped towards the ground, bringing the memory into focus.

The green dragon drifted in the air for a while, allowing Gideon the time to take it all in. They appeared to be in no danger, with neither the dragons nor the men taking any notice of them; they were just visitors in this place. A great city was spread out before them, built partially into the rock amid towering spires decorated with Crissalith.

What is this?

The First War. The war that changed everything.

When is this? Gideon still couldn't believe how real it all felt.

The true history of Verda is not one even the elves can recount. This battle took place thousands of years ago, not long after the creation of the elf.

After the creation of the... Gideon could feel the world he knew tipping upside down.

Mankind created the elves in their image. They were the first attempt at trying to become immortal, but the king failed, and in the process created another species you now know as the elf.

"*We* created elves..." Gideon said the words out loud but he couldn't understand them.

Mankind came first. The king, Atilan, was perhaps the strongest-

Atilan? the mage echoed. **The king of the gods?**

He wasn't always a god. In the beginning he was a man.

Ilargo banked to the left and flew straight for the fortress, in the heart of the city. With a mighty *thud*, the green dragon landed atop the tallest tower and dipped his neck, allowing Gideon to clamber off. Standing by the edge was a man draped in billowing, scarlet robes and a belt laden with scrolls and mage's tools. The Dragorn walked around the man, who was oblivious to the observation, and took him in.

The man had long, white hair and a beard to match and he shouted into the sky, every word eliciting another lightning strike that found a dragon. The staff in his hand was of wood, but the end was adorned with an amber sphere, wrapped within a coil of steel. The shaft was clearly decorated with shards of green Crissalith from top-to-bottom.

This... Gideon looked from Ilargo to the man. **This is Atilan? This is who everyone in the six kingdoms worships above all others? He's just... he's just a man?**

He was the king of the first men and a powerful mage, perhaps the most powerful. The seed was sown by his father, Agandalan, while Atilan was but a child. Agandalan became obsessed with the idea of immortality, an obsession he passed on to his son.

How did he create the elves? Gideon asked.

With magic, and the assistance of his trusted council. But he intended to make mankind immortal, not create an immortal race. Atilan saw the elves as a failure and cast them out of his kingdom, jealous as he was.

How did he get from creating elves to... this? Gideon looked out over the battle between man and dragon.

Dragons are at the heart of Atilan's obsession with immortality. We were the first of the long-lived that mankind met. Before us, they had no concept of life without death.

So he tried to enslave your kind. The mage looked at Atilan in disgust.

He wanted our scales. He believed they held the key to lasting life. Atilan had his right hand, Naius, perform experiments on those he captured. Our scales were used in various spells, but none had the desired effect.

Gideon shook his head. **It's barbaric. How could he believe that would work?**

Ilargo looked from Gideon to the other dragons in the sky. *Because of the Dragorn...*

The mage followed Ilargo's gaze and tracked a golden dragon soaring between the lightning strikes. The dragon had a rider on its back! Gideon rapidly searched the skies and found other dragons with riders nestled between their wings.

Before the elves, dragons chose humans to be their companions. Our bond was significantly stronger and easier to form than it is with an elf. We were natural companions...

They fought against Atilan with you?

Yes. They rebelled against their own kind when the war started. None survived to the end, however.

How did they anger Atilan? Gideon waved his hand out and watched it pass through Atilan's robes as if they weren't there.

Because they are immortal, Gideon.

Gideon wanted to frown but his whole face froze in a blank expression. He wasn't stupid enough not to understand what Ilargo had just said, he just wasn't sure what to do with the information.

All Dragorn, human or elf are immortal.

Immortal... How can I be immortal? I'm human. Gideon had walked away from Atilan now and come to stand before the green dragon.

The magic we naturally expel will be absorbed by you over our time together. You will not appear as you do now forever, but eventually you will cease to age. This can only be achieved with those bonded to us, hence Atilan's jealousy. He was not chosen to be Dragorn.

So... Gideon was finding it all very hard to piece together. **You're saying I'm immortal? I'm never going to die?**

Not if I have anything to say about it. You can still be killed, as any elf can, but time can no longer touch you. Ilargo bent down and Gideon massaged the scales between his eyes. *You are the first immortal man since the end of The First War.*

Gideon turned away and walked across the top of the tower. The wind blew his dark curls and he had to remind himself that none of this was real. He was desperate to wrap his head around the idea of immortality, but it was beyond him. It was impossible to understand something he couldn't touch or see or even measure for years to come.

Is all of this the secret the Dragorn have been keeping? That man came first? That the gods were just people?

If only it were so simple...

Gideon could hear Rainael's wisdom and age in Ilargo's words. It was easy to forget that the green dragon was younger than him, with so much experience available to draw upon from his mother's life.

The war came to an end some years after this battle. My mother and Garganafan rallied the dragons and drove what remained of mankind into The Wild Moores, where they were forced to live, without their castles or magic. Over the millennia they became as wild as the forest that shielded them from us. Malliath wanted to burn it all down, but Garganafan stopped him, preserving your kind. If he had not stopped Malliath, we would not be bonded, and so I am thankful.

Gideon's jaw dropped. **The Outlanders... The Outlanders are the descendants of the first men?**

As are you. When your kind first emerged from the Moores after so many millennia, there were no elves still living who remembered you.

But how did they become gods? Even the elves worshipped them before men did.

Even the elves were wild in the beginning. What facts they had about

Atilan and the others eventually fell into myth and legend. These legends became stories that were taken on as something more, something to be worshipped. Ilargo lifted his head, assuming a regal pose. I have shown you all that my kind has seen. The secret kept by all Dragorn is more of a purpose than a piece of knowledge, but it should only be passed on by another Dragorn.

Gideon could feel the shift in reality coming this time. As Ilargo broke away and the sanctuary became a distant place in his mind, the young mage took a lasting look at the king of the gods, chanting into the sky. The experience was less jarring, and Gideon opened his eyes to see Adriel enter the clearing beside Mournblade.

"I have been in council with Rainael," Adriel announced softly. "You have not been a Dragorn for nearly long enough to learn of the truth, but these are different times... and there are only two of us now." The elf glanced at Ilargo and Gideon felt a brief conversation pass between them. "Ilargo has shared the history of our two people. I know it is a lot to take in; I remember Galandavax imparting those memories to me, so long ago. I assure you, learning that your entire race was made out of one man's greed and lust for power was a lot to take in for me as well."

Gideon needed the missing piece. "What is the real purpose of the Dragorn, Adriel?"

Adriel walked around Mournblade. "In the beginning, when your people were dragon riders, there was no purpose beyond companionship. It was thousands of years later, when my people ruled over Illian, that the Dragorn came into being. The dragons chose their companions from my people, and over time they shared the true history of the world with us. As shocking as the truth was, we all agreed on our singular purpose... we must protect The Veil."

"The Veil?" Gideon had never heard of it.

"When Atilan failed to replicate the immortality he created with elves, and the war with the dragons was tipping against him, he turned to other options. First, he created Crissalith to bring down the dragons and cancel out magic. Only Atilan knew how to use magic in its presence; a secret he guarded jealously. Still the dragons continued to beat his forces, so he had Naius, *the god of magic*, make him something special.

Atilan sent Naius to Kaliban, his personal sanctuary in the mountains, and had him create The Veil. No one knows exactly how long it took Naius, but his work came to fruition as The First War came to an end. Most of humanity had been driven into The Wild Moores by then, but Atilan retreated to Kaliban."

Adriel casually gripped the hilt of Mournblade, but Gideon couldn't tell if the elf was pulling or not.

"What did this Veil do?"

"It granted them immortality." Adriel released his grip and turned back to Gideon. "The Veil opens a gateway to another world, one above this realm. It's hard to say what existence is like there, but they have some level of omniscience that allows them to watch this world. Their ability to affect this world is limited, however. Paldora's Star is said to have been sent by the *goddess*, but there is no proof of that. If they had any real power in this realm, we would all be dead by now."

"So Atilan, Naius, Paldora... all the *gods* are just above us? In some other realm?"

"Yes, and they cannot return. The Veil remained on this side of the gateway, stranding them. There were instances in the past where their influence was evident, but none more so than Valanis. He is proof that they have some reach in Verda."

"So the Dragorn are supposed to protect The Veil?" Gideon frowned. "Shouldn't you have just destroyed it?"

"We tried for years but it was resistant to all our efforts, even dragon's breath. The Veil can only be undone by the magic that created it."

"The pools of Naius..." Gideon said.

"The very place. The Dragorn searched for Kaliban, but the highest peaks of The Vengoran Mountains are not an easy place to explore. Eventually," Adriel glanced at Mournblade, Elandril's fabled sword. "Eventually, it was decided that we would instead keep it safe, so that no one could ever bring them back."

Gideon was putting everything together. "Adilandra told me that Valanis found the pools. That's how he became so powerful."

"Yes, he succeeded where so many of us had failed. The pools of Naius created a bridge between him and the others; their influence undeniable. He started The Dark War for them."

"I thought he wanted the gem? Paldora's."

"The gem was needed to help control the magic of Naius, but his true goal was to locate The Veil and open the gateway. If Atilan and the others were allowed to return, they would wreak chaos across all of Verda. They wouldn't stop until all bowed to them and the dragons were in chains, the secret to immortality theirs."

"So where is it?" Gideon asked, looking from Adriel to Ilargo. "Where's The Veil?"

Adriel took a long breath. "In a safe place..."

CHAPTER 33
SAVAGES

Alidyr stepped through the portal with Nakir and instantly felt the magic resonating from Syla's Gate. It was ominous not just in its incredible size but in the sealing wards that covered the surface. The elf wanted to reach out and touch it, but the sound of the Darkakin could not be ignored. Their war horns and drums echoed inside the canyon, accompanying the thunderous march and guttural chanting.

"You have spoken with these savages?" Nakir didn't appear impressed.

"I have been courting them for years. Mind your tongue, Nakir; they are easily offended."

"You mean they're always looking for a fight..."

Alidyr recognised the albino Overlord Kett, with half a head of white hair and a muscled body layered in red tattoos. The overlord rode up astride a giant lizard, common in Ayda's southern lands.

"The way is shut!" Kett shouted over the roar of his army. "We have travelled a hard road for this fight, ancient one. We want to fight!"

Alidyr couldn't find the words at the sight of four Cave Trolls being dragged alongside the army, laden with thick chains. The lumbering beasts towered over the army and protested with every step, but the Darkakin continued to prod them with spears, pushing them on.

"Where did you find *them*?" Alidyr asked in a harsh tone.

Overlord Kett glanced back at the black Trolls and sneered. "They are mine now."

"But *where* did you get them?" Alidyr tried to keep the concern out of his voice, but he already knew what Kett was going to say.

"These mountains are filled with such beasts." The overlord held up his hand and the entire army of savages came to a stop. "They serve *me* now."

"The Undying Mountains?" Nakir looked beyond Kett to the canyon walls.

Alidyr stepped closer to the giant lizard. "Do not disturb these mountains. There are things that live deep in the rock that should remain there."

Kett puffed out his chiselled torso. "The Darkakin fear nothing!"

"You've never seen an *orc*..." Nakir commented casually.

"A what?"

Alidyr raised his hand to halt the conversation. "Prepare your forces to storm the gate. We will open it."

"Be quick elf." Kett turned his reptilian mount around. "My men haven't killed anything for many days."

Alidyr watched the overlord ride away and turned to Nakir, who was giving him a knowing look from behind his half-mask and hood. "What they lack between their ears they make up for in numbers."

"Their numbers will be for naught if we cannot open Syla's Gate..."

Alidyr took a lasting look at the ten thousand strong army amassing in the canyon and strode towards the gate. The old iron felt alive under his touch, as if the metal was moving. The elves split up, taking a door each, and planted both hands against the symbols and glyphs. Alidyr prayed to Naius and poured his magical will into the gate, drawing on every crystal in his possession. His white robes glowed with all the crystals tucked away, as did Nakir's dark armour and cloak.

The brothers pushed their will into the gate and felt its expanse absorbing their efforts, spreading their energy too thin. Nakir began to growl and roar at the gate as he forced every bit of his magic into it. Alidyr could feel the sweat collecting on his brow and his hair sticking to his temples. There was no counterspell or enchantment designed to halt their efforts, just an enormous amount of magic.

An image flashed before Alidyr's eyes, burning his mind with the terrifying visage of Garganafan, the ancient king of the dragons. Before his demise in the final battle of Elethiah, at the end of The Dark War, the great dragon must have assisted Lady Syla and the elders in sealing the gate. This was a detail Alidyr had not been privy to.

Alidyr ceased his barrage and stepped back, taking in the enormous gate. Nakir did the same and approached his brother with a heaving chest. They were both feeling drained.

"Dawn is upon us..." Nakir looked up, to the top of the eastern canyon and observed the faint light creeping over the stars, fading their beauty.

"This gate has been sealed by more than just elves," Alidyr replied. "Dragon magic has been used."

"I felt it too. Garganafan's breath stains the iron." Nakir stepped back and uncoiled his famous whip. Somewhere between anger and curiosity, the elf lashed out at the gate and struck it with the three sharpened prongs.

Alidyr had seen that whip crack steel and split iron in half. Syla's Gate didn't have so much as a scratch.

Nakir examined his whip as if it were broken before looking to his brother for counsel. "Valanis is expecting us to open these gates..."

"No, brother. Our master is expecting us to provide passage for the Darkakin."

Nakir looked back at the savages before facing Alidyr again. "You cannot mean what I think you do. We are perhaps the most powerful elves in the world, but even we cannot open and maintain a portal big enough and long enough to fit ten thousand Darkakin through!"

"And yet we will, because Valanis demands it. The gods demand it." Alidyr raised his hand to get the attention of Overlord Kett.

"The portals will drain us!" Nakir protested in hushed tones.

Alidyr blinked slowly. "Just stay alive and they will remain open."

"Staying alive in a battle won't be easy with my energy being sapped, brother. And what of the princess and her companion? Both of them have the power to close portals or at least make things harder!"

Alidyr knew his brother had a point there. Valanis had always taught them to never underestimate their opponent. The ancient elf looked up at the gate and let his strategic mind go to work.

"Open your portal up there, atop the gate," Alidyr commanded. "The Darkakin will flood the top and move down the scaffold. The portals will be safe up there."

Alidyr put his fingers into the pouch on his belt and felt the crystals therein. He only had two remaining, but that was all he would need; one to get up there and keep the portal open, and another to get off the gate again.

Nakir appeared to consider his brother's plan. "Fine. But you will have to tell Kett that his Trolls can't go..."

CHAPTER 34

CALAMITY

Reyna parried two oncoming attacks and was thankful for her superior strength over men, as she whipped her leg around and cracked both soldiers across the jaw, sending them flying into the fray. The elf reserved her magic for the moments where her scimitar wouldn't save her life, but was loath to use it in such crowded conditions. The same applied to her magnificent bow. The princess wanted to unleash the weapon and reduce the dark-cloaks as quickly as possible, but the arrow would no doubt take the lives of plenty of owls or even some of Kail's soldiers.

Looking to her right, Reyna could see that Glaide and Asher were tiring, along with the owls, and many of the dark-cloaks had already slowed down. If it weren't for their numbers, Reyna was sure her elven stamina would have her kill them all. She refused to accept that the sharp pain in her sides and joints was exhaustion, however.

The light of dawn was usually a comforting and inspiring view for Reyna, but right now it just reminded her how long they had been fighting. The fires were still burning and the air had filled with smoke and the disgusting aroma of blood and other bodily fluids, that her elven nose couldn't ignore.

A dark-cloak came for her from behind a staggering horse, surprising the elf. There was no time to fall into a defensive stance however, before Bale of the Oakbreaker clan picked the attacker up and rammed him into the side of the horse, bringing all three of them down. The barbarian headbutted the soldier repeatedly until he became very still. Bale stood up laughing and shouting to Krayt, the god of war. Reyna wanted to thank him but the sight of his work took any words from her mouth.

The constant fighting had distracted her from the thought of Nathaniel and Faylen, who were somewhere in the chaos of it all. She knew both were of a skill above the average fighter, but this kind of fighting was new to all of them. Even Asher had avoided battle on this scale, though the ranger appeared to be doing just fine.

"Reyna!" Asher was looking at her with concern marring his haggard features.

The princess didn't realise until too late that the ranger was in fact looking past her, to the dark-cloak. Her scimitar came up to spear the man, but Asher's silvyr short-sword spun past her head and found its end in his face.

That focused the elf.

Reyna ducked and swivelled as she weaved between the various swords, before performing an exotic manoeuvre that had her scimitar claim the lives of three dark-cloaks and the hand of a fourth. Asher stumbled past her and retrieved his silvyr blade from the dead man's face, his blood running down the runes that lined the short-sword. The ranger's injuries were apparent with only a cursory glance. For all his skill, avoiding this many attacks was simply impossible.

"Asher..." Reyna approached him with caution, seeing the wild look in his eye.

The ranger's face was cut in several places and his left eye appeared smaller than the right. His leather armour had taken a beating, with slashes on almost every panel; some had been impaled and seeped blood. What was left of his green cloak was dirty and tattered and streaked with the blood of others. Following Asher's wild gaze, the princess found some wounds of her own, with a particularly nasty gash above her bracer, below the elbow. The more she thought about it, there were several parts of her body that ached and stung.

The reprieve was short, with another cluster of dark-cloaks fighting their way through a group of owls towards them. Glaide was working his way towards them, but the ranger appeared in a worse condition to Asher. His long, tanned coat was weighing him down now and his dark skin was glistening with blood and fresh cuts.

"Look!" The call came from somewhere in the fray and was followed by more calls to look.

Reyna and Asher glanced to the sky, as much of the fighting came to a stop, and gaped at the spectacle in the cloudless blue above. A red streak, brighter than the sun, appeared above the distant horizon. It was a sight none had ever seen during the day.

"Paldora's Star..." Reyna whispered, her expression vacant in awe and exhaustion.

Asher turned to her, his own expression somewhat grave and confused. "What did the prophecy say about this?"

"Paldora's celestial gem graces daylight sky, and in its beauty... ordains calamity."

Asher grunted. "I'd say it's about a day too late for that message."

Reyna was still looking up when her keen eyes caught sight of something other than the streaking comet. "Watch out!" The elf tugged on Asher's arm and pulled him from the spot that would have become his grave.

Dozens of spears fell from the sky, plunging into the desert's hard ground with enough force to keep them standing. Dark-cloaks, owls and Karathan soldiers alike fell under the brutal barrage. With the battle so closely pitched, every *thud* of a falling spear found a victim.

"Move away from the gate!" Reyna yelled.

The fighting on the desert floor had stopped in the mad rush to escape the spears and arrows that followed. Asher grabbed Reyna's arm and pulled her closer to Syla's Gate, where the spears and arrows were sparse.

"Glaide!" Asher called the ranger to him. "Find the others and retreat to Karath."

"What's happening?" Glaide asked, wiping blood from his eyes.

Asher looked to Reyna who examined the top of the gate where her elven eyes could just make out the figures leaning over the edge.

"The Darkakin are here..." Asher said. "Find -"

The ranger stopped when the melee had cleared away from the gate and left the dozens of bodies in the dirt. Bale of the Oakbreaker clan was amid the strewn bodies, on his knees and soaked with blood, with at least five swords and two spears protruding from his thick torso. Both of his axes were buried in the limbs of other dead bodies and his expression was one of glee. There was no time to mourn or even say a decent word for the barbarian, however.

"Find Faylen and Nathaniel," Asher continued. "Get everyone back to the city!"

"Karath will not hold the Darkakin at bay," Reyna offered.

Asher looked away for a second. "Then take everyone north. The road to Alborn is safe and the Velian army will give the Darkakin something to think about. You'll be safe there."

Reyna thought about King Rengar and wondered how accurate that assumption was. "Where are *you* going?"

Asher looked up at the concaved gate.

"That's suicide!" Reyna protested.

"There's nothing to be gained up there!" Glaide added.

"They haven't opened the gate," Asher pointed out. "That means Alidyr and Nakir are using other methods to get them through."

Reyna knew from the way the ranger was looking at her that he was suggesting magical assistance. "They've opened a portal..."

"Well either that or the Darkakin brought some really big ladders." Asher was busy ripping off a strip of his cloak and stuffing it into a gash in his armour, stemming the trickle of blood running down his back.

"At least they can't open the gate," Glaide commented.

Asher looked out at the fleeing forces. "It won't make any difference if there's nobody to push back."

Reyna tore her eyes from the comet and frowned at Asher. "So what do you mean to do up there? Besides getting yourself killed that is."

"Close the portal." The ranger swung his broadsword round, but Reyna could see that he was really testing the strength in his arm.

"You mean to kill Alidyr."

"And Nakir if I can." Asher was already turning for the lift at the base of the scaffold.

"And how are you going to do that without the only weapon that can kill them?" Reyna removed the black bow from her back.

Asher patted the tip of Alidyr's short-sword at the base of his back. "I've got one of my own."

Reyna dashed in front of the ranger. "You're going to need range if you're to kill them all."

Glaide frowned and rubbed his head. "You're talking as if he's actually going to get up there alive."

Indeed, the Darkakin's wild howls could be heard descending the scaffolding on both sides now.

Asher met Reyna's green eyes. "I'm not taking you with me."

The princess raised her eyebrow. "No. *I'm* taking you." Reyna turned to Glaide. "Find Nathaniel and Faylen and make sure they're safe." The princess didn't even want to consider if they were still alive; they simply had to be. Any other outcome would cripple her.

Asher had some final words for Glaide. "Tauren son-of-none will not lightly abandon the city. Make him see sense, Jonus." The two patted each other on the shoulder.

"Just survive, old man." Glaide ran to the east and curved towards the edge of the mountains to find his way back to the masses without running into spears.

Elf and man hopped over the railing, though Reyna took note of Asher's pain as he did so. After a whole night of fighting there couldn't be much left in him. The cries of warring Darkakin narrowed her focus, reminding the princess that her survival was less than likely.

"Without anyone on the pulley, we will have to take the stairs..." Reyna could only imagine what energy either of them would have after such a climb.

"I had a quicker path in mind..."

The princess looked at the taut ropes that Asher was examining on the other side of the lift. "You can't be serious? If you cut those we'll go up so fast our heads will become buried in the ceiling when we reach the top!" Reyna leaned out of the lift and looked up, where the counterweights sat at the top of the gate.

"We'll survive."

"Those weights are huge - they'll destroy the staircase!"

Asher replied with the hint of a smile. "They'll probably destroy the entire scaffold..."

"The scaffold is also the structure that keeps the lift in place. What if it's decimated before we reach the top?"

"Pray to your gods." Asher sheathed his broadsword and went to remove the dagger from his belt. "Just brace yourself against -"

Reyna cursed herself for not hearing his approach, but the Arakesh moved with a speed that left no time for regrets. Ro Dosarn leapt over the railing and barrelled into Asher, taking them both to the floor, while a second Arakesh came up behind the elf. All four were quickly confined to the platform in a struggle to survive.

Asher managed to roll over and put Ro beneath him, but the assassin still had both of his short-swords in his hands. Reyna danced around her own Arakesh, parrying his attacks with her scim-itar and counter-attacking by lashing out with the limbs of the bow. The curved ends were tipped with razor sharp blades that defied the effects of time and never failed to pierce armour.

The ranger was kicked and sent flying into the railing, which cracked under his weight. Reyna could see the man was struggling to keep himself standing, and no doubt Ro Dosarn and the Arakesh had kept out of the battle as much as possible.

"You should have stayed in the wild..." Ro flipped onto his feet and lunged at Asher.

"Hold on!" Reyna couldn't believe what she was doing, but fatigue had curbed her inhibitions. The elf spun around her attacker and lashed out with her scimitar, cutting the taut ropes that kept the counterweights in place.

Asher and Ro collided at the same moment the platform jumped, bringing them both down in a tumble of limbs. Reyna's elven agility and sense of balance did nothing to help her. All four were plastered to the floor as the platform was hurled up the height of the gate. The sound of the counterweights flying past the lift was brief and its descent quickly went wild, until several tons of destruction were battering the scaffold. Darkakin were flung from the upper tiers, while those first out of the portal were crushed by the counter-weights or fractured beams.

Reyna rolled to the side moments before the corner of the lift was torn away in a mess of splintered wood and broken body parts. The Arakesh clawed at her feet, always searching for the kill-angle. A solid kick to the face had the assassin thrown from the platform, where he was intercepted by debris and bent out of any shape that resembled a human.

Asher and Ro were still struggling, but the lift was almost at the top now. Reyna wanted to move and help the ranger, but the acceleration had her pinned to the other side.

"Asher!" Reyna screamed.

The ranger took punch after punch until eventually he rolled with the swing and forced Ro to lie on top of him. It was too late for anything else. The lift came to a stop, as sudden as its lift off, only the end was far more violent. Reyna was launched into the air and saved only by her unrelenting grip on the railing. Asher and Ro however, were flung into the wooden ceiling above and thrown back onto the platform. The princess held her breath, expecting the lift to now fall back to the desert floor and kill them all. The beams *creaked* and the platform *snapped*, but the lift remained in place, for now. Her elven senses detected the slightest of movement, informing her of the ever-increasing lurch. The platform was about to drop.

Asher groaned and rolled Ro Dosarn off him. "You should have stayed in the dark..."

"Asher!" Reyna hissed.

The ranger let go of the assassin's throat and dived for the edge of gate with the elf. Reyna felt the top of the lift brush against the soles of her feet as it plunged back to the base. Ro's screams could only be heard for a second before the destruction and total collapse of the ancient scaffold became deafening.

Reyna recovered first and pulled herself onto the walkway before assisting Asher in climbing up. The pain in her knee suggested she would have a limp and the agonising sting in her shoulder told of torn muscle. The ranger remained crouched, nursing his ribs, while the princess stood defiantly before the horde of Darkakin. The savages had filled out the walkway, shoulder-to-shoulder, and were growling and sneering at the pair, their crude spears and jagged swords baying for blood. Their bodies were covered in thick black tattoos, mixed with piercings and decorated with loose scraps of armour.

"Asher?" Reyna kept her eyes on the Darkakin and her scimitar held up.

"I'm here..." Asher rose slowly to his feet and cracked his back and neck. The ranger's ability to shrug off pain was testament to his life in Nightfall.

The Darkakin quickly thinned out as the masses were redirected to the other side of the gate, now their only way down. As the numbers dropped away, Reyna was given a clear view of Alidyr, standing in the middle of the gate, with his white robes. Nakir was behind him, directing the dozens of savages that poured out of two portals.

"Don't run off this time." Reyna knew they would only succeed if they worked together.

"Don't worry," Asher croaked. "I want him to see what's coming…"

~

Between Syla's Gate and Karath, the stampeding armies that rushed to escape the Darkakin were interrupted by a curious sight, unwitnessed by most mortals. A small patch of reality was ripped apart and replaced by an abyss that had no end.

Valanis stepped through the portal and smiled from behind his mask.

Darkakin could be seen in the distance, clambering over one another to reach the desert floor, while more filled the walkway atop the gate. Oh what a mess of their world he had made, Valanis thought. Smoke rose into the air and fires burned, with horses running in every direction and a field of bodies that stretched across the desert.

The kingdoms of man would crumble under their own weight; savages killing savages. Those of his own kin who survived the war would either bow to the gods or be wiped out by them.

The Karathans stopped in front of him, cautious of the mysterious figure who had come from nowhere. The dark armour that fitted tight against his torso glistened under the morning sun, while his black robes hung lifeless in the still air. Most examined his mask, which concealed his golden glow, but gave them a terrifying reflection.

Valanis looked up, from under his hood, and beheld the red comet. Paldora's Star soared through the sky, much closer than it had ever come before. His fine eyes tracked the streaking star and observed the fragments that broke away and burned to ash.

"Valanis…"

His name was almost whispered and the tone was that of a

woman, but the elf couldn't find the source amidst the throng of soldiers and dirty faces staring at him. The herald of the gods didn't have time for these mortals, though he would have enjoyed wreaking havoc among them with his magic. The power of Atilan coursed through him, keeping the seizures at bay, for now, while he focused on the details. Looking up at Paldora's Star, Valanis knew he was going to need that godly power if he was to do what was required.

The dark elf made for Syla's Gate with confident strides. When the soldiers blocked his path with sheer numbers, Valanis swept his arms from side to side, every movement expelling a crushing wave of telekinetic magic. The soldiers, and even the horses, were pushed away with enough force to break bone and lift them from the ground. His stride never faltered as his spells created a cascade effect to clear a path, kicking up sand and dirt with the body parts that had already been removed in battle.

Behind you! the voice of Krayt, the god of war, hissed in his ear.

In typical human fashion, a man attacked Valanis from behind. His cowardice could be seen as bravery, and was to be commended, since everyone else behind the elf had continued to flee for Karath, but Valanis cared little for courageous humans. The herald spun about and caught the man's sword with his hand mid-swing. A barely perceptible field around his hand prevented any damage or pain, but as soon as the blade was in his grip, Valanis switched from defensive to offensive. The man pressed against him with both hands, desperately trying to regain control of his sword.

"Nathaniel!" a woman cried.

Valanis poured his magic into the blade until the steel turned orange and *crackled* under the immense heat. The waves rising from the blade distorted the man's determined features and the woman who approached him from behind. The ancient elf used his free hand to unleash a blast of energy into the man's chest, launching him into the woman and sending them both hurtling into the fleeing mob.

He is here! Paldora whispered into his ear.

The ranger... Atilan's powerful voice had Valanis looking back at Syla's Gate.

The elf continued to make his way south; the men now giving him a wide berth. It wasn't long before there was nothing but a field of dead bodies between him and the gate.

Paldora's Star flared above him. Now was the time.

Valanis raised his arms to the comet and felt the presence of all twenty gods surround him, keeping him up as he called upon the power of Naius.

Asher used one hand to push a Darkakin over the edge, while swinging round to swipe another savage with his broadsword. As one toppled over the side of the gate, the other lost his head; these were the kind of numbers where an assassin excelled. Asher had the space to move and use his foe's attacks against them. It didn't help that the Darkakin had no style he could adapt to counter. They came at him without any planning or thought of the ally beside them, often resulting in them being the chief cause of death for their friend. The ranger could see how in great numbers this would make them unpredictable and hard to tackle.

Reyna had fired three arrows since the melee began and killed seven Darkakin. The elf was certainly more warrior than princess now, though seeing Reyna in the thick of it was starting to redefine for Asher what a princess actually was.

It only took them a few minutes to reduce the small horde to a pile of bodies. Asher was sure both of them had collected fresh wounds from the encounter, but they could take stock of them later... if there was a later. The ranger pulled his sword free of the last victim and sheathed it on his hip, watching Alidyr as he did. He wanted the elf to see him draw both short-swords from his back, one of silvyr and the other of magic.

"That belongs to me," Alidyr said.

"Don't worry." Asher stalked across the walkway, stepping over the bodies. "I'm going to give it back to you."

Alidyr looked from Asher to Reyna. "You won't close these portals, Princess. The Darkakin *will* bring these lands to its knees."

"Brother!" Nakir stopped directing the savages and ran to the edge of the walkway. "Look!"

Asher hesitated, unsure if this was some kind of ploy, but seeing Alidyr's expression it was clear that the elf hadn't been expecting his brother's actions. Both elf and man approached the side as one, neither looking away from the other.

"By the gods..." Reyna said.

Asher tore his eyes away from Alidyr and looked over the side. In the distance was a lone figure, clad in black, and marching towards the gate. Men and horses alike were being flung away from him by the dozens, adding to the mass of bodies. He eventually broke free of the army and stopped to raise his hands into the air.

"What is it?" Asher asked, his eyes too human to make sense of it.

"Calamity..." Reyna glanced at Paldora's Star before returning her gaze to the figure.

"Now you will witness the power of Valanis!" Alidyr cried over the rush of Darkakin behind him.

A pit opened inside Asher's stomach as he started to put the pieces together. The comet flared above and began to break apart, streaking a brilliant red across the sky. Fragments broke away and dived into the mountain range around the gate. Within seconds the comet had clearly left the heavens and forced its way into Verda.

Regardless of what would happen next, this was the perfect distraction to use against Alidyr. Without warning Reyna, Asher charged over the gate and jumped into the air, his silvyr sword angled down above his head, as if he held a spear. Of course the elf was too fast for such an attack, but Asher had anticipated his counter and spun around, once his feet hit the floor, to whip the magic blade across Alidyr's face. The very tip of the sword cut a perfect line through the elf's cheek, drawing blood.

Alidyr gasped and removed his own short-sword, identical to Asher's, and came at him with a slower, more calculated approach. Paldora's Star had overshot Syla's Gate now and had begun to fall into the southern horizon. The impact could be heard as well as felt, giving Alidyr pause before striking. An explosion, bigger than anything Asher could have imagined, erupted in the distance, reaching the sky and shattering The Undying Mountains.

There was a deep rumble under their feet and the explosion was soon followed by a wave of sand and dust that raced over the mountains and through the canyon. The wave consumed everything in its path, concealing the Darkakin below and blocking out the blue sky above.

"Asher!" Reyna shouted as the wave swept over them.

The ranger saw the princess dive for cover, but the opportunity was robbed from him, as Alidyr planted a foot firmly in his chest and knocked him into the middle of the walkway. The force of the wave dragged him across the gate and had him tumbling and rolling into the side, where the sand and dust pelted him relentlessly. He choked and sputtered trying to catch a breath, but his lungs burned.

Eventually the force died away, leaving an atmosphere of sandy fog and a harsh wind. Something rumbled in the distance and the gate lurched. The sound of heavy rocks falling down the mountains caught up with the ranger and he realised that the noise was coming from either side of the gate. It was hard to see through the fog, but giant boulders smashed into the walkway and broke into a thousand pieces. That meant they were falling from a colossal height.

The gate lurched again.

"Reyna!" Asher yelled, inhaling more sand.

The distant sound of landslides was no longer so distant. The entire northern face of The Undying Mountains was crumbling to dust. The gate shook and the harsh sound of iron bending and twisting found Asher's ears. The comet had caused an earthquake large enough to dislodge the gate. No, Asher thought, Valanis had caused this; the elf had enough power to bring down a star...

Crawling on all fours, the ranger found both of his short-swords and caught a glimpse of Reyna on the other side of the walkway. When he reached her side they picked themselves up and peered over the southern edge, where the Darkakin army was still standing. Even through the fog of sand and swirling winds, their cheers could still be heard. They all knew what was coming.

Syla's Gate was falling.

"We need to get down!" Reyna shouted, turning her head away from the blowing sandstorm.

Asher squinted and looked across the gate, searching for any sign of Alidyr or Nakir. The portals had been closed, but the elves were still shrouded behind a veil of sand and dust. The ranger grabbed the princess's arm and pulled her to follow him across the walkway, heading towards the remaining scaffold. The winding stairs were their only hope of reaching the desert floor again.

Reyna's cry of alarm was the only warning Asher had that Nakir and Alidyr were still up there with them. The princess was pulled away from him and dragged across the walkway by Nakir's whip, its pronged heads wrapped around Reyna's arm. Asher had his hand on the hilt of the magical short-sword when Alidyr emerged from the fog of sand and pounced on him. The elf pushed him back into the side of the gate by the throat and continued to push until Asher's back was arched over the side.

"Where is the rest of the gem?" Alidyr spat, his calm composure cracking. "WHERE IS IT?"

Asher struggled to breathe and fight off the old elf at the same time, all too aware of the unforgiving drop beneath him. With a grip as strong as he could muster, the ranger desperately tried to snap Alidyr's wrist, but the elf was too powerful. Through watery eyes, Asher caught a glimpse of Reyna kicking Nakir away, as she lay on the floor. The princess yanked her arm, pulling the magical whip taut, and lashed out with her bow, using the bladed limbs to sever it. A brilliant flash momentarily blinded them all and Nakir screamed in anger.

Reyna looked at Asher as he hung over the edge. The two held a silent conversation and the ranger knew what he had to do; he could only hope her elven reflexes were up to the challenge after the night they'd had.

"Where is -"

Alidyr's question was cut short when Asher stopped struggling and gripped the back of the elf's head. With all his might, the ranger pushed off with his legs and pulled Alidyr with one hand, sending them both rolling over the side into the empty space beyond. Asher reached out with his free hand, his fingers despairingly grasping at anything to hold onto. The ancient elf swore in his native language and immediately released his grip on the ranger. Falling from a deadly height was always guaranteed to give one a new set of priorities.

"Got you!" Reyna's hands came together around Asher's wrist like a vice.

The ranger dangled for a moment and he watched Alidyr drop to the desert floor with his white robes billowing about him. The falling elf never made it to the ground however, as his entire form was eclipsed by a flash of lightning, a spectacle that had him collapse into nothingness. Asher looked back up to Reyna for some kind of explanation.

"He used a portal!" Reyna was clearly struggling with his weight.

"Pull!" Asher used his free hand to grapple the side after Reyna pulled him up. "Look out!" The ranger pushed the princess away and dropped onto the walkway as Nakir came at them.

"You broke my whip!" Nakir kicked the space where Reyna had been standing.

Asher rolled over, his human reactions not fast enough to get him in the fight. Reyna and Nakir were already trading blows and dancing around each other with enviable speed. The dark elf had abandoned his whip now and was settling for killing the princess with his bare hands. Reyna swung her bow and attacked with every limb, but Nakir was too skilled to fall in hand-to-hand combat with a single opponent.

Asher got to his feet and threw Alidyr's magical blade into the air. "Reyna!"

The princess reacted perfectly, weaving between Nakir's punches and reaching out for the short-sword. Asher paused to pick up the whip as Reyna dropped to one knee and plunged the blade into the dark elf's stomach.

Nakir froze. Only his eyes could be seen behind his black veil, but a degree of torment marred his pale face and golden eyes. Asher wasted no time looping the whip around his neck and squeezing with all the strength he had left. Reyna twisted the blade and Asher pulled on the whip. Nakir's hands gripped the ranger's wrists, but his strength was waning. A few seconds more and the dark elf went limp.

Asher knew what came next, having seen how Adellum left the world, but there was no time to move before Nakir's body began to expel all of its considerable magic. Both the princess and the ranger were thrown backwards, in opposite directions. The dead body of a Darkakin cushioned Asher's tumble, but when he got to his feet again, Reyna had already recovered and was crouched over Nakir's corpse, which was emitting a lot of light and pushing all of the surrounding sand away.

"What are you doing?" Asher shouted, feeling a distinct lurch beneath his feet.

More chunks of the mountain fell over the walkway and the sound of the stone cracking reached the ranger's ears. The only remaining scaffold had been torn asunder by the falling debris, leaving them stranded.

Reyna said nothing as she handed Asher his short-sword back and rummaged through Nakir's belt. She detached a small leather pouch and held it up with the whisper of a prayer on her lips. Relief lit up her face when she removed a single crystal from the pouch.

"It's the only way!"

Asher wasn't convinced. "Have you ever opened a portal before?"

"No! I've always been better with healing magic!"

The gate lurched again and Nakir's body began to shake violently. The first wave of energy he expelled was hot against their skin, but it was only the beginning; soon he would explode and wipe everything off the top of the walkway. Asher looked up at the raining debris of massive rocks and wondered what would kill him first.

"Think of Nathaniel!" The ranger gripped the princess's shoulders. "Think of Faylen! See them in your mind!" Nothing sharpened the mind like the instinct to survive.

Reyna took a breath and threw the crystal away. Asher's hand hovered over her shoulder, ready to drag her through the moment he saw the familiar abyss. the gate tilted and more rocks showered the walkway as Nakir's body expelled wave after wave of magical energy.

Then the crystal exploded.

Asher gripped Reyna's shoulder pad and rushed the two of them through the portal, leaving Syla's Gate to crumble behind them.

CHAPTER 35
A LIFE OF PURPOSE

Adilandra awoke to the concoction of sweet perfumes and sweat. The elf was lying on a bed, wrapped in the finest sheets and entirely without clothes. The last thing she could remember was being drugged and marched through the corridors of the pyramid. After seeing The Goddess waiting for her in the bedchamber, her memories became distorted and then nothing at all. The queen of the elves had yet again been the plaything of the savage witch, forced to satisfy her every desire.

But she was awake...

Never had she awoken in the chamber before. The guards always marched her back to the cells before the drugs wore off. Adilandra sat up and balled her fist, testing her strength. After killing the last Darkakin to use her body, they should have increased the strength of the drugs or given her a higher dose. She was even stronger than the last time. Now Adilandra was awake and felt as if she were her normal self. A part of her had hoped that this would come to pass; that her elven anatomy would adapt and eventually fight off the drugs. The Darkakin had never drugged an elf for so long before, but they had assumed their power came from magic, not simple biology.

Powerful elven ears detected the light breathing beside her, and Adilandra slowly turned around to see The Goddess, asleep. She too was naked, covered in black tattoos from head-to-toe, and completely vulnerable. Adilandra's instinct was to conjure a ball of fire and burn the bitch alive, but no fire could be brought to life. At the base of the bed was a stand, holding another mysterious green crystal. It didn't matter; elven strength was more than enough to end the life of a human.

Adilandra crawled across the bed when three sharp blasts of a horn blared out from somewhere inside the pyramid, followed by the continuous ringing of a large bell. The sudden noise had the elf looking out of the open door, to the balcony and the blue skies beyond. It was a distraction she couldn't afford.

The Goddess whipped her foot into the air and thrust her heel into Adilandra's jaw, knocking her off the bed. The Darkakin queen shouted something in her native tongue and the double-doors exploded open with a flurry of guards to follow. Adilandra flexed her jaw to examine the extent of the damage and rose from the floor, cracking the knuckles of her free hand and spitting blood. The first guard assumed she was too occupied with her jaw - a mistake he would never have the opportunity to regret.

Adilandra moved too fast to follow, her fist already buried deep in the throat of the first guard. Her sensitive, elven skin felt his windpipe collapse, but she ducked out of the way before he could spray her with blood from his mouth. When she came back up, her other hand was already gripping the spear of the second guard and twisting it away to intercept the sword of the third. The elf's foot shot out at a low angle and inverted the knee of the spearman with a satisfying *snap*.

"Don't kill her!" The Goddess screamed over the melee. "I want her alive."

The third guard came again and again with his sword, every swipe too slow to harm the elf. Adilandra evaded every attack with a pivot of the shoulders until the fallen spear was at her feet. The queen deftly flicked the spear up into her hands and deflected the sword at the last second. A simple push-kick was enough to launch the guard across the room, where he collapsed in a heap, desperate for a breath that would never come.

Adilandra turned around, her bloodlust reaching a crescendo now. The ease with which she could kill was still intoxicating, but right now there was no shame to be felt. The Goddess would die!

Adilandra looked every way only to find an empty chamber. Her attention was pulled to the doors, where she heard the sound of heavy feet running towards her. The Goddess was sprinting down the hall, slipping between eight more Darkakin who were charging towards Adilandra.

Three more blasts of a horn could be heard echoing through the halls and outside, with the bells. The alarm had been rung *before* Adilandra tried to kill The Goddess.

"Galanör..." Adilandra both loved and hated the elf for returning.

As the new guards began to fill the chamber, Adilandra picked up the green crystal and casually threw it out of the window, hoping that it would eventually land on some Darkakin's head and kill them instantly. With the crystal gone, Adilandra could feel her sixth sense returning. The eight killers surrounded her with their clubs and swords, each licking their lips with the thought of what they were going to do to her. Adilandra knew there and then that she would never leave Ayda with a single Darkakin left alive. They would all burn.

The queen raised her hands so they were level with her shoulders. "So..." With over a thousand years of experience, the ability to conjure fire came naturally to her, and both of her hands set alight with a brilliant blue flame. "Who's first?"

Galanör had become a creature of instinct. With a scimitar in each hand, the elf released himself of any restraints and unleashed the warrior that he had been trained to embrace since birth. After trekking through The Great Maw and crossing The Trident, he knew that rest should have been his immediate priority before any kind of assault, but the sight of the pyramid infuriated him. The thought of what they could be doing to his queen drove one foot in front of the other, until he was chopping Darkakin down in the street like animals. Had he turned around, the elf would have seen a bloody trail cut through the city, from the edge of the jungle to the base of the pyramid.

The alarm wasn't raised until he breached the palace grounds. Everyone else had made the mistake of attacking him on sight and losing a limb or two. It's hard to ring a bell without arms or legs, and elven scimitars are excellent tools for separating body parts. The Darkakin scurried out of every shadow in the pyramid, vying for his blood. Galanör wasn't in a hurry anymore. The elf strode through the halls, only pausing to dispatch more Darkakin and sever more limbs. The blood sprayed across the golden walls and the cries echoed in every direction, bringing more to him.

Good, he thought. Let them come.

Dancing around the savages was the only thing Galanör did as naturally as breathing. His blades dashed out in every direction, twirling and spinning to deflect, counter and often shatter his enemy's weapon.

"Adilandra!" Galanör shouted at the top of his voice. "If she's dead I'll kill you all!" he growled.

More and more came for him. Spears were thrown and arrows fired, but his speed would always have him one step ahead. After rising through two more levels, the elf became aware of the burning smell. Smoke was slowly filtering through the corridors and the distant sound of fire *crackling* reached his ears. Someone had started a fire...

"Adilandra..." He dared to hope.

Two archers appeared at the other end of the hall and took aim. Galanör threw one scimitar and dropped into a roll, avoiding the arrows, and came up throwing the other scimitar with his momentum. Both swords found their mark in the chest and gut of the archers. Had Galanör not given in to his instincts, he would have instantly regretted throwing his weapons, as the hall quickly filled with a dozen more Darkakin.

The elf balled both of his fists and smiled at the charging horde.

Gideon hugged Ilargo's neck closely as the green dragon raced around The Red Mountains, circling the Reach for the third time. Ilargo had said that regular flying was required to acclimatise the mage to the new form of travel. For once, the dizzying heights were not on Gideon's mind. His head swam with all the history he had taken in, his mind still trying to make sense of which were his memories and which were Ilargo's. Of course, the bulk of his new memories had been passed down from Rainael the emerald star.

The idea that the gods were no more than real people, who had fallen into legend before being idolised, had left Gideon with an empty feeling, but the fact that those people had started off as humans was a revelation he just wasn't ready for. Too much had come the mage's way since he left Korkanath, and now more than ever he wished he had Abigail to talk to. She would know what to do.

The lush trees rushed by beneath them, with Ilargo flying as close to the tops as he could without touching them. Other dragons lounged here and there with a few taking off from between the trees to enjoy the freedom of the skies. Gideon could feel their serenity mingling with apprehension. His connection with Ilargo gave him greater insight and the mage knew instantly that they were collectively concerned about Malliath. The black dragon's presence had them all on edge, his disposition unlike anything they had ever experienced in the Reach.

Gideon tapped into Ilargo's emotions, as the green dragon was less concerned with Malliath.

You're worrying about me...

Of course, Ilargo replied, *you have been initiated far quicker than any Dragorn before you. You have taken on a lot and have few to rely upon.*

I have you. Gideon could feel Ilargo's elation to hear him say that.

You do. But you have only Adriel to guide you as a Dragorn.

Well apparently I have a lot of time to learn...

Gideon hadn't given his new life expectancy much thought. Immortality excited him beyond words, but it also terrified him to think of how alone he would be. Ilargo would always be there, Adriel too, but any connection he formed with another human would always end the same way, eventually. That again brought him back to the fact that he wasn't leaving Dragons' Reach any time soon.

Fate has brought you this far, Gideon. Ilargo was well aware of his feelings. *Trust in yourself to be where you are needed.*

Gideon knew he needed to be in more than one place right now. The mage wanted to be in Malaysai, helping Galanör to find Adilandra and crush the Darkakin. He also wanted to fly west and warn all of Illian that the savages were marching on their land. But after learning of the Dragorn's real purpose from Adriel, Gideon could feel his calling in his gut. The mage knew he had to retrieve The Veil and destroy it in the pools of Naius; it was the only way the Dragorn would be free of the burden.

The Dragorn have never found Kaliban...

Gideon sighed. **You need to stop reading my mind all the time.**

The connection between man and dragon is old. Our bond will always be more intimate than it would if you were an elf.

Gideon didn't know what to think anymore. The responsibility he felt was becoming a crushing weight on his shoulders. Feeling his anxiety, Ilargo gained height and exuded an aura of calm as the dragon tried to soothe his troubled mind. The trees dropped away and the lake soon became smaller than Gideon's hand. Malliath could still be seen in the ruin of trees, surrounded by the larger dragons.

The two soared through the sky for a while, settling into the rhythm of the air currents. Gideon couldn't believe he was actually enjoying it, leading him to suspect Ilargo's meddling in his emotions. The lines between them were becoming awfully grey.

The dragon banked to the west, giving the mage a clear view of Malaysai in the distance. Smoke was rising over The Great Maw, pouring out of the central pyramid; though from this distance it was mostly a blur to Gideon's human eyes.

What can you see, Ilargo?

Fire... Malaysai is burning!

Galanör...

It could only be Galanör. Setting things on fire was a talent he had already proven to be a good distraction. Either that or things had gone horribly wrong and now both he and Adilandra were trapped in the burning pyramid. Gideon's mind raced and thoughts of anything but saving them quickly vanished.

I... I have to go to them. I have to help, Ilargo!

I know. The green dragon banked again and turned back to the Reach.

What are you doing? Gideon hated that Ilargo's thoughts and feelings were better guarded than his own.

The dragon didn't reply, but instead angled them over the crater and dived. Gideon knew enough about the way Ilargo's body moved to know when to expect a dive, but it did nothing for his stomach. The sheer drop kept the mage from arguing with the dragon about flying back to the Reach, as all he could do was hold on.

Ilargo spread his majestic wings at the last second and brought them down in the small clearing that housed Mournblade. The dragon bowed low, signalling to Gideon to get off.

What are you doing, the mage asked.

Take it, Gideon. Ilargo was staring at Mournblade.

Gideon looked from the dragon to the red hilt sticking out of the rock, its golden script shining in the sunlight. *It will only come loose when the Dragorn are needed again.*

Do you feel needed now? Ilargo's blue eyes looked through him.

Was it that simple? Gideon thought. Had Adriel been unable to remove the blade because he didn't *feel* the Dragorn were needed anymore?

Take it, Gideon...

Transfixed as he was, Gideon found himself standing in front of Mournblade with no memory of taking a step. The Dragorn wrapped his hand around the hilt and pulled with no great effort. The scimitar lifted cleanly out of the rock with a satisfying sound, its curved blade glistening in the rays of light.

Gideon was speechless.

The Dragorn marvelled at the blade in his hand, surprised by its lack of weight and comfortable grip. It fitted his hand perfectly. Upon closer inspection, the flat of the blade was engraved with elven glyphs, though their words were lost on the human.

The time of the Dragorn has returned!

Gideon looked at Ilargo and the two shared a moment of pure joy, as if they could glimpse the future that awaited them - a future that they would forge together.

Let's go.

Gideon ran back to Ilargo's side and hopped onto the base of the dragon's neck, with his staff on his back and Mournblade in his hand.

As Ilargo pressed down, ready to shoot into the sky, Adriel stepped into the clearing and locked his eyes with Gideon, before finally resting them on the scimitar. Despite the significance of the scene, the mage was still unable to read the elf's expression. Through Ilargo's link to Galandavax, Gideon could feel a sense of awe and apprehension coming from Adriel. There was no time to debate, however. Ilargo launched into the air, leaving the clearing and Dragon's Reach far behind.

Soaring into the sky astride a dragon, with Mournblade in hand, Gideon began to finally embrace the life that had been thrust upon him, a life of meaning, the life of a Dragorn...

CHAPTER 36

AFTERMATH

Asher ran through the portal, with Reyna gripped in one hand, and hoped that it led to somewhere out of the shadow of Syla's Gate. The ranger's faith in the young elf paid off, but it came at a painful price. With no ground to place his foot, the contents of his stomach shifted dramatically, as the pair fell into the desert outside Karath's southern gate. Reyna had successfully opened the portal, but she had failed to orientate it to the desert floor by ten-feet.

Reyna landed on her feet, with her reflexes adapting easily to the fall... Asher was not so graceful. The old ranger required some assistance finding his feet again, though he had more than one pair of hands picking him up. A new cut above his eye had blood trickling into his vision and the other was hazy with dust and sand, but Faylen's angular face could not be mistaken.

"Where in all the hells have you two been?" Nathaniel appeared by Faylen's side, rushing from the mob of soldiers that crowded through the gate. The Graycoat and the princess came together in a crushing hug and a tender kiss.

Asher wiped his eyes and took in the sight of his companions.

Nathaniel had taken a beating by the looks of his swollen eye and fresh cuts, not to mention his damaged armour and notable limp. Faylen was still standing as regal as ever, despite the blood and dirt that blemished her skin. A cut on her jaw line looked as if it needed attention, but it was nothing elven magic couldn't handle.

"We lost you," Faylen said.

"We were..." Reyna gestured to Syla's Gate, behind them.

They all watched the colossal gates collapse under their own weight. Even the army, flooding through Karath's gate beside them, stopped to watch the spectacle. The mountains either side crumbled, losing their hold on the iron, until eventually there was nothing left to support the ancient gate. The displacement had one side falling flat into the desert with a resounding boom that shook the ground, while the other twisted out of place and remained stuck between the mountain and the ground. The fog of sand clung to the northern face of The Undying Mountains, but it was clear to see that with a few ladders, the Darkakin would scale the fallen gate with ease. There was nothing stopping them now.

"You were on the gate?" Nathaniel asked in disbelief.

"Nakir -" Asher coughed to clear his dry throat. "Nakir is dead."

"He's dead?" Nathaniel echoed. "That would explain all the light we saw."

"The fighting has stopped," Reyna stated, watching the Karathan soldiers enter the city.

"Valanis has given them a common enemy," Faylen replied, her eyes running over Asher with a critical eye. "The Darkakin are too savage to make allies with the men of Illian."

"Oh no..." Reyna was staring into the distance.

Asher spat a loose tooth and a mouthful of blood onto the ground before following everyone's gaze. The first wave of Darkakin had already scaled the fallen gate and were charging into the desert Paldora's Star Reyna stated with audible trepidation.

Faylen's response was grim. "He really is free. Who else could bring down Paldora's star?"

"He is walking death," Reyna said and then, seeing the figure robed in white beside the dark elf, added, "Alidyr survived..."

Asher reached for the magical blade on his back and felt the muscles and tendons in his shoulder protest.

"No," Reyna said. "We cannot face Valanis. He is too powerful." The backdrop to the dark elf was testament to that statement.

"I already tried..." Nathaniel held up his sword. The steel blade had several divots in the middle, as if someone had gripped the sword and changed its shape.

Reyna cupped his face and smiled. "You are a fool, Nathaniel Galfrey, but a brave fool."

The distinct roar of a dwarf pierced the rushing crowd beside them. "What are ye doin'?" Doran pushed his way through the mob until he faced the four of them. "Ye need to ge' inside the walls, now!"

They all looked back at the scrambling army, climbing over the fallen gate and round the mountain debris. Valanis and Alidyr stood defiant in the middle of the desert. Even without an army of Dark-akin behind them, the destruction those ancient elves were capable of was beyond all of them. Asher looked at the high walls and wondered what the point in hiding was. The dark elf had just plucked a star from the heavens and brought down Syla's Gate; what protection could Karath offer?

The four companions filtered into the crowd and found their way behind Karath's walls, guided by Doran. Asher could feel every ache and cut setting in, refusing to be ignored any longer. Before he could give in and slump against the nearest wall, the ranger caught sight of Glaide and Tauren crouching over Salim. He was glad to see that Glaide had made it back to the city, but it was clear to see that Salim had not fared so well. The southerner was lying atop a pile of sacks that were soaked with his blood. Gone was his olive tone, replaced with a pale clammy pallor that Asher had seen many times before.

Salim was going to die.

Tauren held his father's hand and rested his head against it. The son-of-none had lost his aura of rage now, leaving only despair behind. Asher placed a hand on Tauren's shoulder and squeezed, watching Salim take his final breaths. He would have liked to speak with Salim before he left this world, but Asher knew that such moments were always robbed of people in their line of work. Theirs was not a life of sentiment, but action. Seeing Salim die, the ranger could only wonder if it was all worth it. Could they have had a life beyond this one, beyond the fighting and pain? The ranger knew the truth of that question and did the only thing he could in a moment such as this.

"I'm sorry..." Asher offered, his words of little use now.

Tauren closed his father's eyes when Salim failed to draw another breath. "He died with his honour intact."

Asher knew that was more than most would ever get, himself included. He would always choose survival over honour; it just made more sense to him.

The streets were chaotic and rammed with soldiers and citizens alike running in every direction. Some were preparing for battle, while others shouted for their families, intending to flee. There was no order or chain of command to take control anymore.

"Asher..." Faylen's expression was distant but the ranger had come to understand her. The elf could feel Valanis and his over-whelming aura approaching; something Asher couldn't feel anymore without his ring.

Asher spoke directly to Tauren. "You need to get everyone out of the city. The elf approaching us isn't like Alidyr and the others; he's much worse. The city walls won't keep him out and the Darkakin will cross the desert soon." The ranger waited for a response that wasn't coming. "Tauren!"

The son-of-none looked up with the face of a wild animal. He soon found the chaos beyond Asher and his rage slowly melted away. His city was falling into ruin.

Asher crouched down to his level and gripped the young man by the back of the head. "Now isn't the time to fight." The ranger looked down at Salim. "And now isn't the time to mourn. We have to *run*, Tauren."

The son-of-none stood up, much faster than Asher was able to, and looked about, no doubt seeking his fellow owls. "You would have us take The Selk Road north, to Velia?" he asked.

Asher glanced at Jonus Glaide. "The Karathan army is broken; there are too many divides. You need to get behind another army now. If none of your people survive this invasion, there will be no one left to rebuild."

Doran coughed. "That's *if* we win..."

Asher shot the dwarf a glare, silencing any further remarks. "Take your people north. *Survive*. When this is all over, you can return and start again. If you stay and fight for nothing but the bricks, there won't be *any people* left to call it home, Tauren. You have to run..."

Glaide wiped the sweat from his bald head. "Why do I get the feeling you're not coming with us again?"

Asher looked to Reyna and the others. The four of them knew what they had to do.

"Ye don' mean to follow through with *that?*" Doran interjected. "Ye can' go to Nightfall now, not after all this. Ye need rest!"

"We will accompany you, as promised." Glaide squeezed Salim's shoulder before standing up to face them.

"No," Nathaniel replied flatly. "Tauren will need all the help he can get. Help these people instead; they have to leave this place before the Darkakin arrive."

Glaide and Doran looked to Asher, who nodded his approval. The rangers would be an asset on the road to Velia. Taking them to Nightfall would only have them face death again, and losing Bale and Salim would weigh on Asher's conscience enough as it was.

"Wait... Where's Hadavad and Atharia?" Nathaniel asked.

Glaide's eyes went wide as if he were just remembering something. "Atharia took him into the alley..."

Tauren was the last to leave Salim, but the companions moved round the corner to find Atharia crouching over the old mage. Hadavad was sat against the wall with his hand pressed into his abdomen; blood seeped between his fingers. The group approached cautiously before Atharia held up her hand, stopping them from coming any closer.

"Arakesh..." Hadavad could be heard to rasp. "So damn quick..."

"I am ready, Master." Atharia threw her staff down the alley and brushed her hair behind her ears.

Hadavad smiled and coughed, contorting in pain. "Five hundred years... you were my favourite."

Atharia smiled through her tears. "I bet you say that to all of your apprentices."

"The Black Hand... will perish." Hadavad used his free hand to pull the ruby gem out of his shirt. "Your sacrifice will see to it..."

Asher had heard of The Black Hand over the years, mostly from Hadavad, but he had never encountered them in the way Faylen had in The Tower of Gadavance. The mage's grievances with them was entirely beyond him, except for their fondness of necromancy; that was something the ranger would never get behind.

"Do it," Atharia said.

Hadavad let go of his wound and began to whisper an enchantment under his dying breath. The ruby came to life in the same way a crystal would exude light and energy upon use. Both of their faces were illuminated in the red glow, which continued to intensify until neither of them could be seen. Asher shielded his eyes for a moment, desperate to catch a glimpse between his fingers, but before his eyes could adjust, the blinding light vanished, leaving a dead Hadavad behind. Atharia stroked the mage's cheek and removed the ruby necklace with care. The young woman stood up and collected the old mage's staff as she did, claiming it for her own.

"Atharia..." Faylen said, offering her condolences.

"I am not Atharia," the woman replied boldly, "though her sacrifice will go down in history this day."

There was some confusion among the group and Asher looked

from the ruby up to Atharia's eyes, connecting the dots he had been putting together over the years. "Hadavad?"

"None other."

"How?" Tauren appeared the most perplexed of the group. The son-of-none had lived a life devoid of magic and enchantments.

Hadavad, as he now was, tucked the ruby into Atharia's clothing. "'Tis a long tale, older than all of you." The mage eyed Asher. "Almost all of you."

"Is Atharia dead?" Glaide asked, looking at Hadavad's new body as if it were a ghost.

"Yes," was Hadavad's only reply.

The mage's lack of regret or sympathy for his new host didn't escape Asher, but the ranger was not one for judging others and their ways, especially with a past like his own.

Still, the group had a moment's silence for the dead girl who stood before them. Knowing that Hadavad was alive was good, but seeing Atharia's body so obviously alive made it hard to acknowledge her death.

"We're running out of time," Faylen interrupted.

"Valanis is approaching." Reyna looked beyond the alley, to the chaotic streets.

"*Valanis* is here?" Hadavad asked incredulously.

Faylen was already making to move. "We need to get out of the city, now."

"No. Wait here." Tauren dashed out of the alley without explanation.

Asher could feel Faylen's eyes on him, her impatience an ever present shadow. The ranger was eager to abandon the city as well, if not for their own perilous task but to simply survive the wrath of Valanis. A part of him wanted to stay and finish his fight with Alidyr, but it would be suicide with the dark elf by his side. Again, in his moment's pause, the pain of his wounds lashed out and demanded his attention.

"Here!" Tauren came back into the alley holding the reins of a pair of horses. The animals were streaked with blood, their saddles included. "Go to the east gate, past the palace."

Asher had a lot of respect for the young man; there weren't many who could have survived on the streets of Karath, challenged an empire and made a stand before an army of Darkakin. To reward him for such courage, the gods had seen fit to rob him of both his brother and father, not to mention the devastation to his House of Owls. Now, at the end of such a hard road, he still wanted to help them save Illian.

"You have been well met, Tauren son-of-none." The ranger grasped his forearm. "Salim and Halion would be proud."

"Salim and Halion are dead," Tauren replied flatly. "Let us..." The son-of-none took a breath, considering his words. "Let us be concerned with the living; that is what they died for."

The response reminded Asher of something he would say. There was a deep rooted anger inside the man, an anger that would never know release while there was injustice in the world. The ranger admired him for that; at least Tauren's anger had a purpose. Asher was just an angry man. He wanted to leave the son-of-none with some lasting advice or words of wisdom, but such speeches were not among Asher's strengths.

"Asher..." Faylen prompted.

"I'm sorry," Hadavad said. "Between the fighting and the dying I appear to have lost track of what's going on. What's happening?"

Asher wasn't used to hearing him speak with Atharia's voice. "You're going to get these people out of here, before the Darkakin arrive." Asher mounted the horse and offered a hand to Faylen, who sat behind him. "Escort them to Velia. As many as you can. We'll meet you there."

The four companions turned their horses to the end of the alley. Once again he had lost Hector in all the chaos, but Asher decided it was probably for the best, since he had continued to lead the horse into danger, and the mounts they now sat upon weren't heading anywhere good.

Asher looked back at the rangers and Tauren, wondering who he would see again... or if they would see him again. A swift kick had the horses charging into the city streets, where the citizens of Karath were forced to dive out of the way. Asher wasn't waiting for anyone now; they had to reach the east gate and hope the madness concealed their escape.

The eastern side of the city was largely abandoned now, with most of the residents heading to the north gate. Asher and Reyna had their horses gallop through the gates and out into the desert. The ruin of Syla's Gate dominated the mountain range to the south, their peaks hidden within a cloud of sand. Karath was lost, The Arid Lands would follow and, from there, Valanis could march his army of savages into the northern realms.

An overbearing thought weighed down on Asher, a thought he was becoming tired of having. Seeing the Darkakin march over the desert to the south, and the refugees fleeing the city to the north, there was no mistaking it.

They had lost...

Alidyr gave himself over to the fall, instead concentrating his efforts on removing the last crystal from his belt. Throwing the crystal while falling was futile, leaving the elf with only one option. Centuries had passed since he had been forced to use a crystal in this manner, but the pain could never be forgotten. With one hand he crushed the crystal and thought of Valanis. The magic folded Alidyr into nothingness before spitting him back out across the desert floor.

Thanks to his years of training, the elf was able to orientate the direction of his makeshift portal, preventing his momentum from still being the end of him. Humiliatingly however, Alidyr was shot back into existence at the feet of his master. After rolling over the desert and the battlefield of dead bodies, the elf picked himself up and brushed off his tattered, white robes, now stained with blood and dirt.

"Master..." Alidyr bowed his head, though Valanis took little notice of him.

Syla's Gate was falling. The ancient magic that had sealed it for over a thousand years had been for nothing when challenged by Valanis. His master was truly as powerful as the gods. Who but the herald of the creators could bring down a star?

"How did you know?" Alidyr asked. "How did you know we would fail to open the gate?"

Valanis's chest heaved and Alidyr could only imagine the magical strength required to pull off such a feat. He feared his master would suffer for it.

Valanis tilted his head, as if listening to something else. "The gods know the true strength of us all." The dark elf opened his arms to the spectacle before them. "And now man will know the strength of the gods."

A bright light shone from the top of the gate, piercing the fog of sand. Alidyr had only seen a light such as that once before; when Adellum died in West Fellion. It seemed another brother was leaving him now.

"Nakir was weak," Valanis announced. "He could not keep Karath from splintering. Instead they will unify against this threat."

Alidyr cared little for whether Nakir died or not, but Valanis's indifference was disturbing. Would he care so little if Alidyr was to perish? Such doubts were a weakness he could not afford now, not when the war was only just beginning. They were all tools for the gods, Valanis included.

"The forges completed their work before -" Alidyr held his tongue, mesmerised by the sight.

The only remaining monument to the oldest of their kind collapsed into the desert with a deafening roar. The mountains buckled and cracked, raining boulders the size of castles upon the ground. For the first time in over a millennium, the valley of The

Undying Mountains could be seen from The Arid Lands. The ground shook and the elf likened it to Atilan taking his first step on Illian soil. The Echoes of Fate could not be denied...

A new portal opened beside them and Thallan strode out in his dark armour and hood. His jade scimitar was strapped to his waist, as ever, but his appearance was too clean for their surroundings, setting him apart. Only Valanis could have summoned him so accurately, and only a crystal from the pools of Naius could bring him so far. Thallan was speechless at the sight of Syla's Gate.

"Thallan..." Valanis called softly. "You are to take charge of the Darkakin now."

Alidyr didn't like that his brother was receiving so much responsibility, but the idea of leading the savages appalled the elf. Let Thallan deal with the rabble, he thought.

Valanis continued, "They will need a show of strength to take your command. However, the Karathan army will no longer be joining their numbers as planned. With that in mind, cull as few as possible when making your point."

"As you command, Master." Thallan bowed his head, eyeing Alidyr with a smug expression. "I will lead them to Tregaran immediately."

"No." Valanis's tone was even, but his words carried weight. "With Karath laid to waste, The Arid Lands is as good as conquered. I want the next kingdom. I want Velia..."

"I will see it done."

"What of Samandriel and King Merkaris's army to the north?" Alidyr asked.

Valanis whipped around and made for the city, leaving the Darkakin to find their way over the fallen gate. "They will move down from Orith and trap Velia."

Alidyr, the strategist, was always thinking ahead. "What about Queen Isabella and her army? With Felgarn to the west of Velia, they could come to King Rengar's aid and cut off the northern army."

Valanis's smile could be heard through his words. "The alliance between the six kingdoms has never been weaker. The realm of Felgarn will cower when word reaches them of the Darkakin. Let them hide in The Evermoore. When Velia is naught but rubble, Lirian will fall next."

Alidyr knew better than to question his master. "And what of me? What would the gods have me do?"

Valanis stopped and turned on him. Alidyr could see the faint glow from within his mask and the flare of his purple eyes. How his master was commanding so much magic and not falling to it was beyond his understanding. The subtlest of twitches in his left hand betrayed Valanis, however. The exertion was taking its toll.

"As I have always tasked you," Valanis replied. "Find Paldora's Gem. I will need it if I am to see this through to the end."

Valanis continued walking when Alidyr stopped to take in the devastation of Syla's Gate.

"The ranger was on the gate..."

"Was he..?" Valanis's distorted voice echoed from within his mask.

Alidyr feared his master hadn't grasped the gravity of his statement. "Only Asher knew of the gem's location."

Thallan sneered. "And you failed to retrieve that knowledge."

Alidyr shot his brother a look that would reduce even the best of the Arakesh to a withering mess. When he had the time, he would remind Thallan of his place.

"My path to the gem has not been closed." Valanis tilted his head again in the same unusual manner. "The gods would know if Paldora's gem was lost to the world."

Before Alidyr could ask any more questions, an Arakesh ran out from Karath to greet them. The woman was blindfolded and her short-swords were caked in dried blood. Beyond her, through the southern gates, the city was in disarray, with people running wildly though the streets.

"Masters." The woman genuflected in front of them. "The ranger and the princess have been spotted on horseback, leaving through the eastern gate."

Alidyr couldn't fathom how the ranger and the princess kept surviving. "East..." He looked to his right. "There is only one place east of here."

Indeed, a day's ride would have them at Nightfall's entrance, an entrance the ranger would know how to find. Why would they ride east if not for Nightfall; the land was barren. But why Nightfall at all? Unless...

"Master." Alidyr's tone was confident. "When next we meet, I will have the rest of Paldora's gem. Your power will know no bounds."

Valanis reached out and cupped Alidyr's face as a loving father, his voice light. "See that you do, Alidyr, or I will have you dragged to the depths of The Adean." The dark elf took a step closer to his disciple and whispered. "I will not suffer failure."

Alidyr stepped back and bowed. It was all he could do in the face of such power. Valanis's aura was intoxicating but terrifying in its magnitude. Being dragged to the bottom of The Adean was merciful by his master's abilities.

"We need horses!" he barked at the assassin. Without any crystals it was his only option, and he dare not ask Valanis for assistance.

"What will you do, Master?" Alidyr wanted Valanis to return to Kaliban and recover his strength.

"As I promised I would." Valanis looked at the city of Karath. "I'm going to wipe Verda clean..." The dark elf raised his hands and unleashed a fury of magic far beyond anything Alidyr or Nakir could muster. The walls of Karath cracked and mirrored The Undying Mountains.

Now the war could really begin.

Nathaniel could feel the dying sun on the back of his neck and adjusted the cloth wrapped around his head. The desert was painted in orange hues and the temperature continued to drop every minute. Reyna had fallen asleep, slumping back into the knight's chest as they rode ever eastward, her own face shrouded behind white cloth. He was thankful to the gods that the elf had been returned to him safely. It had been the longest night of his life, filled with plenty of opportunities to lose it to the blade of another, but not knowing the fate of Reyna throughout had plagued his mind.

The Graycoat was careful not to move, not wanting to disturb the princess, but also to avoid upsetting his numerous wounds. His skills mastered in West Fellion had certainly kept him alive, but he wasn't invincible. He would have scars to remind him of this battle for the rest of his life.

Whether it was the battle itself or just the thought of its effects on his life, the knight found himself considering his feelings towards Reyna. Their growing love for each other was undeniable, but their circumstances prevented any commitment. He knew that in his exhaustion it would be unwise to dwell on these feelings, but meeting Reyna had changed his life in a way that nothing else ever could. Her bravery and courage to stand up to all was a quality Nathaniel hadn't realised was missing from the world.

The knight sighed, his mind filled to the brim with flashes of death and the feeling of loss for all those who had been claimed in this war. Nathaniel knew that he shouldn't even be thinking about love when there was so much more fighting to come. His exhausted mind was fickle however, and he found himself flipping the argument in his mind. Life was too short to worry about what was to come and what wasn't; he knew he loved Reyna and that was all he needed to know. When this was all over, and Nightfall was behind them, he would tell her of his love. He would rather die an old man in her arms than die an old man, bitter and filled with regret.

No, he thought, he would tell her now! There would be time to sleep, but right now he had to tell her how he felt.

That was when Asher fell from his horse.

Faylen was the first to reach his side, but the commotion had Reyna awake and leaping from their horse in the blink-of-an-eye. Nathaniel's injured leg slowed him down and the drop from the horse wasn't exactly pleasant.

"What's wrong with him?" the knight asked, annoyed that he hadn't seen the ranger deteriorate.

"I'm fine..." Asher groaned.

Faylen checked him over and inspected her hand, soaked with blood. Pulling back his cloak, the ranger had a gash in his leather armour and a piece of ragged cloth hanging out of it. The makeshift bandage had lasted during the battle, but it could no longer stop the flow of blood. Reyna stroked the side of the horse and found fresh blood streaked down the mare's chestnut coat.

"He's been bleeding for some time," the princess commented.

"Can't you heal him?" Nathaniel had seen the elves work miracles with their command of magic, saving his own life among them.

Faylen and Reyna held a silent conversation with their eyes. Nathaniel couldn't decipher their words, but the meaning behind them was clear to see.

"I can heal his wounds, but not all of them. He will still need rest to recover," Faylen said.

"If we stay," Reyna said, "they will catch up with us..."

"Who will catch up with us?" Nathaniel asked.

"The... Arakesh." Asher pulled the cloth from his head. The ranger shrugged off the fuss Faylen made of him and pulled himself up using the horse's saddle.

"You shouldn't move," Faylen said sternly.

Nathaniel still wasn't following. "Why would the Arakesh catch up with us?"

"They watched us leave the city," Reyna replied.

Nathaniel cursed his dull, human eyes. "You think they would know where we're going? They don't even know we're searching for the gem."

Asher was rummaging through pouches on his belt. "Alidyr will put it together. There's nothing else out here."

"Let me heal you," Faylen insisted.

Asher warded her off. "I know where we're going. Trust me; you're going to need all the magic you can muster. We're not stopping until we reach Nightfall. If we don't stop we should find the stairs by dawn." It was clear to see how much pain the ranger was in.

"Stairs?" Nathaniel asked.

"You'll never make it if you don't let me heal you," Faylen continued.

Asher's tone was unwavering. "We've all been awake for two days. By the time we enter the pit, it'll be three days. You need to save whatever strength you have left to find the gem." The ranger climbed back onto the horse with considerable effort and took a swig from the water-skin.

"What is that?" Reyna gestured to the clay-like substance Asher had removed from his belt.

"Dwarven dirt. Something Doran recommended years ago." Asher rubbed the clay into the gash on his lower back, covering the entire wound. "Don't ask me what's in it; I just know it's good for wounds." The ranger winced from beginning to end, until the blood stopped trickling out.

"Are we really doing this?" Nathaniel asked. "Are we going into Nightfall as we are?"

"What choice do we have?" Asher replied. "If we stay out here and rest, the Arakesh will find us and we'll never recover the gem."

"Nathaniel is right," Reyna added. "What hope do we have if we can't even keep our eyes open?"

Asher sighed and looked down at them from his horse. "You're both young, so I understand that hope still plays a part in your thinking, but trust me, *hoping* doesn't get it done. Sometimes you have to grit your teeth and keep fighting..."

Nathaniel could see that fatigue was already taking over their emotions, making them irritable. It was subtle, but the ranger had grown distant and more distressed since the decision to find the gem.

"Going into Nightfall now could be the end of us," Reyna replied with her unyielding tone.

Exasperated, Asher took a deep breath. "Rest here and fight Alidyr and the Arakesh. Go back to Karath and fight Valanis and the Darkakin. Go to Nightfall and enter the pit. All of our options would seemingly spell our doom, Princess. Don't get me wrong. If we're choosing how we die, I say we stay and rest, take our chances with the Arakesh and that worthless shit they call a master. But... if defeating an elf who can pull stars out of the sky is still our course, we cannot stop."

"He's right." Faylen looked back at the horizon, but Karath was no longer in sight. "Too many have died already, and the war has yet to really begin. Forward is our only option now."

Nathaniel could see Reyna's next argument on the edge of her lips. "We can take it in turns to sleep on the ride," he added before she could speak. "Get whatever rest we can before we find these stairs."

Nathaniel hopped back onto his horse and watched Asher with a careful eye. The Graycoat usually admired the ranger's strength in moments like these, hoping in some way that he might be as strong as him in twenty years, but right now he looked at Asher and saw careless choices that would get them killed. Still, there was no arguing that their errand was perhaps the most important in the land. Valanis had the power to bring down the sky now, and if Paldora's gem was the only thing that could undo the dark elf, then Nathaniel Galfrey was going to see it found.

CHAPTER 37
THE PIT

Before the light of dawn could wipe away the last of the stars, Asher held up his hand, placing his fingers and thumb between a particular constellation. They were in the right place, maybe a half mile south of the entrance. Riding through the pain and exhaustion had led the ranger to his past, where he had been rigorously trained to embrace such a state of mind and body. Passing out from the pain had only ever resulted in a harsher punishment, while sleep was a luxury he had to earn.

He had been younger back then, however.

Now he could feel a lifetime of fighting and sleeping rough gnawing at his bones and settling into his muscles like a parasite. He knew that choosing to push on wasn't the wise thing to do, but wisdom was of little use when death surrounded them on all sides. Still, the ranger wasn't sure how much more punishment his body could take. The dwarven clay had healing properties, but its effects on humans were limited.

Nathaniel was half asleep, with his head resting over Reyna's shoulder. The princess was awake, but both elves appeared to have entered some kind of trance overnight, keeping them awake but not present. Before the moon had reached its apex, Asher had seen Reyna healing Nathaniel's leg while he slept. The ranger had wanted to dissuade her, sure that she would need all of her magical strength if they were to survive the pit, but he and the princess had bartered too many harsh words of late, and he knew her stubbornness could not be overcome.

The princess's stubbornness was a quality Asher had come to adore in the elf. Reyna was ready to stand against any and all that would threaten their world. It was a courage he couldn't pin on the recklessness of her age or naivety; the princess was simply a better person than him. Reyna was what Verda needed right now; good people who would do the hard thing and say no to those who ravaged this world. If he was lucky, Asher thought, some of that goodness might rub off on him.

Asher reached for their reins and steered the horse with his own, taking them north along the edge of the gorge. The crack in the earth was deep and ran from north to south as far as the eye could see. There was no way of crossing it without making the long trek through the desert, or climbing down and back up the other side. Asher had glimpsed some of the monsters that called the gorge their home, and knew that way to be folly. The entire area was honey-combed with various entrances, creating a maze of burrows. Somewhere inside all of that, was the pit.

A pale blue sky was creeping over the land when Asher cleared his throat and woke the others. His back stung, but the ranger clenched his jaw and tightened his grip on the hilt of his broadsword. Nathaniel and Reyna got off their horse and joined them by the edge of the gorge. The Graycoat tested the strength in his leg, unaware of the magic that had fixed it during the night. Asher kept his mouth shut and peered over the edge, into the nothingness below. A familiar white owl flew over their heads and circled the gorge.

"That bird is relentless..." Asher said dryly.

"He is loyal. And very smart." Reyna held out her arm so that Ölli could swoop down and land on her leather bracer. The princess stroked his feathers and gave the owl a loving kiss on the head.

"Well he can't come where we're going." Asher removed the water-skins from the saddles before smacking the horses on the rear. "Everyone take a drink."

"What are you doing?" Faylen asked as the horses trotted into the desert.

"There's nowhere to tie them up and we won't be coming back out up here." Asher drank from a skin and passed them round.

"Where will we come out?" Nathaniel asked.

Asher looked across the horizon. "It's always somewhere different."

Reyna gave him a hard look before her fair features softened. "We have followed you this far. If you have the strength to keep going, then so do I."

Her melodic tone was disarming as ever. "You calling me old, Princess?" Asher asked with a hint of a smile. The two had reached a truce, which was the most he could ask for with such frayed emotions.

"Shall we?" Faylen said, checking her blade before sliding the scimitar back into its scabbard.

Asher knew there was no avoiding it; he had come this far. He walked up to the edge and looked down, searching for the top of the stairs. "Follow me." The ranger crouched down and made the short drop onto the outcropping. He used to be able to jump down and run along the stairs without a care.

The stairs were perhaps a natural formation once upon a time, but over the centuries they had been worn down into easy stepping stones that had formed out of the rock face. Here and there were gaps that needed leaping over, but for the most part it was simply a steep decline into the gorge.

"I thought it would be grander..." Nathaniel called from the back of the line.

"Grand things tend to stand out," Asher replied, doing his very best to suppress the memories invoked by the stairs. How many times had he journeyed back to Nightfall after a new kill? The ranger knew the number in his head: he knew how many murders were on his conscience...

It was considerably colder by the time they reached the entrance to Nightfall. It was just as he remembered it. The doorway was a rough triangular crack in the rock, wide enough to fit two grown men side-by-side. It was pitch black inside, but there was a warm breeze drifting out into the gorge. It had felt twice as foreboding when Nasta Nal-Aket had first brought him here, forty years ago. As a child Asher had felt as if he were walking into the mouth of a demon.

Both Faylen and Reyna whispered a spell into their hands and birthed a small orb of light. The orbs floated above them, tethered by magic, and illuminated the entrance floor. Within a few feet, the weathered rock had been replaced with smooth, dressed stone. There were no markings or signs of any kind that one had entered the dwelling of the assassins. Asher inhaled and found his memory tugging at times gone by. His memories of being an Outlander were practically gone now, but his time in Nightfall was as a scar in his mind.

"Keep the light behind me." The ranger walked a few steps ahead of the elves and sank into the thick shadows.

The Nightseye elixir came to life in his veins, exposing every dark corner of the ancient sanctum. Three heartbeats drummed in his ears and his companion's salty sweat found his tongue. The smell of blood came from all of them, though his own blood was familiar, if nauseating. Asher tried to focus through his pain and fatigue and combine his various senses into one complete awareness.

"How big is this place?" Nathaniel asked, drawing his deformed sword.

Asher wanted to tell them all to be quiet, but it would make no difference in these halls. Besides the beating of their hearts, any assassin would smell their wounds or hear their steps on the cool stone. They were flies stuck in a web now.

"It's designed to be a labyrinth." Asher had got lost in the dark more times than he could count.

"Where is everyone?" Reyna asked.

Asher paused at a junction and relied on his age-old senses to show him the way. After fourteen years, many of the identical hallways appeared new to the ranger. His nose detected the distinct odour of rotten flesh and old blood, while his ears heard droplets of water falling down a long shaft.

The pit...

"This way." Asher strode down the next corridor.

"Asher, where is everyone?" Reyna asked again.

The ranger tilted his head, sharpening his senses and pushing them to the limits. He couldn't hear, smell or taste another living body in the area. Even the aroma from the kitchens was absent.

"Alidyr has cleared them out." Asher shook his head. "The Arakesh are just soldiers in a war now."

To the others, the chamber they were passing through was just another shrouding abyss but, to Asher, he could see the throne that had seated countless Mothers and Fathers of Nightfall. The shrine to Ibilis, the god of shadows, was by the far wall, its incense long burned out and forgotten. It had been a long time since he had stepped foot in the Cradle. From this chamber he had been given one murderous task after another, each more despicable than the last.

"Watch the steps," Asher warned, as they descended into the next chamber, another room he would have been happy to never see again.

The ranger came to a stop by the lip of the pit. The orbs floated over the top as the others caught up, their light vanquishing the magic in his veins. It was an odd feeling to be inside Nightfall and be unaware of his surroundings. The darkness was disorientating beyond the light of the orbs.

"I've never taken any Nightseye elixir," Nathaniel said as he looked into the well of black, "but even I can smell that."

"It's a different world down there." Asher's flashbacks were that of a nightmare. "Magic will be our greatest advantage."

"You remember where you left it?" Faylen asked sceptically.

"I went left." Asher recalled the beast that had been waiting for them at the bottom. "We ran until we found the next tunnel..." That creature had shredded two of the students in seconds and pursued them immediately. "There were only three of us left when I hid it. I would remember the tunnel."

"Truly?" Faylen asked.

Asher wasn't proud of the only answer he had. "I killed the other two students and marked the wall with a handprint of blood, just in case I ever needed to find it again."

There was a moment's silence. Asher wondered if they were remembering that he hadn't always been a ranger.

"Why would you need to find it?" Nathaniel asked.

"In case I lost the shard. I didn't know what it was, but I knew it protected me from magic. Back then I just saw it as an advantage."

"And the students?" Reyna asked, but Asher could tell she didn't really want the answer.

"They were competition."

Reyna took a long breath and nodded her head. "Well, talking about it isn't going to get us anywhere." She made for the built-in ladder. "Why don't we just start looking?"

The three of them watched the princess boldly begin the descent into darkness.

Nathaniel looked to Asher. "She's been spending too much time with you..." The knight managed a smile, despite the scowl Faylen gave him.

The companions made their way down the shaft in silence, guided by the descending orbs. The ranger heard their complaints before he met them at the bottom. The ground was littered with bones and rotten body parts. The smell was invasive and the Night-seye elixir wasn't even raising his senses yet.

The atmosphere between the companions changed at the bottom

of the pit. There was no levity in all the world that could distract them from their surroundings. This was a realm of monsters. Asher looked into the darkness beyond the white light of the orbs. As a predator himself, he always knew when something was watching him.

"Faylen..." The ranger kept his eyes forward. "Cast some light." He pointed his chin at the abyss.

The elf wasted no time in raising her hand and unleashing a torrent of fire into the tunnel. The roar was animalistic, but closer to a shrill, as the fire licked the hard shell of a monster that could only be described as teeth and pincers. Its bulk consumed most of the tunnel, as did its maw of razor-sharp teeth.

"Run!" Asher turned about and pushed Nathaniel down the tunnel, where both men were able to avoid the arrow from Reyna's bow.

The group followed the end of Asher's cloak, which was the only part of him caught in the light, as he used his extra senses to navigate the labyrinth. The monster howled with Reyna's arrow lodged deep inside its long body, while Faylen's fire clung to its shell and burned the inside of its mouth. Still it chased them.

Asher darted down the next tunnel and called for them to follow him, concerned that they would miss the change in direction. The monster turned the corner with enough speed to run up the curved walls and pursue them along the roof of the cave. The ranger's senses detected more movement ahead and down the tunnel to the right. Lots of sharp legs digging into the rock hammered in his ears and the smell of toxic secretions stung his nostrils.

"This way!" Asher could see the hole in the ground, where the network of tunnels opened up into a crossroads. The hole was too small for the monster to follow them, but only Asher could sense the true height of the drop.

The ranger stopped at the hole until the orbs caught up and illuminated the jagged entrance for everyone else. There was no time to argue or consider another route; the monster was gaining on them and easy to spot with its fiery shell. It was so close now that Asher could see its mouth was circular and lined with more than one row of teeth.

"Go!" he shouted.

One by one they dropped into the hole, leaving Asher until last. The other tunnels were a cacophony of racing monsters now; their clicking mandibles and gnashing teeth easy to hear, even without the elixir in his veins. The ranger dropped down as the giant monster collided with a cave full of other creatures. Before he could roll across the ground of the cave below, blood dripped down from above and coated his cloak. The monsters were feeding off each other with no other prey.

The companions leapt up and regrouped back-to-back. The orbs had followed them down, rendering Asher blind to the environment. Nathaniel and Reyna had their bows drawn, while Asher and Faylen held their swords high.

"We went the wrong way," Faylen observed through laboured breath.

"I know," Asher replied, favouring his right leg. The left didn't have much life left in it. "These tunnels are all connected. We just need to find our way back."

"And up," Nathaniel added.

Somewhere in the darkness a man cleared his throat. The group spun around to face the direction they thought was a threat, but only an inky abyss stood before them.

Outside the reach of the light, a voice broke the silence. "I am afraid going back the way you came is no longer an option."

Asher knew that voice, that accent...

"Nasta."

"Hello old friend." Nasta Nal-Aket slowly walked into the light. "It has been a long time."

Asher wanted to ask the Father a hundred questions, but the ranger wasn't sure if he was about to run his broadsword through him instead. This man had been a blessing and a curse on his life for as long as he could remember. It was Nasta who had commanded him to complete the contract on the governor's children and Nasta again who had ordered his death when he failed. But the southerner had also kept him alive in the dark and taught him to survive. He had even shown a young Asher some affection and taken to him as a true father.

"You are the Father of Nightfall," Nathaniel stated, his arrow aimed squarely at Nasta's heart.

The southerner moved further into the light, revealing his scarred face, devoid of eyes and lids. His white hair and goatee were still curly, but the man was in a dishevelled state, dressed in tattered robes and streaked with blood. On his belt was the famous Reaver, the sword of the Father, though Nasta was leaning on a long shaft of what appeared to be bone.

"I am afraid that title has been stripped from me. Claimed by Alidyr Yalathanil."

"What..." Asher blinked the unexpected tears from his eyes. "What are you doing down here?"

"Alidyr left me down here for dead, but I have survived the pit more than once. It holds few secrets from me now." Nasta cocked his head. "We must leave here at once. The Razorbacks are coming..."

"Razorbacks?" Reyna asked, her bow lowered now.

"I have had time to name some of the monsters that call this hell their home. Come! And quickly!" Nasta turned around and strode down the nearest tunnel.

Asher was hesitant to follow his old master, but it felt so natural to do as he said. The ranger was confident however, that he could beat Nasta in combat, should he try anything. Nathaniel and the elves followed first, with Asher bringing up the rear, allowing his senses to retune with the darkness. Indeed, there were several things closing in on them, their charging feet vibrating against the rock.

When Asher caught up with them, Nasta had led them to a small cave that could only be entered via a small hole in the wall. Once inside, the southerner covered the gap with a boulder. The orbs illuminated a cave filled with odd bits and pieces collected by Nasta; most of which he had clearly taken from the bodies of fallen students.

The ranger shared a moment with Nasta. Though there were no eyes to connect with, Asher knew that the Father's attention was on him.

"You are wounded," Nasta stated. "You are all wounded." Without any eyes, the southerner would always be acutely aware of those around him.

"War has returned to Illian," Asher replied. "Wounds are to be expected."

Nasta nodded his head and perched on an outcropping of rock. "Valanis... Has he returned also?"

"Yes." Reyna expressed the surprise they all felt. "You know of Valanis?"

"I do. I also know why you are here."

Asher could feel their eyes on him, hoping his familiarity with Nasta would shed some light on his mysterious answers. "Speak plainly, old man."

"I have missed you..." Nasta said absently.

"Explain." Asher had little patience at the best of times.

"You are here for the gem; the one you hid during your final trial." Nasta casually removed a strip of cloth to reveal Paldora's Gem.

The group froze in such a silence that Asher actually heard Reyna's lips part in shock. There it was, the most powerful relic in the world, sat next to an old man with no eyes and no inclination to use it.

"How?" Asher asked, taking a step towards the gem.

"I saw you hide it, of course. Do you not recall wondering where I was before you entered the pit? It was the first thing you asked me upon your return. I had entered the pit hours before your trial. I watched you every step of the way."

"Why?"

Nasta paused. "You know why."

Asher knew why, he just couldn't believe it. The idea that Nasta had intended to protect him during his final trial was a fatherly gesture beyond the southerner's emotional bounds. He was still a killer among killers and the most manipulative person Asher had ever met.

"Wait," Faylen interjected. "How do you know of Valanis?"

"Ever since I was a student at Nightfall, I have been interested in Alidyr. Besides his heritage, the fact that he never wished to rule the assassins was curious. I took several steps over the decades to observe him in secret, to follow him." Nasta turned his head to Asher. "That's why I was at Elethiah when I found you. Alidyr would visit the ruin every now and then. It took me a very long time, too long, to realise that our oldest member had other alliances. Most of his secrets I garnered from his private quarters. It took me years to find a way in without setting off the traps. I found references to Paldora's gem, his true mission, given to him by Valanis."

"You knew I had the gem?" Asher had yet to take his eyes from the relic.

"I suspected for some time. I only believed it when I witnessed your resilience to magic."

"I don't recall that?" Asher was ever suspicious of the Father.

"You were not aware. I had a local mage, in Karath, prepare an elixir enchanted with a deadly spell. It could kill a grown man in seconds, yet you finished off your entire meal and returned to training."

There it was. The other side to Nasta Nal-Aket that Asher would never forget and could never forgive.

"This wasn't the life I wanted for you, Asher," Nasta continued. "I didn't want you to be stuck in the middle of Valanis's war. I was happy when I saw that you rid yourself of the gem."

"But you were happy with me living the life of an Arakesh?" Asher was sure he was only moments away from ending Nasta's life.

"You were untouchable as an assassin. You were the best. You would have replaced me some day. But now, now you're between Valanis and his prize. You cannot beat him alone."

"He isn't alone," Reyna announced. "Take the gem, Asher." The princess reached for the black stone.

"Stop!" Faylen, Asher and even Nasta cried out.

"Don't touch it," Faylen warned. "I touched only the shard in West Fellion and it nearly crippled me."

"Indeed," Nasta agreed. "I was lucky to have remained in one piece when I retrieved it."

"I don't understand." Reyna looked to Asher.

The ranger picked up the gem without any fuss and rolled it around in his hand. "I think my time trapped in the Amber Spell with it has... I don't know, bound us in some way."

Nathaniel added, "A thousand years is a long time to grow an attachment."

"What will you do now?" Nasta asked.

Asher could feel the power of the gem pulsing through his hand and flowing into his body. It was intoxicating. The shard had given him power, but the whole gem had a feeling to it that he had forgotten over the years.

"Get us out of here." The ranger held up his hand and pictured the world above in his mind. He would open a portal to the north, somewhere outside of The Arid Lands.

As he had done before, Asher commanded the magic of the gem to tear through reality and open a gateway.

He might as well have been struck by lightning for all the pain that shot through his head.

The ranger collapsed against the rock and fell into a heap on the floor, convinced that a storm had been conjured inside his mind. The pain was blinding and it didn't stop in his head, but ran down into his body, constricting his limbs and cramping his muscles. He finally let go of the gem and rolled away, desperate for breath.

"What happened?" Reyna and the others were over him in a second, offering their strength.

"I..." Asher couldn't find the words; his mind was a mess.

"It's too much for him," Nasta said.

"Get away!" Reyna exclaimed, holding her hand up to Nasta. "You are not to touch him."

"We have all witnessed him use the gem's magic before," Faylen replied.

"You have seen him use a shard of the gem," Nasta corrected. "As a child he never called upon the gem's magic, it simply defended him. This was never meant to be used by man."

"I'm fine..." Asher didn't fight Nathaniel's assistance in getting up. "But if I can't use the gem, I can't beat Valanis." The ranger felt as if he had just gone ten rounds with a Minotaur.

"Or get us out of here," Nathaniel said, with a concerned glance at Reyna.

Nasta picked up his staff of bone. "I cannot help you with the use of the gem, but I can show you a way out."

"If you know a way out, why haven't you already taken it?" Nathaniel asked, pointedly.

Nasta held up a finger. "I said I can *show* you a way out. I didn't say you could just walk out."

Asher leant against the cave wall and balled his fist, testing the strength of his grip. "The eastern pass..."

"Yes," Nasta agreed. "There is a cave, to the east, which leads onto the beach of The Shining Coast. The entrance back to Nightfall is crawling with monsters, but the eastern pass is home to only one beast."

"There was no creature when *I* escaped," Asher replied, nodding at Faylen to let her know he would be fine.

"There is now. I have been unable to put it down."

"I brought magic..." Asher looked to Faylen and Reyna. "We can put it down."

Nasta slowly nodded his head. "Can you all run?"

"Yes," Nathaniel replied. "Why?"

"Because it's the only way to move around down here." Nasta

shifted the boulder and crouched low, his head tilted. "The way is clear to our right."

"And to our left?" Asher asked.

"A touch of magic may be required..." Nasta stood aside and faced Reyna.

"I will go," Faylen stepped in front of the princess and made for the small hole.

Asher drew his silvyr short-sword, lined with runes that would make slicing monsters open all the easier. The elf rolled into the tunnel and dashed to the side. The beasts of the pit were waiting. Reyna went next and added her own destructive spells to the mix; both elves set the tunnel alight with fire and lightning.

After Nathaniel left the cave, Asher placed a firm hand against Nasta's chest and leaned in to his ear. "Do anything to get them hurt and I will remove your head myself."

With that, Asher collected the gem and exited the cave with Nasta. The tunnel was filled with the carcasses of dog-sized monsters and the smell of burning flesh. Like all the creatures that roamed under Nightfall, they were all teeth and sharp legs with very little to distinguish between head and body.

"More are coming!" Nasta declared. "Follow me!"

Asher had them follow his old master, with him at the back. The orbs drifted away and his extra senses kicked back in, relaying the dire environment through which they ran. Something heavier and larger was chasing them now. His ears picked up the sound of hard shells being crunched under foot. Whatever it was, it had just passed Nasta's cave and run over the bodies.

More magic erupted up ahead, as something akin to a snake dropped out of a hole in the roof. Reyna blasted it with ice and launched another one into the wall. Nathaniel was hacking at it, but the princess's spells were enough to ward the others away. Asher caught up in their wake and decapitated one of the slithering creatures as he ran by.

In the pit it was impossible to keep a track of the time; only exhaustion gave the ranger any indication of how long they had been running. With Nasta still running as if he were a younger man, Asher couldn't let himself fall behind, though he often reminded himself of the battle and the journey he had recently undertaken. More than once he had caught up with Nathaniel and grabbed him by the arm to pull him along. The knight had to keep up with the elves in order to stay in the light.

After another skirmish with a cousin of the Sandstalkers, the group ran out of a cave and entered another, but for the briefest of moments the blue sky could be seen above, as they moved through the gorge. Faylen unleashed a telekinetic spell upon the cave behind them, collapsing the entrance and barring the monsters from following them.

"We're almost there." Nasta said the words at such a level that only Asher's extra senses could hear him.

The eastern pass was easy to detect, if not for the light at the end of the tunnel, but the foul odour that dwelled in the cavern. The group crouched beside Nasta Nal-Aket, taking cover behind a collection of stalagmites.

Nasta gestured to the floating orbs. "Send them out," he whispered.

The elves commanded the orbs to fly out into the cavern and bring light to its darkest corners. Due to the large opening, the ambience inside the cavern was too light for Asher to use his extra senses, but his human eyes found the monster easily enough. The orbs drifted high and revealed the tucked up legs of a creature the ranger had never seen before. The light disturbed it and the monster scurried down the cavern wall, exposing its hideous body and sizable bulk.

"What is that?" Nathaniel wore bravery as if it were his only expression, but Asher could see the cracks. This was a monster no man should ever have to see.

Nasta stroked his goatee. "Man cannot name what it has never seen. I have simply come to call it a *Bastard.*"

Asher could see that it had six legs and a thick body with no discernible head, but its tail was long and ended with three vicious prongs. The ranger examined his silvyr sword and wondered if it would be enough to slay the beast.

"It is foul, no doubt." Faylen stood up with little care. "But it is just another monster..."

"Faylen!" Reyna hissed, but her companion was already striding into the cavern.

Asher groaned and moved to join her. One last push and they would be free of the pit and rest would find them all. Decades of training in Nightfall hadn't prepared him for much more than this.

Reyna rushed out to fight with them and Nathaniel quickly followed with his sword ready. Nasta unsheathed Reaver and swung it round a few times to limber up. It had been a long time since Asher had seen the old man fight.

The Bastard reacted instantly and released an unnatural shrill of alarm. Asher braced himself, as its six legs propelled it across the cavern with a speed that wouldn't be stopped by any blade. Faylen was an elf of four hundred years however, and she wasn't wielding any blade. She raised both of her arms and thrust the Bastard into the stalactites above. The spell was so powerful that the beast broke through the rock and dented the cavern roof.

When it fell back to the ground, Reyna was already waiting with a fire spell. Burning it didn't stop the bastard from trying to get back up, however. Its four unbroken legs had it coming for the elves with a vengeance - and a gnashing of teeth surrounding a thick tongue with a large sucker on the end. Faylen cast a spell of ice which had the monster's tongue pinned to the ground with an icicle.

"Asher!" Nasta's call was too late to warn the ranger.

A short-sword flew out of the darkness behind them, its tip heading for Asher's head. Nasta stepped in and cut the sword down mid-flight with the flick of his bone staff. The blade careered away, but it was followed by a group of Arakesh.

The Bastard whipped its tail about and had the elves diving for cover in the same moment the assassins descended on them. The monster was screaming in pain and fury, its ire aimed at Faylen. The Arakesh paid it little heed however, and attacked only the group.

"Give me the gem, Asher!" Alidyr entered the cavern with his magical blade in hand. "At this point a swift death is all I can promise."

Asher headbutted the closest assassin and threw him under the scurrying monster tackling Faylen. The assassin was trampled to death, as the elf danced about the Bastard, firing spell after spell. The ranger allowed Nathaniel to intercept the next Arakesh so that he could remove the other short-sword from his back.

"Together." Nasta joined him.

"No. Help them!" Asher shoved his old master away and ran for Alidyr.

The two collided in a flurry of sparks, as the twin blades met one another for the first time in combat. Asher used his silvyr sword to take advantage of Alidyr's exposed areas, always keeping him busy with the magical blade. After three days without rest and the wounds of a battle still plaguing his body, the ranger might as well have been fighting in a lake of mud. His attacks were sloppy and predictable, making it easy for the elf to evade his extra sword.

Reyna's bow could be heard over the melee, every arrow bringing an end to an assassin. Nasta weaved between the princess and the Graycoat, offering his deadly talents wherever possible. Had Asher not been in a fight for his life, he would have marvelled at the old man's abilities. As it was, the ranger could only glimpse his extraordinary skills. Alidyr side-stepped his next attack and kicked Asher in the gut, throwing him further down the cavern, towards the light. They had all been pushed towards the light, with the Arakesh coming at them with relentless force.

Only Faylen was stuck in the recesses of the cavern, locked in battle with the Bastard. Her spells ignited the cave and created flashes of light that wiped away the shadows.

"You can't save them, ranger." Alidyr push-kicked Asher to the ground. "You can't even save yourself."

Asher wasn't one for words; instead he roared in defiance and launched himself at the elf. His blades slashed in every direction, but found only Alidyr's white robes.

"Asher!" Nathaniel ducked and sliced his opponent's gut before charging Alidyr.

The third blade kept the elf on the defensive, but it only took a few evasions for the elf to land an elbow in the knight's face, knocking him to the ground. Reyna was torn between helping him and helping Faylen. Asher wanted to send her to Faylen's side, but if he wavered for just a second, Alidyr would claim his life. It mattered not, as two Arakesh set upon the princess and forced her towards the light, where the sea air was finally breaking through the Bastard's musk.

Nasta dispatched his attackers with apparent ease and moved to assist Reyna, while simultaneously dragging Nathaniel out of the way, before Alidyr could plunge his sword into his gut. Asher made sure he was between them, with his companions and the light to his back.

"Is this what you wanted?" Alidyr spat. "You wanted to fight me? It is only the skills that I have taught you that have kept you on your feet thus far."

Asher wiped the blood from his eye and blinked slowly. "You talk too much..." The ranger's next swing was far too wide and too slow. Alidyr kicked him again before the swing could fall, sending him to the ground with another painful impact.

The Bastard screamed in the background and Asher caught a glimpse of the elf burying her scimitar into its hard shell. The monster's outcry was quickly followed by her own screams, as its wicked tail curled about and speared her leg.

"Faylen!" Reyna shouted over the melee.

Asher was no longer watching Alidyr, who was only a few feet away and closing in with his short-sword. Instead, the ranger had locked eyes with Faylen, who had limped forwards and fallen to the ground at the back of the cavern. The Bastard was dead behind her, but the elf could barely stand. Everything happened at once then, and Asher knew what was coming; he could see it in her eyes.

The elf raised her hand and brought down the stalactite between Asher and Alidyr, separating them momentarily and giving the ranger a chance to escape. Her telekinetic spell didn't stop there, however. Alidyr, caught off guard by the falling stalactite, was hurled backwards, into the cavern.

"Run..." Faylen hissed. "RUN!"

Alidyr was already recovering and heading back to Asher, when Faylen screamed her last spell, unleashing a powerful wave of telekinetic energy into the cavern.

"NO!" Reyna yelled over the breaking of rock.

Asher tried to pull himself up, intending to run back into the cavern, but a hand grasped the straps on his back and dragged him towards the light, away from Faylen. Reyna continued to scream in protest as Nathaniel pulled her back with both arms, careful not to trip over the dead Arakesh. The ranger kicked out and attempted to break free of Nasta's grip, but there was no energy left in him.

Alidyr ran for the light, seeing his own doom in the crumbling cavern. The smaller rocks were quickly followed by larger, immovable boulders and slabs that dropped to the ground. Within seconds, both Alidyr and Faylen were hidden behind a new wall of rock.

"Quickly!" Nasta shouted over the collapse.

The rest of the cavern imploded behind them. They ran until they were back under the sky and the eastern pass was completely buried. The air, filled with dust, pushed them further onto the beach to escape its suffocating effects. Nasta released Asher, but the ranger couldn't find his legs to stand, as all strength had finally left him. Reyna broke free of Nathaniel and ran back to the collapsed tunnel, her tears and screams all mixing into one.

Faylen was gone...

Asher knew that neither of them could have survived that, but he could take no solace in knowing that Alidyr was dead when it came at such a price.

Nathaniel ran to Reyna and the two fell on their knees in a tight embrace. The knight cupped her head to his chest and let his own tears streak down his cheeks. Nasta walked away, towards the lapping sea, his own emotions impossible to tell.

Asher pulled Paldora's gem out of his belt and inspected it through teary eyes. Was it worth it? Was the gem worth Faylen's life? He had the only weapon capable of stopping Valanis and he couldn't use it. The urge to throw it into The Adean was overwhelming. He gripped the gem tight as new tears ran down his face, clearing the dirt and blood. No, he wouldn't throw it away; Faylen's life would have been for nothing then. Asher knew that if it was the last thing he ever did, he would learn how to master Paldora's gem, and then... he would destroy Valanis.

After a lasting look at Reyna and Nathaniel, the ranger let his head fall back onto the sand. He let go and allowed the empty abyss of his subconscious to take over his senses. Faylen's face was the last thing he imagined before rest finally found him.

CHAPTER 38
THE ECHOES

The king of elves sat on his balcony and gazed into the sky, as he had done for most of the day. After his servants had dressed him in the finest armour, word had quickly reached him of the spectacle in the heavens above. Seeing Paldora's Star break its eternal cycle and reveal itself in the light of day had been a harrowing sight. Unlike the mortals of the world, Elym had seen the star soar through the night sky every century without fail.

This wasn't supposed to happen.

The rest of his kin had seen the phenomenon, but their reaction had yet to reach him. Elym had spent his centuries as king convincing his people that the Echoes of Fate were not to be believed, and that his sister had been in her death throes at the hands of the vicious Outlanders. Time and time again he had been justified in his abandonment of the gods, as Paldora's Star continued to grace a starlit sky, but now...

The king had been trying to recall every detail of that fateful moment when Nalana, his sister, had said the prophetic words out loud. He was still young at the time of the Amber Spell, and a very young ruler by elven standards, but when Nalana had failed to return from her search for Asher and Paldora's Gem, he had commanded the current High Guardian to assemble his best warriors and accompany him into The Wild Moores, to search for his sister.

Elym's frustration with his sister had always been trumped by his adoration of her. Not only a princess, but a Dragorn, Nalana was loved and respected by all who met her. Being a Dragorn however, Elym had been powerless to stop her from entering that wild forest. It had all been for the boy, Asher. At the time it had been believed that the young boy had fled back into The Wild Moores with Paldora's gem, after escaping the battle of Elethiah. Of course, Elym knew the truth of it now.

For days the young king and his warriors had scoured the forest of man. Elym had been sure his sister had already found the boy and doubled back, and would be looking for him in the new palace, in The Evermoore. She hadn't. That wretched forest would be the last thing she ever saw. On the sixth day, Nalana had stumbled across the search party, covered in blood and sweat, her agony easy to see. Elym had taken her in his arms, while his escort spread out and prepared for any ambush.

"Where is Tovun?" Elym had asked his sister, believing that had her dragon been present, she would never have come to such harm.

Nalana groaned. "He did... not come. The council..."

Elym had recalled that the dragons were in deep council to decide who should succeed Garganafan, who had perished in the Amber Spell. Of course, wherever Tovun was right now, he would be suffering the same wounds as Nalana; such was their bond.

"Where have you been?" Elym had asked, tears running freely from his eyes.

"I couldn't find him," Nalana croaked. "Asher..."

"It doesn't matter." Elym remembered stroking her face and feeling how cold she was. "Valanis is vanquished. The gem no longer matters."

The warriors had closed in now, finding no threat in the area. They had all known that the wounds Nalana had suffered would be the end of her; even magic could not defeat what death had so obviously claimed.

"I... found something. There's more to... the Outlanders... than we thought." Nalana's face crumpled in pain. "I found the Echoes. The Echoes... of Fate."

Elym had looked to his High Guardian, but all the elves had worn the same expression of confusion. The young king had seen others on the edge of death and knew well that their final words could be unintelligible. He held his sister close and bade her to hush, hoping to give her a peaceful passage.

"Valanis will return..." Nalana managed. Her crystal eyes glazed over and she took a breath, as if the princess was gasping for her last hope at life. *"These favoured elves fall and lose their way, as man's anger devours all dragons' fire. The immortal man is set to rise, bringing the dark one closer to his most dangerous desire... Paldora's celestial gem graces daylight sky, and in its beauty ordains calamity. Only alliance and trust between two shores offers an intimation of hope and a glimpse of eternity.... Children of fire and flame offer great promise, but only one perceives the time we will fall. As the gods recast their fortune and power, one will suffer the burden of destiny for all..."*

Nalana's final effort robbed her of another breath.

Elym had seen the impression her words had had on his soldiers, as if the gods themselves had just spoken to them. The king had only wanted to hold his sister, the young elf unaware of the impact those words would have on his people. It had certainly made his task all the harder in the years to come, and Elym had no doubt that there were still those in his kingdom who held faith in the gods, but they hadn't seen what he had seen that day.

In the waning sun, as the group was preparing to depart The Wild Moores with Nalana's body, they had been set upon by a band of Outlanders. Elym had been more than happy to cut them all down, his anger bubbling over, but the skirmish had been bloody and more violent than he had anticipated, resulting in the king being separated from the High Guardian and his warriors. Not far from where they had found Nalana stumbling through the trees, Elym had found the entrance to a cave, adorned with skulls and various animal bones on pikes. A typical Outlander home in his eyes. The cave however, had been filled with pieces of canvas, that upon closer inspection were in fact pieces of human skin.

The nearest human leather had been stretched between two wooden poles and used as parchment. Elym's command of the human language had been very basic, having only picked up some of their words from Nalana, but the writing on the skin was familiar. It was the Echoes of Fate, scribed in blood and signed at the bottom with a black hand, like all the others. Those words were not from the gods, but from the humans. His sister had found the prophecy and had clearly been studying it, but they were not godly words, as his warriors had then believed.

This scene had fuelled his own belief over the centuries that the gods were not real - that any god who could support Valanis or give prophetic words to savages was not a divine creator. Elym had kept his own findings that day to himself. He could not stain the memory of his sister any more than he already had. It had been a burden in itself to convince the elven people that her last words were that of the dying, and not to be misinterpreted as holy.

Elym looked down at the chest resting on his table. The rectangular box was engraved with ancient symbols and elven glyphs, keeping the chest shut to all but him. To the king's touch, it was as if the chest had never been locked, opening with the greatest of ease. Inside he found the rolled up scroll he had taken from The Wild Moores so long ago. Unravelling it, he found the Echoes of Fate and the black hand print in the corner. For years he had kept it hidden. The scroll's existence wasn't proof that the gods were fake, but it would have seen his sister made a fool of in her dying moments.

Elym quickly rolled it back up and tucked it into his belt, under his robes. It would remind him in the coming days that he determined his own fate and that of his people, not some god in the sky.

"My Lord..." Varö was in the doorway to his balcony.

Elym retired his reverie and tore his eyes from the empty chest. "Are we ready?"

Varö straightened his back. "We are, my Lord. The ships have been assembled and stocked; the army is on the beach awaiting your command."

The king glanced at the sky and looked back at his High Guardian. "You saw it?"

Varö hesitated. "Yes, my Lord. We all saw it; a beautiful display of nature, nothing more."

Elym smiled, though he didn't quite believe the elf. "You have put your faith in me, Varö. You have put your faith in my vision for this world." The king stood up and clasped the High Guardian's forearm. "We will rule Verda as the true gods, the only gods that matter."

With that, Varö threw a crystal into the king's room and opened a portal. Elym strode through and stepped onto the beach of The Opal Coast, on Ayda's western shore. Hundreds of ships edged the ocean with white and blue sails, while the beach itself was occupied by six thousand elves, all lined up and ready to go. Elym admired his warriors, who stood in complete silence, the epitome of discipline. The only sound came from the lapping waves and the trees in the breeze.

Elym turned to Varö. "I always envisioned this scene to have dragons in it..."

"Even with the Dragon Wall closed to us, we will still claim victory, my Lord."

"Seeing the army you have trained I don't doubt it. When Illian is ours and some measure of peace is accomplished, I will return to Ayda and discover the secrets of Mount Garganafan. I would see the dragon eggs recovered and their kind returned to these lands." Elym hoped that would see the return of Adilandra, his wife. He could only push away his thoughts of her for so long.

Varö bowed his head. "We will see Verda returned to its natural state."

Elym paced the sandy beach, meeting the eyes of his warriors. "The gods are false..." he whispered to himself, before announcing, "The gods are false! We, the immortals, are the true rulers of Verda!" The army cheered in response. "We set sail today to forge a new world for our people, a world free of Valanis and his evil, a world free of man and its corruption! The elven nation will rise! We will bring about a time of peace and prosperity! If man must be wiped away to achieve this, then so be it!" The army cheered again. "GO NOW! TO WAR! TO VICTORY!"

The army continued to cheer as they turned about and made for the ships. For the first time in history, elves would go to war with man...

EPILOGUE

Faylen dragged herself over the sharp rocks and the warm carcass of the dead monster. Everything hurt. Breathing had become a laborious effort with little reward. The elf had more cuts than she could count, and healing wasn't an option right now; what was left of her magic had a single purpose.

Killing Alidyr Yalathanil.

The head of Valanis's Hand was only feet away, stuck on his knees, wedged between the collapsing cavern and the slab of hard ground beneath him. Both of his hands were raised as he exuded enough force to keep the tons of broken stalactites from crushing him. The shield of pure magic flared against the jagged rocks, generating the only source of light and guiding Faylen.

It took some time before she made it through the narrow gaps, but her final effort in life was worth it. Before her now, and helpless to defend himself, was Alidyr. The elf was dripping with sweat and blood, his own injuries not far from mirroring Faylen's. His arms shook and his teeth were firmly clenched as he watched her crawl ever closer. Faylen hoped he could see the look in her eye.

Despite her long life, there hadn't been anything Faylen could say she hated. Looking at the elf responsible for so many deaths however, she knew there was room in her heart for such a feeling after all. With every inch she crawled, that rage Faylen had been told lived inside of her was finally bubbling to the surface. For years she had clung to the ideology of her queen, Adilandra, believing that they could be more than that. Not now, not after everything Alidyr had put them through.

It took everything the elf had left to get to her knees and face him. Killing Alidyr would be the sweetest way to leave this world, she thought. The two locked eyes in the flaring light, both aware that this would be their grave.

"If..." Alidyr struggled to speak. "If you kill me... we both die."

Faylen glanced at the mountain of rock that threatened to bury them. "So be it..."

With a wicked grin, the elf looked back at Alidyr and opened both of her hands, igniting them with brilliant, blue flames.

THE SAGA CONTINUES...

PHILIP C. QUAINTRELL

THE ECHOES SAGA

RELIC OF THE GODS

BOOK III

PHILIP C. QUAINTRELL

———

Hear more from Philip C. Quaintrell including book releases and exclusive content:

 PHILIPCQUAINTRELL.COM

 FACEBOOK.COM/PHILIPCQUAINTRELL

 @PHILIPCQUAINTRELL.AUTHOR

 @PCQUAINTRELL

AUTHOR NOTES

If you're reading this then you've enjoyed Rise of the Ranger enough to buy and read Empire of Dirt. Thank you! I was overjoyed with the response to this series, with Rise of the Ranger going into the top 1,000 best sellers in three continents in its first two months of life.

I envision The Echoes Saga to comprise of nine books. Some of you may find the clues here and there as to what is to ultimately follow on, but it will take some of the characters you've come to love in this trilogy, and a few new ones, into a world of new adventures.

Anyway... there will be more details on that to come, but I just had to put it out there because the things to come are very exciting and I can't wait for you all to read it. I just wish I could write as fast as I can think!

This is my fifth book now and I feel like I'm starting to get the swing of it; I certainly don't think I'm at the top of my game yet. I read a lot and am always comparing the writing style of the great authors with my own, but I'm enjoying the learning curve and can't wait to see how and what I'm writing in another 5 years from now.

So, Empire of Dirt... I loved diving into this story and I find it very hard to come out; my wife always says I'm a little detached for half an hour when I come back to reality (sorry Emma!). Sometimes when I get into the characters' head for a while, I can adopt their mood for a short time too. This is a process I probably need to work on! Like with all of my books, or my writing style in general, the characters make a lot of the decisions based upon their personality and circumstances. I obviously have particular scenes and set pieces that I know will be in the books, but getting there is a journey for the characters and I've found it's the most organic way of creating a story with believable characters. That might sound a little weird and out of control, but trust me; it's worked so far... I think.

Valanis has returned! I always enjoy fleshing out a villain and making them in some way relatable and flawed. I get bored of bad guys who have unlimited power and dastardly plans that always go their way. I prefer it when things don't go to plan for either side and improvisation is required. It just makes it more real to me and somehow less scripted. I did for a short while consider writing a prequel with Valanis, going through his life and what led to him starting the Dark War etc, but I'm not really a prequel kind of guy, at least not right now. I have enough ideas to keep this ship moving forward, but who knows, maybe I'll write a story about him or some other time in Verda's history - that timeline's pretty big. I guess that's what I love about having this whole world at my fingertips; anything can happen!

So you can probably tell by now, having read the first two books, that The Echoes Saga isn't a one man show. I did start with the intention of Asher being 'the guy', and yes his role is integral to the story and he's certainly a main character, but the story demands more than just one person's role.

From some of the reviews and the feedback I've had, it's clear that some people actually prefer Gideon Thorn (one of my favourites) and I hope after reading Empire of Dirt you like him even more. In terms of character growth and development, Gideon has definitely come a long way. I added a couple of new characters, chiefly Tauren son-of-none and Tai'garn of the elven council. Obviously some have bigger roles than others at different times of the story, but all are integral to getting us to that final epilogue. Tauren had a big impact on book 2, whereas Tai'garn's actions will have consequences in book 3 – it's all connected!

And of course, I couldn't not mention the rangers. You haven't seen the last of them, those that survived that is, so I hope you enjoyed Doran Heavybelly et al. I really like the idea that despite Asher's 14 years of solitude on the road, there was some evidence that he's had an impact and hasn't been the ghost he wanted to be. Some back stories have been explained and some haven't, but like I said, there's more to come from the rangers.

As always, if you could find the time to leave a review on Amazon I would be most appreciative – every one counts! The self-publishing business is a little different to traditional. I don't have the marketing power of Random House or the editors of Penguin Books, so word of mouth and reviews online really help to give the book more reach.

Until the next time...

APPENDICIES

Kingdoms of Illian:

1. **Alborn** (eastern region) - Ruled by King Rengar of house Marek. Capital city: *Velia*. Other Towns and Cities: Palios, Galosha, and Barossh.

2. **The Arid Lands** (southern region) - Ruled by Emperor Faros. Capital city: *Karath*. Other Towns and Cities: Ameeraska, Calmardra and Tregaran.

3. **The Ice Vales** (western region) - Ruled by King Gregorn of house Orvish. Capital city: *Grey Stone*. Other Towns and Cities: Bleak, Kelp Town and Snowfell.

4. **Orith** (northern region) - Ruled by King Merkaris of house Tion. Capital city: *Namdhor*. Other Towns and Cities: Skystead, Dunwich, Darkwell and Longdale.

5. *Felgarn* (central region) - Ruled by Queen Isabella of house Harg. Capital city: *Lirian*. Other Towns and Cities: Vangarth, Wood Vale and Whistle Town.

6. *Dragorn* (island nation off The Shining Coast to the east) - Ruled by the four crime families; the Trigorns, Fenrigs, Yarls, and the Danathors.

~

Significant Wars: Chronologically

The Great War - Fought during the First Age, around 5,000 years ago. The only recorded time in history that elves and dwarves have united. They fought against the orcs with the help of the Dragorn, the first elvish dragon riders. This war ended the First age.

The Dark War - Fought during the Second Age, around 1,000 years ago. Considered the elvish civil war. Valanis, the dark elf, tried to take over Illian in the name of the gods. This war ended the Second Age.

The Dragon War - Fought in the beginning of the Third Age, only a few years after The Dark War. The surviving elves left Illian for Ayda's shores, fleeing any more violence. Having emerged from The Wild Moores, the humans, under King Gal Tion's rule, went to war with the dragons over their treasure. This saw the exile of the surviving dragons and the beginning of human dominance over Illian.